PRAISE FOR
Diamond Rings Are Deadly Things

"I love Rachelle J. Christensen's stories and characters, and *Diamond Rings Are Deadly Things* is another thrilling mystery to add to my collection. Don't be surprised if you have to stay up all night to finish the book!"
—Rachel Ann Nunes, author of *Before I Say Goodbye*

"*Diamond Rings Are Deadly Things* pulled me right in from the first page and held me captive until the very end. Great characters, a compelling plot, a surprising twist at the end . . . Rachelle J. Christensen knows how to craft a great mystery."
—Tristi Pinkston, author of the Secret Sisters Mysteries

"This terrific story with quirky characters, fun craft ideas, and a mystery will keep you wondering through all the twists and turns."
—Heather Justesen, author of *Brownies and Betrayal*

"A cunningly crafty mystery with just the right mix of romance. You won't be able to get enough of Adrielle Pyper."
—Nichole Giles, author of *Descendant*

Diamond Rings are ~ Deadly Things

Diamond Rings are Deadly Things

A WEDDING PLANNER MYSTERY

RACHELLE J. CHRISTENSEN

SHADOW
MOUNTAIN

Visit us at ShadowMountain.com

Library of Congress Cataloging-in-Publication Data
CIP data on file
ISBN 978-1-60907-861-4

Printed in the United States of America
Lake Book Manufacturing, Inc., Melrose Park, IL

10 9 8 7 6 5 4 3 2 1

For Steve
Thank you for the diamond ring—
loving you has made my life
a beautiful adventure

Acknowledgments

Thank you to Heidi Taylor, my product manager, Suzanne Brady, my editor, and all the other wonderful people at Shadow Mountain. I have dreamed of being a part of this phenomenal publishing team since my very first writing conference. I can say that hard work, determination, and perseverance make dreams come true.

I have a list of wonderful people to thank when it comes to the critiquing and revising of this novel. Patrick and Necia Jolley were my first readers and as usual provided excellent insight. Andrea Jolley, Sarah Winn, and Stephanie Johnson helped me brainstorm craft ideas to help build the storyline, and we had fun talking about title ideas.

Thank you to Heather Justesen, Nichole Giles, Tristi Pinkston, Shirley Bahlmann, Cindy Beck, Rachel Ann Nunes, Melanie Jacobson, Michelle Packard, and Jennifer Nielsen, who read all or part of the manuscript and offered excellent advice to make the plot stronger. Thank you to Josi Kilpack, Connie Sokol, and Julie Wright for their savvy advice and encouragement. To LDStorymakers and Authors Incognito I owe a debt of gratitude for putting me on this pathway and helping me through the obstacle course of writing and publishing.

I'm so thankful for my readers, who waited patiently for this novel and encouraged me with their eagerness to read the words I've written. Thank you to knowledgeable friends and family who constantly give my writing a boost and lift my spirits. A special thanks to my dear husband, Steve, for making writing retreats possible and for my beautiful children who provide me with inspiration daily.

I'm grateful to my Father in Heaven. Sometimes it's hard to be patient and it's tough to understand this journey, but I'm thankful for His guiding hand in my life and for the gifts and talents He has blessed me with.

Chapter 1

BRIDAL HEIRLOOM CREATIONS: RING PILLOW

Using fabric that is the same or similar to the fabric of the bride's gown, make a small pillow. Add a personal touch by hand-embroidering the names of the bride and groom on the fabric. To complement the wedding dress, decorate the top of the pillow with lace, sequins, beading, rhinestones, or a satin bow. To add a splash of color, select narrow ribbon that coordinates with or repeats the wedding colors. Stitch the ribbons to the top of the pillow, and then tie the rings to the pillow before the ceremony.

Courtesy of www.mashedpotatoesandcrafts.com.

The air was charged with an expectant current as I unlocked the back door of my wedding planning headquarters. Pausing for half a second, I ran my fingers along the smooth vinyl lettering printed in teal on the metal door: *Adrielle Pyper's Dream Weddings, Where happily ever after is your destination.* Those words were the

1

realization of a lifelong dream for me, even though I never would have guessed I'd be setting up shop in Sun Valley, Idaho. I had loved my life in San Francisco, but after what happened, I needed to get out of the city and back home to my Idaho roots.

The anxiety that had plagued me for over a year was finally fading. For once, I wasn't afraid to step into the darkened room and flip the switch—the fluorescent lights illuminated everything I'd worked so hard for, and I felt like today might be the beginning of something different. The soft scent of lavender filtered through the air. It smelled like hope.

My assistant, Lorea Zubiondo, arrived at the shop minutes after I came through the back door. Her dark hair looked glossy under the lights, almost black. The short layers were teased in the back—I joked that she was trying to make up for her five-foot-two height impairment.

"Morning, Adri." Her voice sounded chipper, and there was a lightness to her step. I noticed a bit of eyeliner and dark green eye shadow accenting her deep brown eyes and barely kept myself from gaping. Lorea was a no-frills girl, so why did she have makeup on?

I glanced at the clock—fifteen minutes after eight. "You're early today."

"Couldn't sleep." Lorea tugged the measuring tape hanging from her dress mannequin. A few minutes later, I caught her looking at the clock. The eye shadow suddenly made sense.

"Ah, I see why you couldn't sleep. It's Wednesday. Guess I'd better open the front door in case we get a special delivery."

"I'm excited about seeing the dresses, that's all." Lorea's gaze flicked to the clock again.

"Me too." I didn't push the issue, even when I saw the hint of a smile lift the corners of her mouth. My own anticipation buzzed happily in the back of my mind as I turned the locks on the front door. I was ready to embrace this new venture, and I ignored the nagging thoughts of "What if?" that kept trying to creep in and overshadow my visions of success.

I tidied up the front of the shop, winding the satin ribbon in shades of forest green and burgundy on a spool. A customized ring pillow with coordinating ribbon to match the accent colors might be just the thing for one of my June weddings. I tucked an errant strand of blonde hair behind my ear, my fingers brushing my favorite pair of sapphire earrings. With my sketch pencil, I outlined ideas for the ring pillow.

Ten minutes later, wedding chimes rang, and I heard a familiar whistle. Lorea and I hurried to the front of the shop, pushing each other aside in hopes of getting there first. At the last second, I let her pass—she was going for the guy. I just wanted to see if the shipment had arrived. A man dressed in a brown uniform waited out front, holding a scanner.

"Hi, Colton," we greeted the delivery man simultaneously.

"Hi, ladies. Your wait is over." Colton motioned to the long box behind him. "I have a couple more boxes like this in the truck."

Lorea pumped her fist in the air. "They're finally here. I'll sign for them."

Colton flourished his scanner, and Lorea signed, her grin widening. He took back the scanner, studying it for a moment before pushing a couple of buttons. "Zubiondo. I've been meaning to ask you. Where does that name come from?"

"From Spain. I'm Basque." Lorea's face lit up as it always did when she spoke of her heritage. Bonus points for Colton—I rooted for anyone who might improve Lorea's attitude toward dating.

Colton nodded. "That's great. You ever been there?"

"No, but I will someday."

I couldn't be sure, but it seemed like Lorea was on the verge of flirting with the delivery guy. If only Colton would get up the nerve to ask her out. He pushed the large box forward on a dolly, and I pointed to the back of the store. "Can you roll those to the back room so we don't have to carry them?"

"Anything for you, Adri." He followed me and set the box down. "What's in here?"

"Wedding dresses," I said.

Lorea ran her hand lovingly over the box and then pushed it farther into the back room. As she ripped the packing tape to open the box, my stomach flipped in anticipation.

"Dresses now, too? I thought you mostly planned the weddings." Colton stopped and surveyed our showroom. "You like to stay busy, don't you?"

"Actually, the dresses are for Lorea. She's getting married this weekend."

"What?" Colton fumbled with his scanner.

"Don't believe a word she says." Lorea hurried out from the back, carrying a vacuum-sealed package of beads and lace that I was sure made up a beautiful gown.

"But I think she'd look great in that dress, don't you?" I ignored the death stare coming from my friend.

Colton's cheeks flushed. "I'll get the other boxes." He hurried out the door.

"You *txori buru!*" Lorea reverted to Euskara once Colton had gone. "What are you trying to do to me?"

I laughed—she had called me a birdbrain in her native Basque language at least a hundred times. "Just proving my point." I smirked. "You like each other."

Lorea turned with a huff and went back to unpacking dresses.

Colton brought two more boxes inside, and I kept my mouth shut.

"Thank you, Colton," Lorea said.

"Good luck with everything, ladies." Colton winked at Lorea as he walked away.

I waited until I heard the door close to say, "See, I told you."

Lorea shook her head and pulled out several more bags containing the dresses. "Four, five, and that one makes six." She gestured to the third box. "The last four are in there."

The bag rustled as I opened the tight packaging and pulled out a gown. The dress seemed to breathe as it broke free and I hung it on the clothes rack. My fingers fluttered, struggling with the zipper. For a moment, I wished that Briette could be with me to enjoy this moment. I blinked to clear the moisture in my eyes and continued unveiling the dress.

"Careful," Lorea murmured, edging closer.

Folds of creamy satin hung like graceful dancers surrounded by tulle and sparkle. We both sighed as I unfastened the train. The satin rustled, trailing from the bodice to the floor. A dusting of pearl glitter covered the gown, and intricate beadwork and embroidery adorned the bodice and hem.

"Lorea, this is perfect." I rubbed the satin between my fingers. "Sylvia is going to be so excited to try it on."

I saw her flinch at the mention of our least favorite client, Sylvia Rockfort. At twenty-eight, Sylvia was close to my age, but that was about the only thing we had in common. She was a soap star diva. Sylvia had had her ten minutes of fame in a now-cancelled soap opera and enough plastic surgery to make sure everyone remembered it.

Lorea kept her focus on the dress. "It's exquisite. And when Sylvia sees this, she'll tell all her friends." Lorea clenched her hand around the necklace she always wore, her thumb tracing each of the four comma-shaped heads of the silver Basque cross she referred to as a *Lauburu*. "Her wedding will be absolutely gorgeous."

"Can you believe how heavy this hem is?" I knelt down to examine the beadwork fastened to the thick lines of embroidery. Shimmering rhinestones were sewn in five-petal flower arrangements along the hem. The fancy stitching matched a rhinestone-encrusted clip at the hip of the gown and the tight-fitting bodice. "Sylvia will probably want you to try to take it in around the waist—even if it fits perfectly."

Lorea frowned. "It's a size four, but I'll call her. Should we time how long it takes her to get here for her first fitting?"

"Wasn't she coming in at one o'clock anyway?"

"Yeah, to check on how the bridesmaid dresses are coming," Lorea answered. "I guess she can wait until then."

"If you do call her, I bet she'll be here in less than an hour."

"My bet is on thirty-seven minutes."

My fingers snagged on an uneven part of the hem. "Please tell me this isn't—" I covered my mouth when I saw the gaping hole in the hemline of Sylvia's dress. The frayed edge of the fabric loomed before me, and I felt like I was choking on eighteen thousand dollars, the price tag on Sylvia's gown. Lorea and I were banking on the sale to launch our new dress business.

Lorea knelt beside me and examined the hole. "You'd better pray that Sylvia doesn't stop by for a surprise visit."

My stomach churned. "There isn't time to order another."

"Hang on, we can still make this work." Lorea ran the material through her fingers. The corners of her eyes crinkled in concentration. "Give me an hour, and you won't be able to tell me where the hole was."

"Are you sure?" The hole looked more like a slit in the fabric, about six inches long.

"I have to be." Lorea jerked her head toward the clock.

I followed the motion and cringed. It was nine forty-five. Sylvia had been known to stop by the boutique to start her day. "I'm taking a picture of that damage first. I can't imagine how it could have made it through their quality checkpoint." I stalked to my desk and grabbed my camera. Wriggling my shoulders, I imagined the stress rolling off and melting into the carpet.

Lorea held the bottom of the hem so I could take pictures, and then she ripped the tape off the final box. She stood and surprised me with a hug. "Before I finish unpacking, I just wanted to say thank you so much for giving this dress business a chance."

I returned the embrace. "Thank *you*. I think this will give the shop the special flair I've been looking for." I had been reluctant to add one more line of expense to my wedding planning business, but the wisdom of becoming a full-service bridal boutique couldn't be ignored. In my expanded new business, I would plan the weddings and also give the bride the opportunity to buy wedding amenities directly from me. The two meshed seamlessly in the small town of Ketchum, where residents were used to driving more than an hour to get to a large department store.

Lorea nodded. "I can see my dream of someday owning a dress shop coming true."

"Me, too. As long as we're in the same building."

"For sure." Lorea pulled up the flaps of the last box.

My eyes kept straying to the hole in Sylvia's gown. I ran through the conversation I'd be having with the dressmakers in China, and it wasn't pretty. When I opened my boutique, I used every last cent of my savings and borrowed a few thousand dollars from my parents. Adding the dress business was a wise decision, and Lorea was carrying the brunt of the loan for that, but I didn't have a backup plan if it failed. At that moment, I saw just how easily Sylvia Rockfort could ruin me—if she didn't like her gown, then we wouldn't get the coveted endorsement we needed in *Country Bride Magazine*. The referral would be wonderful, but if Sylvia decided the gown didn't suit her, Lorea and I would be left holding the bill.

"Wait a minute." Lorea ran her hand along each of the gowns hanging in their individual garment bags. "Please tell me I can't count."

"Um, math isn't my favorite subject, either."

Shaking her head, Lorea began pulling all the packing material from the box.

"What's wrong?"

"There are only nine dresses." Her chin trembled slightly as she hurriedly recounted the gowns. "One is missing. I think it might be the one with the beaded hem."

My throat felt chalky. "The one Sylvia ordered in case she didn't like her gown?"

Lorea kept pulling packing material out of the box. Long strips of brown paper were quickly strewn across the floor. I dropped to the ground and dug through the box. Then I stood and recounted the gowns.

"Let's open up each bag and pull them out. Maybe there are two gowns in the same bag."

Lorea's eyes lit up with hope. "That's probably it."

Neither of us spoke, and the sound of plastic and rustling satin covered the dull roar of blood pumping in my ears. We were working against the clock for Sylvia's wedding, and we couldn't afford to upset her.

"It's not here. I can't believe it," Lorea cried. "Of all the dresses to go missing, it would be Sylvia's alternate."

My imagined conversation with the dressmakers took a drastic turn, but I slowly breathed in and out. "You know what? She's going to love her first choice. You'll steer her in the right direction. Maybe convince her it would be bad luck to try on the other dress when the first one was obviously designed for her."

Lorea's face had red splotches, and she blinked her eyes to clear them.

I pointed at the gown with the gaping hole. "Let's concentrate on one problem at a time. You fix the hole. I know you can work with that diva. I'll back you up."

I knelt next to the box and began tossing the packing paper back in, but I froze when I focused on something caught in the tape lining the bottom of the box. Leaning forward, I reached for the tiny pearl. Three more beads were stuck in the corner. "Did any of the other dresses have pearl beading?"

"No, it was just that one."

"Let's empty the box and see if we can find any more of these beads."

"Huh?" Lorea studied the bead in my hand and gasped as I picked up the others.

A powdery residue hugged the corners of the cardboard. The packing tape glimmered in the light with the same fine particles.

"What's this?" Lorea held up a shiny piece of metal.

My skin prickled with goosebumps. "That looks like part of a razor blade." I closed my eyes, but not before the image of blood trickling down a knife point seared my consciousness. A foreboding sense of discomfort broke through my dam of positive thinking. A million negative outcomes flowed through my mind, and I felt cords of tension tightening my shoulders. Taking a deep breath, I opened my eyes, commanding myself to stay in the present and focus on Lorea. "I don't understand. Do you think our shipment was tampered with?"

Lorea tilted the silver blade. "How fast can you get China on the phone?"

Chapter 2

VINTAGE BRIDAL SHOWER FAVORS: FIVE-MINUTE LAVENDER SACHETS

Lay flat one doily or lace-edged handkerchief, and arrange lavender buds in center. Bring fabric up around the buds and tie off with ribbon or string to form a small bundle of buds. Your guests will enjoy these unique favors, which can be used to refresh a drawer, a car, a closet, or even a coat pocket.

Courtesy of www.mashedpotatoesandcrafts.com.

An hour later, my hands were still shaking from the tension radiating through my body. The dress-making company in China assured me that all the gowns had been shipped, so something must have happened in transit.

I gripped the edge of the countertop and studied the gray and black flecks of paint. My customers didn't know it was paint; my mother had helped me mask it to look like granite. The flecks of colors turned into so many dollar symbols before my eyes. With a shake of my head, I told Lorea, "They're opening a case for investigation with the shipping company, and I'll do the same from my end. They won't charge us for the dress, but we won't be seeing it anytime soon, either."

Lorea frowned as she snipped off a piece of thread. "So as long as Sylvia likes this dress, we'll survive." She continued working her tiny stitches to repair the hole in the gown.

I knew Lorea was struggling to look on the bright side. That was usually my game. Rolling my shoulders back, I put on my best fake smile. "This is nothing we can't handle, right?" I swaggered over to her side, flipped one of my blonde curls over my shoulder, and splayed my fingers, pretending to adjust a diamond on my left hand. "Beauty is no accident," I said with a sniff.

Lorea looked at me and laughed. She knew I was imitating Sylvia Rockfort, which made the situation even more hilarious because Lorea was usually the one poking fun at her least-favorite client. "You're terrible, you know that?"

The laughter zapped some of my stress, and I slid down into one of the office chairs we'd recovered with my signature teal, cream, and purple fabrics. "It really is strange to think that someone might have stolen that gown en route. How much were you going to sell it for?"

"We weren't sure because of the pearl beading, but I was thinking around six thousand." Lorea smoothed the edge of the gown and examined it with a furrowed brow. "What do you think?"

"You're amazing." I leaned forward and could barely make out the tiny stitches in the hemline. "No one will ever know the difference."

"You'd better hope so because Sylvia will be here soon."

"Okay, let's stow these boxes first. We're supposed to give them back to Colton as part of the shipping inquiry."

After I helped her haul out the boxes, Lorea called Sylvia so that she could prepare for her first bridal fitting.

"She said she'll try to get here before one o'clock." Lorea replaced the phone and began a thorough inspection of each wedding gown.

"Do you need my help?"

"I got this." Lorea's fingers moved rapidly along the bodice of a dress, checking for imperfections.

"Good. I've got some craft work to do before I run errands."

An hour later, my eyes were watering from scheduling several posts on the website I had created with my mom: mashed potatoesandcrafts.com. It was a hit in the virtual sphere of crafting, recipes, and DIY wedding tips. My mom still couldn't believe that people from all over the world flocked to the site where country girls from Idaho shared their penchant for spuds and crafts. A craft blog was my guilty pleasure but one that worked perfectly with my wedding planning certification. I had created the site to share my favorite things with everyone, not just those in wedding mode, and so far it had been a lot of fun. Mashedpotatoesand crafts.com had also given me one more way to document ideas I could share with prospective clients.

I read through the simple steps needed to create favors for a vintage bridal shower. The pictures of "Five-Minute Lavender Sachets" made with antique hankies or lace doilies matched up perfectly with the instructions. My readers would love the idea, and I thought Lorea might like to do something similar for Natalie Berlin's bridal shower.

Clicking off the site, I stood and stretched, ignoring the dull pain in the small of my back. "I'm going to the post office, bank, and a couple other places. Do you need anything?"

"I'm certain we will both need chocolate by the end of the day." Lorea's expression was completely serious.

"You read my mind. The Rocky Mountain Chocolate Factory is one of my stops." I grabbed my purse. "I hope I don't miss our customer with the excited nostril."

Lorea laughed. "I'll be sure to give you details if you miss her."

"I guess we should let Walter know that most of the shipment came through," I said.

"Good idea. I'll give him a call." Lorea picked up the phone.

Walter Mayfield was the best jeweler in Ketchum. I had made it a point to check out his shop early on because I knew that part of being a successful wedding planner was in connections with other business owners. Plenty of couples visited Mayfield Diamonds, and Walter might be just the person to drop my name.

Luckily for me, Walter and I had hit it off, and the older gentlemen had already referred some clients. In turn, I encouraged prospective brides to visit his store and view his fine creations. It was convenient that my shop was only two doors down from Mayfield Diamonds. When Lorea had taken a happy couple over to meet Walter nearly three months ago, she mentioned her dream of opening a wedding dress shop.

A couple of weeks later, Walter told Lorea about his cousin Roland, who had connections with a clothing manufacturer in China. Elaborate wedding dresses were available for a fraction of the price, but they were still too expensive for Lorea's meager budget.

I ran my hand along the line of dresses now taking up space in the back room of my bridal boutique. The ten dresses we ordered had cost nearly eight thousand dollars. That was an incredible bargain, but with my savings already invested in a new business, I wasn't able to front the cost. Walter offered to help Lorea get started by giving her a loan. He said that Roland would benefit, and he wanted to see her achieve her dreams.

"Hmm. No one answers." Lorea hung up the phone.

"Maybe I can run over there and tell him on my way out," I offered.

"That's a good idea." Lorea smoothed the fabric on one of the gowns. "I have to keep pinching myself, Adri. They are so beautiful."

"It almost makes you want to get married, huh?"

Lorea wrinkled her nose. "Not yet. But our brides will be happy."

"That's right. When a bride-to-be sees these dresses, she'll fall in love all over again."

Most of the gowns would be priced at around five thousand dollars each, but Sylvia's dress flaunted a price tag of eighteen thousand dollars. We had special ordered it for less than twenty percent of the price she would be charged, which is why Lorea felt she could take the risk. With the profit from that one dress, she'd be able to pay back Walter and have enough cash to place an order for more. As long as Sylvia liked the dress and didn't want to try on the missing gown. Banking on a diva's nuptials was a risk, but as I examined another gown, I felt confident it was a risk well taken.

Tinkling bells signaled a customer entering the shop as I headed for the back door. Lorea was entrenched in satin and tulle, so I dropped my purse and hurried out front. A man with neatly trimmed black hair stood by the window display. He was leaning over the elegant fondant wedding cake, his fingers barely brushing the soft-pink satin roses surrounding the second tier. The cake was a sample brought in by a bakery in Hailey, the town bordering Ketchum; the owner had hopes of being on my preferred associates list. Everyone who had seen the cake thought it was wonderful. Of course Lorea and I still needed to taste it, but that would have to wait until later.

I recognized the man's profile. My stomach flipped as I thought of our date Saturday night. Dallas Reynolds had waited on my table for the girls' night Lorea and I had celebrated last Tuesday. When he asked me out, I surprised myself by agreeing. It was basically a blind date, and although I hated first-date jitters, I felt like we'd gotten through it quite nicely. He'd asked me out again for last night, but I had too much work to do, not to mention a bit of apprehension over treading into second-date territory.

I straightened and flicked a piece of white thread from my black pants. "Dallas! I didn't expect to see you here."

He turned and smiled. "I had to run some errands on this end of town and thought I'd drop by to say hello." He cleared his throat. "That is, if you're not too busy right now."

His green eyes were incongruent with his Asian features, and I found myself staring into them for half a second too long, just as I had on Saturday night. He raised his left eyebrow, and his smile widened. Immediately, my face felt warm.

"I was just heading out to run errands, but I'd love to show you around." It was flattering that he had stopped by to see me—that he wanted to get to know me. The tingles riding along my nerves weren't unpleasant, but it had been a long time since I'd been on a second date. I stepped forward and motioned to the desk where I helped clients sort through fabric swatches for centerpieces, type fonts for wedding invitations, and myriad other things. "This might bore you. Guys aren't usually into the whole planning of the fairy-tale wedding."

Dallas ducked his head. "You're right. I just needed an excuse to see you, but I am interested to know why you like being a wedding planner. I also love weddings—or at least, the cake they serve."

"Typical male. That's why we have food—to get the best man to attend."

He laughed. It was a nice laugh.

"Look, there's an ice show this Thursday. A special event. You might have heard." He shoved his hands in his jeans pockets. "Sasha Cohen is coming to town."

My heart skipped a beat. I remembered watching the talented skater when she won her first silver medal in the Olympics. I nodded. "I heard. She's amazing."

"Would you like to come with me? I know it's not much notice since it's tomorrow."

I shot him a mega-watt grin. "I love figure skating."

Dallas returned the smile. "And dinner before?"

This was it. I was committing to go on a second date with someone—after almost a year, I was finding strength to step forward. "Sure."

"I'll pick you up at six?"

"Sounds great. See you then."

He waved as he pulled the door open. The front door whooshed shut. My smile widened as I watched Dallas cross the street. I thought about why I had so readily agreed to go out with him. Of course, Sasha Cohen was hard to turn down. Usually after one date, however, I found enough excuses to keep from going out again. That was before Briette. Things were different now. I had promises to keep.

I headed to the back to see how much of the conversation Lorea had overheard. My grin stretched ear to ear as I reentered the sewing room. Lorea raised her eyebrows, and the pins in her mouth wobbled as she tried to keep from smiling back.

"Did you hear?"

Placing a few more pins in the hem of the dress, Lorea let out a sigh. "You're going to the ice show."

"To see Sasha Cohen!"

"That almost makes me wish I had a date."

"You could, you know, if you would stop turning down every guy who asks you out." I picked up a stray pin from the floor.

"I've seen too much behind-the-scenes action to want to date anyone seriously."

"Who would think a wedding planner could be a cynic?"

Lorea waved her pincushion at me. "I'm not a wedding planner; I'm your assistant. And I'm not a cynic. I'm just realistic."

I straightened a pile of fabric swatches and thought about how my promises included an attitude change. "I used to say that. But now I'm a 'glass is half full' kind of girl."

"Aren't you forgetting Brett Hansen the night of his rehearsal dinner?"

"Now, don't blame that on me. Friend to friend, I tried to warn Gwen not to marry him." I had a personal policy of honesty that Lorea liked to call "brazen bluntness." Whatever it was called, it meant that I didn't care about the money enough to help one of my friends make a mistake. I wasn't afraid to break up an engagement—I wouldn't stand idly by and let a girl marry a jerk if I could help it.

"It's too bad she didn't listen to you before the wedding was planned instead of after she found her fiancé making out with the caterer. That would've saved her parents a lot of money."

I cringed. "That reminds me. We really need to look into some new catering businesses."

"Glad I'm in charge of dresses," Lorea said.

I made a note on my to-do list before scrolling through the images of the wedding gowns we were thinking of ordering for the next shipment. My eyes lingered on one of the dresses, and I tried not to think of how it reminded me of Briette's gown. I looked down at my hands and saw that they were clenched into fists. The familiar strands of anxiety tightened my stomach. I straightened my shoulders and forced myself to relax. Not today. She would want me to be happy in my new business venture.

Briette would have been excited for my date with Dallas. It was time for me to open my heart to new possibilities. I hoped I could find the courage to do so.

Chapter 3

COFFEE FILTER ROSES

For each rose, gather three four-cup and three eight- to twelve-cup unused basket-style coffee filters. Dye them using watercolors or watered-down acrylic paint. Dip and then dry.

Stack the three large filters together. Flatten them out, then fold in half and in half again to form a triangular wedge. Using scissors, cut along the open end of the triangle to create a scalloped line. Do the same with the three small filters.

Open the cut filters and place the small stack on top of the large stack. With your fingers, pinch the underside of the stack in the center, where the folds meet, which will cause the filters to crinkle together. Using a stapler, staple just above where your fingers have pulled the filters together.

Turn the flower over and open up the filters. Beginning with the outermost filter, gather the filter at the base and pinch around the base to pull the circle tighter, forming ruffles and petal-like fullness. Repeat with each of the six filters, gathering them at the base and pinching along the bottom to create a stem-like bump on the bottom.

Wind masking tape around the base to hold the shape. Fluff out the flower.

Use coffee filter roses as table décor, hang from the backdrops or ceiling, or use them to create floral wreaths.

Courtesy of www.mashedpotatoesandcrafts.com.

Chatting with Dallas had put me a little behind, and the line at the post office was longer than I'd hoped. When I stopped by Walter's store to tell him about the shipment, I found the store closed. A hand-written sign taped to the front door stated he was sick. It seemed strange that he didn't have someone covering for him. I couldn't recall a time when Mayfield Jewelers had ever been closed during regular business hours. Walter was looking forward to seeing the gowns, and Lorea and I were just as excited to show him, but it would have to wait.

The sun burned off the cool mountain morning as I walked down the block to my building. Summer was fast approaching, but the temperatures were still sluggish, even this late in May. I unlocked the back door of my shop and stepped inside. Before I could greet Lorea, the wedding bells above the front door rang, and I recognized the click-click of stilettos.

"Hello, darlings," a familiar voice called out.

Glancing at Lorea, I suppressed an eye-roll and went to greet our client.

"Sylvia, how are you?"

"I'm feeling radiant. Isn't that how people describe a lovely bride?" Her hand fluttered, and the flash from a gargantuan diamond crossed my showroom as Sylvia Rockfort approached.

As usual, I struggled to come up with an appropriate response to her self-aggrandizing behavior. So I settled for a nod and a smile.

Sylvia looked as if she'd just stepped off a movie set. Her auburn hair was straight with just the right amount of shine, and the jeweled belt she wore with a light blue sundress accentuated her tiny waist. She directed one of her glamour-girl smiles my way. "I can't wait to see my dress, although it probably will need to be taken in around the waist."

I thought I heard Lorea groan from the back room.

"Lorea will be happy to help make it a perfect fit," I answered Sylvia with a plastic smile. Depending on who you asked, I had either done something very good or very bad to deserve a bride like Sylvia. Her Hollywood-style wedding at the end of June would bring in a fat paycheck, but would I be sane enough when it was over to cash it? I fidgeted, smoothing out invisible wrinkles on my lime-green blouse.

"Adrielle, I really wish you'd consider trying out my hair stylist." Sylvia leaned toward me and lifted one of my blonde strands, letting the length of it slip through her fingers. "Not quite curly, not quite straight."

"It's called relaxed, Sylvia," Lorea said as she came to the front of the shop. "You should try it. Adri's hair is beautiful."

Sylvia's blue eyes narrowed. They were set too close together, and the plastic surgeon's symmetry must have been off when he fixed her nose because one of the nostrils flared in a crooked slant when she was annoyed or angry. I cleared my throat and accidentally elbowed Lorea. "What she means is, my hair stylist thinks it's beautiful, and I'm not due for another trim yet."

"Follow me," Lorea said. "I have everything ready for your first fitting."

I hung back and listened to Sylvia's exclamations of delight as she examined the gown, and Lorea helped her try it on. We didn't have a private fitting room in the bungalow-turned-wedding head-quarters, but I had set up a partition which offered the look and feel we were after.

"We're ready," Lorea called.

I thought I heard a note of satisfaction in her voice, and when I entered the room I could see why. Lorea held a measuring tape and slowly twirled the bride-to-be in front of our full-length mirror. The satin bodice was tight-fitting against Sylvia's small waist, and the dress flared at the hip line, flattering her tall physique. Lorea put on a tiny pair of reading glasses she kept on a beaded chain around her neck to magnify her work. She examined the hem carefully.

Sylvia leaned over and looked at the hem as well. "I love the design, don't you?"

Lorea nodded, and I could see her shoulders relax. "It's lovely."

"We need to get a couple more mirrors to do that gown justice," I said. "You look beautiful."

"Isn't it divine?" Sylvia fingered the delicate beadwork on the bodice. "I love how it sparkles. Lorea said it would be bad luck to try on the other gown when this one is so obviously me, but I just have to make sure."

"I think I agree with Lorea." I inclined my head slightly and lifted a brow. Lorea shrugged and held up her crossed fingers.

The creamy strapless gown showed off Sylvia's tanned skin. She had pulled her auburn locks into a chignon for the fitting. Sylvia did look beautiful. Even though she hadn't been lovely to deal with, it was a nice change to see a smile and relaxed brows instead of the spoiled slant I had come to expect.

"I feel like everything is going to be perfect now," Sylvia said. "Oh, Adri, I know I've been difficult. Things have just been so stressful with Natalie planning her wedding the same time as mine." Sylvia stepped forward and grasped my hands. "But now it just feels like everything is coming together like I dreamed it would."

My nerves tingled at the mention of the person Sylvia considered her rival and worst enemy, Natalie Berlin. I hurried to change the subject. "Everything is on schedule, and I'm meeting with a couple new caterers for your bridal shower. I think one of them might be perfect for the theme you've selected."

"What about the country club?" The familiar slant returned. "Will they budge on the time at all?" She straightened, trying to appear taller, but my five-foot-ten inch height couldn't be matched by her high heels.

My head began to throb. "They were firm about their time frame, but I was able to reserve the club starting at two o'clock as a special circumstance."

"Wonderful!" Sylvia clapped her hands, and I noticed Lorea's attempt at a fake smile.

"I'm almost finished, Sylvia," Lorea said. "The dress seems to have been made for you. Only a few minor alterations will be needed."

I looked at the gown again. It *was* beautiful.

"Adri, can you pull out the other gown while Lorea finishes up? My friend Lisa says that she could be getting a ring any day. I thought she might like the other dress."

I opened my mouth to speak, but Lorea interrupted. "It's the third dress hanging over there." She pointed, and her eyes seemed to scream at me, *Just play along!*

24

My steps were hesitant as I approached the line of garment bags. Each wedding gown was a possibility and a risk at the same time. Did Lorea think that one of the gowns was close enough to Sylvia's alternate? If so, I hoped she wouldn't be able to tell the difference. For half a second, a part of me thought about coming clean, but I swallowed hard and choked on the painful truth. Lorea knew what she was doing: avoid making Sylvia angry, at any cost.

I would have to play along. The click of the zipper was akin to a timer counting down to an explosion. The dress was eager to escape the confines of plastic and spill its tulle and satin onto the floor. I noted the train on the back and hefted the fifteen pounds of fabric, moving slowly toward Sylvia.

She narrowed her eyes. "That isn't my backup dress. Lorea, don't you remember, it had a bell skirt."

"That's right." Lorea nodded. "Hmm, now I remember the problem. That particular dress was discontinued, and there was a mix-up with the order."

"What?" Sylvia's eyes flashed with anger. "But we ordered it. How could they discontinue it? And why didn't you say so in the first place?"

I felt my heart rate increase, but Lorea held up her hand to stop Sylvia's protest and spoke rapidly. "Tell you what. Let's get you out of this dress, and you can take a look at the other gowns. I know for a fact that none of them comes close to how extraordinary this gown is, but that way you will know for sure."

Sylvia's gaze flicked to the gowns hanging innocently in their dress bags, and then she turned her head and looked in the mirror again. The sneer was replaced with a demure smile. "I think you're right, Lorea."

She had echoed my words of earlier, but I knew we had barely missed a diva-sized tantrum. "I'll be at my desk if you need me." I wanted to breathe in my own level-headed space for a while.

"Thanks, Adri," Lorea called. I heard the relief in her voice.

I sat in my office chair and retrieved one of the cream binders with turquoise accents and silver embossed words on the front: *Adrielle Pyper's Dream Weddings, Where happily ever after is your destination.* I ran my fingers over the words and smiled. When I designed my shop, I had selected some of Briette's and my favorite colors to decorate with—turquoise and purple. The signature mix made it easy to recognize my mark on the otherwise boring pages I filled out for my clients.

Each of my clients was assigned a binder when we began preparations for her wedding. I looked at the other three binders stacked neatly on the bookshelf beside the desk and thought about the fifth one tucked away in the office safe. Two weddings during the month of June and three more in July. It didn't sound like much, but I handled everything from the typeface on the invitations to the musicians playing the couple's first dance.

A twelve percent commission might not sound like much, either, but with clients like Sylvia Rockfort, a wedding costing 100,000 dollars was well below what her incredibly rich parents thought their daughter deserved. So I put up with Miss Nostril because twelve percent of her projected 175,000-dollar expense sheet would go a long way in my business.

I flipped through a few pages of Sylvia's wedding binder and glanced back at the safe. The Rockfort-Porter wedding had come to me with only a two-month lead time. Because of the time crunch, I added a rush fee of five thousand dollars. The Rockforts had expected as much and signed the contract happily, which left me wishing I'd charged ten thousand extra.

Several indicators led me to assume I wasn't selected merely for my skill or charm. Word leaked out that I was planning the prestigious nuptials of movie star Brock Grafton and homegrown Natalie Berlin, which generated some interest in future wedding dates and new clientele. For the Rockforts, it generated a definite need to hire me as their wedding coordinator. Brock Grafton was Sylvia's ex-boyfriend, and rumor had it that at one time they had been close to tying the knot. Maybe he hadn't been able to get over that crooked nostril.

When Mrs. Bonnie Rockfort grilled me for details about the Berlin-Grafton wedding, I had to cite client privilege. "You wouldn't want me telling people your daughter's unique plans for her centerpieces, would you?" That shut her up, but the Rockforts kept a sharp eye on my list of vendors, trying to analyze which one Natalie would choose so they could best her. That was why I kept her wedding details under lock and key.

Thirty minutes later, I heard Lorea finishing up with Sylvia and decided to check on her. I stepped into the back room. "Is there anything else you need?"

"Actually, yes." Sylvia pivoted toward Lorea, who was bent over a piece of fabric with a mouthful of pins. "It's short notice, but I need another bridesmaid dress. My best friend from high school divorced her husband." Sylvia lowered her voice. "Jeff was *my* boyfriend clear through senior year. I don't think he ever got over me." She sighed. "Anyway, she's seen the error of her ways and we're best-ies again—just like the old days. She *must* be in my wedding." Sylvia leaned closer to Lorea. "That won't be a problem, right?"

The inside of my cheek stung from biting it. I couldn't make eye contact with Lorea or I might say something I'd regret—or worse, my contained laugh might come out as a snort. Lorea's skin practically buzzed with anger, but she pulled the pins from her mouth and gave Sylvia a stiff smile. "Have her call and give me her measurements, and I'll get started on it."

"I just knew you'd come through." Sylvia patted the top of Lorea's head. "Such a sweet little thing."

It was fortunate Sylvia was so oblivious to everyone around her—otherwise she couldn't have missed the smolder in Lorea's eyes or the way Lorea flinched when Sylvia patted her head.

"I'm betting the magazine will want to do a feature on my dress," Sylvia said. "I'll have my people call their people and get back with you."

"That would be wonderful. Thank you, Sylvia," I gushed.

"Ta, ta, darlings." Sylvia waved, and her twelve-carat diamond ring just missed Lorea's forehead. I covered a laugh as Lorea yanked another pin from the pincushion around her wrist. After the door closed and I checked to be sure Sylvia was on her way, I turned to Lorea. "So, how did it go?"

Lorea stabbed her pincushion with a needle. "When I envisioned my future as a dressmaker, Sylvia was never in those dreams."

"We'll get through it," I said. "When I lived in San Francisco, there were a few bridezillas I worked with at Bellissima." I thought about the difference of owning my business. The clients I dealt with on a monthly basis when I lived in California were mostly pleasant and there was always someone to assist me—here it was just Lorea and me. Not to mention that in addition to our current work load of wedding planning, the two of us had decided to venture into the wedding dress side of the business.

Lorea pulled out a dress and grumbled, "If I have to pick out this hem one more time . . ."

I drummed my nails on the counter. "Just think how much Sylvia is paying for each additional alteration."

Lorea scowled. She adjusted the silver chain holding the Basque cross, each arm of the cross curved, angling into the next in a sweeping pattern. Her frown lines reverted to a smirk. "Not to mention the price of her wedding dress."

I raised my eyebrows. "Yes, there is that to consider."

"But now I have to deal with fitting another one of her lovely friends." Lorea kicked her shoes off, kneeling on the floor to cut fabric. She wore five-inch wedge sandals so clients wouldn't tower over her, but she always took them off when she was sewing.

"I'm surprised we've made it this far. I thought she would've called it off by now," I said.

Lorea shook her head. "I might win that bet. It shouldn't be hard to believe, but I can't fathom getting engaged to try to make Brock jealous."

We'd discussed our secret theory a few times, but I still wasn't sure if Sylvia was out to get Brock back or if she just wanted to win the competition for Most Glorious Wedding.

"She doesn't have a chance with Brock. He and Natalie are a perfect match," Lorea said. "I wish we didn't have to deal with Sylvia at all."

"At least we have Natalie, thanks to you."

Lorea's shoulders relaxed when I mentioned the other wedding we were planning, the one for her best friend. "I might quit if it weren't for Natalie." She sighed. "But Sylvia's dress really is perfect. I'm so glad she liked it."

"It probably helped that you told her it was one of a kind and the most expensive dress coming into the store."

Lorea nodded, and then she looked at me, her eyes scrunching in the corners as if deciding to share a secret.

"Whatever you want to say, just say it." I tilted my head in her direction.

Lorea laughed. "I keep thinking about the dress with the organza frills. I know Natalie has something else picked out, but I can just see her in it." She pulled the measuring tape through her fingers. "Would it be totally inappropriate to ask her to come down and try it on?"

My gaze traveled over Lorea's head to the gown in question hanging for display. The bodice was fitted, embellished with thousands of sparkling sequins outlining the embroidered roses that reached to the hipline. Then the ruffles started, and I loved every one of them. The lightweight organza kissed the glittering tulle skirt with nearly thirty layers of frills covering the wide bell skirt of the princess dress. Natalie would look exquisite in it.

I sighed. "I couldn't live with myself if we didn't let her at least see it."

Lorea grinned, and I noticed her squeezing the pincushion. "I'll call and tell her it's my duty as her bridesmaid to introduce her to this dress." She dashed off to make the call, her reading glasses swinging haphazardly from their chain. A few minutes later, she returned. "Natalie will be here in an hour. She told me she was just looking at bridal magazines, wondering if she really was in love with the dress she was thinking of buying. She sounded so happy I called."

"That's great. Can you imagine if we could sell that dress, too? We'd have enough money to pay cash for the next shipment."

Lorea nodded, and I knew she was mentally calculating how far the gown's price tag of eleven thousand dollars would take us.

Moving to my desk, I clicked through a few spreadsheets and brought up my to-do list. I enjoyed planning weddings, and working on Natalie's had been more satisfying than most. But my feelings differed for my other major client. To say that Sylvia's wedding plans had been exhausting would be an understatement. She had pushed the limits on every aspect of her dream wedding. One thing was certain, though—the Rockfort-Porter wedding would be absolutely gorgeous. I scrolled through my contact list and pulled up Frankie Lawson's number.

"Hello, you've reached Francesca Lawson, wedding coordinator for the Sun Valley Lodge. We'd love to make your day unforgettable, so please leave a message, and I'll get back with you soon."

I waited for the beep. "Hi, Frankie. This is Adri. I wondered if you'd talked to the chef yet about the possibility of making a second wedding cake shaped out of the fourteen different cheeses Sylvia selected. I'll have some color samples ready for you later today so the crackers don't clash with the linen."

Biting the inside of my cheek again, I ended the call. I took my job seriously, but a wedding for someone like Miss Nostril only happens once a decade. I relaxed and let the smile creep across my face as I pictured Frankie laughing when she heard the message. Sometimes I had to remind myself to enjoy the small moments.

"Before you ask, I'm planning to finish Sylvia's centerpieces by tonight," Lorea said.

"Are you sure? I can help you."

"All I need to do is stab another magic wand in each of those hideous things. Don't worry."

I shook my head. Lorea hated themed weddings, and the Rockfort-Porter event was all about the magic of true love—celebrity style. Even though the clients were hard to please, I enjoyed the change of pace that went into the details of the wedding plans for a unique celebration.

Taking advantage of the unplanned meeting with Natalie, I arranged the three swatches of fabric we were contemplating for the accent color in the centerpieces. The major decisions had all been made, but Natalie had struggled with selecting the perfect shade of ivory to complete the burgundy and forest green that would highlight the wedding decor.

"A wedding I went to last year had strands of paper roses hanging from the ceiling," Lorea said as she fitted her dress mannequin with a swath of cream-colored silk. She looked over at me. "Fishing line makes them look as if they are floating in the air. It might be the perfect thing for Natalie's reception."

An image of blood-spattered emerald roses filled my mind. Delicate silk roses threaded with silver string. I swallowed hard.

"Adri, are you okay?" Lorea hurried over to my desk. "You look pale."

"Those were—I made hundreds of them." I looked at my hands. My purple glitter polish sparkled in the overhead light, another reminder of her. "Stayed up until three in the morning watching movies and sewing with Briette so we could finish."

Lorea sucked in a breath. "Oh, I had no idea. Let me get you some water."

I grasped Lorea's hand. "I'm sorry—it shouldn't matter. Natalie would love it."

"No way, Adri." She shook her head and her dark hair brushed the nape of her neck. "There are lots of other ideas. In fact, I thought of one for the bridal shower invitations. Is there any way you could use a button on the card?" She released my hand and gave me a water bottle.

I knew Lorea was changing the subject, but I was happy to push those memories back and focus on another aspect of the business that I loved—the bridal shower. I took a sip of the water Lorea offered me and forced a smile. "Can we use *buttons* on the card?" I winked. "Do you know who you're talking to?"

Lorea laughed and held up her pincushion. "Good. I think it'll give them some personality."

"And everyone will know that Natalie's best friend is throwing the party before they even open the invitation."

"Hey, girls." Natalie walked through the door. It had only been forty minutes since Lorea phoned her. She carried an over-sized purse that I knew contained several bridal magazines and notebooks. Hefting the purse, she waved one of the magazines at me. "Can you believe this farm girl is getting nervous about what those movie stars think?"

"Whatever. You *look* like a movie star. Just worry about what Brock thinks," I said.

"She's right. You're gorgeous." Lorea motioned for Natalie to follow her to the back of the shop. Brock had admitted he was initially drawn to Natalie for her tall and slender model-type build and clear blue eyes, but he fell in love with her kind and generous nature.

Natalie swept back a loose curl of soft, brown hair, tucking it behind her ear. "My stomach is doing backflips, I'm so excited to see this dress."

"Right this way," Lorea said. She led Natalie into the makeshift gown-fitting area we had set up in the back. The dress hung a few feet off the ground, trailing with layer upon layer of gorgeous frills.

Natalie gasped and covered her mouth. I noted how her eyes sparkled as she stared at the dress. She dropped her purse and approached the gown with tentative steps. "Lorea, this is beautiful. Help me try it on."

Lorea and I laughed. I waited as Lorea helped Natalie into the dress and tugged on the invisible zipper sewn artfully into the snug bodice. I straightened the mirror and caught Natalie's smile as she looked at herself.

The dress was a size six and a bit on the short side for the bride's long legs. Lorea could let out the hem and take in the bodice, but otherwise, it appeared to have been created for Natalie.

"Oh, I love it." She turned slowly, craning her neck to see each side of the gown.

"I can do some alterations," Lorea said. "And then it'll be perfect for you."

"I know Brock will love it," Natalie responded.

"It does fit right in with the choices you two have made for the wedding." I grabbed a clipboard and jotted down a few notes about how the materials in this dress would flow with the backdrop of the reception.

"How much is it?" Natalie glanced at me and then at Lorea, who paused a moment before answering.

"We were going to mark it for eleven thousand, but you can have it for nine." The price hung in the air between us, and I remembered the discussions we'd had with Brock and his bride-to-be. He continually assured her that he wanted to pay for the wedding, and she kept reminding him that it was the bride's responsibility. She selected simple, elegant designs to keep prices low and Brock didn't mind, as long as he could foot the bill—and he had won that argument.

"I don't want you to give me a discount." Natalie bit her lip. "I don't know. It's just so expensive."

"You're right. It is," Lorea said. "But you have to wear something you love on your wedding day. I know you don't want Brock to help you pay for things—and I know it's because people have accused you of being a gold digger, but honey, sometimes you just have to swallow your pride."

Natalie shook her head. "Good thing you're my best friend, or I might think you were just trying to make a sale."

I suppressed a laugh as Lorea's eyebrows shot up. "I'm trying to make a sale *and* help my friend have the most beautiful wedding possible." She smoothed down one of the frills and grinned at Natalie. "Everyone knows the dress is the focal point."

"She's right. If you're going to splurge, do it on the dress." I made myself a note to remind Brock that Natalie was hopelessly in love with him.

Lorea began measuring, pinning, and writing down what needed to be done to the dress as Natalie smiled into the mirror. I showed her the fabric swatches, and she selected a chiffon lace, just as I had thought she would.

"I'll have some samples ready for you in a week." I checked that off my list.

"Are you bringing a date to my wedding, Adri?" Natalie asked with a teasing lilt to her voice.

Lorea answered before I could. "Yes, and he's taking her to the ice show this week."

I glared at Lorea, but Natalie's face lit up. "To see Sasha Cohen? Brock's taking me—we're going to that fancy dinner at the lodge before the show, too. So, who is he?"

My brows relaxed as Natalie's contagious joy swept over me. "His name is Dallas Reynolds. I met him at the Roosevelt Grille. He's very nice, but I don't usually bring dates to the weddings I plan."

"Well, see if you can make an exception this time, won't you?" Natalie asked. "Someone as talented as you should be planning her own wedding."

I wrinkled my nose. "Thanks, Natalie, but I think your sentiments should be directed toward Lorea, don't you?" With a wink in her direction, I hurried back to my computer to order the fabric Natalie had selected. I could hear Lorea grumbling about "too many romantics." Natalie was right—someday I hoped to plan my own wedding. I just needed to find the right groom first.

Chapter 4

GUEST BOOK QUILT

Prepare or purchase 4-inch quilt squares and place on the wedding reception entry table. Invite each guest to share their love by signing a quilt square with a permanent fabric marker. Construct a quilt from the signed quilt squares and present it to the married couple as a special "guest book" that will be both useful and memorable.

Courtesy of www.mashedpotatoesandcrafts.com

"Ready to go home and veg?" I asked Lorea. The hands of the mantle clock were nearing the five. "We've worked too hard today."

Lorea pulled her bottom lip through her teeth. "With Sylvia's new order for another bridesmaid's dress, I won't have time to finish this hem for Natalie, and I'd really like to get it done by next week."

"I can help. Why don't I take it home and start undoing it for you?"

"Would you?"

"Sure. My hot date isn't until tomorrow, remember?"

"That's true." Lorea smirked. Then she reminded me how to handle the gown and the best method to take out the blind hem. "And no chocolate. Don't let this gown get near your stash."

"Yes, sir." I saluted.

"See you in the morning, boss."

The lights hummed for a moment after I turned them off, and I hurried out to the parking lot behind Lorea. It took me less than ten minutes to drive home and kick off my black leather sandals.

I didn't run in the evenings very often, but I definitely needed an endorphin high after the barely contained dress disaster. I ate a light dinner of broiled salmon, broccoli, and rice and gave myself a few minutes to decompress. Thirty minutes later, I laced up my neon green running shoes and forced myself out the door.

For the past year, I'd been the one-date wonder, never getting close enough to open up my heart and spill my painful secrets. I gave myself a mental pat on the back for agreeing to go on a second date with Dallas, while at the same time wishing it wasn't so hard. My natural fun-loving nature had been obscured by the tragedy in California.

All that was behind me now. My wedding planning skills meshed with my thriving craft business. Fate had frowned on me last year, but she must have been smiling when she nudged me toward Sun Valley.

The brisk mountain air raised goose bumps on my skin, and I shivered. It was late May, but the nights still cooled considerably, and the Sawtooth Mountains clung to the last remnants of winter snow. Breathing deeply, I paused, relishing the feel of the cooled oxygen in my lungs. Tension threaded my shoulders and I rolled them back, wincing when my right shoulder popped. The missing gown and the potential nightmare with the hole in Sylvia's dress had definitely strained my nervous system. I could feel every stitch in my tired bones.

After a few more stretches focusing on my high arches, I turned up the volume on my iPod and broke into a run. I was doing so much better now—not running away from everything, like before, but running toward a future filled with promise.

The bike paths of the Sun Valley area were never lonely, and the paved trails topped my list of reasons to live there. With the ski slopes in view and the lush scent of evergreen forests filling my nose, it didn't take long for my sluggish body to feel energized.

As I neared the first mile of my run, I couldn't help but wonder if I might see him again today. I chided myself. Several times in the past few weeks, I had sprinted past "the hottie," as Lorea had named him. She had been teasing me mercilessly since I told her about my encounter with the sexy, sculpted runner. Denial was my best defense when Lorea asked me why I had been so diligent in my running lately, but I found myself looking for him more than I cared to admit.

And there he was, rounding the next bend with his hat on backwards, chrome sunglasses reflecting the fading light. Maybe he was bald. I had never dared turn around and look for fear he might catch me looking at him, but I secretly hoped he used the hat to keep the sweat out of his eyes instead of to prevent sunburn on a shiny scalp. As he drew nearer and I watched his delts flexing in tandem with his six-pack abs, I decided baldness would be just fine.

When I first mentioned him to Lorea, she said she might have to take up running, if only to stop me from making a fool of myself. Three or four runs a week was enough for me, but I wondered how many nights found him pounding the pavement. Bright yellow running shorts with a black racing stripe sans shirt revealed his muscular body. So hot. My heart sped up as the distance between us disappeared.

I tried to suppress the goofy grin threatening to cross my face by reminding myself that my cheeks were flushed dark red and I hadn't shaved my legs for two days. Who was I kidding? I was a sweaty mess. All the same, I couldn't resist staring at those chrome sunglasses as he ran past, wondering what color his eyes might be.

"Great night for a run," he said between breaths.

"Yeah, it is." I lifted my fingers in a wave. Inside I screamed, *He talked to me! You idiot! And all you could say is, yeah, it is?* Oh well, he had initiated conversation. I couldn't wait to tell Lorea.

I wondered what the chances were that I might bump into him somewhere else in town but fully dressed. The Ketchum–Sun Valley area wasn't a metropolis—the population was less than four thousand—so it could happen. *Calm down, Adri.*

I thought about my own appearance. The large black sunglasses I wore covered one of my best features. People always commented on my dark brown eyes, remarking how they contrasted nicely with my honey blonde hair. My soft curls were hidden when I pulled my hair back into a ponytail. There was a chance he would recognize me, but could I pick him out of a lineup? I hoped so. I found myself smiling for the rest of my run.

When I returned home and showered, my thoughts strayed to Dallas versus "the hottie." It was nice to think of something besides wedding dresses, and I didn't need to make a decision yet, especially since I'd only been asked out by one of the guys. All the same, it was fun to imagine possibilities. The pillow on my bed looked inviting, but I knew I needed to start picking out that hem. Instead of sleeping, I washed my hands thoroughly, gathered my seam ripper, and lifted Natalie's heavy dress.

Fingering the soft folds of the gown, I plopped onto my sofa and flicked through my DVR list until I found a bunch of *Antiques Roadshow* episodes I had recorded. I pushed play, donned a pair of white cotton gloves, and started the tedious job of picking out the blind hem sewn into the satin underlying the last frilled layer. Forty-five minutes later, I had made it more than halfway around the dress. I was pleased to see the extra fabric folded neatly into the hem for just such an alteration as Natalie needed. Smoothing out the folds, I measured about four inches with my fingers and was satisfied that Lorea would be able to include a beautiful hemline for Natalie's tall figure.

The seam ripper slipped on a stubborn stitch, and I jabbed myself in the palm of the hand. "Ouch!" I cried as the point broke through the material of my glove. I checked my hand for any sign of blood. That would be more than I could take right now— blood stains on a wedding gown. I wasn't bleeding, so I put the glove back on and returned to the thick thread holding the hem in place. Scissors did the trick, and with a few snips the hem began to unroll again. As my fingers dug inside the hem to pull the stitching apart, they came in contact with something solid. I put my seam ripper down next to the scissors and examined the material with both hands.

There was something hard in that portion of the material. Pressing the hemline, I squinted, trying to see what had gone wrong. The hem bulged with some kind of solid mass. I inserted the sharp tip of the seam ripper and cut through the thread holding the hem together. I worked faster trying to free it, wondering all the while if I had stumbled upon some seamstress's secret.

The wad of material came loose, and I pulled it out, feeling the hard bumps inside. At first, I thought it might be extra fabric, but it was something else. My chest tightened. The gown had come all the way from China—what if it was infested with cockroaches or something even worse? I shuddered and then commanded myself to stop being a wimp.

A tiny slit with my scissors assured me that the roll of fabric was not filled with insects or vermin. Instead, hundreds of little rocks had been packed neatly inside the bundle. What in the world? The tube of material was only about six inches long. Why would anyone put rocks in a wedding dress? Was this some kind of ancient Chinese folklore or good luck charm?

I took off my gloves and emptied a handful of the rocks into my hand. I studied them under the light, and a nervous feeling wound its way up my throat. The rocks were yellowish and brown and all about the size of pea gravel, but there was something about them that set a warning bell off in my head. Sucking in a breath, I lifted one of the stones and held it up to the light. It definitely wasn't a rock. The light glinted off it, reminding me of crystal, but something told me that wasn't it, either.

Moving the wedding dress aside, I cupped my hand and carried the mysterious stones over to my computer desk. I had an idea of what I thought the stones might be—in my wildest imagination—but I felt a little foolish as I toggled my mouse. Using Google, I brought up an image of uncut diamonds and gasped. My hands shook and I clutched the stones tightly until they jabbed the soft skin of my palms.

The images were of rough-looking stones with tints of yellow,

brown, and mottled gray. Looking closely at the pictures, I could
see that most resembled a rough caricature of the diamond shape,
and I opened my hand to look at the stones again. Most of them
had four distinct edges like a diamond. A few appeared more like
a triangle, but none of them were round, like you might find in a
collection of rocks or gravel. I shook my head—this couldn't be
happening.

My breath came in short puffs as I hurried into the kitchen
and grabbed a Ziploc bag. I dumped the diamonds—if that's what
they were—inside, emptying them all from the fabric tube. As
they cascaded on top of each other, the light glinted from the
rough edges, and I reminded myself to be calm and think about
what my brother Wes would do. I had seen him in stressful situations—his mind alert and his ability to make good decisions
seemingly unhindered by anxiety, the same kind that was clouding
mine at the moment.

Would he call the police? No, not yet. If they weren't real
diamonds, the police would just laugh at me, and even worse
they might take Natalie's dress in for examination. I sucked in a
breath—I couldn't do that to her or to her exquisite gown.

Maybe I could call Walter and have him look at the stones. A
glance at the clock told me that option was also out. It was almost
midnight. I'd have to use Google to help me figure out my problem. Typing in searches for checking the authenticity of diamonds
brought up several pictures and pages of details. There was way
more information than I could sift through in a night. I decided to
try the easiest test first—scratching glass.

According to the Internet, cubic zirconium or moissanite,
types of man-made stones, could also cut glass, so that test wasn't
as reliable if you were trying to see how cheap your fiancé was

before you said "I do." But I already knew these rocks weren't man-made diamonds, so I picked out one yellowish gold stone and walked over to my patio door.

It took a second for my hand to stop shaking enough that I wouldn't drop the gem. I located an area right near the handle that I thought might be inconspicuous. Pushing hard on the glass, I was rewarded with a tiny scraping noise. I continued pushing for about an inch, then traced the smooth cut I had just made in my glass window. I flicked on the large Mag flashlight I kept by the back door and shone into the blemish I'd created. It wasn't just a surface scratch, like a rock might make—it was straight and deep.

I returned the diamond to the bag and stared for a minute, estimating that my quart-sized Ziploc held nearly two hundred rough diamonds. And since rough diamonds usually come from Africa (according to Google), I wondered how they had made their way into a wedding dress from China. The only explanation I could come up with was that someone was smuggling diamonds in wedding gowns, and Lorea just happened to order the wrong dress. Or dresses.

A sick feeling caused a sweat to break out on my forehead. What about the missing wedding gown from the shipment and the hole in Sylvia's gown?

I grabbed my phone, thinking of calling Lorea. I had a moment of self-doubt. It couldn't possibly be connected, could it? Natalie's and Sylvia's gowns were the most extravagant and unique that Lorea had ordered. Had someone planned to steal the dresses all along and just taken the wrong ones?

My windpipe suddenly felt tight, and I checked to make sure my front and back doors were locked. The bag of diamonds in my hand felt ominous. I should call the police. My mind sped forward over the chain of events that might take place if I put in a call to Tony, my brother's childhood friend now turned police officer. If I told him I found diamonds in Natalie's dress, he would surely confiscate it for the investigation. Then I wouldn't have one missing wedding gown but two. The pearl beading in the bottom of the box came to mind, and I wondered if something bigger was going on with the dress shipment. It didn't matter. I couldn't report this yet. I had to protect Natalie's gown and Lorea's future. My future.

But Tony would definitely want to know. I wondered if I could call him as a friend. No, he was a police officer and a good detective. He would have to do his job. Lorea's dream of her own dress shop would be crushed instantly in this tight-knit community. No one would risk getting attached to a dress if it might turn up missing or be placed under investigation for diamond smuggling.

I needed to keep Natalie's dress until her wedding. The bag of diamonds crinkled as I tightened my grip, thinking of how I could do the right thing for Natalie, Lorea, and the police. What if I could hide the bag of diamonds in one of the boxes from the shipment? Nervous energy spun around me as a hundred different scenarios marched through my head. Could I lie to the police, to Tony, for the sake of a wedding dress?

Tomorrow, I would study the box and figure out if my idea might work. I thought about taking the diamonds with me to work and stowing them for Lorea to discover, but my throat tightened with fear. It felt too risky to carry the diamonds back and forth. I would have to formulate a solid plan first. Until then I needed a hiding place for the diamonds, and it had to be a good one. My mind ran through all the common scenarios I'd seen in movies. Under a loose floorboard or a piece of carpet, even taped to the inside of the lamp shade. Then I thought of the perfect place.

I walked into my front room and stood in front of the gorgeous quilt folded neatly on a wrought iron stand near my sofa. Light spilled from the hallway onto the quilt. I purposely left the light off in the room as I thought about what I would do next.

The quilt had been a gift from my mother when I completed my wedding planner certification. The varied shades of fabric in maroon, sea foam green, and cream formed circles that intertwined across the fabric in the famous Wedding Ring pattern—my mom felt it was the perfect symbol of success.

My aunt Dana had helped her piece the quilt and hand-stitch the binding. I carefully unfolded the quilt, turning over one corner to reveal one of my favorite pieces. On the bottom right-hand corner a block of hunter green material had been stitched over the lighter green backing. I held it up close, reading the screen-printed cursive writing, *Created by Mashed Potatoes and Crafts.* Then I ran my index finger along the embroidered signature of Laurel Pyper, my mom. Many quilters put such signature blocks with their name and date on the backs of their masterpieces. Most people wouldn't know what a signature block was, let alone where to look for one.

I placed the quilt back on the rack and returned to my living room, where Natalie's dress covered most of the couch like a ghostly bride. I grabbed my sewing basket and seam ripper and headed to the darkened front room.

Clutching the bag of diamonds tightly, I focused on the shades covering my front window. Was someone lurking outside, waiting for the chance to find the diamonds? I shivered and checked the seal on my Ziploc, then rolled the bag carefully into a long tube. I allowed the extra air to escape and then retightened the seal. Grabbing my seam ripper, I sat cross-legged on the floor with my wedding ring quilt. I paused for half a second before picking out the stitches along the side of the signature block.

The first threads popped and I winced, but I continued until I had opened the seam about three inches. I wondered briefly about stashing the diamonds somewhere else and leaving the police an anonymous tip, but what if someone found them first? With a shake of my head, I slid the bag of diamonds inside the signature block. They settled nicely along the bottom seam of the fabric where the cotton batting inside bulged naturally next to the tight edge of binding.

My fingers shook as I threaded a needle and hurriedly stitched the hole shut. With a snip of my scissors, I held the quilt up and examined my hiding place. I doubted that my own aunt Dana— the expert quilter—would even think of looking inside the signature block. I hoped that my game of hide and seek would be good enough to buy me some time to figure out what kind of mess I was in.

I rearranged the quilt on the stand, willing my heartbeat to slow to a normal rhythm. The clock ticked loudly in time with the blood pumping through my veins. It was half past midnight, and I needed to calm down so I could get some sleep—there was work to be done in the morning.

After I checked the locks again, I walked through my house just in case a diamond thief was hiding somewhere. I scanned the rooms with my heavy flashlight and my cell phone ready to dial 911. Within a few minutes, I was completely freaked out. I turned on several lights in my house and walked back to my bedroom. I did some stretches and focused on breathing deep to slow my heart rate.

Half an hour later, I slipped between my covers, pulling the blanket up to my chin, and grabbed my iPod from my night-stand. I selected a playlist I had titled "Relaxation" and pushed play. Forcing myself to follow the cadence of the music, I felt my breathing slow. With my eyes scrunched shut, I drifted off to sleep while listening to my favorite melodies played by talented violinists.

Chapter 5

CALMING SPRITZER

Fill a small spritz bottle (about 4 to 6 ounces) with water. Add three drops lavender and one drop melaleuca essential oils (certified pure therapeutic grade). Lightly spray a refreshing mist over face, hair, or clothes.

Courtesy of www.mashedpotatoesandcrafts.com.

A strange noise awakened me, and I peeked out from under my covers to see light streaming through the blinds. The noise was a mixture of one song being played in my right ear, which still had an earbud in it, and the alarm on my cell phone playing on the pillow near my left ear.

After I pulled out the earbud and rubbed the sleep from my eyes, my thoughts immediately turned to the package sewn into my quilt. Those diamonds were probably worth a lot of money, maybe close to a million dollars, and it made my stomach turn over with dread when I thought about who might be looking for them. I again considered calling the police, but I couldn't, not yet. I thought of what Wes would say—he'd definitely tell me to call Tony, but I felt there were no good options at the moment that wouldn't hurt my business or my friends. Best to scope out my idea of making it seem the diamonds were in the box, but I'd have to do that when I was certain Lorea wasn't around.

I felt guilty just thinking about my plan. It was barely seven o'clock and I hadn't slept well, but I knew that action would be the only thing to put my nerves at ease.

I had hoped to take some time before breakfast to undo more of the hem. Instead I stowed Natalie's gown in my spare bedroom, covered it with a quilt, and hurried out the door. I double-checked that it was locked. The panicked feeling kneading the back of my neck was hard to ignore. What if there were more diamonds in the dress? I rolled my shoulders back and commanded myself to focus on what I could accomplish *and* control: my to-do list.

As I drove to Pyper's Dream Weddings, I concentrated on the good things happening with my shop. The location was perfect. Two blocks from Main Street and one block from Sun Valley Road put me in prime real estate territory, but the two-bedroom bungalow-turned-boutique was too small for most merchants. It was just right for a wedding planner's headquarters.

I stopped by Iconoclast Books & Café, another great perk around the corner, to buy one of their delicious Thursday special bran-berry muffins and an apple juice. I decided a reward for the diamond drama was due—the dense muffins with a hint of sweet honey were perfect.

With a mouthful of goodness, I opened the back door of my shop. Something wasn't right. My heart sped up, and I tensed as a feeling of unease lifted the hairs on the back of my neck. I flipped on the light and stood near the doorway, eyes flicking nervously around the room. For half a second, I blamed my nerves on my upcoming date with Dallas that evening. Then I took another step forward, and my breath stilled. Sylvia's closet was open, and I could see that something was missing.

Organization being key to a wedding planner's success, I had installed several clothing racks with sliding doors to keep out dust. Each wedding party was assigned a closet, where we stored samples for tablecloths, centerpieces, clothing for the wedding party, tuxedos, and now wedding gowns. I pulled the door all the way to the side and rummaged through Sylvia's closet. No dress.

"Don't panic. Maybe Lorea has it," I whispered to myself as I frantically dialed her number.

Lorea didn't answer, and I ended the call, not trusting myself to speak calmly in a message. I hurried to the rack of wedding gowns in the corner and counted six. Two were missing. Struggling not to freak out, I slid open the closet labeled Berlin-Grafton. Nothing had been touched.

Natalie's dress was at my home, hidden safely away in my spare room. Now I thanked myself for offering to take out the hem, even if it did involve illegal diamonds, or her gown might be missing as well.

But were the dresses really gone? I rummaged through every corner in the back room, searching, and then returned and counted the dress bags again. I unzipped each one to make sure there weren't two in one bag.

A knock at the front door brought my attention to the fact that I hadn't yet opened the shop. I peeked around the corner and was horrified to see Sylvia standing outside the glass double doors, tapping her foot.

A key turned in the lock behind me, and Lorea came in humming. "Hi, Adri. Did you—" She stopped when she saw my face. "What's wrong?"

"Please tell me you have Sylvia's dress."

Lorea shook her head slowly. The knocking on the front door increased. Lorea moved to look, and I grabbed her arm. "It's Sylvia. She's probably here to try on her dress again, but it's gone."

"She didn't make an appointment. And what do you mean, it's gone?" Lorea ran to the closet rack and pawed through the items. Then she repeated what I had done and searched the hanging bags of gowns. "Where is it?"

"I don't know. When I came in this morning, something felt off, and then I noticed the closet door was halfway open." I motioned to the closet and tried to ignore Sylvia's tapping and obnoxious "Hello?" outside the store.

Lorea pressed her fingers against her temples. "Okay, you go talk to Sylvia. Tell her I'm still working on her dress, and we'll have to reschedule for later."

What was happening? The dress missing from the shipment, the hole in Sylvia's gown, rough diamonds, and now this? I swallowed and walked toward the front of the shop. But I halted before I entered the main showroom. My office safe was gone. Someone had hacked through the floor mount and taken the entire thing. I cried out, "Lorea, call the police. My safe is gone!"

Grabbing a sheet of paper and a Sharpie, I wrote a note and headed for the door. My foot slid, and I grabbed a chair before I lost my balance. Looking down, I sucked in a breath. Bits of chocolate cake and frosting stuck to the bottom of my white sandals. The beautiful wedding cake had been smashed, pink satin roses stained dark with chocolate dotted the floor, and fury licked the back of my throat. The gooey pudding infused with raspberry that had once filled the top layer of the cake was now splattered up the side of the wall. I hadn't even tasted it!

The thought made me pause, and I realized I was one breath away from losing it. The paper in my hand crinkled as I clenched my fist. Taking a deep breath, I smoothed out the paper, stepped forward, and taped it to the glass. I watched as Sylvia read it.

Please excuse us while we take care of a minor emergency. A broken pipe was discovered this morning.

Leaning close to the door, I called out, "I'm sorry, Sylvia. We'll make it up to you if you'll come by Monday. There's a wonderful surprise for you."

"I really wanted to try on my dress again. I felt a little heavy yesterday, and I've been dieting since then."

"I understand, but we have to get this fixed."

Her right nostril flared but then relaxed as my words sank in. Sylvia nodded and waved. "Good luck, darling."

I scrambled to the back of the store to hear the remnants of Lorea's conversation with the police.

"They're on their way."

Fighting back tears, I thought about the contents of the safe. There wasn't much—a pair of diamond earrings Walter had lent me to show a potential client, two hundred dollars cash, and the most important item: Natalie Berlin's wedding binder. Every speck of personal information about her tastes and desires was recorded in that book. I did have a file on my computer for the Berlin-Grafton event with a spreadsheet of all the vendors involved, but I couldn't get back those personal details. The wedding would go on just fine, but I often perused the binders for a spark of inspiration to give each ceremony that special touch.

My throat tightened when I heard another tap on the glass. I hoped Sylvia hadn't come back. With relief I saw a tall man with light brown hair waving at me as I approached. He wore a dark suit, and his badge was clipped to the front of his belt. My shoulders drooped as I unlocked the door to greet the detective from the Ketchum police department.

"Tony, I'm glad you came." My throat was thick with unshed tears, and I struggled to retain my composure.

"Hey, Adri. I wish we were with Wes meeting over fried pickles instead."

One corner of my mouth turned up. "Me too." It seemed a long time since I was tagging along with my older brother and his friends in our hometown of Rupert.

Anthony Ford patted my shoulder as he walked inside. "So your shop was robbed." He stepped over a gooey blob of frosting and pink roses. "And vandalized?"

"Makes me so mad. Lorea and I were going to eat that today."

Tony raised an eyebrow and his lips twitched. I knew he was trying not to smile, and somehow that made me feel better.

I motioned to the back door. "At first I wasn't sure because nothing looked out of place, and then I noticed three missing wedding gowns out of the nine that were delivered yesterday. I was double-checking to see if the dresses were somewhere else in the store when I noticed that my safe was gone." I pointed to the sharp edge of metal protruding from the floor.

Tony knelt down. "Hmm. Cut right through it. This must be the broken pipe you referred to in the note on your door."

Wrinkling my nose, I tried to keep the flush from heating up my cheeks, but Tony just laughed. I shrugged. "I'm not a good liar, but I thought it'd be better to keep it quiet for now."

"Your shop is an odd target for a burglary, but you never can figure out a criminal's mind," Tony muttered.

I wondered if I should tell him about the little rocks I found in Natalie's dress. *Yes, that would be great. Why don't you just turn over all of the gowns now?* I answered my thoughts. I opted for a vague reference. "Strange things have been happening with this shipment of dresses." I told him about the hole in Sylvia's gown and the dress that didn't arrive.

"Those are good things to take into account." Tony scribbled in his notepad. "Can I take a look at the shipment?"

"Sure. Lorea and I unpacked all the gowns over here." I motioned to the gowns hanging, ready to be steamed, and those still tucked in their packaging.

"What about the boxes?"

I swallowed. "We stacked them over here. I want to keep them for my claim." To my chagrin, Tony nodded and headed over to the stack of boxes. He looked inside each one, made a note on his pad, and continued to the dresses.

If only I could've hidden the diamonds in the box. Tony would have found them and Natalie's dress wouldn't be in danger. Stupid, stupid, stupid.

"What did you keep in the safe?" Tony asked.

"Not much. Two hundred dollars in cash. The most valuable items were a pair of diamond earrings from Mayfield Jewelers and a binder full of wedding plans." I frowned. "Irreplaceable, but it will probably be thrown out by the thief."

"How much do you think the diamond earrings were worth?"

I could taste the muffin in the back of my throat. "At least a thousand. Walter will know. I'm pretty sure my insurance will cover that."

"Okay, give me a description of the earrings," Tony said.

"They were half a carat each, I think. In a white-gold setting. Walter probably has another pair exactly like them in his store. Maybe you could take a picture," I offered.

"Good idea. Can you describe the binder?" Tony jotted notes on a spiral pad.

"I'll do better than that." I pulled an empty planner from a storage closet. "It looked just like this, but with swatches of fabric, some beading, pictures, and other items in each of these clear pockets."

Tony flipped through the binder, trying his best to look interested, but he didn't fool me. "Follow me, and I'll show you where we keep the wedding gowns."

Lorea stood in front of Sylvia's closet staring at the space where the wedding dress should have been hanging. "She'll kill me."

I frowned. "No, she'll kill *us*."

"Who will?" Tony asked.

"One of the gowns belonged to Sylvia Rockfort." I cleared my throat and pushed down the panic threatening to overtake me. "She's getting married in three weeks."

Sylvia's B-star rating wasn't enough to attract her a lot of attention, but most residents of Sun Valley had seen their fair city highlighted in the tabloids when she dated Brock Grafton.

Tony grimaced.

"She's going to be so angry when she finds out. We'd like to keep this quiet for a few days, if possible," I said.

"We'll file a report, but the most important thing to do now is contact your insurance adjuster. You do have theft insurance?"

"Not enough to cover everything." My parents had insisted

I invest in good insurance, but I hadn't upped the merchandise value before the shipment of wedding gowns arrived. That error in my planning now hung like a huge flashing "I told you so" beacon in the empty space of the closet where Sylvia's dress should have been. Again the panic crawled up the back of my throat as I calculated how much the insurance might cover and what Lorea and I would do with the balance. I clamped down on the fear and reassured myself that everything would work out—there would be time to dry-heave later. I definitely would not think about multicolored stones in a quilt.

After Tony left, Lorea and I tidied up and attempted to get some work done, but neither of us was very successful. I heard a sniffle and walked to the back room where Lorea was sewing.

"Lorea?" I crouched beside her and put my arm around her slim frame.

She attempted a smile but failed. She wiped at the tears escaping the corners of her eyes. "Sylvia's going to kill me," Lorea sobbed. "She'll ruin us. You know how she is with her lawsuits."

"Maybe we should call a lawyer." It was something I didn't want to do, but I couldn't soothe Lorea's fears when the same thought had crossed my mind.

She lifted her head. "Do you know any who could scare her off in case she tried to sue us?"

"First of all, I'm going to find that dress. And second, Sylvia wouldn't have grounds to sue if we offer her a full refund and a replacement dress."

Lorea didn't look convinced, but she wiped her face and let out an angry huff. "I can't believe this is happening when we were so close to making this dream a reality."

"Your dream is still coming true. We'll figure this out, and don't forget we have Natalie's dress." *Not thinking of diamonds*, I repeated to myself. I pulled out my cell phone and started scrolling through contacts.

"What are you doing?"

"I'm trying to see if I know any lawyers." My mouth turned down. "But the only one I know lives in Phoenix."

Lorea stood and picked up her pincushion. "Have you heard about the new divorce lawyer in town?"

"No, should I have?"

"Natalie's mom, Kaly, was telling me he's been keeping the courts busy."

Stowing my phone in my purse, I lifted my shoulders. "Well, people do get divorced—they say over half of all marriages end in divorce these days."

Lorea tsked. "I know. It's just that he's such a cynic that Kaly swears he could make even someone like Natalie want to get a divorce. He hates the idea of marriage."

"And how did she come by all this info?"

"Kaly's brother is in the process of getting divorced. His wife hired the new lawyer." Lorea smoothed the fabric on one of the gowns. "Anyway, Kaly warned me about him because she was concerned. He's been advertising his services for prenuptial agreements."

"Why is that a concern?" I toggled through a list of expenses on my computer and tried to figure out how much I could afford to spend on a security camera.

"Because when people meet with him for a prenup, he talks them out of getting married. But the bigger reason is, he's friends with Brock. I guess he's doing the prenup for Natalie."

"I can see why that would have Kaly worried." Natalie's

mother was a born-and-raised Idahoan, and she was as genuine as you could find. It was probably hard for her to wrap her mind around why a prenuptial agreement would be needed in the case of her sweet daughter. "And who is he?"

"I can't remember his name," Lorea replied. "People are saying he's pretty tight-lipped about his past. They're not even sure where he came from because he's so vague, but he's good at what he does."

"Well, let's just hope Sylvia's dress turns up so we don't have to worry about lawyers. I'm going to make a few calls about installing a security system."

Thirty minutes later, I had an appointment scheduled on Saturday for installation of a surveillance camera. Just before noon, Walter Mayfield tapped on the glass. He wore a concerned look, so it was a safe bet he had come to offer his condolences or perhaps to check on the future payback of his loan.

"Hi, Walter." I opened the door for him. "I guess you heard the bad news."

"No specifics. Tony said there was a break-in, and he needed to check the area."

"Some of our wedding gowns were stolen," I said.

Walter flinched and his forehead creased with worry, but in the next breath he composed himself, giving us his usual smile. "The important thing is that you girls are okay."

"Thanks, Walter," Lorea said.

His smile was the thing I liked most about his appearance. Walter was in his fifties, with silver streaks running through his dark hair. He wore an ornate wedding band he had designed himself. Mayfield Jewelers was known for the outstanding quality of their diamonds, and his ring had three beautiful stones embedded in the band. "I have some insurance, so I'll help Lorea pay you back," I said.

Walter waved his hand. "I'm not worried. I wanted to check on you and let you know I'm heading out of town for a diamond-buying trip to Belgium. Hopefully, things will be looking better by the time I get back."

"Oh, I thought you weren't leaving until October," Lorea said. Walter usually went to Belgium twice a year, so it was surprising for him to leave during wedding season.

"That was my original plan, but my cousin had some frequent-flier miles that were about to expire. He also invited me to a family reunion in Wisconsin on my way out, so I moved things up."

"That sounds nice," I said. "But we'll miss you."

"Gracie is running the store for me. She has a great eye for matching each bride to the perfect ring, so keep sending your clients over." He lifted his hand. "I'll be back in two weeks."

"Bring us back a souvenir," Lorea said with a wave. "Like a diamond."

"Or chocolate," I said.

After letting Walter out the front door, I made the decision to take a much-needed lunch break. It was silly, but I wanted to try to find Sylvia's dress, and I needed some brain food in order to think up some ideas. "I'm frazzled. I'm going to Smokehouse BBQ for some fried pickles. Do you want to come?"

Lorea laughed. "No, thanks. Stress relief for me doesn't have anything to do with pickles."

"Here, let me give you some stress relief before you go." She grabbed a spritz bottle, and I closed my eyes as she sprayed a combination of lavender and melaleuca oils on my face and hair. "Take a deep breath."

The calming scent of lavender tickled my nose, and I smiled.

"See, that helps," Lorea said. "Of course, you'll have to rinse and repeat after you get back from your smelly barbeque joint."

I laughed. "Now, if only they could bottle *that* smell . . ."

Lorea frowned. I waved at her as I headed out the door. "I won't be too long."

I rolled down my window as I approached the intersection for the Smokehouse BBQ and inhaled when the aroma of wood smoke filled my nose. A large rust-colored smoker belched out smoldering trails of mouth-watering aromas. The place was a dive, but the succulent ribs falling off the bone and dripping with his signature "smoke sauce" had given Clay Anderson a cult following.

With limited parking, I slid in next to a decked out Harley Davidson Road Glide. I regarded the dark blue and silver insignia on the Screamin' Eagle version. I had an eye for Harleys, and I hadn't seen this one around town before. I paused to admire it with more deserving attention. I grew up riding dirt bikes through the fields to move pipe, and the wide-open stretches of flat deserts provided plenty of great recreation for motorcycle enthusiasts in this part of Idaho. To say I had a thing for a fancy ride was putting it mildly.

If I hadn't been so sensible, my first ride would have been a Harley with a purple glitter helmet. Instead, I drove a used Mercury Mountaineer with plenty of space in the back for hauling wedding décor. My fingers grazed the leather saddlebags attached to the bike, and then I curled them inward and wondered who the lucky owner might be. My parents didn't know about my secret desire to date a biker. Briette had always teased about setting me up with a Harley owner, but it had never happened.

The biker would be in for a treat if this was his first time at

Smokehouse BBQ. Clay's burnt ends, a marvelously slow-cooked beef brisket with a bark full of so much flavor it could make any barbeque enthusiast cry, was the Thursday special.

The restaurant was actually an old house remodeled into a barbeque joint, and I squeezed between two ranchers in the entryway and walked toward the front to place my order. A glance through the four booth seats and three tables didn't satisfy my curiosity regarding the owner of the Harley, as I didn't spot any leather-clad bikers.

Two senior citizen couples, a few golfers, and a heavy-set man chomping through some ribs and brisket sandwiches made up the lunch crowd at the moment. The bike could belong to anyone, but I held out hope that I hadn't spotted him yet. With a ride like that, he had to be interesting. Clay was skilled at moving people through the joint, though, and the weather was warm enough for the outdoor patio to be in use. I'd have to check.

A line of take-out orders flanked the cash register, and I lifted my fingers in a wave as Clay shimmied through the kitchen with a billowing pan of Smokehouse pork.

"Hey, Adri. I'll throw some pickles in the juice for ya," Clay hollered. "What else would you like today?"

"That pork looks delicious. I'll have a Clay's special sauce sandwich."

He grinned and gave me a wink. His ruddy face perspired, and he continually wiped it with a white towel as he dodged the sizzling grease that enveloped the sweet potato fries and pickles.

After I placed my order, I meandered over to the patio door but was still unable to sate my curiosity. No one occupied the deck chairs under the bright red Coca-Cola umbrellas, so I turned back toward the empty corner booth I had passed. Only it wasn't empty anymore.

I came up short as I locked eyes with a man whose deep blue gaze fastened on me. Thick black hair curled at his temples and rimless glasses sat lightly on the bridge of his nose. The muscles in his forearms tightened as he lowered a copy of *The Idaho Mountain Express*, Ketchum's most reliable newspaper. I guessed he was about thirty and noted the absence of a wedding band. The corners of his eyes crinkled when he smiled. "Sorry, did I take your spot? Clay likes to keep this house full."

"Oh, not at all. I—uh . . ." I stuttered and looked around to find that the ranchers had just taken residence at the last table and a group of tittering ladies were heading out to the patio.

"Rack of ribs, burnt-end special for Luke, and a side of onion rings and slaw," Clay hollered.

Blue-Eyes stood at the call, proving his name was Luke. I tried not to stare, but he was well over six feet and made an imposing figure in the low-ceilinged barbeque joint. He wore carpenter jeans and hiking boots with a moss-green, V-neck tee that accentuated his muscular build.

"Why don't you sit down? There's room for both of us." Luke thumbed toward the booth.

"Are you sure?"

That smile appeared again as he nodded. "Definitely."

The booth could comfortably fit four, so I considered his offer. I turned to watch him pay for his order and felt my stomach flip. Luke headed toward me with his steaming plate. I was just about to sit down when Clay hollered, "Order's up, Adri."

I nodded at Luke as I approached the counter. Clay slid a tray full of hot fried pickles alongside a sandwich overflowing with carnivorous delight. I hurried forward, glad for the interruption to my awkwardness.

"Thanks. I really needed some comfort food today." I pushed two dollars in his tip jar, grabbed a stack of napkins, and turned back around.

Luke nodded as I set my tray down and slid in close to the window. I wanted to bite into one of my fried pickles to wipe the stupid grin off my face, but they were still too hot.

"I'm Luke." He pushed his tray to the side and extended a hand.

I gave him a firm handshake. "Adrielle Pyper, but you can call me Adri. Everyone does. Thanks for letting me sit here."

"My pleasure. This place has amazing food, doesn't it?" Luke lifted his burnt-end special and inhaled slowly, closing his eyes as he took a saucy bite.

I laughed but followed suit with my sandwich. "Mmm. The best barbeque I've ever had." I felt self-conscious eating the messy sandwich in front of him, but the aromas caressing my nose had kicked my hunger into high gear, and not even the best-looking guy could make me miss out on this meal. When I bit into the fried pickle, steam escaped from the hot vegetable turned to the artery-clogging dark side. I chewed slowly, savoring the flavors. Luke's face split into a grin.

"I haven't ever tried the fried pickles. They just sound weird, but from the look on your face, they must taste good."

He was forward. First inviting me to sit with him and now practically asking for one of my deep-fried delicacies. Chewing slowly, I picked the smallest breaded pickle and edged it onto his plate. "I dare you."

Luke's eyebrows lifted, and he set down the rib he'd been

gnawing. He grabbed the pickle and took a bite. I heard the slight crunch and saw the steam release from the fried shell. "That's hot!" He chewed quickly and swigged some water. "But tasty." He examined the crusty exterior and took another bite. "Thanks."

"You're welcome." I took another bite of Clay's special sandwich and savored how the pork separated in meaty chunks with each mouthful. "Are you from around here?"

Luke wiped his face with a paper towel he snagged from the roll sitting on our table. "Not really. I'm a transplant. But I found this place the first weekend I moved to town. I love coming on burnt-end special days."

"I come here when I need comfort food. It's been a while."

"Why? What do you do?"

"I'm a wedding planner. I own Pyper's Dream Weddings, and this is the busiest time of year for me." The missing wedding dresses were the real reason I needed fried pickles, but I wasn't about to make that public knowledge.

He wrinkled his nose. "I can see why you need comfort food. Maybe you should order some more pickles."

"Hey, I love what I do. I make people's dreams come true."

Luke popped an onion ring into his mouth, chewed, and mumbled, "Or their worst nightmare."

"Wow." I leaned back with a frown. "Remind me never to let one of my prospective clients come within ten yards of you."

"Probably not a bad idea, considering . . ."

"Considering what?"

"I'm just giving you a hard time." Luke took a monstrous bite of his sandwich.

I knew my face was red, and if he had half a brain, he could see my hackles were raised in defense of every girl's fairy-tale wedding.

He chewed for a few seconds, and when I didn't respond to his rather brusque jab at my line of work, he reached across the table and brushed his fingers over the back of my hand. "I shouldn't have said that. I apologize. I don't even know you, and I shouldn't make fun, no matter what I think of marriage."

The glass of water became my focal point and I took a drink, clinking the ice cubes around noisily.

"You must be very good at what you do. I know why your name sounds familiar. You're doing Sylvia Rockfort's *and* Brock Grafton's weddings, aren't you?"

I tried unsuccessfully to hide the grimace that belied my feelings of Ketchum's own soap-star diva. Luke slapped his thigh as he laughed. I gave in and laughed with him.

"See, now *that* would be my worst nightmare," he said.

If he was new to the area, I wondered if he'd experienced Sylvia's charm personally, or if he was only going by what the tabloids presented. "That's not fair. I've worked with many brides who are wonderful and kind. You can't knock marriage just because someone like Sylvia is doing it."

"Whatever you say."

I grumbled and finished the last bite of fried pickle. A glance at my watch made my throat tighten. It was already past one o'clock, and I had plenty of work to do. "My goodness, I'm a slow eater today."

"Me too. I'd better be on my way." He stood and swept a few crumbs from his pant legs. "It was fun talking to you. Do you ever give out your number to strange men set against marriage?"

I couldn't help smiling, but I wasn't sure about him. "Well, you know where to find me."

"Ah, gonna make me grovel, huh?"

He rubbed his hand along the shadow of stubble on his jaw, and I almost relented when I noticed the dimple in his chin. But my pride kept me to the sticking point.

"I don't think I got your last name."

He paused. "It's Stetson." He waited as if to see how I would react, and then his shoulders relaxed. "Have a great weekend, Adri."

I was confused with his reticence just before he left and wondered why he'd been reluctant to give his last name. The way his broad shoulders filled the doorframe tucked the question in the back of my brain, though, especially when he turned and lifted two fingers in a wave. When he walked out the door and straddled the Harley, I knew I was in trouble.

Chapter 6

SIMPLE WEDDING CARD

1. Fold a 4¼" x 11" piece of white cardstock in half to make a 4¼" x 5½" card base.

2. Stamp a flower image on white cardstock. Using scissors or a shaped punch, cut around the image. Attach the flower image to the front of the card, about ⅓ of the way down on the left side of the card base, using self-adhesive foam dimensional.

3. Using the same color ink as the flower image, stamp a greeting on white cardstock. Cut out the greeting by using a medium oval punch or decorative-edged scissors.

4. Use a large scallop oval punch to create an oval piece from the same color cardstock as the flower image. Attach the smaller greeting oval on top of the larger oval, then attach the larger oval to the card front, lower right corner, using self-adhesive foam dimensional.

Courtesy of www.mashedpotatoesandcrafts.com.

A twinge of guilt struck my heart when my phone vibrated with a text message from Dallas.

Looking forward to seeing you tonight.

I tapped out a response:

Me too.

I tried not to think about how I wished I'd given Luke my number. I smoothed the emotions from my face before I entered the shop. Hopefully Lorea wouldn't see anything in my eyes that hinted at a story to tell. I was saving Luke the Harley owner for later.

"You look better. Maybe Clay puts something in your fried pickles." Lorea stepped forward and wrinkled her nose. "You smell like a barbeque, though."

I laughed. "Someday I'll get you to come with me."

Lorea waved me off and smoothed out the fabric she was stitching. "Thanks for listening to me whine earlier."

"We'll figure this out," I said. "For now, I'm going to concentrate on finishing those bridal shower invitations someone tricked me into making." I hoped that keeping my hands busy would give my mind a break from worrying about the missing dresses and my looming financial ruin.

Lorea lifted her chin. "I didn't trick you. You practically begged me to let you design them."

"Ha! If I left it up to you, Natalie's shower guests would have received an invite on dollar store party notes."

With a snort, Lorea tossed a wad of packing tape at me. "I would never, not when I have a mashed crafts expert within spitting distance."

I shook my head at Lorea's nickname for mashedpotatoesand

crafts.com. She knew that I'd been creating handmade cards with my family long before rubber stamping hit the big time. Some of my mom's stamp sets were more than twenty years old, and she still used them for her thank you cards. "Wait until you see the finished product. I'm using vintage buttons as an accent."

That got the seamstress to look up. "Thanks, Adri. I would be a pretty wretched bridesmaid without you."

"You know that isn't true. Natalie is lucky to have you as a friend *and* her assistant wedding planner."

Lorea smiled as I carried a basket full of card-making supplies to my desk. Within thirty minutes, I had creased all the cards, added a punched lace edging, and stamped a bouquet of roses onto nearly fifty cream-colored squares of paper. I rounded the edges of each square and glued the image of the roses to the front of the cards. Then I attached a button near the right edge of each card, threaded burgundy embroidery floss through the back, and looped it over the button. The guests would unwind the simple closure to open the card and read the details of Natalie's bridal shower. The date and time were printed on vellum and attached with a flower-shaped brad to the inside of the card.

"I can feel you peeking," I said.

"Well, aren't you going to show me?" Lorea leaned over my shoulder. "Those are gorgeous."

I handed her a finished invitation. "Tell me what you think about the inside."

Lorea read the details and nodded. "Thank you for making these. They're perfect."

"I'm glad you like them." I gave in to a yawn as I finished cleaning up scraps of paper and stamp supplies. "I'm bushed. I think I'll head out early."

"Have fun on your date tonight," Lorea said. "You deserve a break. Oh, and shut off your inner critic and give Dallas a chance. He was so cute the other day when he stopped by the shop."

"I'll try," I replied. "I forgot I wanted to straighten my hair." I tugged at an unruly curl. "I'm going to have to hurry to get ready." At least there would be a silver lining to my cloudy day. "Try not to worry about Sylvia. We'll figure something out, and maybe the police will find the dress."

"Natalie's coming Monday afternoon for her fitting. Can I stop by tomorrow and pick up her gown?"

"Yes. I'm sorry I didn't finish taking out that hem yet." *Not thinking of diamonds!* I gave her a half smile.

Lorea nodded. "I might have to forgive you, especially since you made all of those invites."

With a grimace, I stacked the cards. "What was I thinking when I offered to help you with that hem?"

"That you love me. Also, you're very kind, and I would never turn down service." Lorea laughed and backed away as I tried to swat her with a stack of paper.

"I think I'll let you handle Sylvia's next tantrum."

Lorea rolled her eyes. "I want to hear all about your date."

I headed for the back door, jingling my keys. "Let's hope I have something good to tell."

It was difficult to relax when scenes of murderous rage—starring Sylvia Rockfort with me as the victim—kept flitting through my mind. Lorea had called Sylvia, hoping to schedule an appointment for Tuesday, but Sylvia insisted on coming first thing Monday morning. If the dress hadn't turned up by then, we would have to tell her. And there was the other problem concerning a certain quilt in my living room, but I wasn't thinking about that right now. It all felt too overwhelming.

At fifteen minutes to six, I sat at my kitchen table trying to reconstruct some of the details from Natalie's stolen wedding binder. My fingers kept wandering to a loose string near the hem of my minidress, or extra-long shirt, depending on who was describing the outfit—my mother or me. With black leggings under the turquoise dress, my clothing was appropriate for an evening ice show.

The night breathed cool air from the peaks of the mountains down on the valley, keeping the evenings crisp and just right for cuddling. My thoughts wandered to the sexy biker guy I'd met at lunch. Luke was attractive, but it was probably better if I didn't pursue my initial fascination. His obvious lack of appreciation for marriage should have kept thoughts of him at bay, so I was frustrated with myself for even contemplating him.

I forced myself to think of Dallas and the dark lashes that rimmed his green eyes. I wondered if he would kiss me good night at the door, or hope for an invitation inside. The latter definitely wouldn't happen—I hadn't dated him long enough to let him see my living space.

The doorbell rang. I swept my papers into a pile and grabbed my purse. When I opened the door, I had to command myself not to grin like an idiot. Dallas definitely looked kissable. He wore a dark-blue dress shirt and khakis, and I loved the way he spiked the front of his black hair. "You look pretty, Adri."

"Thank you." Excitement thrummed in my chest. "You look nice too."

He held his hand out just as I swung the door shut behind

me. Before I could take it, his nerves got the better of him, and he shoved it into his pocket. "The weather's perfect."

My eyes lifted to the cloudless sky above us. "It is. I bet the stars will be bright later on."

"Maybe we'll have a few minutes to stargaze after the show."

I thought of linking my arm through his as we strolled to the car, but my own courage was faltering for some reason. He held my door for me, and his eyes lingered on my legs as I tucked them in. As Dallas shut my door and walked around to the driver's side, I thought about the night we had met less than two weeks before.

A vendor from my preferred list had given me a gift certificate to the Roosevelt Grille. It was a place where I had always wanted to dine, but the thirty-dollar-a-plate price tag was outside my budget. Lorea and I used the gift certificate to celebrate our fourth month in business and our two major clients—Sylvia and Natalie. Our waiter was Dallas Reynolds, and in what I could tell was a bold move for him, he asked for my number when he left the bill.

Dallas cleared his throat, interrupting my thoughts. "I hope you're in the mood for Italian because I wanted to take you to Rico's."

"I love that place." A lot had changed in the Ketchum–Sun Valley area since my teenage years, so I'd enjoyed walking up and down the streets and getting to know the merchants. Six months of living here had given me a taste for fine cuisine, as well as fried pickles, but I wasn't sure if I was ready to confide that guilty secret to Dallas yet. As I watched him, something passed over his face. He clenched and unclenched the steering wheel as if trying to remind himself to relax. I had never struggled with shyness, but I could see that Dallas was definitely out of his element.

"So, you mentioned that you're hoping your second job will

take off this summer?" I ventured—maybe talking about his new job as a realtor would help him relax.

"Yes, the housing economy is still down, but the agency I'm with is projecting a strong season. I'm scheduled to show quite a few homes next week, and tomorrow I'm helping with an open house on a mansion that went into foreclosure." His face lit up as he spoke, all nervousness seeming to dissipate.

"Sounds great. That's how I came by my condo. It was a short sale."

"Looks like you chose wisely. I bet it's nice being so close to your shop."

I nodded. "It does help to be close to Sun Valley. I never dreamed I could afford a place here—then I found my house." Ketchum and Sun Valley were interlaced. The resort hugged the Ketchum streets, and the businesses all catered to the tourists who traveled to the area year round. And I did feel fortunate that things had fallen into place so nicely, as if I was meant to start over in Sun Valley.

Dallas and I talked easily through a dinner of linguine with prosciutto and sun-dried tomatoes. Rico's signature toasted bread-sticks tasted delicious. There were a few moments where I could see Dallas's nerves return, and I did my best to steer the conversation to light topics to ease the tension.

He unfolded his napkin, and I noticed the ring finger on his left hand. When we'd first met, I'd checked to see if he wore a ring—he didn't, but what surprised me was that his ring finger was just a nub.

"I'm sure you've noticed." Dallas held up his hand.

I nodded.

"I appreciate that you didn't ask, although I'm certain you were curious."

I shrugged. "I thought you'd tell me if you wanted me to know." I *was* curious. I'm observant, and I've always felt like you can tell a lot about people from the details—especially the little ones they don't think you notice.

"Well, it was an accident in wood shop class in high school," Dallas explained as he showed me the stub of finger on his left hand. "Nothing really exciting, and most of the time I forget until I see someone staring at my hand."

"Maybe they're just checking to see if you're available." I winked and then laughed when I saw a bit of color creep up his neck.

"We have time to walk around the lodge before the show if you'd like."

"Yes, that'd be fun. Thanks for dinner, Dallas."

I drank the last of my ice water while he paid the bill and noticed the nice tip he left for the waitress. I wondered if he felt nervous socializing with someone he'd waited on. He seemed more at ease as we drove to the ice show. We parked, and when Dallas started to reach for my hand, I grasped his before he could change his mind. He smiled and gave my fingers a gentle squeeze as we walked toward the Sun Valley Lodge. Three swans floated gracefully across a pond in front of the main entrance. The temperature was perfect for the end of May—the summer heat wasn't far off, though.

"Do you plan many weddings here?" Dallas motioned toward the building.

Wood paneling spanned the huge hotel as we walked through the covered entryway. "The lodge actually has a wedding coordinator who schedules for here and the Sun Valley Country Club." I nodded at the doorman. "But I'm working with her for a wedding the end of this month."

"I bet it will be magical," Dallas said.

Tilting my head, I laughed. "Actually, it will. The theme is, 'The Magic of True Love.'"

The interior of the Sun Valley Lodge exuded an aristocratic feel from days gone by. Low lighting was enhanced by the giant wall of windows at the back of the lobby, which looked onto the ice arena. Dallas and I turned down a hallway lined with antique wallpaper and decorated with dozens of picture frames.

I had never stayed at the hotel, but plenty of Hollywood superstars enjoyed the rustic mountain retreat. The placard below a photo of the founder, Averill Harriman, stated that the lodge was opened in 1936, driven by the enthusiasm of Count Felix Schaffgotsch of Austria, who purchased 4,300 acres that would become the resort town. When he had happened upon the old mining town of Ketchum, the count declared the area rivaled Switzerland or Austria for a winter resort.

Although I had been down this hallway several times in my youth, I never tired of looking at the old black-and-white photos of such entertainment legends as Lucille Ball with her two children and Louis Armstrong on skis. A shot of Marilyn Monroe from 1956 and Ginger Rogers in 1938 always made me wonder what it must have been like to be in the spotlight back then. I motioned for Dallas to notice more recent photos of Clint Eastwood and Arnold Schwarzenegger, who stood by a ski run named after him. Dozens of photos of ice skaters and other Olympic athletes as well as presidents and dignitaries covered the wall. I took my time examining both sides of the hallway.

Dallas squinted to read Ernest Hemingway's letter dated June 15, 1961, not long before his suicide. Fans of the great writer enjoyed visiting a memorial not far from the lodge. "This is interesting," Dallas murmured. "No indication from the letter that he felt unhappy."

"I know." I motioned to the array of pictures. "I'd forgotten how many different celebrities came here."

"It was definitely a happening place by the looks of these." Dallas motioned to a picture of Jackie Kennedy on a horse-drawn sleigh.

The hallway ended near the entrance to the hotel's spa and guest services, so we walked back toward the lobby and observed the crowd of people enjoying the extravagant buffet set up for the ice show. Dallas and I would sit on the bleachers right by the rink, while nearly two hundred people would watch the show from the patio after their dinner.

"I think there's still time for us to look around back." I linked my arm through his and was rewarded with a smile. "Have you seen the pavilion where they hold the summer symphony?"

"No. This is actually only my second time up here. The first time, I didn't walk around much because it was too cold."

Dallas had mentioned that he was a newcomer, having moved here from New Hampshire in March, not quite three months earlier. It was fun to see through his eyes as he observed his surroundings for the first time in a way that left me wondering what was going through his head. He noticed a bunch of daffodils late in bloom and surprised me by calling the flower by name. Then he pointed out a chipmunk dashing up a fir tree and laughed. His boyish curiosity was contagious, and I congratulated myself on how comfortable I felt on our second date.

The sidewalks lined freshly manicured grass, and several older couples strolled by with wraps and blankets, probably for the ice show. I was grateful I had remembered at the last minute to grab an old quilt—the bleachers by the rink could become quite cold as the night progressed.

"Here it is, the Sun Valley Pavilion." I waved my arm with a flourish. "I think this would be a beautiful setting for a wedding."

"And have the symphony play the 'Wedding March'?" Dallas asked.

"That would make it pretty special." I leaned over the edge of the wall separating us from the stage. It was crafted out of dark brown wood and flanked by chairs for the musicians. It would be fun to see a musical performed there. I admired the backdrop of mountains and greenery behind the pavilion. "I've always loved weddings."

"Me too," Dallas said and cleared his throat. "I mean, the idea of two people starting a new life together always holds so much promise."

He shuffled his feet and his cheeks reddened, but I touched his arm and looked into his eyes. "That's just how I feel."

He stared at the ground. "Well, we'd better get seated. I'm looking forward to my first ice show."

Most men would be embarrassed to have spouted such romantic notions, but I thought it was sweet that Dallas shared his feelings anyway. It was a welcome difference from the way Luke had reacted to my wedding business. Another point in Dallas's favor.

Chapter 7

KEEP YOUR DIAMONDS SPARKLING

Soak your diamond ring in a warm solution of liquid dish detergent and water for five minutes. Use a soft brush if necessary to remove dirt. Soft is the key—don't use a brush with bristles that are stiff enough to scratch the ring's metal setting. Swish the ring around in the solution and then place it in a colander (so you don't lose it down the drain). Rinse it thoroughly in warm water. Dry with a lint-free cloth.

Courtesy of www.mashedpotatoesandcrafts.com.

Shivers of excitement zipped through me when the ice show began. I'd been to a handful of the summer performances, but the last had been more than ten years ago. The professional ice rink stayed open year-round, and nothing quite compared to skating outdoors in the heat of the summer. Dallas put his arm around me when a cool breeze drifted through the arena, and I let my thoughts wander. At barely six feet, he was shorter than my ideal guy, but that was mostly because I knew if I wore my three-inch heels I might be taller than he was. I glanced at his fine profile and the glossy blackness of his hair and mused that I might be okay with the height issue.

Several figure skaters entertained us with performances to popular music. They each had their own flair, but I could hardly wait for Sasha Cohen to hit the ice. The audience applauded as another skater finished a rendition to a movie theme song.

"This is great. I never would've thought this kind of entertainment could be found so far off the beaten path," Dallas said. "I can see why people want vacation homes here."

"Ah, that's the realtor speaking, isn't it?"

"It is." He covered my hand with his. "Thanks for coming with me, Adri. I hope we can go out again soon."

"Thanks. Me too," I whispered. Surprisingly, I meant it.

Dallas scooted closer, and I noticed a slight tremor in his left hand, particularly the shortened ring finger. I hoped his shyness would dissipate as we continued to get to know each other, but if it didn't, that would be a deal breaker for me. I hated feeling like I had to tone down my vivaciousness so I wouldn't overshadow the quieter types. I wanted someone who could steal a kiss without having a panic attack.

His arm tightened around me, and I noted that he was strong, an impression his lanky figure didn't give at first. I was just about to ask him what he liked to do for exercise—maybe running, like me—when the announcer shouted Sasha's name.

The Olympic medalist circled the ice with grace, and my arms tingled when I heard the scrape of ice as she catapulted into a double axel. I cheered when she landed in perfect form and sped past us on her way to the other side of the rink.

"Isn't she fantastic?" I asked Dallas.

He applauded along with me. "It's different watching in real life. I don't know how they do it."

The performance ended all too soon and had my feet itching to skate around the rink, even if I could do so only in clunky rental skates. "Have you ever been ice skating?"

Dallas shook his head. "You know how people say there are some things that are better left undone?" He pulled his thumb toward his chest. "That goes for me and any slippery surface."

My hopes deflated. Guess there wouldn't be an ice-skating date in the near future. He must have noticed because he took my hand. "But I'd be willing to try it. Who knows? Maybe I just need the right teacher."

I smiled. "Maybe so."

We walked back to his car in a relaxed silence—or at least, *I* felt comfortable. I glanced at Dallas, wondering if his hands trembled with nerves again. He seemed to be deep in thought, maybe trying to figure out what he wanted to say.

We passed under a stand of blue spruce trees and the night sky twinkled above us. Dallas lifted his face toward the heavens. "Look, there's Cassiopeia."

"And there's the Big Dipper." I pointed toward another area of the northern sky. "That's the extent of my stargazing skills, but you sound like you have more expertise."

"The Big Dipper is also known as the Plough, or the Saptarshi, after the seven rishis or sages in Hindu literature."

Leaning back, I widened my eyes in appreciation of his knowledge. I couldn't resist teasing, "I'm impressed, Professor Reynolds."

"Astronomy is a hobby of mine. I have a telescope. Maybe I could show you the sky sometime."

"Do you use that line with all your dates?"

Dallas stiffened. "Well, no, I, uh—"

"I'm teasing. But it is a good line." He relaxed and gave me an easy smile. He really was good-looking, and I'd had a great evening. Probably in part due to Lorea's advice.

I could be patient. His shyness was no problem with his killer good looks and sweet personality, but I did wonder if he had enough confidence for my taste. My dad told me that confidence was definitely my strong suit, and my brother just said I was full of myself. I called it independence and knowing what I wanted out of life. I knew I couldn't reach my goals if I reined in my natural "conquer the world" attitude.

We stared at the sky for a few more minutes, and then Dallas led me to the car and opened my door. "I had a great time tonight," he said. "Those figure skaters were awesome."

"They were. I loved it when that guy did a back flip—I thought you were going to fall off your seat."

Dallas laughed. "He surprised me, that's for sure."

We continued to talk during the ten-minute drive to my house. He pulled up beside my condo and put his car in park, leaving the engine running as he hurried to open my door.

"Thanks for being a gentleman." I allowed him to help me from the car. "And thanks for the nice evening."

"My pleasure."

He looked at me and a strange flicker of emotion crossed his face. I had noticed it before, and now I wondered if it might be fear. Was he that anxious about the doorstep scene? If so, it was kind of cute. For half a second I thought about initiating a kiss myself.

"I'd really like to take you out again, Adri." He hesitated and then leaned toward me and kissed my cheek.

Dallas and his insecurities passed through my mind, and even though I wanted to, I wondered if I should accept his invitation for another date. I considered the effort he was obviously making to get past his shyness and decided to challenge myself as well. "I'd like that." I hugged him briefly and leaned back.

"Good night, and may the stars shower good dreams on you." He gave my hand a gentle squeeze and returned to his car, humming a tune I couldn't quite catch.

Barely eleven o'clock and he didn't try to invite himself in? Dallas might be reserved and a bit cautious, but he had definitely just scored some major points in my book.

With a hand on my freshly kissed cheek, I moved through my home, trying to analyze my feelings about Dallas. I started to get ready for bed, but after I slipped into my comfy pajamas, I knew I was too keyed up to sleep. Natalie's wedding dress still needed my attention. Maybe I could think about my potential love life while I finished taking out the hem and figured out what to do with those rocks in my quilt.

On my way out of my bedroom, I paused, lifting the silver-framed picture of Briette and me at her bridal shower. Her grin was contagious, and my own smile was full of laughter as best friends celebrated childhood dreams of fairy-tale weddings coming true.

The corners of my mouth lifted, but my heart still hurt. "Oh, Briette. I miss you," I whispered. Swallowing, I set the frame back on my dresser with the hope that she was proud of me for keeping my dream alive. Briette had always been my biggest supporter, and she'd done so much to help me make a name for myself.

After completing my wedding planner certification four years ago, I couldn't stop pinching myself when I landed a job at the ritzy Bellissima Wedding Dreams in San Francisco. Grueling hours of pampering spoiled brides by fulfilling their every wish eventually earned my place as an assistant to one of the associate wedding planners. Then karma had intervened in my behalf—or so it seemed at the time.

Briette Nelson was engaged to marry Caleb Rice, a southern boy with old money, and his family wanted to spare no expense when it came to the wedding. Briette hired me, her best friend from college, as her wedding planner. The news of her engagement made it into the social sections of the major newspapers, and Bellissima was thrilled. Overnight, I was promoted to the position of associate wedding planner.

Six months of preparation passed as I oversaw every detail of Briette's bridal showers, gown fittings, flower choices, and twinkle light displays. More accounts piled up with young women hoping to garner Briette's wedding planner next. The Nelson-Rice wedding would be the highlight of the year for Bellissima.

Tears stung my eyes as I relived the moment that had dammed the course of the river my life had taken. My throat clenched, and even this many months later, it was still hard to swallow when I thought of how Briette was murdered. The sharp pain of sorrow enveloped me as I thought about Briette's dreams—about her life. Stolen.

Only three days before the big day, I had found Briette strangled and stabbed to death in her wedding gown. There were no suspects. No one was arrested. And someone got away with murder, because even a year later the police didn't have any leads and were moving the investigation to the cold-case file.

Caleb was trying to come to terms with the fact that he might never see the murderer brought to justice, the person who ripped his happiness away and left an aching hole in both our hearts. I knew I shouldn't do this to myself, but I still hoped that the killer would be found and punished.

My mind went to those days after the tragedy, even though I resisted the memories. I had collapsed after Briette's murder. The news surrounding her death, the subsequent cancellations of accounts, and the horrible realization of loss proved too much for me. I packed up and moved back home to Idaho.

With another glance at the picture, I left the room. At least the best parts of Briette would live on. Her cheerful, optimistic attitude crept into my thoughts and reminded me that she wouldn't be happy to see me dwelling on the sad ending of her life.

I wondered what Briette would think of Dallas. Immediately I knew she would have been sympathetic to his shy nature. She'd consider him adorable, definitely worth several dates because of his quiet charm and chivalrous ways.

My cell phone sang "Marry Me" by Train—Lorea thought it was perfect when it rang at the shop. I wondered who might be calling so late and bit my bottom lip when I saw Dallas's name float across the screen. My heart fluttered as a tiny thrill of excitement changed my solemn mood.

"Miss me already?" I answered.

A nervous cough preceded his voice. "Uh—yes, actually. Adri, can I see you again tomorrow?"

He liked me, and I surprised myself because I was okay with him liking me enough to ask for a third date less than an hour after dropping me off after our second date. "What time?" I wiggled my toes and watched the purple nail polish shimmer as the fluorescent light in my kitchen reflected off the glitter.

"I, um—I just can't stop thinking about you," Dallas stuttered.

I couldn't help but smile. "I was thinking about you too."

"Really?"

"You're a great guy." And if he had been in front of me at that moment, I would definitely have kissed him for being so genuine. What a change from the arrogant men I'd dated.

"Thanks. I—well, what would you like to do?"

I eyed Natalie's gown and frowned. It would take nearly two hours to pick out the hem—I couldn't pull the seams to pop the threads or it would damage the material. I had to undo each and every stitch. "It'll have to be something fast. I'll be working past six tomorrow, and then I have some work I need to finish up tomorrow night on a wedding gown. How about meeting for an ice cream around seven?"

"Sure. I love ice cream."

"Have you ever tried a frozen mud pie?" My sweet tooth started aching just thinking about the sugar-laden treat.

"No, but it sounds like something I should. Where do you get one?"

"At Frozen Tundra Treats, just past Roxy's grocery store."

"I'll see you tomorrow."

I grinned at the phone for a full minute before moving myself to the spare bedroom to work on Natalie's dress. There was a lightness in my step as I thought about what tomorrow might bring. I found myself smiling over the memory of Luke trying a fried pickle and pushed him from my mind. Tomorrow would be date number three with Dallas, and I hoped a kiss might be in order.

Dallas had sounded a bit more confident on the phone. Maybe he just needed time to find his footing. An hour later, I picked out the last stitch, releasing the hem on Natalie's gown. Thankfully, I'd finished the task much faster than I anticipated. Maybe I'd have a little more time to get ready for my date with Dallas. There had been no more surprises. I still didn't have any ideas for dealing with the diamonds, but my mental energy was shot. They were safe enough in the quilt, at least that's what I told myself. I prepared for bed, reprimanding my thoughts whenever they strayed to the mystery of Natalie's gown.

Chapter 8

SAVE THE DRESS! STAIN REMOVER

Mix together ⅔ cup dishwashing liquid, ⅔ cup ammonia, six tablespoons baking soda, and two cups warm water. Pour mixture into a spray bottle. Shake before use. Spray on stains and let sit for one minute. Launder as usual. *I always keep a bottle handy at the shop for accidents!

Courtesy of www.mashedpotatoesandcrafts.com.

Lorea was waiting for me when I opened the back door of the shop at eight fifteen the next morning.

"Dish," she demanded, handing me a peppermint tea with a sleeve from the Iconoclast Bookstore. The cinnamon mocha latte she sipped reminded me of Christmastime.

"We had so much fun. Sasha Cohen is amazing, and Dallas is a romantic. We did a little stargazing after the ice show."

Lorea looked at the ceiling and pursed her lips, deep in

thought. "Yeah, I can see that. He seems like the sentimental type. Did he kiss you?"

"On the cheek." I slid my bag under the desk and sipped my tea.

"That's it?"

"He's pretty shy. I was kind of worried halfway into our date about how nervous he seemed, but he was such a gentleman and so sweet that I agreed to see him again tonight."

"Wow, you must like him if you're making time for him on June first—the beginning of insanity for all wedding planners."

"It's just ice cream. I told him I have too much work to do."

"Don't let work rule your life," Lorea said. "If you like this guy, I can help you more."

"I know you would, but I also know you're just as busy as I am right now. Besides, I take breaks. Remember I went for barbeque yesterday?"

"Wait a minute. You never told me why you were smiling so big when you came in yesterday."

Nothing got by Lorea. I hesitated, wondering if I should tell her about Luke.

"Oh, I know that look." Lorea clapped her hands. "'Fess up."

I shrugged. "Clay's place was crowded, as usual, so I shared a booth with this good-looking guy and ended up giving him one of my fried pickles."

"Did he like it?"

I nodded, and Lorea chuckled. "So what's his name?"

"Luke Stetson."

"Hmm, that sounds familiar." Lorea fiddled with the chain holding her glasses. "Or maybe it's just one of those names that makes you think of something else. So, is he hot?"

"Um. He rides a Harley."

Lorea squealed. "Tell me."

I felt a bit disloyal to Dallas. "Maybe you could go out with him."

Lorea frowned. "You're not engaged to Dallas. You can date two guys at once. Just tell me what he looks like."

"Okay, okay."

I described Luke's gorgeous cobalt blue eyes, imposing height, and dark curly hair, and Lorea listened with a grin on her face. I was just about to mention the dimple in his chin when my phone started chirping a reminder. I snatched it off the counter and groaned. "Good thing I set this alarm in my phone. I'm supposed to be meeting that new caterer in ten minutes." I swiped my finger across the screen to silence the alarm. "I'm going to be late."

"I'm sure they'll understand." Lorea shooed me out the door. "Bring me back a sample."

"Will do," I said. "I probably won't be back until after lunch."

It was hard not to speed across town, but I made myself take a few cleansing breaths with a mental reminder that the caterer was probably just as busy as I was. Decadent Catering was housed in another remodeled bungalow with a charming yellow and pink foyer. Valerie Garner was prepared for my visit with professional-looking brochures, delicious ribbon sandwiches, and chocolate mint truffles.

"These look beautiful, and they taste even better," I said around a bite of sandwich.

"Thank you. I promised my husband an extra batch of mint truffles if he would help me design these brochures." Valerie traced a finger along the pink and yellow font of Decadent Catering.

"I'm sure it wasn't hard for him to agree to your terms." I snagged a truffle and let it melt in my mouth while I studied her pricing suggestions. "Let's talk about how you might be able to help me with an upcoming bridal shower."

Valerie's face lit up with a smile. "I'd love to. Have a seat." She motioned to a few whitewashed chairs, and we spent the next two hours discussing Natalie's and Sylvia's bridal showers and what they were hoping for. Valerie had already prepared bids for specific layouts, and we talked about how adjustments would change the bids. Overall, we were both happy with the ideas she had prepared.

I left Decadent Catering with a package of mint truffles, ribbon sandwiches, a container of Valerie's specialty herb and spinach salad, and a smile on my face. Valerie was organized, confident, and from what I'd sampled so far, talented enough to pull off catering Sylvia's bridal shower. It was a relief to find someone I felt was competent enough to help me through the summer.

On the way back to my shop, I turned sharply into the post office when I remembered that I hadn't checked the P.O. box for a couple days. With keys jangling, I hurried inside to grab my mail. There wasn't anything interesting in the little silver box, and I crammed the bills into my purse. I turned to go but halted when I recognized the profile of Luke from Clay's Barbeque. Should I say hello? I recalled our conversation from yesterday and frowned.

He turned at that moment, and his eyes brightened with a smile when he saw me. "Hello, there. It's Adri, right?"

I nodded.

"What's the matter, no fried pickles today?" He winked, and I felt my cheeks flushing. What was I, thirteen?

"Just bills, unfortunately." I patted my purse and immediately felt even more juvenile. I racked my brain for something witty to say.

He stepped toward me and all wittiness left my brain when I focused on the dark blue of his eyes. "Hey, I'm sorry if I came off rude yesterday," he said.

"Oh, uh—"

He grimaced. "I didn't mean to make fun of your profession. I've got a chip on my shoulder, and it carries over where it shouldn't."

I felt myself softening, but my stronger side resisted. "You weren't very nice, and I even shared my pickle with you."

He chuckled. "Maybe we should start over." He held out his hand. "My name is Luke Stetson."

I tilted my head and my lips twitched as I tried to suppress a grin. Finally, I reached out my hand. "Hi, Luke. I'm Adrielle Pyper, but my *friends* call me Adri."

"Well, *Adri*, would you consider letting a big-mouth take you out for an early lunch?"

My surprise must have been evident because he laughed. "C'mon, I promise I'm not all bad."

"I guess you'll have to prove it to me."

Luke adjusted his glasses. "I'm up for a challenge." He grabbed my hand and tugged me out the door toward his shiny Harley. "Mind if I drive?"

Dang, was I ever in trouble.

At first I thought I'd be just fine if I sat up tall and kept my hands on my thighs, but as soon as Luke pulled out on the street and revved the engine, my hands flew forward of their own accord, gripping his waist. I could almost feel Luke smiling as we cruised down Main Street. Or maybe that was me. Why was I smiling so big? My hair brushed against the back of my neck, and I felt the cool breeze tickle my arms as we buzzed through town. I was just about to ask where we were headed when Luke pulled up in front of Honey's Pizza Cafe.

"Have you ever had the pizza pockets here?" he asked as I got off the bike.

"No, but I love pizza, so I'm in."

"What did you think of the ride?" Luke twirled the keys on his index finger.

His grin told me he already knew the answer. "Pretty smooth." I hoped he caught my double meaning. "How long have you had it?"

"Only about six months. I've been saving for one of these since I was a teenager."

"Lucky." I put my hand on the leather seat. "I had my eye on a Road Glide custom painted to match my shop, but I didn't think my brides and their mothers would be too keen on a Harley-riding wedding planner."

"I'm impressed that you knew this was a Road Glide."

"I may be a wedding planner, but I'm a country girl first," I replied.

Luke smiled appreciatively. "You're full of surprises, aren't you?"

I shrugged and turned toward the restaurant so he wouldn't notice the heat in my cheeks. He took my cue and opened the door for me. As we entered, he placed his hand briefly on the small of my back. The gesture startled me, mostly because of the way my middle began flitting with butterflies. What was happening here?

I studied Luke as we stood in line. He seemed relaxed, and when he smiled at me, I was struck by the sincerity there. Maybe yesterday he was just having a bad day. He had apologized for his comment. I wondered about the chip on his shoulder he'd mentioned—maybe he'd been dumped recently. We moved into a line with about four people ahead of us. The line was for the pizza pockets, set up similar to a sandwich bar, and it seemed to be moving at a good pace.

"I'll have the supreme with jalapenos, please." Luke pointed at the menu and then turned to me. "I've tried about half of them, if you need a recommendation."

I stepped forward and squinted at the menu printed on glossy cardstock hanging from the wall. "I'll try the Hawaiian with extra cheese."

The pizza pocket was delicious. Ham and pineapple encased in delicious rosemary garlic bread that had a slight crunch on the outside but was absolutely moist on the inside. "Mmm, this is incredible. Thanks for lunch."

"Glad you approve. I know the owners, and they are great people. It's fun living in a small town like this, feeling like you're supporting each other."

"It is. Idaho is full of great little towns like this one." I took another bite of my pizza pocket.

"So what great little town do you hail from?" Luke took a sip of his lemonade and waited for me to finish chewing.

"Rupert. It's about the best place to grow up in the whole world."

He chuckled. "That's only what, an hour and a half from here?"

I nodded. "Have you been there?"

"Just passed through. It's a beautiful route for a bike ride between here and there. Sometimes I take off Fridays and go for a long ride." He leaned back in his chair, and I saw his eyes flit to his bike parked outside.

"It is a beautiful drive. Where are you from?"

Luke grimaced and rubbed the back of his neck. "North Carolina. This is a good change for me. How about you? Is this where you wanted to end up?"

"Um. Well, I was living in San Francisco for the past five years, so it's good to get back to my roots." I watched Luke closely for any explanation of the hurt I saw behind his eyes. There must be something painful in his past. At the same time, I felt him studying me, and I realized he could see the same thing in my eyes.

"Well, thanks for giving me a second chance. I hope I was better behaved today." Luke crumpled up his napkin and swigged the last of his lemonade.

"This was very nice. Thank you." I glanced at my watch. It was almost noon, and I had a mountain of work ahead of me, yet a part of me wished I could sit here longer and talk to Luke. Or maybe just memorize that endearing dimple in his chin, or the hundred different shades of blue in his eyes. "Sometime you should stop by my shop. Weddings are pretty fabulous."

He opened his mouth to speak but stopped himself. He reached across the table and patted my hand. "I think that sounds like a good idea."

I couldn't help but laugh at his obvious struggle not to tease me, but it was nice that he didn't take the bait I'd offered him.

"You were teasing me, weren't you?" he asked a second later, the realization crossing his features.

I waggled my eyebrows. "Maybe."

Luke stood up and held out his hand. "This was fun. Do you think I could have your number now?"

I took his hand and let him help me from my chair. He was gorgeous, appearing even taller when I stood so close to him.

My insides were melting, and the butterflies had morphed into an explosion of fireworks that threatened to obliterate my self-awareness. I needed to remember to play a little hard to get. Luke had given me a great apology, but he needed to grovel just a bit more. I ignored the manly woodsy scent that had me wanting to close my eyes and inhale. Instead I gave him a coy smile and began walking toward the door.

"You still know where to find me."

Luke hesitated a moment before grinning and following me out the door. On the ride back to the post office, I might have leaned a little closer to him, but I blamed that on the sharp left turn he took just after we left Honey's Pizza Cafe.

Chapter 9

BERRY-LICIOUS CUPCAKES WITH MAGIC GLITTER

Mix cupcake batter as directed on a box of white cake mix and fill cupcake wrappers with batter. Push one large blackberry or raspberry into the center of each cupcake, making sure that the batter covers the berry, then follow box instructions for baking. When cupcakes have cooled, use a frosting bag to fill centers with whipped cream and then pipe additional whipped cream on the top of each cupcake. Sprinkle with edible glitter.

Courtesy of www.mashedpotatoesandcrafts.com.

It was only after I was headed back to work that I remembered to feel guilty about Dallas. I remembered what Lorea had said: I wasn't engaged to Dallas, we had just started dating, and I decided to give myself a break where Luke was concerned. The attraction I felt toward him was intriguing, and I could tell he was a little confused by the sparks flying between us as well. It left a warm feeling in my chest, and I walked into my shop with a huge smile on my face. I knew it would give me away, but I didn't care.

"Holy cow! That must have been some caterer? Did she lace her samples with happy tonic?" Lorea asked as soon as she saw me.

"Oh, the samples!" I put a hand to my forehead. "Be right back." I dashed out the door, hoping that the mint truffles hadn't melted in my vehicle. I had stowed them inside an insulated lunch bag, and it was a good thing, since I hadn't planned on going on an impromptu date with Luke. I returned to the shop, where Lorea held the door with an expectant quirk in her smile.

"I brought you some goodies from Decadent Catering and hired Valerie to do Natalie's bridal shower."

Lorea clapped. "That's great news. Now spill the rest."

I handed Lorea a truffle. "First try this."

Her eyes widened as she bit into the chocolate. "Mint. That is yummy!"

"I stopped at the post office and ran into Luke. He apologized for making fun of my profession and then asked me to lunch. We went to Honey's Pizza Cafe and had these delicious pizza pockets and I got to ride on his Harley." My words came out in a jumble, and we both squealed. I shouldn't admit that, but apparently I'm not too old to feel giddy over a good-looking guy.

"So, do you think you're going to go out with him again?" Lorea asked.

I lifted one shoulder. "He asked me for my number again, and I told him he still knew where to find me."

"You didn't?"

I nodded.

"You go, girl." She bumped my shoulder. "What are you going to do about Dallas?"

I bit my lip. "I guess I'll wait and see what happens."

"Good plan." Lorea opened the container of salad from Valerie. "This looks divine. I didn't stop for lunch."

I tsked and was about to say more when my phone began singing.

"It's the police department!" I nearly shouted when I saw the caller ID. Hopefully it was news about our stolen gowns and not anything to do with diamonds. An image of a jail cell flashed through my mind. How much trouble could I get into for holding onto the stones I'd found in Natalie's dress? Deciding that I could claim a blonde moment, I answered the phone. "Hello, this is Adri."

"Adri, two of your wedding dresses were found today." Tony's voice didn't sound happy.

"Can you bring them back here?"

"Unfortunately, they've been vandalized. We need you to come down to the station to have a look."

My heart sank. "I'll be right down," I mumbled and hung up.

"Good news?" Lorea asked.

With a shake of my head, I repeated the short conversation. "Do you want to come with me?"

"Of course," Lorea said. "Maybe there will be something we can salvage."

I didn't answer, and she didn't say anything else. I figured it was because we both felt the doom and gloom settling over the shop as we imagined scenes of Sylvia Rockfort in a rage.

The Ketchum police department was housed in a new red brick building only three blocks away. Tony ushered us into a little office, where folds of white satin and tulle billowed from a table near his desk.

Lorea cried out when she saw the damage. I covered my mouth. The dresses had dirt and grass stains on them, and bits of twigs and dried leaves stuck in the tulle skirt. But that wasn't the worst part. I touched the ragged hemline of the sleek form-fitting gown made for a princess. It had been crudely slit open, strips of fine silk hanging in a jagged line.

The other dress had a bell skirt and a graduated train over layers of tulle. Its hemline was in similar condition. The gowns were destroyed. But Sylvia's dress wasn't one of them. I wondered where it could be.

"Why would someone do this?" Lorea whispered, and I noted the husky sound of tears under her breath.

The back of my throat burned as disappointment washed over me. I couldn't look at Lorea until I got myself under control. Crying was definitely not something I liked to do in public. This seemed like a personal attack on my dream, not to mention Lorea's.

"I'm sorry, ladies," Tony said. "A fly fisher on Trail Creek found them under some bushes. I don't understand it, either."

So the thief had vandalized the wedding gowns and then dumped them barely a mile from my store. Was someone trying to ruin my wedding business? It seemed so pointless, and my head spun with the implications. I shoved down the rising paranoia and reminded myself that Ketchum was a good, wholesome community filled with caring individuals. The thieves were after the diamonds I'd hidden in my quilt. That thought terrified me.

My mouth went dry, and I grabbed Lorea's arm to steady myself as I stared again at the ripped hemlines. The diamonds. I needed to tell Tony about Natalie's dress, but how could I do that without getting myself and her dress into trouble?

"I wonder where Sylvia's dress is," Lorea said. "It just doesn't make sense. The thief could have sold these dresses for a lot of money. Sylvia's dress would have easily brought a few thousand dollars to even the most unknowledgeable person."

Lorea was right. Where was Sylvia's dress? The thief, or thieves, had only taken three of the nine wedding gowns, and although I felt grateful they hadn't all been stolen, I was confused as to their motive. "Can we take the dresses with us?" I asked. "Lorea might be able to salvage some of the beadwork on this one."

"These are going to the lab to see if we can pick up any trace evidence," Tony said. "I'll let you know as soon as I find anything."

"How long will that be?"

"I'm not sure. Maybe a couple of weeks."

"That's a long time. Good thing these dresses weren't scheduled to make an appearance at a wedding yet," Lorea said.

With difficulty, I swallowed my confession. Natalie's wedding was in three weeks—not enough time to go to the lab and make it back.

My phone rang, and Tony laughed. "Great song."

"I know. My clients like it too." I recognized the caller as one of the caterers I had contacted about Natalie's wedding. "I'll take this outside if we're finished here?"

Tony nodded, and I walked out of the station, grateful for an escape from the guilt coming like heat waves from my body. I declined a meeting with the potential caterer, happy all over again that I had found Valerie, and ended the call with a deep breath.

The sun glinted off the windshield of my Mountaineer, and I didn't relish getting inside the oven-like interior. As I moved toward it, Lorea came out the front entrance, accompanied by Tony.

"Adri, I forgot to ask you one more question about the other stolen dress," Tony called.

I paused. "Shoot."

He pulled out his notebook. "Do you have any idea how many might've been made like it?"

"I can answer that one," Lorea said. "It's supposed to be one of a kind. I'm sure there are dresses with similarities, but we chose the design especially for our shop."

Tony nodded. "We're concentrating on pawn shops or other places where someone might have tried to sell that dress. If it's online, we have a better chance, but we haven't seen anything yet. We'll keep searching with the pictures you provided."

"Thanks." I fished out my keys as I passed the car parked next to my Mountaineer but stopped when I noticed the fancy motorcycle on the other side of the parking lot. The blue and silver were the same design I'd admired at the Smokehouse BBQ and taken a ride on just an hour earlier.

"Hey, I've seen that Harley before." I indicated the motorcycle with a smile, and both Tony and Lorea took a step forward.

"Yeah, it belongs to that new lawyer." Tony whistled. "It's a nice ride."

"A lawyer?" I looked at Tony, and then back at the Harley. "Is his name Luke?"

"Yeah, Luke Stetson. He's that divorce lawyer with the new office on the other side of the bookstore."

"Uh-oh," Lorea whispered.

"Divorce lawyer." I ground my teeth. "I can't believe it. That's what he meant by 'considering.'"

Tony gave me a confused look, and Lorea hurried to explain.

"Adri met him the other day and uh—they kind of hit it off, but he didn't tell her he was a divorce lawyer."

"Oh, right. Guess he'd be equivalent to the dark side for you." Tony patted my shoulder. "Seems like a nice guy. Kind of serious, though."

I glared at the motorcycle. "No wonder he was hesitant to tell me his last name was Stetson. He was probably afraid I'd recognize his profession." And too late, I realized that he hadn't said much about himself earlier today.

"He's a nice guy, Adri," Tony repeated in a soothing tone. "You have to admit, you come off kind of strong. He was probably afraid he'd get a tongue-lashing."

My head jerked up. I caught Lorea shaking her head and giving Tony a pleading look. She stopped and said, "You know, this day isn't getting any better standing here. Let's grab some chocolate before we go back to work."

"I'm a wedding planner, Tony. You know, as in people getting married—that 'til death do us part sort of thing."

Tony held up his hands. "I get it. I'll let you know if we find anything new." He retreated a few steps. "Good luck with the chocolate." He smirked and hurried inside.

I growled. Tony knew he could tease me because I'd grown up with my brother, Wes, and him tormenting me. But if I ever saw Luke again, he'd find out exactly what I thought about his silence regarding his profession.

The shop was quiet that afternoon. I could tell Lorea was upset about the damaged gowns, but she went right to work, only surfacing when the door opened at three o'clock. I glanced at

Colton and swallowed my grin as Lorea leveled a cool stare in my direction that I was sure meant "Keep your mouth shut."

"Hi, ladies." Colton carried in two boxes. "Sorry, I don't have any news on the shipping inquiry."

He had anticipated my question, but his news wasn't surprising as I knew the investigation was going through the corporate offices. I frowned. "That's okay. I kind of figured we wouldn't find the dress. When I talked to the supervisor, he said to expect at least six weeks before they can come to a conclusion." I didn't mention that my contacts in China had said the same thing. My focus had shifted from the botched shipment to the stolen gowns, anyway.

"Yeah, that probably will be the case, but you never know." He shifted the boxes, and the larger one dropped with a thud on the floor. I flinched, hoping everything inside was packed tightly. He set the smaller box on the counter and handed over his electronic pen. "What do we have today?"

Colton always acted interested to know what was inside our boxes. Today it rubbed me the wrong way because I was in a bad mood over the dresses and in a lesser way the revelation about Luke. Besides, delivery guys weren't supposed to be nosy, anyway. Deciding to let Lorea answer, I smiled and reminded myself that Colton wasn't at fault—a certain fried-pickle-eating divorce lawyer was my problem. The silence stretched on, and I hesitated, leaning back to watch Lorea pull back the tape on the large box.

"Don't sign for that, Adri. This box is damaged."

"Just the outside corner. I'm sure the stuff inside is okay." Colton crouched beside Lorea as she opened the box and moved aside some crumbled Styrofoam.

"Uh-oh." She lifted out a jagged piece of cream-colored ceramic.

My heart sank as I realized what was in the box. "The cupcake stand for Sylvia's bridal shower!"

Lorea held up another piece with a scalloped edge. "The one she wanted to hold those cupcakes with the magic glitter. Please say this wasn't one of a kind."

"I'm going to have an ulcer for sure. I ordered that six weeks ago." My nerves were buzzing, and I shoved the signing device back at Colton, clenching my teeth together because my training at Bellisima would never let me forget: *a wedding planner always exhibits self-control.*

"Hey, I'm sure the company will get you a new one." He held out the pen again. "Just sign here."

"It's broken. I'm not signing. I need a claim slip, or whatever. Your company will have to take care of the damages."

I turned back to Lorea and heard Colton swear under his breath.

"Excuse me?" Lorea stood up, holding the broken cupcake platter in her hand. The fire in her eyes put Colton in his place.

His shoulders slumped. "Sorry, I'm under a lot of pressure. Boss threatened to change my route if I couldn't take care of the boxes. He expects me to look the other way and let things slide. I'm supposed to encourage the customers to sign no matter what."

"Do you have a lot of damaged boxes?"

"We've been getting our fair share." He rubbed his hand across his forehead. "I'll get you some paperwork." He hurried out to the van.

"I don't buy that," I said. "They have insurance for these types of accidents."

"Maybe his boss is trying to cut through the red tape." Lorea put the broken pieces of ceramic back inside the box.

My frown deepened. "I guess he found out what was in the delivery again."

"What do you mean?"

I shrugged. "Just thinking it was kind of odd how Colton always asks us what's in the boxes."

"Isn't he just making conversation?"

"I don't know. Can you take care of this?" I motioned to the box and then to Colton returning with a handful of papers. "There must be one similar online I can get here with expedited shipping. As long as it doesn't get broken too." I glared at Colton, and his eyes went hard in return. I hurried to my computer. I'd never seen him act that way before. Maybe his boss *was* on his case, or maybe he felt embarrassed about the damage because he thought Lorea might blame him. It was obvious he liked her. With a deep breath, I pushed down my anger and began clicking through images of cupcake stands. There was no way I was going to deliver more bad news to Sylvia.

An hour later, some of my tension drained away as I clicked on the box that would summon a new cupcake stand almost identical to the broken one Colton had delivered—and it would be here within three days. Then the bells chimed, and I turned to greet the customer entering the shop. My mouth dropped open when I saw Luke standing next to the new cake display—in almost the same place Dallas had been when he'd visited earlier in the week.

My lips pressed into a hard line. "What can I do for you, Mr. Stetson?"

He smiled, and the dimple in his chin was so endearing I thought for half a second about forgiving him. Then I remembered the fried pickle I had wasted on a divorce attorney who mocked my line of work. I imagined an iron gate falling into place around my heart.

"You said I knew where to find you. Turns out, you were right."

"Convenient, since I'm just a few blocks away from your office."

His smile faltered, but he straightened his shoulders and glanced toward the back. I wondered if Lorea was peeking around the corner but resisted the urge to look.

"This is a nice setup you have here." He rested his hand on the back of a cream-colored chair with turquoise buttons. It sat next to the desk where I planned weddings with my clients.

So he was going to pretend it was no big deal that I knew he was a divorce lawyer. I narrowed my eyes. Or maybe he thought I didn't know he specialized in divorce. When I checked the business listings, it only identified him as an attorney with emphasis in family law.

"Thank you." It came out sounding like I was clenching my jaw, probably because I was.

Luke picked up one of my business cards and then a pamphlet explaining the different types of weddings I helped arrange and the plans couples could choose. He gave a low whistle and jabbed the description of the Destination Wedding Package. "People really pay this much to get married?"

"And usually fly the wedding planner to the location two weeks before for last-minute arrangements."

"Man, maybe I'm in the wrong business." He started to laugh but stopped, probably because I wasn't laughing with him.

"What do you want, Luke?"

He took a step back. "I was hoping to get your phone number so I could take you on a date. Is something wrong? You seem—uh—upset."

"You think?" I folded my arms and tapped my right foot. The anger bubbling beneath the surface was about to explode. I ignored the voice that told me to take a deep breath. How could he ask me on a date after the way he'd mocked my wedding planning business? A niggling thought reminded me that he *had* apologized and rather lavishly, but I was too ticked to listen.

Luke eyed my stance and adjusted his glasses. "Are you upset with *me?*"

"I told you I was a wedding planner, so you purposely didn't tell me you were a divorce lawyer."

"Why does my profession matter?"

"I help people get married, and you help people get divorced. You don't see any problem with that?"

"It only has to be a problem if you make it a problem," Luke replied. "I apologized, remember? And I said *I* don't believe in marriage—that doesn't mean I think no one else should."

Tightening my hands into fists, I could feel the anger rising. I tried to keep the venom from my voice. "Then why would you ask me out?"

"I don't care what your job is—I just wanted to get to know you. You seemed nice." He tossed my business card and the pamphlet back onto the desk. "My mistake."

"What?" Flames would spurt from my mouth any second if I stayed near the creep. I couldn't trust someone who didn't tell the whole truth. I pointed to the door. "I've got to get back to work."

Luke shook his head and dropped his hands to his sides. He turned and left my store without another word.

"*Tontua*," Lorea muttered in Basque behind me. She *had* been peeking. "You're better off. Dallas is a sweet guy—maybe not as good looking, but that's what you get." She watched Luke crossing the street. "Dang, he's fine."

She was right, but part of me still wondered about the initial connection I'd felt to Luke. When he'd said he didn't believe in marriage, I thought it was just a front. Lots of guys say they're not interested, so girls fishing for a ring won't put them on their radar. But now, considering Luke's occupation, maybe he really was against wedded bliss. I wondered why.

Chapter 10

STORING YOUR WEDDING DRESS

Have your gown professionally cleaned immediately after use, even if it looks spotless. Do not hang the dress. Keep it in a storage box in a room or closet with constant temperatures and humidity levels (attics, basements, and closets next to exterior walls usually fluctuate too much). Where possible, line any folds with nonacidic, undyed tissue paper. Check your dress once a year for yellowing. Always wash your hands before handling the gown.
Courtesy of www.mashedpotatoesandcrafts.com.

After the incident with Luke, I felt doubly grateful that I had a date with Dallas to distract me from what had happened. Sylvia's bridal shower was coming up, so I worked myself into a frenzy checking every detail and trying not to dwell on the fact that she didn't know yet that her wedding gown was missing.

In light of the vandalized dresses, Lorea and I decided we shouldn't wait any longer to tell Sylvia. It was Friday, so Lorea put off making the call until nearly four o'clock—hoping the weekend would find Sylvia too busy to come and personally harass us. Her fingers shook as she dialed Sylvia's number. She kissed the Lauburu cross hanging from her neck before launching into the details of the robbery and subsequent vandalism of the gowns. I could hear Sylvia shrieking through the phone.

"I understand. That's why we're prepared to offer you another gown at no charge. We'll refund your money completely, and if you'd like to purchase a gown elsewhere, I'd be happy to offer my services to get the perfect fit." Lorea ran a section of silk through her fingers as she spoke, struggling to keep her voice soothing and calm.

My own hands were shaking as I listened to Lorea explain over and over again that even if Sylvia's wedding gown could be found, it might also be ruined. Not to mention the time needed to complete the alterations.

When Lorea hung up the phone, she took a deep breath and let it out slowly, wadding the piece of silk into a ball. Then she cursed. Loudly. I tensed, waiting until she finished.

"It went that well, huh?"

Lorea tried not to smile, but her lips twitched. Then she scowled. "She's on her way over."

"Now?"

"I hoped it would be too late, that she'd have other plans. Apparently she's canceling whatever she had and coming right now to look at our other gowns."

"And to chew me out." This day definitely wasn't going well. Lorea and I scurried around the shop, pulling out the dresses and tidying up the fitting room. Exactly sixteen minutes after Lorea ended the call with Sylvia, the woman arrived at the store, her nostril flaring.

"If my wedding wasn't a mere three weeks away, I'd find a new planner." Sylvia lifted a bright red polished nail in my direction and sniffed.

I had been preparing myself for her. "Your wedding will be featured in bridal magazines years from now because of how absolutely stunning you are, Sylvia. I can't begin to explain how sorry I am that this happened. Lorea and I are crushed and frightened that someone would attack us in this way." I took a step forward and handed Sylvia the pink rose I'd cut from the antique rosebush next to my shop. "We are determined to be successful, to make your dreams come true."

Sylvia took the rose and eyed me suspiciously. My offering was dramatic, but I was talking to a former soap opera actress and piling it on any other way wasn't an option. "Well, show me the other gowns." She smelled the rose and then followed Lorea to the rack where the six remaining dresses hung.

We both knew they paled in comparison to the countless beads and embroidery that encumbered Sylvia's missing gown. The dresses were beautiful, but the price tag on Sylvia's dress had been eighteen thousand dollars, and the most expensive of these gowns was seven thousand.

She stalked along, trailing her fingers over the dresses, and then whirled around to face Lorea, her look somewhere between a glare and a sneer. Her nose gave every look its own interpretation.

"I saw another dress here when I came for my fitting. It had lots of frills. Was that one stolen?"

Oh, no. Just what we needed. Lorea gave me a pleading look, and I cleared my throat. "We sold that gown last week."

"To whom?"

I ignored her question, speaking rapidly so she couldn't interrupt. "Lorea has the magic touch when it comes to dresses, and she's picked out two we'd like you to try. They are both one of a kind, and she has a few ideas to make them even more unique."

"Yes, this one here." Lorea held a dress up in front of Sylvia. "It could be worn as is, or I was considering adding a detachable train." She reached for a swath of fabric and held it up to the dress. "And I've ordered a belt studded with three hundred cubic zirconium brilliant cut stones. They're all the rage in Hollywood this year."

"I might as well try it on. Could you put this in water for me, darling?" Sylvia handed me the rose, and I obeyed, eager to put some distance between the diva and me.

It was nearly six o'clock when Sylvia left. She had selected a gown but wasn't "feeling the magic," she said, and wanted a chance to continue her search. Lorea assured her that as long as she found a gown ten days before the wedding, there would be enough time for alterations and the multiple fitting sessions needed.

The café around the corner delivered croissant sandwiches, which Lorea and I devoured as we discussed the financial ramifications of the robbery.

"I talked to my insurance agent, and almost half the value of the stolen dresses are covered. But I don't want you to worry about anything. We'll continue making payments to Walter and go ahead with ordering the next shipment."

Lorea folded her napkin into something akin to a bird. "Maybe we should wait to order more."

I shook my head. "Natalie's dress is worth enough to cover the setback with Sylvia's gown, and because of insurance, it's almost as if it were sold anyway. I don't think you should wait."

"I'm just worried about how everything will go if Sylvia bad-mouths us too much."

"Forget Sylvia for now." I tossed my wrapper in the garbage. "When people see Natalie's gown, I think you'll see new customers."

"I hope so. Speaking of Natalie's dress . . ." Lorea raised her eyebrows at me.

I hadn't told Lorea that I was practically finished but that I was scared about moving the gown. What if someone was looking for it and watching the shop? I held up my hand. "I know, I know. I promise I'll finish with it tonight."

"Good, because I'll be working into the wee hours trying to finish Natalie's bridesmaids' dresses." Lorea crossed her fingers. "I hope she likes them."

"She'll love them. She picked out the pattern, didn't she?"

"Yes, but I made a couple of alterations so they fit better and to accentuate the design."

"Then I'm sure they'll be perfect."

Lorea and I cleaned up, and I was able to schedule another meeting with a caterer the following week, as well as a meeting with the local florist who would be doing both Natalie's and Sylvia's weddings. I rushed out the door at five minutes past seven to meet Dallas, grateful again for the small town of Ketchum. Frozen Tundra Treats was only six minutes away.

Dallas seemed more talkative as we ordered our treats and settled into a cherry-red booth. "Thanks for introducing me to the finer side of Ketchum." Dallas motioned to the ice cream parlor. "I've been waiting all day to find out what a frozen mud pies tastes like."

"You'll love it." I didn't tell him that it was a new twist on a brownie sundae. That could wait until the double-chocolate brownie layered with peanut butter and frozen between slabs of vanilla ice cream was served. I took a deep breath. "I need to tell you what happened at my shop before you hear it through the grapevine."

Dallas tilted his head. "Something bad?"

"Yes. Someone broke in and stole my safe and three wedding gowns."

"But you didn't mention it last night." He reached for my hand. "Are you okay?"

"Pretty stressed. I was trying to pretend I could deal with it yesterday, and I didn't want to burden you with my problems."

"It's not a burden. What will happen with your shop?"

"I have insurance to cover some of the loss, but it's really put me on edge." I described to him the details of the vandalized dresses, and he listened intently. He didn't grill me, and I was grateful, even though I saw the curiosity in his eyes.

"I can tell you'd rather think about something else, so let's change the subject," Dallas said after I'd finished my depressing report. "The important thing is that you're safe."

"Thank you." I squeezed his hand, touched by his kindness and intuition.

Our server brought out the frozen mud pie in a bright red dish with two long silver spoons. Dallas dug into the hot fudge and ate a huge bite. "That's delicious."

And it was. I ate my fill of the chocolate concoction drenched in melting ice cream as Dallas told me about the homes he was showing in the area and how real estate seemed to be picking up for the summer, allowing him to cut back on his hours as a waiter.

After we finished dessert, we went out to the parking lot. The sun inched toward the horizon, casting rays of pinkish light across the Sawtooths.

"So, tell me about your family," Dallas said.

"They're great. My parents are Carl and Laurel Pyper. Dad is a semiretired farmer, and my mom is basically amazing in every way."

"Sounds like you're pretty close to them." Dallas gave me his full attention, and I found myself pausing to admire his handsome face. His black eyebrows curved down slightly near his temples, accentuating the straight black lashes framing his eyes.

"We are. Well, when I'm not working myself to death. I have an older brother, Wesley, who has always been a mentor to me. Even though Wesley returned home after college to manage the farm and allow Dad to retire, the two enjoy working together. Wes can't keep Dad off the tractor." An image of my dad in overalls came to mind, and I smiled. "Wes and his wife, Jenna, have the cutest little girl, Bryn. She's three, and I just adore her."

"I bet you're a fun aunt."

"It's not hard to impress a three year old." I shrugged. "What about your family?"

"I don't have any nieces or nephews yet. But I'm curious. Does your family wish you had started your business in Rupert?"

I leaned forward, impressed that he had remembered where I grew up from the brief introduction I'd given him on our first date. "My family has really been rooting for me to succeed here with my wedding planning business, especially since . . ." I stopped before I mentioned Briette's murder. Dallas seemed like the type who would understand, but it was still hard for me to talk about that, and after the week I'd had, I didn't trust my emotions. Dallas looked expectant, and I coughed before continuing. "Especially since they know how important my dreams are to me."

"That's wonderful. So did your family help you get started up here?"

"They did—each in their own way. My mom tends to go a little overboard with things, and she can be a bit overbearing, but it all works out. Dad and Wes helped me move, and Jenna helped me with a few contacts she has through her business. She pitches in with the crafting blog I run with my mom."

"Crafts?" Dallas's eyebrows scrunched in confusion, and I couldn't suppress my giggle.

"Good thing my mom's not here now. She'd find the nearest computer and show you our site and what's trending on Pinterest."

Dallas appeared mystified. "So, like sewing and those little statues you paint?"

"Not really. Think anything creative and beautiful for the home, for the kids, for the stomach. We love to make cards, share sewing tips, gardening ideas, cleaning tips, recipes—even a little crochet. My website is called mashedpotatoesandcrafts.com."

Dallas laughed. "Serious?"

"Yep, we do everything from cooking to crafting, so it fits. I've actually posted some specialty items for my weddings that my mom and I created."

Dallas shook his head. "It's amazing what you can find online, huh?"

"Totally. My family gets pretty excited about crafts. My mom, especially. She's always coming up with new ideas for things that I might be able to use for a wedding or bridal shower. Which reminds me, I'd better hurry or I'll never get everything on my list done."

"I'm glad we could see each other tonight." Dallas interlaced my fingers with his as we walked outside. "I'd like to take you back to the Roosevelt Grille while I can still get the employee discount."

"I would love to go with you," I said. And I meant it. The food was fabulous there, and the sugar I'd just consumed made me feel a bit giddy on the heels of the stressful day I had endured. That was the only explanation I could think of for agreeing to another date, besides the obvious one that I was starting to like Dallas more than I wanted to admit. We leaned against my Mountaineer, and he put his arm around me. Scooting closer to him, I speculated what he was working up the nerve to say or possibly do. Somehow I doubted he would kiss me in the parking lot of Frozen Tundra Treats.

"I wish you didn't have to go," he murmured.

"Me too. Believe me, I'd much rather do anything than what I have ahead of me tonight, picking out thousands of tiny threads."

Dallas laughed and then leaned closer, his face inches from mine. "Thanks for giving me a chance, Adri. I really like you. I get nervous around girls as pretty as you, but I want to get this right."

"You're doing fine so far."

He smiled, and I noticed his teeth were small and even. His flawless skin was a reminder of his Asian heritage. I admired his startlingly green eyes, and Dallas chose that moment to close the distance between us and brush a feather-light kiss across my lips. Before I could react, the kiss was over, and he pulled me into an embrace. I relaxed into his chest, enjoying the closeness of the moment and wishing he would kiss me again. Then I stepped back.

"When can I see you again?" Dallas asked.

"Maybe Monday? As long as I'm caught up on everything." I pushed back the loose tendrils of hair tickling the sides of my face. "Thanks for tonight."

Dallas rubbed his stomach. "Definitely my pleasure."

As I drove home, I relived the nanosecond-long first kiss and felt a keen disappointment. There weren't any fireworks yet, but maybe next time there would be time to light the fuse. If Dallas hadn't been so nervous, I might've even invited him over for a movie while I worked on Natalie's bridal shower details. I frowned. Oh, well. At least this way there would be nothing to distract me from getting the job done.

Lorea texted me as I was changing my clothes.

So? How was date #3?

I wasn't sure how I felt about Dallas, so I didn't want to give her too much info. My hesitant nature in the dating arena had me overanalyzing everything, and that kiss hadn't quite swept me off my feet.

Short. Sweet. One peck. Now back to work.

Hmm, he def. likes you, sounds like you still don't know.
Okay, I won't bug you. Get that hem done!

Lorea had me figured out. I pulled on a pair of green-and-white cotton pajama pants. They had been a gift from my grandma, and I felt so relaxed I wished I could just fall into bed. But first I needed to make sure that all the windows and doors were securely locked, and then I felt for the bulge in the quilt. The diamonds were still safe. With careful steps, I walked into my spare bedroom to check on Natalie's gown. I tried to laugh at myself for sneaking around my own house, but I was too worried for laughter.

The dress was just as I had left it. I reexamined the hem and spent some time trimming and pulling out the remnants of thread that had held the hem together. When the task was finally complete I tucked the gown away. I walked through my house again, double-checking the locks. Satisfied that my home was secure, I crawled into bed thinking about my plans for the next morning.

Chapter 11

CONVERSATION STARTERS

Print quotations on paper silverware wrappers or along the bottom of place cards for fun conversation starters. Example: "Better a diamond with a flaw than a pebble without one." —Chinese proverb Courtesy of www.mashedpotatoesandcrafts.com.

My dreams were haunted by wedding gowns that were all too heavy to lift because they were weighted down with smuggled diamonds. The morning sunshine was a welcome change from the nightmares. I changed into a pair of old jeans and a long-sleeved, quick-dry shirt that felt soft against my skin. On my way out of the house, I grabbed a banana and a granola bar. There was always a box of water bottles in my trunk; growing up in the Idaho desert near the boonies had taught me well. I retrieved a bottle and guzzled half of it before sliding into the cool interior of my vehicle. The Mountaineer had a great stereo system, and I selected one of my favorite running mixes for the ride over to the shop. What I was about to do would not be pleasant.

The music heightened my spirits, and I was able to shed a little worry as I drove. Eight minutes later, I pulled into the parking lot behind Pyper's Dream Weddings. A quick walk-through of the building calmed my frazzled nerves—everything was as I'd left it the day before.

Rolling my shoulders back, I headed outside. I eyed the garbage cans lined up behind the shops and cringed. Garbage day was Monday, so they were full and foul smelling this clear Saturday morning. The police had performed a perimeter search of the area after the break-in, including a search of these trash cans and dumpsters, but they were looking for wedding gowns. I needed to search for any remnants of material that a male police officer, who had no idea about fabric, might have missed. Hoping for a clue to the whereabouts of Sylvia's gown, specifically, I stared at the dumpster and swallowed. The pair of blue latex gloves I'd pulled on didn't seem like enough of a barrier for searching through trash, so I put an old pair of work gloves over them.

With a shudder, I checked the trash from my shop. Not surprised that I didn't find anything of significance, I moved toward the next building. It was one of many realty agencies in Ketchum, and I figured it was a good place to continue my search. I lifted the lid of the big black garbage can and began sifting through the trash. Most of the bags were white or clear plastic, so it was easier work than I'd feared it would be. Breathing through my mouth instead of my nose made the task bearable, and because the dress had been stolen in the last two days, I didn't feel the need to dig down to the bottom of the garbage bins. It only took a few minutes, and I moved to the next bin.

Mayfield Jewelers didn't have much trash, so I pretty much eye-balled that can. I was just closing the lid when something caught my eye. A corner of lovely cream and turquoise cardstock, similar to my company's letterhead peeked out from underneath a cardboard box. The lid banged against the back of the can when I threw it open. Leaning into the trash can, I grunted at the unpleasant feeling of pressure against my ribs from the hard edge of the container.

My fingers grazed the corner of the paper, and I stretched my arms just enough to get hold of it and pull. The paper wouldn't budge, and I let out a cry of frustration. I would have to tip the can on its side. I prepared to push the garbage can over, but something brushed against my leg, and I shrieked.

"Meow."

I looked down to see an innocent black kitten nuzzling my leg. I nudged it away. "You scared me to death. Don't you know you're not supposed to sneak up on someone when they're digging through trash?"

The kitten paid no attention to my scolding and wound its way between my ankles. I stooped and picked it up. I was partial to cats—growing up on a farm we had plenty of them—and this one was quite friendly. I could tell it was at least three months old and didn't need its mama anymore. "Who do you belong to?" I asked as I examined the white markings on its throat and feet. I scratched between his ears, and he purred and snuggled against my chest. The vibrations from his purr brought back hundreds of memories of my farm-girl days when I loved playing with kittens near the haystack on our farm. This one didn't have a collar, but for how friendly he was, I imagined he belonged to someone. I set him down and eyed the garbage again.

"Meow." The kitten peered up at me and then batted at my leg as I put my hands against the garbage can and pushed. With a loud thump, the can landed on the pavement, and some of the trash bags fell out. I squatted near the opening and looked for that elusive piece of paper. I inhaled sharply when I found not one page but a whole stack of pages with turquoise and purple trim. They were *my* pages, with the Pyper's Dream Weddings logo, and each of them had three holes punched in the side. One of the pages had writing on it, and I held it with a trembling hand.

Simple, yet elegant and close to nature describes Natalie's dream wedding.

My handwriting flowed across the bottom of the page. I brushed off some dirt, and my eyes flicked to the words written on the top lines.

Sunshine, blue skies, meadowlarks, silk, pink diamonds, pink glassware settings, Warm Springs, Brock . . .

When I had first interviewed Natalie about what she wanted for her wedding day, I gave her two minutes to write down whatever came to mind. This was her list, and I knew it was also the third page of the wedding binder I had locked in my office safe.

I glanced at the back door of Mayfield Jewelers and tried to swallow the knot in my throat. Then I shook my head. Walter wouldn't have had anything to do with the crime. The thief probably just dumped what he didn't want in the first trash can available. But even though I told myself that, it didn't make sense that the thief would have cracked open my safe and disposed of its contents in the vicinity. Why hadn't Tony found any of these pages before?

The kitten pawed at the page in my hand, and I stroked his back absentmindedly. Then I pulled out my cell phone and called Detective Ford.

"Yo, Adri. How are you?" Tony answered on the second ring, chipper even though it was only seven o'clock in the morning.

"I'm going through the trash on the street behind my shop, and I found some of the contents of my safe in the can behind Mayfield Jewelers."

"I'm on my way," Tony said. "Don't touch anything until I get there."

"Too late, but I'm wearing gloves."

"Good girl. See you in ten."

So he was already at the station—three blocks away from my shop. He might be here in less than ten minutes, but I hated waiting, and some of the trash spilling out of one of the bags had soda cups dripping sticky liquid all over the rest of the garbage. I wanted to salvage as many of Natalie's pages as I could.

Gravel bit into the thin fabric of my running pants and pinched my knees as I leaned farther into the garbage can and collected the pages. Why were they loose? Wouldn't the thief have chucked the whole binder at once, not seeing anything of value in my wedding plans?

The stack of pages appeared a bit rumpled, and smears of dirt and debris clung to a few of them. I started putting them in order in an attempt to recall what might be missing. Soon there were sixteen pages of information about Natalie's wedding stacked next to the kitten. I was relieved to have found the pages that were vital to creating a perfect wedding, but that relief vanished when I realized one of the pages was gone.

I flicked through them again to see if I had missed it but

knowing that I hadn't. Wednesday just before closing, I had attached a picture of the layered-frill wedding gown Natalie had selected to the dress section of her binder. The page was covered with sketches, stapled fabric swatches, and clippings of dresses Natalie loved. That page was gone. So were the first and second pages, which contained all of Natalie and Brock's contact information.

Panic shot through my head as several different theories collided at once. The two dresses with shredded hem lines flicked through my mind. I recalled how heavy Sylvia's dress felt, and then Lorea wondering how to lighten the underskirt.

Did the thief know which dresses had diamonds sewn into them? Had he searched for Natalie's dress, and not finding it, grabbed others that seemed similar? If the idea forming in my mind was correct, he now had proof that we were in possession of the smuggled diamonds. He also had Natalie's contact information.

Brock had hired bodyguards and had surveillance cameras installed at their homes after news of their engagement covered the tabloids. I felt that Natalie was safe, but her dress was not. I had to find somewhere secure to keep it until the big day.

The kitten batted playfully at something inside the overturned garbage can. It looked like a scrap of material, and I leaned forward for a closer look. The kitten mewed softly and retreated farther inside.

"Here, kitty, kitty," I called.

"Adri, what are you doing?"

I screamed and sat upright—or tried to, but my head bumped the inside of the trash can. "Ouch."

"Are you okay?" Tony leaned over me and offered his hand.

Rubbing my head, I scowled. "Why'd you sneak up on me like that?"

He grinned. "I thought I told you not to touch anything."

"I had to. There was soda dripping all over my papers. I couldn't just sit here and watch them get ruined."

Tony raised an eyebrow. "What did you find?"

I showed him the stack of papers and told him that the personal information pages were missing, as well as the photo of Natalie's wedding dress.

"Hmm. I don't think these were here Thursday. Were any other pages missing?"

"I didn't find the binder, and I know we had jotted down random notes and sketches on some other pages, but all of the vital wedding planning information is here." My conscience nagged at me to spill the beans about the diamonds I had found, but I resisted.

Tony pulled out a clear plastic sack marked 'Evidence' and dropped the pages inside.

My shoulders slumped. "You have to take the pages, too?"

"I can get photocopies of everything, and as soon as we're finished with the investigation, they'll be returned."

"So anything related to this crime has to go in for processing?"

"Yes." Tony eyed me curiously. "Why do you ask?"

"Because I need those other two gowns back so Lorea and I can salvage at least the bodice for a new dress. How soon can we have them?" I gave Tony my best stern glare which was supposed to be hiding my honest eyes screaming, *I have diamonds in my house, and I should tell you about them but now I know for certain I can't!*

Tony rubbed his forehead. "They said it'd be three weeks."

"Three weeks!"

Tony held out his hands. "Not my fault. It takes a while to get test results back. This isn't *CSI Miami*."

Any confession I might've made died on my lips. I couldn't sabotage Natalie's wedding. Three weeks. She would be married in three weeks, and the dress would be sent to the cleaners. I could offer to take care of that for her, and then I would tell Tony everything and hand the gown over to their crime lab.

I often used the quilt in my front room to cozy up with a book and get lost in the pages. Good thing it was summertime because the quilt would have to stay put in my spare room. There would be no warm cozy feelings associated with my crime of withholding information from a criminal investigation.

My actions might be wrong and dangerous, but I wasn't going to let some criminal ruin my wedding business again. I had been on the threshold of success before Briette's murder, and my career had been yanked out from under me. Every painstaking moment of detailed work had led to this chance of success for my business. Natalie was a sweet and genuinely nice person who deserved to have her happiness. Not to mention our own happiness in planning her wedding after all we had had to put up with from Sylvia Rockfort.

Maybe there was a way to let Tony know what was happening without giving up Natalie's wedding gown.

Tony interrupted my guilty train of thought. "How many cans have you searched?"

I pointed down the street to two large dumpsters. "Those are the only ones left."

"Would you care to search with me?" Tony asked. "Then you can tell me if anything looks relevant."

"Okay."

"You know, you could've called me before you started digging, and I would've come and·helped you." Tony looked at me, and I withered under his gaze.

Scuffing my shoe along the asphalt, I murmured, "I'm not trying to mess up your investigation. I just didn't know how thoroughly those other officers dug through the trash. I thought maybe I'd find something that hadn't seemed important."

"Can you give me a chance next time? I'm a good cop. If you think it's important, I'll listen." Tony pulled on a pair of work gloves and opened the next trash can.

That guilty feeling tickled the back of my throat, but I bit down on my tongue so I wouldn't tell Tony anything. I needed time to think, and I couldn't do that until we'd finished searching. "I'm sorry. If I think of anything else, I'll tell you."

After an hour of looking, we hadn't found anything useful. The smell of rotten food and moldy garbage can innards left me feeling sick to my stomach. The nagging guilt over withholding information probably contributed to that, but I did my best to ignore it.

"Sorry about all this, Adri. We'll be patrolling this area heavily, keeping an eye on your shop."

"Thanks, Tony." I hurried home to take a shower before I changed my mind and confessed.

Natalie's wedding gown looked ethereal hanging in the dim light of my spare bedroom. Although I was relieved it was still safe, it seemed to emanate tension as I thought about the diamonds in my quilt.

Lorea texted me to say she was on her way over to pick up the dress. I couldn't put her in danger, but I knew she needed to finish the alterations. Tony said a patrol would be watching my shop. The scene of the crime might be the safest place for now. I replied to her text asking if she could meet me at work. Then I carefully zipped Natalie's gown into the dress bag and rolled it up inside a thick quilt—I had at least six handmade beauties. My mom and Aunt Dana made sure I was warm and prepared for company. Holding the bundle close to my chest, I paused. I didn't want anyone to see me with the gown, and the idea that the thief could be watching me sent a chill down my spine.

I loaded it into the cargo space and told myself to remain calm. Turning around, I scanned the parking lot. It felt as if someone were watching me, but I told myself it was just nerves. My body felt sore from lack of sleep and crawling through trash. I rolled my shoulders and stretched out my legs before climbing into my vehicle and locking the door.

Chapter 12

HANDMADE CANDLES

Measure the depth of a Styrofoam cup or other heat-resistant but temporary container. Cut cotton wicking one and a half times the depth of the container. Melt paraffin wax (one pound of paraffin melts to about 20 fluid ounces) in a double boiler. Add essential oils for your favorite scent. Stir in dried rose petals, eucalyptus leaves, berries, or wood shavings, using about four parts wax to one part mix-ins. Wrap one end of cotton wicking to a pencil that is slightly longer than the diameter of your container, and tape the other end to the inside bottom of the container. The wick should be slightly taut. Pour wax into your container and adjust the wick as needed. Once the wick is centered and taut, allow 24 hours for the wax to harden. Then cut the container and peel it away to reveal the candle. Trim the wick to ¾ inch. Wrap twine or ribbon around the candle.

Courtesy of www.mashedpotatoesandcrafts.com.

The trash cans looked foreboding when I arrived at the shop. I swear the smell of garbage still lingered on me even after a shower. My nerves were popping as I unlocked the back door. Everything was as I'd left it that morning. Lorea arrived a few minutes later, and I handed her Natalie's dress.

"I'm sorry to make you come in, but I'm really worried, and I don't want whoever vandalized those dresses to do something to you."

"Why would they do something to me?

"To get Natalie's dress." I looked directly at Lorea with what I hoped conveyed the importance of what I was about to say. "I've been thinking that maybe her dress was the one they intended to take. When they realized they took the wrong ones, they trashed them."

"But why would they want it?"

"Sylvia's and Natalie's are the most expensive dresses." We both stared at the bag holding Natalie's gown. "Maybe that's why we haven't found Sylvia's yet."

"You're making me nervous." Lorea clenched her hands together.

"Tony said the police will be keeping an eye on the shop, and I'm having someone come by later today to install a surveillance camera. Promise me you'll be careful and keep that dress locked in the closet."

"Okay."

Lorea seemed scared, but that's what I wanted, so I didn't try to reassure her. If she was frightened, hopefully she would be more cautious.

It was almost noon by the time I got back to my condo. Dallas texted me and asked if I wanted to go to lunch. I wanted to see him, but I needed time to think through what to do with the diamonds and searching for Sylvia's gown. I texted a reply as I approached my front door.

I really want to, but I'm swamped. Rain check?

Sure. See you soon. Don't work too hard.

My heart fluttered when I read his reply and reached for the door, where a manila envelope taped near the door handle caught my attention. I pushed Send on the text and stuffed my phone into my pocket. ADRIELLE PYPER. I read my name in all caps and turned to look behind me before snatching the envelope from the door and hurrying inside. I didn't like the feeling I had just now of being watched. With a shudder, I opened the envelope and emptied the contents onto the side table.

My heart froze for an instant, and goose bumps rose on my arms. Glossy eight-by-ten pictures of me in my jeans and light blue shirt caught my eye first. I leafed through the photos quickly, fingers shaking. A close-up of me stuffing the quilt containing Natalie's dress in my trunk made my heart pound in fear. The pictures were from this morning, barely an hour ago.

I focused on a close-up of my face, pensive in thought. I'd been thinking about the stolen wedding gown when the picture was taken. Is that why I'd missed the pervert?

Flipping over the last picture, I sucked in a breath. The photo had been taken through the front window of my shop, and I could see a faint outline of myself behind the desk. On the bottom of the picture, someone had scrawled, *I hear wedding bells ringing.*

The photo dropped to the floor as I covered my mouth. Who was doing this?

Scrambling into my front room, I grabbed the quilt, pawing through the thick folds until I found the signature block. I ran my fingers along the bottom seam and felt the distinct bump of the gems I had hidden. They were still there, but someone was watching me. A thorough search of the rest of my house assured me that no one had been inside, but I didn't feel safe.

My thoughts strayed to the farm in Rupert, and I craved the comfort and safety I always felt with my family. I could be there in less than two hours. I'd been meaning to go home to meet with an old friend of mine who had started a business designing wedding invitations, hand addressed with beautiful calligraphy. But I also had plenty of work to do here to prepare for Sylvia's and Natalie's bridal showers. For a moment, I vacillated between the two options. Then I grabbed a bag and began tossing in everything I needed for a quick jaunt to my hometown.

I'd have to report this to Tony, of course, but not until I was safely on my way. I considered taking the quilt with me, but I didn't want to draw any attention to the hiding place, so I left it sitting conspicuously in my front room. The bag of diamonds threatened all kinds of trouble to me for interfering in a police investigation, but I ignored that and hoped a way would present itself soon for me to come clean and still keep Natalie's dress.

As I pulled out of my parking space, I dialed Tony's number. "Tony, can you have someone drive by my house? I'm going to Rupert for the weekend."

"Sure, but I think your home is safe," Tony said. "Are you worried about something in particular?"

I struggled for a moment, unsure of what to do. "Someone left a picture of me taped to my front door." I swallowed back tears. "It was from this morning."

"Where are you?"

"I'm just pulling out of my parking lot."

"Stay there. I'll be over in five."

I groaned as he hung up, and I looked at my shaking hands. Even though I was trying to be brave, I was scared, but I still couldn't tell Tony about the diamonds. Closing my eyes, I braced myself for his questions and turned off the engine. Wait. Could someone be out there watching me now? I looked around, but no one was in sight. I locked the doors anyway before texting Lorea to let her know I'd be back first thing Monday morning. Better to keep busy.

Tony arrived in four minutes. After I let him in the house and showed him the pictures, he did a thorough search of every room. "I think it's a good idea for you to go to Rupert. This is strange, but I'll find the connection."

My face paled as I thought of the connection I had already made. Tony referred to the wedding gowns, but it was probably all related to the diamonds hidden in my quilt.

He patted my arm. "Try not to worry. We'll get to the bottom of this. And tell Wes hello for me."

"I will."

Ten minutes later, I stopped for a sandwich in Hailey. I sent a text to my mom:

Surprise! I'm coming home for the weekend.

I opted to eat my sandwich while driving, pushing to get home and see my family. For the first twenty minutes of the drive, I constantly checked my rearview mirror, but then I laughed at myself. What did a diamond smuggler look like? And what would

I do if the criminal did decide to follow me? It was better not to think about it, so I pushed down on the gas pedal and continued on the back roads toward Minidoka County.

My mind kept wandering to the missing wedding gowns, diamonds, and the pictures taped to my door. I was pretty sure not telling the police was a bad idea, but I didn't know what else to do at the moment.

As I entered the quiet streets of Shoshone, I reminded myself to slow to the twenty-five-mile-per-hour crawl through town. The cops here were relentless with the tourists on their way to Sun Valley, and a ticket wouldn't help my insurance rates.

As I approached the turnoff to the old highway that would take me to my hometown, I couldn't help but smile. When I first moved home from California and began investigating the possibility of starting a wedding business in Sun Valley, it had been ten years since I'd visited the American Shangri-La, as some locals liked to refer to the resort town. My sense of direction was a bit rusty, so I consulted Dad. He loved to give directions, and when he told me about the shortcut to Sun Valley, at first I thought he was kidding. "It's three stop signs and you're there."

It really was that simple. Over one hundred miles of road, and I only had to make a right, a left, and another right. My path home led through fields of potatoes and sugar beets bright green under the warm sunshine.

I loved being away from the freeways and traffic jams of San Francisco. When I talked to Dallas about my family, he had hit on a point that I'd often asked myself. Was it the right decision to move to a tourist town where I didn't know anyone? Back home, I was surrounded by people who knew my parents and my grandparents. My ancestors had homesteaded in Rupert at the root of its foundation. But then I thought about Lorea and the friends I'd made, the clients I'd served in the four short months I'd been in business in Ketchum. It was different, but I felt like I was in my element. And I knew Briette would approve.

When I pulled into the lane, our golden retriever ran up to my Mountaineer, barking and bumping into the fender. I honked and rolled down the window. "Hey, Samson." The big dog's tongue lolled to the side, and he dashed back to the house and then ran circles in the yard. My vehicle fit perfectly in the third space next to the garage. I hopped out and gave Samson a good scratch behind the ears.

"Adri, I just saw your text twenty minutes ago." My mother, Laurel Pyper, opened the front door of the brick rambler and hurried across the wraparound porch. She wore denim capris and an old T-shirt emblazoned with *She who dies with the most fabric wins!* I couldn't help but giggle and remind myself that I needed to have Jenna design a cute polo shirt for Pyper's Dream Weddings and give my mom a few. As Mom explained it, she had lost her figure somewhere among all her pins and needles, so her capris had an elastic waistband and relaxed fit. Her blonde hair hid the few strands of gray that had sneaked in over the years, and she wore it shoulder length, the natural curl styled with extra-hold gel.

"It's so good to see you." Mom hugged me and then held me at arm's length, her dark eyes piercing. "What's wrong? More bad news about the stolen dresses?"

Mom had nearly been frantic when I'd told her and Dad about the burglary of my shop. I leaned in for another hug. "No. I figured I'd better come see what you and Jenna have cooked up for Sylvia Rockfort's wedding. I probably won't be able to come back until the end of the summer."

"You're not going to miss the Fourth of July!" Mom tugged on my arm, and I followed her to the porch. "I've already planned the family picnic, and your dad just bought new water guns for our annual soak-fest. I can't believe you'd be so busy you'd have to miss out on our family celebration."

My mom was always so dramatic, but Rupert did put on a great celebration for Independence Day, and my family had attended every summer for forty-three years. Farmers tend to stay close to home during the growing season, and my dad was no exception. The few vacations we did take were planned around grain and potato harvest. Besides, once my dad spent money on a boat we could use on the Snake River, less than ten minutes from our home, we didn't need to go anywhere else.

But at least my announcement had diverted her from grilling me about why I'd suddenly come home. "Mom, I have two weddings before the end of June, and people are just starting to find out about Natalie and Brock. I expect a lot more bookings once word spreads."

"Oh, how is Natalie? She always looks so pretty in the tabloid pictures," Mom gushed. "I hope you'll let me create something for her wedding."

"Natalie is as sweet and down-to-earth as they come. Brock's lucky to have found her. I just hope the reporters don't infringe on their happiness."

Mom gave me a pointed look.

"And yes, I've already given her your portfolio of centerpieces."

Mom punched the air and gave a whoop. I laughed. She did have a knack for pulling together extraordinary decorations. Fishbowls with the bride and groom's name etched in the glass with rose petals floating on the water and a live beta fish swimming

137

in it was just one example of her foray into the creative world of weddings. When a bride was looking for something unique, I'd find it after a brainstorming session with my mom.

The hook where my dad hung his cowboy hat caught my attention. "What's Dad up to?"

"He's out back checking the fence."

I followed Mom across the great room into her spacious kitchen that overlooked the backyard and horse pasture. She and Dad had remodeled five years ago, knocking out a wall and doubling the size of the kitchen. My mom's favorite part of the remodel was the large room just off the kitchen which had become Craft Central.

I could see the top of my dad's cowboy hat bobbing along the irrigation ditch as he restrung electric fencing on the digger links that lined the bank. A part of me longed to kick off my shoes and run outside through the lush green grass in my bare feet. The poplar trees towered over the pasture, and I wondered how far I could climb, given the chance. I'd spent plenty of days with my brother scrambling up those trees and shouting across the open fields at the top of our lungs.

Thoughts of my big brother warmed my heart, and I turned from the window to the direction of his house. He and Jenna had built a new home two years ago on the eastern edge of the farm only half a mile from my parents. My brother knew how lucky he was, so it was hard to feel anything but happiness for him, even though a small part of me wondered when I would have a family of my own.

"Are Wes and Jenna around?"

"I already invited them to dinner so you could play with Bryn."

I grinned, and Mom laughed. "What did you bring her this time?"

"Well, this visit was kind of spur of the moment, so I grabbed a box of Reese's Pieces from my stash."

"I'm sure Jenna will love that."

"I can share with Jenna, too. Wes is probably out spraying, right?"

"Yes. He loves listening to those epic fantasy novels on his iPod while he works."

I had given Wes his iPod Touch for Christmas with a subscription to Audible and a special pair of noise-cancelling headphones that he wore in his tractor. The machinery was so incredibly loud that he couldn't hear a thing otherwise. He worked long days, spraying all the five hundred sixty acres planted in potatoes and grain each year with a tractor equipped with a huge spraying contraption that spanned twenty-five yards.

"I'm glad he likes it. And I'm glad we can all get together. It'll be fun to hang out." I put my arm around my mom. "Do you want me to help you make supper?"

"You mean we have to eat?" Mom looked longingly at her craft room and then frowned at the kitchen. "I wanted to show you my latest creation."

"If we set foot in that room, it'll swallow us whole, and then Dad will be hungry and grumbling about his need for a personal chef."

We both laughed. "You're right," Mom said. "Let's see what we can whip up."

She'd already pulled some chicken out of the freezer, and we opted to cut it up and marinate it for stir-fry with ham fried rice. It was too early in the summer to eat anything from the garden, though my mouth watered when I thought of the juicy cherry tomatoes that would be ready to munch by the end of next month.

Once the water was bubbling in the rice cooker and the chicken strips were floating in their marinade, Mom pulled me into her craft room. My eye was immediately drawn to a beautiful piece of furniture against the back wall. It stood at least six feet tall and three feet wide. "What is that?"

"The pièce de résistance. Remember Mother's Day, when Dad said he had a surprise for me? Well, this came a week later." Mom placed a loving hand against the cabinet. "He said it should do for at least the next five years."

"Dad's always trying to find an easy out when it comes to gifts. There's no way he got this for you himself."

"You know your father well." Mom tugged on the handles of the cabinet and slowly opened it. "Jenna helped him."

The knotty alder doors swung open and then folded out to reveal hundreds of compartments, drawers, and bags filled with paper, rubber stamps, buttons, stickers, inks, fabric, and dozens of others things I couldn't see.

"Mom, this is amazing." I examined a drawer full of vintage buttons. "I can't believe Jenna kept this a secret from me. I want one."

"It's called a Workbox, and it's made by a company called The Original Scrapbox." Mom patted my arm. "Just wait until I show you what else they have. They've thought of everything for crafters."

With a shake of my head, I fingered the bags of rubber stamps attached by Velcro to a wall of the cabinet. "Dad must really love you."

For all my dad's teasing about Mom and her craft addictions,

I knew he was proud of her. "I'll have to make sure Jenna knows what I want for Christmas." I motioned to the rows of drawers. "So, which one of these compartments has something for me?"

"Right here." Mom pulled out a ceramic dish lined with smooth river rocks and pine cones glued to the rocks. An herbal candle added a splash of color with dark green leaves and burgundy flowers mixed into the wax.

"This is perfect, Mom." I examined the glitter spray on the pinecone that would catch the light of the candle when it was lit. Natalie wanted her wedding to be unpretentious, close to nature, reminiscent of where she first met Brock at Warm Springs. Lorea and I gave each other knowing looks every time we saw how hard Sylvia struggled with outdoing Natalie. If only she knew how minimal Natalie's decorations would be. The Berlin-Grafton wedding would be elegant (and bring in a good commission) but in a much simpler way.

Mom was showing me how she thought some of the June wildflowers could be used in the centerpiece when we heard my dad stomping his boots outside. I hurried to greet him with a hug.

"Hi, Dad. How are you?"

"Looks like the weekend has finally started." Dad kissed my cheek and tugged on my ponytail.

"I saw you out there working away, but Mom took me into the craft room before I could offer any help."

"She showed you the Craft Monster for her role in that mashed potato business?"

I lifted my eyebrows in Mom's direction.

"That's what he calls my Workbox," she offered.

Dad took off his hat and hung it on its peg by the door. Then he sat down with a grunt and unlaced his boots. His head of dark brown hair was still full, though the hairline was starting to recede a bit, but he would probably escape the baldness his father had experienced. His middle had thickened over the years, but at just over six feet he stood strong, still full of energy—a combination of good genes and Idaho farm stamina. Dad stretched his back. "So how are you holding up?"

"This month will pretty much put the mark of success or failure on my business. It's a challenge, but I'm up for it." I hoped I sounded convincing.

"I'm proud of you." Dad stood and crossed the kitchen, grabbing a glass and turning on the tap. "Just make sure you know when to ask for help. Don't get in over your head."

With a nod, I ignored my conscience as it piped up about the layers of meaning in my father's words. I savored Dad's compliment. For all his teasing about my choosing to be a wedding planner for "hoity-toity celebrities," his confidence in me was reassuring.

"I need to give Shayla Fitzgerald a call. She has some calligraphy samples for me to take back for display."

"Oh, that would be wonderful. Dennis has been out of work for over a year now, and they've both been doing all they can to keep their home." Mom twisted a dishtowel as she spoke. "They're basically living off their farm and odd jobs right now."

"I knew Dennis was out of work, but I didn't realize it was that bad." The grandfather clock in the living room tolled four times, and I checked my watch to be sure it was accurate. "If I hurry, I can get over there and back before dinner. Do you mind?"

My dad waved his hand at me. "Go on. We'll make sure you don't miss anything. Wes won't get here until close to seven, anyway."

I dialed Shayla's number to make sure she was home. She was—no surprise. With her three young children, she didn't get out much. She was a year older than I, so we hadn't hung out in high school, but I knew she came from a good family, and her work ethic was impressive. It wouldn't be ideal to have my calligrapher out of town, but everything was done so far in advance that I felt confident we could make it work. When I had told Lorea about Shayla, she suggested shipping the invitations back and forth, and I wasted no time in accusing her of ulterior motives, especially one named Colton, the delivery man.

The Fitzgerald home was only about ten minutes from my parents', and it was surrounded by fields. Taking a shortcut through the untamed sagebrush that covered the grazing grounds north of my parents' fields, I bumped along for about a half mile before cresting a hill that overlooked the mellow green waves of wheat that banked Shayla's property. The lane going up to her house blended into the sagebrush, and I slowed so I wouldn't miss the turn.

As I pressed on my brakes, I glanced in my rearview mirror and was surprised to see a silver sedan come around the curve behind me. Not many people knew about this shortcut, so I wondered if Shayla had visitors coming. As I turned right down the lane, the sedan slowed and then sped past me. The dust hung thick in the air, so I didn't catch a glimpse of the driver.

I felt a bit rattled as I entered Shayla's home, but she immediately put me at ease. She introduced me to her kids with a wave of her hand, and I admired the three towheads. "They have your dimples."

She grinned. "I have to admit, I was hoping they would."

The two boys and the girl continued watching cartoons in

the family room while Shayla led me back to the sitting room where an old desk served as her calligraphy headquarters. I leafed through a binder of samples done on different types of envelopes, cardstock, vellum, and even handmade paper.

"These are beautiful, Shayla. It's just the thing I'm looking for to make my business stand out. I want to be able to offer my clients anything and everything their hearts desire." I tapped a piece of vellum monogrammed with a swirly 'F.' "And this is what both my brides will want."

"Really?" She blinked rapidly, and I was happy that her work was the quality I needed.

At least Sylvia would be satisfied, for once. We'd already examined the work of a few locals, but she had rejected them for one reason or another. Looking at what Shayla had to offer, with her more elegant handwriting, I felt confident my search was over.

"I'll show these samples to my clients. And hopefully be contacting you next week about getting started on hand addressing five hundred place cards."

Shayla gripped my hand. "Thank you, Adri."

On my way home, I kept a sharp eye out for the silver sedan but didn't see anything. I breathed a little easier when I reached home and pulled in next to Jenna's car. Bryn's squeals reached my ears before I made it to the front steps. Her red pigtails danced as she burst through the front door and into my arms.

"Aunt Adri!" she screamed. "I'm so glad you're here."

"Hi, Brynnie!" I squealed right back at her.

"Let's play," she commanded.

"Okay, but I want to say hello to your mommy first." I found Jenna sitting in the kitchen sipping a glass of water. Her auburn hair contrasted with her fair skin, which looked a bit paler than usual, but she smiled brightly when she saw me.

"Adri! I'm so excited you're here."

"Wow! Now I know where Bryn gets her enthusiasm." I gave Jenna a hug.

"I *am* excited, but mostly because I wanted to tell you that Wes and I are going to be extremely busy this December."

Winter was my brother's chance for a little downtime, so I wondered what project they had cooked up. Then I noticed the saltine crackers beside Jenna's water glass. "What do you have planned?"

"A new baby." Jenna beamed.

I cheered and hugged her again. "That's incredible news, but you must be feeling rotten," I said, indicating the crackers.

"The worst should be over soon. I'm almost eleven weeks." Jenna touched her stomach, but besides a little puffiness in her face, she didn't look pregnant yet.

"Aunt Adri, we need to play now. I've been waiting forever," Bryn said.

I obliged and helped her make a blanket fort in the living room. We earned a few raised eyebrows from Grandma when we almost tipped over her lamp. The soft flannel on the quilt we used for the floor of the tent looked inviting. Bryn and I pretended to sleep, and I actually started to doze off. The stress of the past week had zapped my energy.

The sizzle of ham hitting the wok awakened my growling stomach, and I hoped today would be a lucky day for Wes so we could eat on time. My brother and I had both grown up working the fields, either moving pipe or weeding endless rows of vegetables. It was hard to do much with my friends during the growing season when potatoes needed to be irrigated three times a day. My friends and I would call it a lucky day if we finished in time to do anything fun. Occasionally, I still texted Wes and wished him a lucky day in the fields.

At fifteen minutes to seven, I heard the diesel engine of Wes's pickup as he pulled into the driveway. Bryn tripped over the blanket in her hurry to meet him, and I caught Grandma's lamp one more time before it hit the ground. I decided to adjust our blanket fort to exclude the table with the lamp on it.

Wes came in through the garage, leaving his work boots by the door. The back of his neck was turning a dark brown with his farmer's tan, and I noticed how his sandy brown hair curled at the nape of his neck just as it had when he was younger. Wes carried Bryn into the kitchen and kissed Jenna before turning to me. "How's my little sis?"

"Hey, brosky. I don't smell like fertilizer, so that's always a plus." I wrinkled my nose when I hugged him, and he laughed.

"At least I don't have to deal with spoiled divas. The potatoes don't talk back."

"You're right, but spuds aren't as interesting."

"So tell me, is wedding planning really better than being in the great outdoors, producing food for the world?"

"Well, when you put it that way . . . yes, I enjoy it. All the blood, sweat, toil, and tears leading up to the final event, and then the look on the groom's face when his bride says, 'I do,' and then the kiss, the reception, the cake."

"Oh, gag me." Wes made choking noises, and Bryn giggled.

"Hey, better quit knocking the wedding business," Mom piped up. "Adri might be able to use some of Jenna's creations from our

Mashed Potatoes and Crafts website, and those clients pay top dollar."

Wes glanced at me and then at Jenna. "Really? That's great, sis."

"Belly up to the bar, folks. Soup's on." My dad brought the steaming dish of ham fried rice to the table, and Mom followed with the chicken and stir-fried veggies. In the Pyper household, you didn't need to be told twice that supper was ready. We gathered around the oversized table. After Dad said grace, we dug in. Bryn focused on picking the peas out of her rice and examining each one before chewing it. The meal reminded me of how boring it is to cook for one person. It was hard to want to go to the effort of making a nice meal for myself.

"Oh, I almost forgot. Tony says hello." I waved my fork in Wes's direction.

He nodded. "Tell him to keep an eye on you. Can't believe he let someone rob you on his watch."

"I'll be sure to tell him." Wes and Tony had teased each other mercilessly as boys. Not much had changed.

"Seriously, though. Be careful, Adri." Wes held a forkful of chicken in midair. "Tony said people often get a false sense of security in small towns."

"It's not like I left my doors unlocked, but I am getting a security system installed today."

"That's a good idea," Dad said.

Wes leaned in for a second helping. "When are we gonna see a ring on your finger?"

Jenna smacked his arm. "He means, are you dating anyone?"

Unbidden, Luke's face came to mind, and I frowned. Then I thought of Dallas and replaced the grimace with a smile.

"Must be something going on with that look," Wes said and earned another jab from Jenna.

I had purposely left Dallas out of the conversations with my mother. If there was one thing that irked her, it was that her talented twenty-six-year-old daughter, who ran her own wedding planning business, had not yet planned her own wedding. If Mom caught wind of the dates I'd been on with Dallas, she'd hound me nonstop for the next level of commitment.

I decided I'd tell my family about Luke in hopes of throwing Mom off the trail. My family waited for me to spill the details of my pathetically single life like a cat watching a canary. I lifted one shoulder and directed my gaze at Wes. "I met this good-looking guy. He was really nice and fun, and he asked me for my number." I paused, to increase the anticipation, and Mom leaned forward. I cleared my throat. "And then I found out he's a divorce lawyer."

"So?" Wes said.

"So?" I glared at my brother. "Wes, that would be like you marrying a John Deere tractor salesman while wearing your favorite Massey Ferguson hat."

My dad laughed and slapped his knee. "She got you there."

"Carl." Mom set down her fork. "Wes has a point. Adri, you should give this guy a chance. Being a divorce lawyer doesn't mean he's against marriage."

That was my cue and my perfect out of this discussion. I lifted my chin. "Actually, according to Luke, that's exactly what it means. He made fun of my occupation and said he didn't believe in marriage."

Jenna gasped. "He didn't."

I nodded and gave Wes a sharp look. Of course my brother could never let a simple explanation suffice. He shook his head.

"Maybe he's just saying that. You have to admit there's a little pressure for a guy who wants to date a wedding planner."

"I agree," Mom said around a mouthful of food. "Give this boy another chance."

My shoulders slumped. And now I'd have to tell them about Dallas. Mom wouldn't be satisfied otherwise. My plan for discretion had backfired again. "I don't have to worry about Luke. There's another guy, Dallas, who's interested in me *and* my wedding business."

Mom clapped her hands. "Well, why didn't you say so earlier?" She squeezed my hand, her brown eyes sparkling. I suppressed a groan along with my explanation for why I hadn't shared any dating details with her.

Jenna murmured, "Because she doesn't like Dallas. She likes Luke."

I felt heat rise in my cheeks. Jenna's piercing blue eyes were dancing with laughter. She lifted her eyebrows and giggled.

"I like Dallas. He's very sweet. He took me to see Sasha Cohen at the ice show Thursday."

"I think it's time for dessert," Dad said as he tugged on one of Bryn's pigtails. "What do you say, Your Highness? Is it time for ice cream?"

Bryn's cheers effectively changed the subject. Dad grinned in my direction and then headed for the freezer. I jumped up to follow him. "I'll help."

Jenna's words and the look on her face had me undone. I did not like Luke Stetson. He was rude and insulting. It took more than a Harley Davidson Road Glide and a dimpled chin to impress me, even if he did like Smokehouse BBQ.

We all went outside for a walk after the ice cream. Jenna

decided to take Bryn home to bed. "I'm exhausted. I'll see you in the morning, Adri."

Bryn gave me a sticky kiss, and I waved as they drove away. It was nearly eight-thirty and the temperatures were dropping, cooling off the earth. The click-shush sound of the sprinklers that watered the corner of Dad's alfalfa field soothed my mind. Let my family think what they wanted about my life. It didn't really matter, because Ketchum was far enough away to be outside my mother's radar.

As we walked up the canal bank, I could hear the horses whinny from the corral. I turned to watch my dad's quarter horse, Fellar, kick up dirt as he raced across the pasture. Samson barked and brought my attention back to the canal. Irrigation water churned slowly with its greenish hue, pushing for the next culvert to open so the flow of water could sprinkle the fields. Following the canal back for several miles would lead to the mammoth Snake River wending its way through southern Idaho.

We passed a bunch of cattails, and I heard a sound just before Samson dived into the water. "Samson, get back here right now," Dad hollered.

The golden retriever stopped, and I watched as a mother duck and five brown tufts of fluff swam to the other side of the canal. The ducklings hid in the tall grasses, and Samson gazed longingly after them before climbing out of the water. I broke into a run to escape the inevitable dog shake and continued down the road another hundred yards. The evening was still, and it seemed every sound echoed against the next, creating a country harmony that couldn't be replicated. The sun hung low on the horizon, and I gazed across the flat expanse of fields, most holding giant pivots, or circulars—sprinklers on a great arm rotating around the field.

I turned around to see Wes and Dad pointing at something in the water and Mom heading toward me. Then I saw something out of my peripheral vision and jerked my head to the right. A silver car had pulled up to the stop sign on the canal bridge. My throat tightened as I studied the vehicle, wondering if it was the same car I had noticed on my way to Shayla's. The car was only about fifty yards from me. It was time to find out if this man was following me. I took off in a dead run toward the car, my eyes glued to the driver.

Chapter 13

BRYN'S RASPBERRY
CHEESECAKE SQUARES

Spread cream cheese on one graham cracker. Top with raspberries and chocolate chips.
Courtesy of www.mashedpotatoesandcrafts.com.

"What are you doing, Adri?" Mom called after me.

The stop sign on the bridge stood just before the slope so the driver could see down the country road before descending into oncoming traffic. A fertilizer truck approached from the west, and the car was forced to wait at the stop sign. Pushing myself, I closed in on the sedan, which I now recognized as a Toyota Camry. I wondered if the driver had seen me or if I was making a fool of myself.

Twenty-five yards from the car, I saw the driver turn to look behind him and to the right. We made eye contact. As I continued running toward him, his eyes widened, and then he punched the gas and zoomed out in front of the truck. His tires screeched as he made a sharp left turn and then accelerated up the road. The truck honked and swerved to the right, the tanks of fertilizer sloshing as it came to a stop.

The panic ratcheted up my heart rate even though I told myself to remain calm. I didn't know for sure that the car had anything to do with me, but at the same time, I couldn't convince myself it was a coincidence.

"What the—" Wes ran up beside me and craned his neck, peering after the car. I heard my dad cuss and felt Mom's hand on my arm.

"What were you doing?" she asked.

How could I explain that I had spotted a suspicious car and wanted to see who was driving it? And I was right. The man driving that car had been looking for me. The way his eyes widened when our eyes met explained away any false hopes I might have had in my own paranoia.

With a deep breath, I closed my eyes. I wanted to capture the man's features before they melted into the adrenaline of the moment. His hair was dark, his face clean-shaven. There had been something sparkling near his face as he turned his head, and I struggled to reconstruct what I had seen in that split second.

"Adri, are you okay?" Mom grabbed hold of my elbow, and my eyes flew open.

"I'm fine, just trying to remember details," I mumbled.

"Did anyone catch the plate number?" Wes asked.

"No, and the truck left, so I doubt the police would come out here anyway. That car is long gone." Dad gestured to the truck farther down the road. I watched as it grew smaller in the distance, then I turned back toward the direction the Camry had taken to escape.

"Why were you running?" Wes asked.

"That car looked suspicious. I wanted to see who was driving it."

Dad chuckled. "Do you have some mobster after you or something?"

I forced a laugh and ignored the concern creasing the wrinkles near Mom's eyes. "No, it was just the way he pulled up to the stop sign. He wasn't watching the road—he seemed to be looking for something."

"Probably just rubber-necking," Dad offered. "People always think there's something better to look at than the road."

"We should head back," Mom said. She tugged at my hand, and we turned toward home.

"Yeah, I stuck around to see if you're up for a game." Wes bumped my arm, and I bumped him back.

"You're on. Hope you're ready to lose."

When we returned to the house, Mom served us what she called a new delicacy inspired by Bryn. We laughed as we ate the graham crackers spread with cream cheese and topped with raspberries and chocolate chips. I took a few pictures to post on my website because they were incredibly yummy.

We played *Settlers of Catan*. After Wes won two games in a row, Mom said it was time to play *Sorry*. Wes ribbed me about losing, and normally it would've bothered my competitive streak, but my head wasn't in the game. Worry over the man who might have followed me from Ketchum kept the tendons in my shoulders taut. He had to be connected to the diamonds. I admitted to myself that I was dealing with more than I'd originally thought. Whoever had smuggled those gems into the country surely didn't mean for them to be delivered to me. So who was supposed to receive them?

Wes interrupted my disjointed thoughts. "Adri, you lost again? This must be a record for you."

He was right. I decided I'd better call it quits. "I'm bushed."

"Ah, it's only ten o'clock," Wes protested. "Plenty of time for more games."

"I know, but my brain is struggling. It needs sleep."

"Adri's had a busy week, and so have you, Wes," Mom said. "Let's call it a night."

"What time do you have to leave tomorrow?" Dad asked.

I bit my bottom lip. Originally I'd planned to leave right after dinner, but now I wondered if being here was putting my family in danger. "I want to go to church with you in the morning, but I'd better leave after lunch. If the police find out anything about Sylvia's missing gown, I want to be there."

"Well, I'm glad you could come, even for a short visit," Mom said.

"Thanks for staying to play, brosky." I gave Wes a hug. We all walked out to the front porch and stared up at the stars twinkling in the cloudless sky. I thought about Dallas naming constellations and smiled. He had texted earlier, wishing me a good weekend. I hoped I'd have time to see him in the next few days. Maybe I could give him a call.

After Wes left, I stayed outside and dialed Dallas.

"Hey, Adri. How are you?"

"I'm good. It's nice to see my family, and it's beautiful here in Rupert." I could hear the sprinklers in the background and the crickets trying to compete with other night noises.

"Are you doing okay? You sound different," Dallas asked.

I don't know why but it made me happy that Dallas was intuitive enough to recognize the stress underlying my words. For a moment, I wished I could tell him about the diamonds, but I thought better of it. "I'm worried about Sylvia's missing wedding gown."

"I'm sorry. I wish I could help you. Maybe I could check back at the pawn shops. Or do you think someone dumped her dress like they did the others?"

I sat on the front step. "I hope not, but it's a definite possibility."

"Have the police checked the thrift stores?"

"I'm not sure, but that's a good idea. I'll give Tony a call."

"Adri, will you let me help you?" Dallas's voice was soft, yet I could feel his strength through the phone.

He was so thoughtful and kind. It was evident he cared about me and could tell I was struggling. I cleared my throat. "Just knowing you care is a help to me. Thanks for worrying over me, Dallas."

"My pleasure," he replied.

I could hear his smile through the phone and also my mother's approaching footsteps. "I've got to go now, but I'll call you tomorrow."

"Sweet dreams. I'll be thinking of you," Dallas said.

I clicked *end* just as the front door opened. "Ready to call it a night?" Mom asked.

I stood and stretched. "Yep, I'm dead tired."

Even though talking to Dallas had soothed some of my stress, my nerves were jittery as I got ready for bed. My mind wandered back to my question of who was supposed to receive, or maybe intercept, the wedding dresses carrying the rough diamonds.

The dresses were specially made for Lorea's new business. It seemed unlikely the smugglers could make such a mistake.

Then a thought came that made my gut twist with anxiety. Walter Mayfield. He had approached Lorea with the idea of bringing in the dresses from China, and then he offered to lend her the money for the first order. His cousin Roland had been eager to help and waived part of the shipping fee.

I recalled the pages from Natalie's wedding binder dumped in Walter's trash. Tony and I had both figured they had been put there by the thief, but what if the thief was Walter? He had been sick the day the dresses were delivered. His store was closed when I went to tell him the good news about the shipment. Then the dresses were stolen, so he'd never even seen Sylvia's gown. I racked my brain to recall just how much Walter knew about the dresses beforehand. Did he know that Sylvia had already put a deposit on hers? We had been expecting the shipment, so if the plan was to smuggle the diamonds in specific gowns, the person would have to know enough about the gowns to select the right ones and plan on robbing my store.

My head churned with conversations I'd had with Walter. He was well-spoken, kind, and genuinely seemed to love his business. A dull ache started behind my eyes. I massaged my temples, trying to relieve the stress. It couldn't be Walter. But I had heard him mention how the price of diamonds continued to rise, making it difficult for him to be competitive with larger jewelry stores.

If Walter *was* involved, Roland surely had to be the mastermind behind the crime. His ties to the shipping industry and the actual dressmakers pointed to him as the more plausible criminal. But Roland lived somewhere on the east coast, so why would he ship the diamonds to Idaho? Unless Walter knew someone close by who could cut the stones and be discreet about it.

Even with my limited knowledge of diamonds, I had heard enough about jewelry in my training to know that there were few master craftsmen in the world qualified to cut and shape diamonds. Specialized equipment and years of training were needed to perform more than fifty cuts with precision for a brilliant, or round, diamond—my favorite cut.

There was also the coincidence of Walter moving up his trip to Belgium right after the dresses were stolen. Tony hadn't been able to reach him when I found the papers in his trash.

The possibilities continued to spin through my mind, but my focus always came back to the mystery man driving the Camry. An unsettled feeling wouldn't leave me, and I knew I didn't want to wait until something bad happened. The diamonds were calling, and the man who wanted them had followed me—had located my parents' home. I didn't want to think that the man could have been Roland. I'd never met him, but I knew Walter cared about him a great deal. I wondered just how many people were involved.

That thought led me to consider how many more people could be involved if things went wrong. Bryn's happy face came to mind, and I imagined what a desperate diamond smuggler could do to my family. I clenched my teeth and frowned. Tomorrow I would do what I should have done already—call Tony. He could help me figure out what to do.

Chapter 14

DON'T PEEL THE POTATOES!

 When making Idaho mashed potatoes, scrub the potatoes thoroughly and then use a paring knife or peeler to remove three strips of skin, one on each end and one in the middle. Cut, boil, and mash the potatoes.
Courtesy of www.mashedpotatoesandcrafts.com.

❧

Sunday morning was a blur. My lack of sleep and the tension I was feeling made it difficult to put on a happy face and attend church services with my family, but I did my best. After church, I enjoyed another delicious meal of my mom's home cooking complete with her signature recipe of mashed potatoes. Even though I wanted to stay longer, the worry of putting my family in danger was too great.

It always tugged on my heartstrings to pack up and leave my family in Rupert. Each time, I would picture my little shop with its antique rosebushes growing out front and the weddings I had on the docket. Dreams took hard work and sacrifice, and I did feel fortunate to work in the Sun Valley area.

Before I left, Jenna pulled me aside. "I meant what I said about Luke, even if you didn't like it. I could tell you feel something for him."

"But I don't—"

She put her hand on my arm. "It's okay if you don't want to date him. I just don't want you to talk yourself into dating someone else for spite, or whatever reason. Love can't be forced. You either feel it, or you don't."

I didn't know what I felt for Luke or Dallas, but I was looking forward to seeing Dallas again. "I'll keep that in mind."

"But do have fun." Jenna smiled, and her blue eyes lit up with mischief. "And kiss plenty while you can."

"Jenna!" We both laughed, and I gave her a hug. "Take care of yourself and that baby."

I tucked a few more items behind my seat, and Mom stashed some frozen meals and a loaf of homemade bread beside my suitcase. "Thanks, Mom. You're the best."

"I worry about you." Mom took my hand and looked me in the eye. "I see the part of you that still aches. I know it was hard to pick up and start over. Please don't overdo it. If you need something, I'm only a phone call away." She patted my cheek. "Your dad and I want to come up for a visit again, so let us know a good time."

"That'd be great." I hugged Mom and saw Dad step out onto the porch. "I have a honey-do list for you, Dad."

He shook his head. "Just tell me which tools to bring." He put his arm around my shoulder. "You be careful."

"I love you." I waved as I got into the Mountaineer.

"We'll see you on the Fourth of July," Mom said. I noted that it wasn't a request.

I blew Bryn a kiss and backed out onto the road. As soon as I put the Mountaineer in drive, I felt a pang of loneliness. A passenger would be the perfect thing to keep my mind off the worry overpowering me. I swallowed and pushed play on my favorite Rascal Flatts CD. The music took the edge off, and even though I kept a lookout for suspicious vehicles, I sang at the top of my lungs.

My cell rang about forty-five minutes into the drive, and I clicked off the music when I saw it was my mom.

"Adri, I'd love to hear more about that Dallas fellow you mentioned. And don't you dare roll your eyes. I'm your mother, and you're my only daughter. We only get to do this once, and I want to enjoy it."

I didn't roll my eyes. Instead, I filled my mom in on all the details of my three dates with Dallas. She demanded a full physical description, and I was happy that he wasn't lacking in that area. Part of me wondered if Jenna was right as I described how kind yet nervous Dallas was, and how hesitant he'd been even to kiss me. Still, a part of me kept thinking of Briette and how she wanted me to give guys a chance so that I could find love one day. She was the reason I had decided to give Dallas a fighting chance.

Mom and I talked until my Bluetooth told me I only had ten minutes of talk time left. A few minutes later, I pulled up to my condo and got out of the vehicle smiling—grateful for her mother's intuition. She might be nosy, but I needed her love and attention all the same.

My throat clenched when I noticed the paper flapping in the doorjamb. Goosebumps scattered across my arms. The pictures left on my door passed through my mind, and I wished I didn't live alone. The loose board on my steps creaked as I took tentative steps toward the front door.

I pulled the paper out and unfolded it, then breathed a sigh of relief. It was an announcement for a community yard sale taking place next week. Unlocking the door, I tossed my bags on the floor and hurried back out to grab my suitcase from the Mountaineer. When I reached out to put my keys on the side table in the hall, my hand froze. A note was tucked under the lamp. I grabbed it and scanned it quickly. This one wasn't about yard sales.

The note was handwritten, and there were no pictures this time. My jaw tightened as I read the script in all caps:

YOU HAVE MY DIAMONDS. NO ONE WILL BE HURT IF YOU RETURN THEM TO ME. I'M WATCHING YOU. PUT THE DIAMONDS INSIDE THE LUNCH BAG YOU TAKE TO WORK. LEAVE THE BAG BEHIND THE DUMPSTER AT ROXY'S TOMORROW MORNING. DON'T CALL THE POLICE. I'LL KNOW IF YOU DO.

A wave of fear overtook me, and I felt tears welling up inside. At any moment, the delicate dam holding back my hysteria would break. I struggled to think clearly. He needed the diamonds. If I called the police, he couldn't do anything to me because he still needed the diamonds.

Criminals always tell you not to call the police. Anger flared in my chest, and I dialed the cell number Tony had given me. It went to his voice mail, and I hung up. I dialed 911 but didn't push the call button. Holding the phone so tight it hurt my fingers, I walked through my house.

It had been searched, but no one would know that but me.

The cushion on my secondhand couch had a nickel-sized stain on one side, and I always put that side down. The dark brown spot caught my attention as soon as I entered my living room. Whoever had searched my house had done so methodically and carefully. They didn't want the search reported to the police.

But I had an eye for detail. Wes often teased me about my anal-retentive qualities, but it served me well in the wedding business—and now. The afghan that draped over my grandma's chair had been shifted to the left side. In my room, the picture of Briette and me had been moved just enough that it caught the glare from the light. I reached out to move it back but stopped. Would the police dust for fingerprints?

No. If this person had searched my home so carefully that only I would know, he wouldn't be dumb enough to leave a fingerprint. My house was empty. I hadn't noticed anything amiss when I first entered. Hopefully that meant the quilt still kept my secrets.

I could taste the fear as I entered my front room and stared at the interlocking rings of cream and sea-foam green fabric spread across the wine-red background. Each circle had a dark green square where it intersected with another ring. The squares reminded me of a diamond sitting atop a solitaire engagement ring.

The quilt was folded exactly as I'd left it. I knelt down and pulled back the edge until I could see the signature block. A whoosh of breath escaped when I felt the bump sewn into the fabric. The diamonds were still safe, but what about me?

I leaned back and took deep cleansing breaths, trying to settle my nerves, which were going ballistic. Then my skin tingled with a new fear. What if my house was bugged or under surveillance? There was no time to consider the ramifications of what I was about to do. I had to act. I tried Tony's cell again with no luck.

I thought of calling Dallas, but he'd probably tell me to call the police.

After I double-checked that my doors were locked, I grabbed my seam ripper and prepared to assault my quilt once more. I ripped open the stitches holding the diamonds in place. When my fingers closed around the diamonds, I let out the breath I'd been holding and stuffed the bag down my shirt. Holding my cell phone, I returned to my bedroom. The house was quiet, and the stillness added to the tension. I could hear my heart pounding in my ears as I tried to think of a plan.

It was almost five-thirty. I needed to get rid of the diamonds. The thief hadn't found them in my house, but if he came back, I knew I would turn them over in a heartbeat. I also knew what a bad idea that would be, because in the movies, the person playing me—the girl who took the diamond smuggler's cache and then returned them at gunpoint—always ended up dead.

My closet door was slightly ajar, and I noticed that the toes of my running shoes were turned away from the wall. They weren't where I'd left them, either, but it gave me an idea. Slipping into the bathroom, I changed into running gear, rolled the bag of diamonds into a tube, and tucked it in my sports bra. I pulled on a jacket and a pair of jeans over my running shorts.

If they were watching me, I needed to think ahead, and I wanted it to look like I was heading for the mountain. On my way out, I grabbed an apple, a cheese stick, and some crackers. At the last minute, I remembered the dinners from Mom and shoved them into my cramped freezer space.

Keeping my head down, I hurried out to my vehicle, jumped inside, and locked the doors. I drove up Warm Springs Road. The traffic was light, as usual on Sunday, and I kept an eye out for anyone tailing me. The road narrowed as I drew closer to the mountain pass that led to the natural hot springs.

When the stretch of road was clear both ways, I jammed my foot on the gas pedal and careened to the right into a dead end just past a section of cabin-like homes. I whipped the Mountaineer around and put it in park. Watching the dashboard clock, I waited five full minutes and counted four cars, none of which included a silver Toyota Camry. If I was being followed, it was likely in a different vehicle. I nosed the Mountaineer back on to the road and sped off in the direction I'd just come.

Purposefully driving on the quiet side roads kept me away from the traffic of Main Street. The back roads made it easier to check for someone who might be following me. When I had weaved through town, I backtracked, stopped at Rotary Park, and took off my jeans and jacket. Grabbing a water bottle, I scanned the area. The park wasn't crowded—a few families and older couples dotted the grass.

Towering pine trees surrounded the parking lot, and I darted between them, sprinting toward the paved bike trail that would take me close to my usual running route. If anyone had kept up with me, they would hopefully think I was just out for a run.

With my destination over two miles away, I slowed to a comfortable pace and tried not to think about the diamonds pressing against my chest. My watch showed that I had already been gone for an hour. It was almost seven, and by the time I finished the run and diamond drop, it would be eight o'clock. The list of things I needed to do during the week cycled through my mind. Stressing over it wouldn't get the job done, so I forced myself to count steps in an attempt to keep my running cadence even.

The bushes near the trail grew thick this time of year, and I had to dodge a few low branches. The path curved slightly, and I saw "the hottie" coming toward me. My heart rate increased, and I panicked. What if he was the diamond smuggler? It would have been easy for him to figure out my running route because we'd passed each other at several different points over the past few months.

But we hadn't passed each other for a few days. My runs had been more sporadic with everything going on at the shop and wedding season in full swing. Maybe he'd been busy stealing wedding gowns.

He approached at a fast pace, and with a quick glance I knew that this part of the trail offered no access to hiding places. We were about a half mile from any sort of business. If he had come to get his diamonds, there was little I could do about it. He had his shirt off. Today would have been a perfect day to admire his firm abs if he wasn't a diamond smuggler. Instead, he'd probably kill me.

I felt my face tighten as we closed the distance between us. Odd, I thought—something about him seemed familiar today. Thirty feet from me, he yanked out his earbuds.

"Adri. How are you?"

I nearly tripped as he stopped beside me. Grateful that my sunglasses gave me time to hide the confusion in my gaze, I sucked in a breath and choked when he pulled off his sunglasses.

"Luke?"

I was so surprised and grateful that I wasn't about to be murdered on a bike trail that I nearly hugged him. I took a step forward and remembered this was Luke Stetson, divorce lawyer against marriage, and leaned back. My balance was off, and I wobbled. Luke grabbed hold of me.

"Are you okay? I didn't mean to scare you."

All this time, "the hottie" was Luke. Lorea would never let me hear the end of this one. He stared at me. "I kept wondering why you seemed familiar."

"I didn't recognize you with your sunglasses and hat." My words sounded clipped, and it was a good thing my face was already red from running because I felt mortified to think how many months I'd been admiring him. Every time we'd run past each other, I had secretly hoped for a chance to meet him. My fantasy crumbled.

Luke let go of my arm and pulled off his hat. He squeezed the brim and rubbed a hand over his face. "I've been thinking about last week. I'm really sorry."

The words I wanted to say burned on my tongue, but I waited a moment.

"You have a right to be angry with me," he said. "I was out of line. And then I heard about your wedding dresses getting stolen—it was bad timing. I was rude."

I realized I had stopped breathing and took a big gulp of air. "You were. I don't understand why."

Luke's stance relaxed, and he looked at the ground for a moment. I watched him swallow, and he lifted his eyes to mine. "I need to explain. It's not something I want to do, but I owe it to you if you'll give me a chance."

"I'm listening."

"I haven't always been so cynical about marriage." He lifted his left hand. "I *was* married—I mean, I'm a widower—my wife died." He stumbled over his words, and the pain etched across his face made my heart hurt.

I opened my mouth to speak, but he shook his head. "Please don't say anything. Don't say you're sorry. Just listen."

My mouth clamped shut, and I blinked rapidly, chiding myself for the tears threatening to fall at his display of grief. It was easy to see that the pain was still raw, and I wondered how long it had been. He cleared his throat and answered my unspoken question.

"Three years ago. Hodgkin's disease. She was supposed to get better." Luke closed his eyes, and his jaw tensed as he blew out a deep breath. "We were married for five years—she helped put me through law school. Our whole life was just beginning. A few months before the diagnosis, we were talking about starting a family."

My throat seemed to collapse on itself as I struggled to swallow the anguish I felt for him.

He clutched his hat, turning it over and over in his hands. "It's not something I want people in this town to know. I've been able to keep my past a secret, and I want it to stay that way—it's easier."

I wanted to speak, but I didn't want him to shush me again, so I waited.

Luke lifted his head and met my gaze. "I'm sure it doesn't make sense to you."

I lifted my shoulders and then let them drop.

"People say if I was happy once, then I could be again, but I can't go there. It's not worth the hurt." His face tightened, and I noticed moisture on his dark lashes.

"Then why ask me out?"

"I wasn't going to, but you were so fun and easy to talk to that day over fried pickles, and then our little date with the pizza pockets was even better. I thought . . ." He didn't finish the sentence. He smiled, but it didn't reach his eyes. "I'm sorry."

I wanted to reach out and embrace him—try to take away some of his hurt—but instead I reached for his hand, pressing my fingers against his. Luke glanced at my hand and then at me, his eyes misting with emotion.

"Thank you for telling me," I said. "I'm sorry I was so angry. I was out of line too." I gave his hand another squeeze and let go.

Luke stepped closer and his shoulder brushed mine, sending a spark of electricity through me. His breath came in short puffs, and I could see him still struggling to maintain composure. "Thanks," he whispered. Then he turned and sprinted down the hill. I watched him go and wondered what else I could say to ease his pain. I wanted to say, "I'm here if you need me." But I was still confused.

He didn't want to ask me out, but he made the effort to come to my store anyway? It was almost like he sabotaged himself by being rude to me, so he would have a way out. But he'd just apologized and explained because he cared about what I thought of him. He *cared.*

I watched his back disappear around a copse of bushes and scowled. Now he'd gone and given me a reason to forgive him. My heart fluttered when I thought about how close I'd stood to his bare chest. I took a deep breath and felt the bag of diamonds against my sports bra. *Dang you, Luke.* With a glance around to check that no one was approaching, I picked up my pace and tried not to think about Luke Stetson.

Chapter 15

SPARKLER SEND-OFF

THE BIG SEND-OFF IS AT 11:00 P.M.!

Print announcement of the send-off on 4 x 6-inch pieces of heavy-weight cardstock. Cut two slits, one at the top and one at the bottom of the announcement. Slide one sparkler through the slits. Arrange sparklers and announcements in a vintage bucket or basket. Have helpers ready with torch lighters just before the time of the send-off.

Courtesy of www.mashedpotatoesandcrafts.com.

Die-hard literature fans often visited the Ketchum cemetery to view the final resting place of Ernest Hemingway and his granddaughter, actress Margaux Hemingway. A plain granite slab stood between two fir trees in the shadow of the hill that banked the cemetery. The marker engraved with only Hemingway's name and dates was the main attraction in the cemetery.

The two tragic deaths brought some notoriety to the well-manicured cemetery, but most people stopped at the memorial off Sun Valley Road to pay homage to a bust of the literary hero.

A late-night visit to the cemetery usually had something to do with spooks and spirits, but since I didn't believe that nonsense, it didn't scare me to run through a graveyard at twilight. I chose to focus on the peaceful feeling I felt from most of the people who rested under the tombstones. The thing that scared me had nothing to do with granite and everything to do with diamonds. Keeping a steady running cadence was difficult with trepidation chasing at my heels. I struggled to breathe evenly and ignore the bulge of diamonds tucked in my sports bra. I also struggled to stop the flow of thoughts about Luke from overtaking my consciousness.

Running a full loop of the cemetery reassured me that no one had followed. Solitude blanketed the landscape, so I decided it was safe to follow through with my plan. I crisscrossed through the pine trees flanking the headstones until I reached one with a bird feeder hanging from a low limb. It was constructed of metal that had rusted over in a deep brown patina.

I had run past it before and wondered about the empty feeder swinging in the breeze. When I inspected the family headstone beneath it, I found two names—a woman, who had passed on twelve years before, and her husband, who had been dead for only three years. I imagined the old man filling the bird feeder so his wife's favorite songbirds would sing over her in her final slumber.

The bird feeder would be the next hiding place for the diamonds. I had wanted to tell Tony everything, and maybe I should have taken the diamonds directly to the police station, but the note scared me into questioning my earlier resolve. Besides, I still hadn't figured out how to report the diamonds without losing Natalie's dress. I'd find a way to talk to Tony and tell him about the diamonds as soon as they were out of my possession.

Before I pulled the bag from my sports bra, I checked behind me. The cemetery was fading into darkness, and no one was around. I stepped under the low-hanging branches of the fir tree and stuffed the diamonds inside the rusty shell of the bird feeder. The chain holding the feeder made a tiny squeaking noise until I stilled the movement with my hand.

Peeking out from underneath the tree, I took off running, faster now that the foreboding weight of the diamonds no longer pressed against my heart. Hopefully Tony would not arrest me when I could finally tell him what I had done.

Meeting up with Luke had delayed me enough that when I ran the full distance back to my vehicle, the sun's last rays had disappeared. I hurried to unlock the door and get out of the open. My cell phone pinged with a new message from Dallas.

Missed you this weekend. Can I see you tonight?

It was already nine-thirty, and I didn't know what to think of the conflicted feelings I had for Luke. But I was scared and didn't want to go back inside my empty house alone again. The idea to call Lorea and have her come over had briefly crossed my mind, but she knew me too well. She would know something was up and quiz me until she found out. I decided to be impulsive.

Can you come over right now? I'm just getting back from a run. Would love to see you.

My phone pinged with his answer.

Be there in 5.

Dallas responded so fast it made me smile. Good. We should get to my condo about the same time, and he could go inside with me. If there were any bad guys, hopefully Dallas could save me.

I pulled into my parking space and grabbed my stuff out of the back just as Dallas pulled in beside me. He jumped out of his Hyundai Accent with a big grin. I smiled back—I was happy to see him. *So there, Jenna.* I ignored the niggling thought that I was only happy because I was scared spitless to go in my own house.

He put his hands in the pockets of his cargo shorts and tipped his head toward me. "Adri, you continue to amaze me. You run yourself ragged planning weddings, and then you run some more."

"I know. It seems crazy, but it's my stress relief." And tonight I'd had a certain bag of diamonds worth hundreds of thousands of dollars I needed to hide in a cemetery. No stress there.

Dallas touched my shoulder as we approached my front door. "You're my stress relief."

I looked over my shoulder at him and lifted one eyebrow. "I don't know. Lately, I'm emanating stress, so you'd better watch out."

Breathing through my fear and relying on Dallas's presence helped me as I unlocked my door and walked inside. There weren't any notes on the side table, and my house seemed just as I left it. The wedding ring quilt hanging in my front room was folded neatly so the gaping hole near the signature block was hidden from view. The erratic beating of my heart struggled to return to normal. I dropped my stuff on the table and filled a glass with water, guzzled it, and then refilled it. "Would you like anything to drink?"

"I'm good. This is a nice place," Dallas said, and I was reminded that this was the first time he'd been inside my house. "Everything is so clean."

"My mother taught me well. And I'm a little obsessive—I make sure my house is 'spring clean' because once summer hits, I don't have time for anything but wedding plans." I tried not to think of my garage, because it definitely wasn't up to my standard. It was full of boxes and every scrap I had brought from my days working weddings in San Francisco. Parking outside now wasn't a problem, but in a few short months, the weather would turn cold and the garage would have to be cleared out. Scraping windshields was an activity that just didn't suit me.

"I like it." Dallas stepped closer and stared at me with those alluring green eyes. He put his arms around me and pulled me in to his chest. "I missed you."

I rested my head on his shoulder. The back of my ponytail felt sweaty. A quick shower would have been nice, but Dallas didn't seem to mind my running gear. "I missed you too. Thanks for coming over. Sorry I've been so stressed."

He leaned toward me, and his lips caressed mine softly, cutting off my rambling apology.

I kissed him back, eager for his closeness, and wrapped my arms around his neck. His face was clean-shaven, and I could smell his minty aftershave. He put his hand on the small of my back and brought me closer, deepening the kiss. My fingers brushed the coarse hair at the nape of his neck, and I felt my pulse quicken. His kiss was gentle, yet insistent, and when I finally pulled away, I could see a fire in his eyes that made me wonder if Dallas was finally getting over his shyness. He leaned in for another light kiss and then held me close.

We stood there for a moment until the mantel clock chimed ten. I sensed that Dallas wanted to keep kissing me, but I didn't want to get carried away.

"Do you want to watch something? I know it's kind of boring, but I need to sort through some fabric swatches and see if I can find one that will work as an accent for Natalie and Brock's wedding. I'm trying to re-create the binder that was stolen."

"I'd love to." Dallas clasped my hand and followed me to the living room, just off my kitchen. "It's pretty impressive that you're doing a wedding for such a famous person."

"Yeah, Lady Luck decided to shine on me for once." Lorea was my Lady Luck because she and Natalie had been friends since childhood, and Lorea had started working for me just two weeks before Natalie got engaged.

"Why do you say that?"

I grabbed the binder of fabric swatches and settled on the couch next to Dallas. "Oh, it's just been a particularly difficult year, and then to have those wedding gowns stolen . . ."

"Do the police have any suspects?"

"No, and things don't look good for finding Sylvia's gown."

"I keep trying to think of something I could do to help."

"Don't worry. I've done enough to get myself in trouble." I laughed when Dallas lifted a brow. I definitely was not going to tell him about the diamonds. "I searched through the trash around my shop, and one of the cops wasn't too happy when I called to tell him I found some of the wedding pages that had been stolen from my safe."

"But wasn't that a good thing, to find something?"

"Yes, but Tony doesn't want me to do any investigative work on my own." Too bad I was already in over my head by the time Tony gave me that admonition.

"Will your business survive the loss?" Dallas asked.

"We'll manage. What I'm really worried about is Sylvia. She didn't take the news of her stolen dress too well."

"I can imagine. I met the realtor who helped find her home. It was a lot of commission, but he wasn't sure it was worth it in the end."

I tried not to laugh. Sylvia was a pain, but she was also my client, and I had learned that you should always be careful what you say because it could come back to haunt you. Thinking of Lorea, my smile widened. I could say whatever I wanted to my fiery friend, and it would never equal the grumbling she did about picky customers.

Dallas and I hadn't selected anything to watch, and the ten o'clock news rolled past. The weather report was on, and the forecast looked beautiful for the next ten days with just a couple of insignificant rain showers that probably wouldn't amount to much. No matter how lush and green the lawns and golf course in Sun Valley appeared, we still lived in a desert. That fact was a great benefit and stress relief when planning an outdoor wedding, which is what Natalie wanted. Sylvia's reception would be partly outdoors at the Sun Valley Club, but in the case of inclement weather, we could move indoors.

A commercial for an online dating service came on, and I flipped through fabric swatches, fingering the textures and scrutinizing the weave that might work best with the fabrics and colors Natalie had already selected. Since most of Natalie's wedding book remained in police custody, I didn't have the full list of fabric ideas she had written down, so I marked several that I remembered.

Dallas put his arm around me, and I enjoyed the level of comfort his presence afforded me that night. I glanced at his profile. His face seemed relaxed, devoid of the prominent cheekbones I'd admired on Luke earlier.

My mind flashed to our chance meeting, and I still couldn't get over the fact that Luke was "the hottie." I thought of the times I'd noticed his toned chest and muscular build, but today I had been more focused on the emotion in his dark blue eyes. I frowned. I didn't want Luke infiltrating my thoughts, especially while I sat by Dallas, who had finally gotten the nerve to show some affection.

I hadn't tried calling Tony again. With a sinking feeling, I realized time had slipped away after I moved the diamonds. Maybe it could wait until morning—the diamonds were safe now. Hopefully nothing would change before then. I marked a swatch and compared it to one I thought Natalie had selected. The cream-colored linen with a hint of blush would look perfect against the bouquets of pink antique roses we had planned.

I worked for another twenty minutes, sketching the layout of Natalie's wedding, and then I moved to another project— Sylvia and Elliott's sparkler send-off. Lorea had found the idea on Pinterest, and Sylvia actually squealed she was so excited. Each four-by-six-inch piece of cardstock was printed with an announcement:

> *Let the magic of true love shine!*
> *Light the way for Sylvia & Elliott*
> *The big send-off is at 11:00 p.m.!*

I cut two small slits in the top and bottom of the cardstock so that later I could slide a sparkler into each piece to be lit for the send-off. I caught Dallas smirking after he read the card. "Don't laugh, or you'll be enlisted." I waved my scissors at him, and he smoothed the grin off his face.

Dallas flipped through the stations until he settled on an episode of *Diners, Drive-Ins, and Dives* from the Food Network. My mouth watered over a barbeque chicken sandwich and fresh coleslaw while Dallas seemed particularly excited about a fried corned beef sandwich.

"Boy, we're exciting, aren't we?" I said as the show ended.

Dallas brushed my cheek with a kiss. "Do you have time this week to do anything *more* exciting?"

My stomach flipped as I breathed in his closeness. "Maybe. I just have so much to do."

"It looks like you got something accomplished tonight." Dallas motioned to the pile of fabric swatches and papers in my lap.

Notes were scrawled all over my sketches, and I'd marked several pieces of fabric with brightly colored paper clips. "Anyone else would call this a mess." I set my stuff on the coffee table and leaned back against the couch. "Thanks for understanding."

Dallas pulled me closer, smiling as if he knew a secret he wanted to share with me. He touched my cheek and let his fingers trail along my jaw line, and then he cupped my chin and pressed his lips softly against mine. He retreated enough that he could look into my eyes.

"I really like you, Adri."

I lowered my eyes and tried to think how I would describe my feelings for him. I recalled what Jenna had said about Luke and thought of my own expectations for a man who measured up to my list of qualities. I still didn't know enough about Dallas to make that call, but I did like spending time with him. "I like you too." My voice wavered a little, and I broke eye contact.

He wrapped his arms around me, and I relaxed against him, listening to his heartbeat thrum against my temple. His lips caressed the skin on my forehead, and I tipped my head back and allowed him to kiss me again. I let myself indulge in the moment—he was a pretty good kisser, and it had been a while since I'd been this close to a man.

A flash of heat went through me when I felt his lips on my neck. His fingers tangled in my hair as he moved the blonde curls off my shoulder and pressed a kiss there. Each kiss lasted longer than the one before, and when Dallas lowered my head to the couch cushion, I noticed his breath was no longer silent and even.

I was just thinking we'd better cool it when Dallas stopped kissing me. His face hovered above mine with a question.

I answered it before he could ask. "Um, now would probably be a good time to let you know that I won't ever invite you to stay over."

He hesitated, and his eyes softened. "I can respect that."

Relief flooded through me. I'd made decisions long ago about my future, and even though sometimes it was hard, I still knew that I wanted to wait until marriage to share the most intimate part of me. Some of my boyfriends had called me old-fashioned and prudish, but my headstrong nature had taken that as a challenge and made it easier to keep my promise to myself. Once I became a wedding planner, it seemed even more important for me to have the perfect wedding, and that included saving myself for the wedding night. I felt my face flush thinking about how close I was to Dallas at the moment.

His face was almost touching mine, and he cleared his throat. "I care about you too much to do otherwise." He nuzzled my cheek. "But I'll admit, kissing you is like nothing I've ever felt before." He kissed me once more, and for a moment as his mouth moved against mine, I wondered if he realized how serious I was about no sleepovers. He sucked on my lower lip and then broke contact. He pulled me to a sitting position beside him and stood up. I felt surprised that part of me wanted to keep kissing him, but I let him pull me to a standing position beside him.

"Thanks for coming," I murmured. I walked toward the front door. We stared at each other for a moment, and I leaned forward and kissed his cheek. "And thanks for that fine kissing."

"Have a good night, Adri." His mouth curved into a smile that seemed irresistible, but his hand was already on the door knob, so I resisted the urge to kiss him again.

"Good night." I lifted my fingers in a wave. Then I closed the door, locked it, and hurried to get ready for bed before the feelings of euphoria were replaced with cold dread and diamonds.

Chapter 16

GARDEN PARTY CENTERPIECE

Fill a Mason jar half to three-quarters full of water. Add slices of lemon and a bouquet of your favorite flowers—try white lilacs, daisies, freesia, or daffodils for a great contrast.
Courtesy of www.mashedpotatoesandcrafts.com.

Over breakfast, I considered my options for communicating with the diamond smuggler. My mother's delicious homemade bread and a soft-boiled egg were one of my favorite meals, and it irked me that my worry over the diamonds was still giving me indigestion.

I pulled out my favorite lunch bag and frowned. On a sticky note, I wrote:

I don't have any diamonds. What are you talking about? If you're the one who stole my dresses, the police will find you.

It was the best I could do, and I didn't even want to think of what Tony would say to me when he found out. I tucked the note in the bag and zipped it shut. The list of things I needed to do buzzed like a ticker tape through my brain as I got ready for the day. At fifteen minutes to seven, I grabbed my purse and lunch bag on the way out the door. The ping of my phone and Dallas's name next to a text made me smile.

I'm in the mood for more kissing. Can we do lunch?

His newfound confidence surprised me. Part of me wondered—was the shyness all an act to get me to fall for him? He seemed plenty forward now. It was okay with me, though. My toes were still tingling after last night's makeout session. I sent a reply before I dashed out the door.

Wish I could. I may need resuscitation by the day's end, though. :)

Roxy's grocery store was less than ten minutes from my condo. The store was well loved by the tourists and locals alike for its wide selection of organic food, but it definitely wasn't a location I would've picked for a diamond drop-off. I guessed that was why the thief had selected it. Trying to appear inconspicuous, I pulled into the parking lot and walked around to the back of the store. I saw a delivery van parked there, and a man pushed a cart stacked with crates of whole-grain bread toward the store. I nodded at him and made a beeline for the dumpster.

Please don't shoot me, I thought as I pulled the lunch bag from my shoulder and surveyed the area for anyone who might be a diamond-smuggler-turned- murderer. I didn't see or hear anything out of the ordinary, so I dropped the bag behind the dark green trash bin and hurried away.

My heart pounded, and my breakfast was thinking of making a reappearance by the time I reached my vehicle. I was the girl who couldn't deliver Secret Santa treats to the neighbors without having a panic attack. How had I gotten myself into this mess?

The parking lot didn't have any silver Toyota Camrys in residence, and I felt pretty certain that if he had any kind of criminal training, the man would have switched vehicles by now. The inside of my cheek was sore from clenching my teeth on it.

I reached for the door handle of my Mountaineer but jumped back when I noticed Colton reflected in the window. I whirled around and watched as he jogged toward the store. He was in uniform, but he didn't have any packages to deliver. Hurrying after him, I caught a glimpse of him as he passed by the carts and headed through the produce section empty-handed to the back of the store.

My throat went dry, and it took several tries before I could swallow. I shook my head and returned to my vehicle. *It's a grocery store, Adri, you know—where people buy groceries.* I tried to tell myself that Colton wasn't involved with the diamonds, but my pounding heart disagreed. He probably wasn't working alone *if* it was him. I jerked my head around, surveying the parking lot for an accomplice. I needed to get out of here. I started the engine, took a deep breath, and headed for my shop.

On the way, I told myself to calm down. Colton was a delivery man who liked Lorea, that was all. I called Tony and grumbled when it went to his voice mail. If I was being watched or if my vehicle had been bugged, I couldn't leave him a message, but I really needed to talk to him. I decided to call the police station directly. After waiting on hold for a few minutes, the secretary came back on to say that Tony was unavailable and would I like to leave him a message? I declined and ended the call.

Where was he? I told myself that if I couldn't reach him on his cell by that afternoon, I'd stop by the station on my way home and track him down.

It was hard not to look suspiciously at every corner and trash can behind my building. My nerves were already frazzled, so when a black streak ran past me, I screamed. Telling myself to quit being jumpy didn't help, and when I saw what had scared me, I felt like an idiot.

The black-and-white kitten who had been my trash-digging companion waited by the shop door. He meowed and rubbed against my legs as I unlocked the building. His fur looked soft and clean, but he was skinny. I wondered how he had ended up behind my shop. He cried and gave me the same look that cats have perfected to get what they want. "Okay." I relented and picked him up. He immediately began purring, and I rubbed behind his ears. "You've definitely missed a few meals," I said to him as I walked inside.

A mini-fridge and microwave stacked in the corner of the back room made up our "employee lounge," and I rummaged around in the fridge, sorting through Lorea's leftovers. The girl never threw anything out. The cat perked up, his whiskers twitched, and he squirmed in my arms. A Styrofoam box with last week's burrito from the La Paparilla Mexican restaurant would do. I went back outside and set the leftovers and the kitten down. He pounced on it like it was a scurrying mouse, and I laughed when he made grumbling noises as he chowed down.

I read the notes Lorea had jotted down on the instruction

manual for the new surveillance camera that had been installed. It was digital and efficient, which pretty much ensured that the bad guys wouldn't come back because why would I be that lucky? My computer hummed to life thirty seconds after I pushed the button, and I started checking the details of my task list for Sylvia's bridal shower.

"What is that cat doing out there?" Lorea demanded as she came in lugging a dress bag. "And why are you feeding him my leftovers?"

I tilted my head to see around my widescreen. "He volunteered to save you from food poisoning. You know leftovers aren't good after three days."

"Hmmph. I have a strong stomach," Lorea countered. "You're the one telling me I need to eat."

"Look, I'll buy lunch today. You choose. Just have it delivered." I hoped we would have time to stop for lunch.

Lorea grumbled as she unlocked the closet holding Natalie's dress. She hung the bag on a rack next to the gown, and her mood immediately improved. "What do you think?"

I couldn't resist checking the hem line. "It's beautiful. This dress is perfect for her. And you did a great job on the hem." The sheer frills hung gracefully over the skirt and trailed to the floor.

"So how was your weekend in Rupert?"

"Too short. I always have to remind myself why I decided to move here when I'm getting ready to leave."

Lorea stopped fussing with the gown for a moment. "Angels sent you my way. Don't ever doubt that."

"Thank you." My throat felt thick with emotion, and I tried to think of something to lighten the mood. "You'll never believe what I did Sunday night."

"What? Another date with Dallas?"

"Well, that too." I could feel my cheeks heating up as I thought of the "date" Dallas and I had on my living room couch. I wasn't going to share those details with Lorea yet. "I went running, and I saw 'the hottie.' "

"Oh, you still need to get a picture of him for me."

"Turns out you've already seen him."

Lorea stood up and grabbed my arm. "You know who he is? Did you talk to him?"

I struggled to keep a straight face. "You ready for this?"

"Um, yeah. Is he available?"

I thought about that for a minute, how Luke had confided in me. "I guess so. 'The hottie' is Luke Stetson, divorce attorney."

"You're kidding."

I pressed my lips together and raised my eyebrows.

"The jerk lawyer? Did you recognize him?"

"No, he recognized *me*." I didn't tell her how I thought he was going to kill me for the diamonds. "I was just going to do my usual run-by admiring, but he stopped and told me he wondered why I had looked so familiar. Then, get this—he apologized."

"No. Freakin'. Way."

I laughed. "Way. And it was a sincere apology."

Lorea narrowed her eyes. "Did you tell him where to go?"

"Actually, I'm thinking about forgiving him."

"He must have had his shirt off again, huh?"

I knew my cheeks were pink, but I didn't care. "He said he has a difficult time with dating." For a moment, I thought about telling Lorea the truth behind Luke's apology, but I swallowed the secret and kept his confidence.

"So he asks you out and then is incredibly rude so he won't have to go through with it?"

"That pretty much sums it up."

Lorea unzipped the garment bag and pulled out two of Natalie's bridesmaid dresses. "Are you going to go out with him if he asks again?"

"I don't think I have to worry about that." A speck of lint on my computer keys drew my attention, and I busied myself with dusting off the keyboard.

Lorea patted my cheek. "But you are, just the same."

I didn't try to argue with Lorea, because she was right. I had been thinking about Luke *and* Dallas. Luke's tortured expression when he told me about his wife kept haunting me. I could forgive him, but I didn't know if I should go further than that.

Twenty minutes later, Natalie showed up for her fitting, her light brown curls twisted in an updo. "I'm trying to decide if I should wear my hair up or down."

"You'll look beautiful either way, so do what makes you most comfortable," I said.

When she put the gown on, both Lorea and I sighed. Natalie's full smile showed her white, even teeth. "I love this dress. It's perfect, and the length is just right." She turned slowly and Lorea followed, checking the circumference of the dress.

"I feel like a princess," Natalie said. She swayed in front of the mirror and let the organza frill trail through her fingers. "I also feel a little guilty about how much this dress costs."

Lorea's smile faltered, and I knew she was fretting over the price and the conversation we'd had at the first fitting. Natalie was a native of this valley, and she knew the hard work required to earn every dollar on a farm.

I stepped forward and turned Natalie toward the mirror. "Brock called me and said you would be worried. He wants to do this for you, so let him. I think you two bring out the best in each other, and you need to keep reminding yourself of that. The dress is expensive, but you only get married once."

Natalie laughed. "Hopefully."

Lorea snorted, and I shot her a look that she knew meant, "Quiet the cynic."

Natalie swished her gown back and forth in front of the mirror. "That is so sweet that he would call. This is all like a dream. I've always wanted a beautiful wedding."

"Yours will be so lovely, it'll take your breath away," I said. "As soon as you're finished with Lorea, I have a few more things I want to go over with you."

"I want to check the waistline. You'd better not get any skinnier." Lorea indicated Natalie's thin figure, and Natalie blushed.

"Oh, I almost forgot to show you the latest idea for your garden party, Natalie." I lifted a Mason jar bouquet off a filing cabinet. "You've met the florist, Melissa, right?"

"Yes, she's fantastic." Natalie eyed the flower arrangement with a smile.

I rotated the Mason jar slowly in front of Natalie. "She and I were brainstorming, and we put slices of lemon in the water. Melissa had some white lilacs and daisies handy, but she said that freesia or daffodils would look lovely as well."

"I love the fresh look," Natalie said.

The front door chimed, and I heard someone call, "Yoo-hoo! Where are you, darlings?"

"Oh, no." I saw Lorea's mouth drop open and several pins

scatter to the floor. I set the Mason jar down and hurried out to the front, but I knew this wasn't going to end well.

"Good morning, Sylvia."

She wore a creamy yellow sundress that set off her auburn curls. When she waved a hand in my direction, her bracelets jingled. "I wish it was a good morning. I tried contacting the police, but they wouldn't give me any information on whether my dress had been found or not."

My shoulders slumped. This woman would be the death of me. "I'm sorry, Sylvia, but they still haven't found it, and as Lorea explained, it will most likely be damaged like the others. It's best not to pin our hopes on that gown."

"But it was designed for me. There's nothing else that even compares to it." Sylvia's nostril flared, and I looked away.

"I'm sorry. Is there something else I can help you with right now?"

Sylvia pushed past me. "I want to take a look at that detachable train Lorea showed me."

"But . . ." Sylvia had already entered the back of the shop before I could do anything to stop her.

"You stole my wedding dress!" Sylvia screeched.

Lorea stepped forward to protect Natalie. "Sylvia, please."

"I did not." Natalie's voice was quiet, yet firm.

"And now you've taken the next best dress. You conniving piece of white trash. You think you'll be happy as Mrs. Brock Grafton? Well, think again." Sylvia held up her left hand and ripped the ring off her finger. She stuffed the gaudy engagement ring in her purse. "I'm available, and I'm going to make sure Brock knows it."

Natalie's chin wobbled, but before she could say anything, Lorea took over.

"Did you know that Adri has a picture of you and your mother before your plastic surgery?"

I cringed as I watched the fury of Sylvia's gaze redirect to me.

"I'm going to press charges against your business for all the trouble you've caused."

My jaw clenched, and I felt anger shoot through me. I straightened my shoulders—no one talks to me that way and gets away with it. I stepped forward, catching her in a withering stare. "Sylvia, I'm sorry things haven't worked out, but I'm certain you'll be glad this happened later on. What if you had married a man you didn't love?"

"How dare you?" she cried.

I took another step closer. "The police brought the old pictures of your family, so you might want to take it up with them if you're concerned about how they are conducting their investigation." I lifted my cell phone, selected Anthony Ford from my contact list, and then turned the screen toward Sylvia. "With this latest outburst, they might wonder if you stole the dress to sabotage your own wedding—you know, the wedding you set up to try to make your ex-boyfriend jealous enough to want you back?"

Sylvia pursed her lips and clenched her fists. She glanced toward Natalie and Lorea and then back at me, gnashed her teeth, and screamed. Natalie cowered in the back, and Lorea's eyes widened as Sylvia bolted for the door.

The wedding bells above the door chimed, and I turned to Lorea. "I think we just officially made our first enemy in business."

Lorea shook her head. "Another *txori buru*."

Natalie sat on the loveseat in the back room, sobbing. I knelt in front of her and took her hands from her face. "Don't you let her bully you. I've seen you and Brock together, and if there's one thing I'm sure of, it's that he adores you. He loves you, Nat. I can see it in the twitch of his eye, that dimple in his cheek, even the way he stands up straighter when you're near. You're a perfect match for him. Don't you ever forget that."

"Really?" Natalie wiped her nose, her face a picture of hope. I nodded.

"Girl, he loves you like a fish loves water," Lorea said.

Natalie hugged me. "Thank you. I'm so sorry."

"You don't have anything to be sorry about," I said. "Be happy. You're getting married in three weeks to an incredibly handsome man who wants to be with *you*, not some plastic surgeon's pro-bono experiments."

Natalie shrieked and covered her mouth. "I can't believe you said that." We all laughed. Until the police arrived.

Chapter 17

VINTAGE HANKIE WEDDING FAVORS

Collect vintage handkerchiefs in assorted colors. Arrange in a basket, on a cake stand, or in a cut-glass bowl with a placard that reads "For Your Happy Tears!"
Courtesy of www.mashedpotatoesandcrafts.com

Tony poked his head around the dividing wall of the back room. "Adri, do you have a minute?"

"Did you really call the police?" Natalie whispered.

I shook my head and put a finger to my lips. Lorea snorted, and I left the two of them on the couch, Natalie's dress rustling as she laughed.

Tony's suit looked freshly pressed, and the badge clipped to his belt glimmered under the fluorescent lights as he turned.

"Hey, I've been trying to call you," I said.

"I know. I've had some problems with my cell phone, but I got it working again." He patted the phone clipped to his belt. "I came by to tell you we found something significant with one of the wedding dresses."

"What?"

He held up a clear plastic bag that appeared empty at first glance. With his index finger, he touched the corner of the bag, and I leaned closer. As he tilted the bag I noticed a yellow-brown rock that was definitely not a rock.

"You found—" Cursing myself for opening my mouth, I glanced at Tony.

"Do you know what that is?" He gave me a curious look.

The carpet suddenly held my interest, and I studied the flecks of dark brown and tan in the cream fibers until Tony cleared his throat. The uncut diamond in his evidence bag changed everything. I had to tell him. Now.

Straightening my shoulders, I met his confused stare. "I need to talk to you but not here. Can we go somewhere private—not the police station?"

"Adri, what's going on?"

I clenched my eyes shut and then opened them. "This is going to sound crazy."

"I'm listening."

I lowered my voice and pointed at the bag. "That is an uncut diamond, and I'm betting you found it along the hemline of one of my stolen wedding gowns. I know that because the people who smuggled those diamonds want them back, and they're watching me."

Tony's fingers grazed the handle of his gun as he looked out the front doors. "Where would you like to go?"

"I have a meeting at noon with the wedding planner at the

Sun Valley Lodge. It won't throw up any red flags if you come—as long as you don't look like a cop."

Tony shook his head. "I don't like this."

"Me neither."

"I want to ask why you didn't tell me this sooner." He frowned. "But I'll see you in a couple of hours. Please be careful."

With a nod, I headed back to check on Natalie and Lorea. Natalie had changed out of the wedding dress and looked through the notes I'd made by the fabric swatches in her new wedding binder. She held up the piece with the rose blush on cream linen. "This one is perfect."

"Let's get to work, then." We finalized the details of her wedding, and I showed her the calligraphy samples from Shayla. Natalie loved them.

"I wish I could've used her for my invitations." Natalie studied the portfolio of elegant writing.

"I think it would be a nice touch for the place cards, though, don't you?"

"Can she have it done in time?" Natalie tapped one of the cards. "If she could do this style on paper that matched the fabric sample you gave me, it'd be lovely."

"I agree. Shayla can do this for us, guaranteed."

"Oh, I almost forgot to tell you that my mom found about fifty more vintage handkerchiefs." Natalie's face brightened. "If we keep hunting, I'm certain we'll have enough for the wedding."

"Everyone is going to love that idea." We had all been collecting vintage hankies for two months to use as wedding favors. I had already hand-painted a sign with dark green lettering that read *For Your Happy Tears!* I had sanded the edges and given the coat of paint a few distress marks by pounding a flat-edged screwdriver into the wood to mar the surface. The result was a new sign that sported a vintage look to match the hankies, which would be arranged in a basket for the wedding guests.

"I can't believe it's less than four weeks away now." Natalie's gaze settled on her gown hanging over a dress form while Lorea worked. "I'm glad I had a hard time finding the right dress, because that one is remarkable."

"Lorea knew it was yours as soon as it came out of the box."

Natalie bit her bottom lip. "I'm so sorry about all the trouble with Sylvia."

"Don't be." I patted her arm. "It's not your fault."

"But maybe if I hadn't been here today, she wouldn't have called off her wedding."

"I don't want you to think about her anymore, and I mean it. Every time you worry about her, you're letting her win. That's all this is to her—a game."

Natalie twisted her ring around her finger. "Okay. You're right." Her phone beeped and she glanced at the screen. Her face split into a wide grin. "Brock is coming to get me for lunch."

I couldn't help smiling in return. "Sounds like fun."

"He says he wants to pay for the wedding dress now—full price, no discounts."

Lorea opened her mouth as if to protest, paused, and said, "Thanks, Nat."

Natalie squeezed Lorea's hand. "Thank *you*."

"I'll print up a receipt," I said.

Brock had already put down a hefty deposit for the wedding, so Lorea hadn't waited for payment before getting started on Natalie's dress. His check in the amount of eleven thousand dollars would pay off the loan to Walter Mayfield but wasn't quite enough to order the next shipment of dresses. Unfortunately, I wasn't sure Lorea would be able to place another order anyway, with all the criminal activity attached to these dresses.

A white Cadillac Escalade pulled in front of my shop, and Brock jumped out. His close-cut light brown hair and megawatt smile reminded me of Matt Damon. He was so down-to-earth that if I hadn't seen him in the movies, I never would have believed he was a millionaire. He greeted Natalie with a kiss and flashed another grin in Lorea's direction.

"Do I get to see the dress?"

"No, sir. You don't," Lorea shook her finger at Brock. "It's bad luck."

"But couldn't you make an exception? I'm a pretty lucky guy—just look at this beautiful woman who agreed to marry me." Brock put his arm around Natalie's waist and pulled her to him. She looked at him with adoration, and he gave her another light kiss.

Watching the lovebirds, I was more determined than ever to create the wedding of Natalie's dreams. If Sylvia stayed out of the way, I'd have plenty of time to devote to the rest of the preparations.

I had barely sat down when someone entered the shop. Turning slowly, I caught sight of a beautiful bouquet of red roses against the backdrop of a familiar brown uniform. Colton lowered the roses and smiled at me, his cheeks darkening with what must have been as close to a blush as his brown skin would show.

"I'm sorry," he said as he approached with the bouquet. A wave of relief washed over me as he lifted a grocery sack from Roxy's. "And here's some chocolate to go with my peace offering."

"Thank you, Colton," Lorea murmured from behind me. She was always sneaking up on me.

"Yes, thank you," I echoed. "It all worked out. I was able to order another cupcake stand. I bet you'll be back with it tomorrow."

"I'll be extra careful." He handed the roses to Lorea, and I saw the way his eyes met hers for a half second.

I felt my face redden as I thought how crazy I had been earlier. Colton wasn't going to fetch the diamonds. He went to buy an apology, and I was about to meet with Tony and tell him my suspicions. I shivered. Someone was still after me. Fear pricked my heart when I thought of how close the danger might be, and I didn't have a hint of who might be stalking me.

At noon, I met with Frankie Lawson of Sun Valley Lodge and gave her the bad news that Sylvia's wedding had been cancelled.

"I wouldn't be surprised if she changed her mind tomorrow," Frankie said. "She's so dramatic, she's probably doing it to get attention."

"She seemed pretty serious." Then I thought about the way Sylvia had taken off her ring and carefully tucked it into her purse. Frankie could be right.

Frankie flicked off an invisible speck of dust from the cuff of her black business suit. "I'll call Mrs. Rockfort and see if she would like me to hold the date. It might be interesting to get her reaction."

"You're a saint. I purposely have not called her yet." That woman had me on a pathway to an ulcer. Delegation was something I had perfected in my contacts with her. "I need your help for something else, though." I explained as briefly as possible the theft of the wedding gowns and subsequent police investigation, including my need to meet with Tony in private.

Frankie nodded. "Sure. I'll just put you in an empty guest room off the main floor."

"Thank you." I was so grateful for Frankie's tact and ability to stifle her curiosity. She probably wondered why I hadn't met Tony at the police station but accepted my vague explanation. A moment later, a knock sounded at the door, and I recognized Tony through the frosted glass.

Frankie escorted Tony and me into an empty room. Before I spilled the beans on my unlucky part in the business of diamond smuggling, I needed to have some assurances.

"I have some information that I should have told you, but please don't be angry with me."

Tony lifted his eyes to the ceiling and huffed. "Adri, I already asked you not to play detective."

"And I wasn't. Honest. I know about the diamonds because of something I found, but I didn't—*couldn't*—tell you."

"You can tell me. I'm a police officer, but I'm also your friend."

"I want to tell you, but I need a promise from you first."

Tony held up his hands. "What's this about?"

"Just promise me that you will not take any more of my wedding dresses for the investigation."

"I can't make a promise like that. I could take all of them now, based on that one diamond we found."

I crossed my arms over my chest. "Fine."

Tony narrowed his eyes, and I could hear him noisily exhale as he scrutinized me. "I can't make any promises, but I'll listen."

"Don't you understand? I want to tell you, but if you're going to confiscate my wedding dresses, then I can't. Lorea is trying to start a brand-new business alongside mine, and we can't afford any more setbacks. We're doing some high-profile weddings, and we can't have a wedding without a gown."

"Okay. I promise I won't take any more of your wedding dresses, but you have to make *me* a promise."

I lifted my eyebrows. "What?"

"That you won't do any more sleuthing unless you call me first."

"You say that like I'm out looking for trouble."

Tony lifted an eyebrow.

"Fine. Whatever. I promise—no more sleuthing." We shook hands, and I sat in the straight-backed chair next to the bed. I took a deep breath and told Tony how I had found the diamonds in the hem of Natalie's dress.

Tony shook his head when I told him about hiding the diamonds in the quilt my mother made. "And where are they now?"

He was good. I hadn't gotten to the part about the cemetery yet, but his police antenna had picked up on my anxiety. Letting my head fall to my chest, I murmured, "I moved them because someone searched my house and left me a note."

"Someone searched your house, and you didn't report it?" Tony ran his fingers through his hair.

"I tried to call you first, but when I couldn't reach you, I was sure no one else would believe me."

"They might if you showed them a bag of diamonds."

"I know, but the smugglers had searched my house so carefully that if I wasn't so particular, I wouldn't even have noticed." I unzipped my purse and pulled out the note the criminal had left on my entryway table. While Tony studied it, I told him about the pictures and my evening run to the cemetery. He was silent for a moment as he clenched the note tightly.

"You are in way over your head." He paced across the room. "I'll have to talk to the other detective—his name's Hamilton—but I have an idea. So where are the diamonds now?"

I dragged my sandal against the nap of the carpet and whispered, "In a bird feeder."

Tony frowned but listened intently as I explained the current hiding place of the smuggled gems and the delivery I had made early that morning. His frown deepened when I told him the specifics of my lunch bag being left behind the store, empty. I could see his jaw working as he processed the turn of events.

"Have you mentioned this to anyone else?"

"Of course not."

"Let's keep it that way. I'm going to see if I can find a way to have someone watch your place."

"I don't think that's a good idea. I don't want whoever is after me to know I talked to you, remember?" The police station in Ketchum wasn't large, so it would be relatively easy for someone with resources to find out who was on the force and keep a lookout for them, even if they were in unmarked vehicles.

"Your safety is my priority. Let me take care of the details." Tony reached out his hand and helped me to my feet. "Those diamonds are worth a lot of money. So far these people have played nice, but I'm worried about what they'll do now that you didn't turn the gems over. Call me if anything happens or if you notice anything out of the ordinary."

I swallowed and met Tony's gaze. He appeared genuinely worried, and that made me even more uneasy because I had been trying to convince myself that things weren't as bad as they seemed.

I was crazy busy for the rest of the day. I delayed cancelling Sylvia's wedding plans. It could wait until tomorrow after Frankie had talked to Mrs. Rockfort. Lorea finished up the alterations to Natalie's gown just before five o'clock.

She cleaned up the shop and looked through the back window before opening the door. "That cat is still outside. What are you going to do with him?"

I cracked open the door to peek at the kitten. He meowed and pushed his nose into the space. Opening the door wider, I swooped him into my arms and rubbed the soft black fur between his ears. His purr resonated against my chest. "Maybe I'll take him home with me. I thought he belonged to someone, but I guess not."

Lorea wrinkled her nose. "Black cat hair doesn't mix well with white wedding dresses."

"Don't worry. He can stay in the garage."

I'd have to do some reorganizing. I wondered if he would hang around my back patio if I fed him gourmet cat food. I found a cardboard box, questioning my decision a half second before the kitten rubbed against my legs, purring. My heart melted, and I picked him up again. The white patch of fur under his neck reminded me of a tuxedo. "I think I'll call him Tux." I patted his head and put him inside the box, where he commenced mewing loudly.

"Have fun with that," Lorea said.

"If Sylvia is engaged again in the morning, you owe me dark chocolate." I headed out the door with Lorea's laughter trailing behind.

The air conditioner in the Mountaineer felt delicious on my tired body, and I switched it to full blast as I drove home. My heart rate accelerated as I approached my front door—I wished for the hundredth time that my garage weren't so small.

There wasn't anything taped to the door. I breathed a sigh of relief and unlocked it, balancing the box with Tux on my hip. Just inside the door, I set the box down and allowed Tux to jump out. My senses were on full alert as I walked through my house, the kitten following me. Once I had deemed my home safe, I rummaged through my cupboards and found some old containers that would work for cat food and water. I set them outside my patio door and put Tux just outside with the sliding glass door open a sliver so he could hear me talk.

"You stay right there, and I'll bring you something good to eat."

A search of my fridge produced some leftover chicken casserole that Tux pounced on happily. I'd have to make a run to the store for kitty litter and cat food, but for now I needed to put my feet up. I slumped onto my couch and mentally ran through my to-do list. Natalie's bridal shower was in two days—no stress. If only every bride were as delightful to work with as Natalie. Immediately, an image of Briette came to my mind, and tears welled up in my eyes.

My best friend had been the perfect client. Everything was new, exciting, and special. I had reveled in every moment of planning for Briette and Caleb. Three elaborate bridal showers, one of which was held in Georgia, and Briette flew me there to help coordinate and to attend. She had been so happy. The night she died had been the Babe Bash she threw for her six bridesmaids and me, the maid of honor. She had completely surprised me with that one, using one of my associates to plan it so I could attend stress free.

I'd never forget the glow of happiness on her face when she dropped me off after the party. "You're the best friend a girl could have, Adri." She hugged me fiercely and then giggled. "That guy was totally into you tonight. You better answer if he calls."

I remembered rolling my eyes. "When would I have time to date?"

"You make time. Speaking of which, I'd better go." She blew me a kiss. "Love your guts!" she called out as she drove away.

My bottom lip trembled, and I swiped at the tears weighing down my lashes. Caleb hadn't checked in for two months. I considered calling him to see if there were any new leads with the private investigators he'd hired to look into Briette's murder. My fingers grazed the screen of my phone. No, if Caleb knew anything, I would be one of the first people he would call. I leaned my head back against the couch and closed my eyes. A few minutes later, the jangle of my phone startled me awake.

Chapter 18

1,000 REASONS I PICKED YOU

Select flowers of the same variety as those in the bridal bouquet and separate petals from the stems.

Open journal so that the outside front and back covers lie flat. Brush a light coat of Mod Podge glue over the entire cover and spine of a hardbound journal and press petals onto the cover. Apply a second coat of Mod Podge and allow to dry. Once dry, add one more coat of Mod Podge or shellac for a glossy look. On the first page of the journal, print "1,000 Reasons I Picked You . . ."

Ask the bride and the groom for three reasons they picked the other and write those on the first few pages of the journal, as well as instructions for the couple to continue to remember and write other reasons in the journal over the first few years of their marriage.

Courtesy of www.mashedpotatoesandcrafts.com.

I fumbled to answer the phone, which had slid between the couch cushions. A glance at the clock on my mantel had me rubbing my eyes. Somehow I had lost track of twenty minutes—an unplanned power nap was probably just what I needed, though. I answered the call on the third ring. "Hey, Dallas."

"Adri, are you okay? Why haven't you answered my texts?" His voice sounded tense.

"Huh? I—let me check. I just got home and fell asleep on my couch. It's been a stressful day." I switched the phone to speaker and scrolled through my text messages. There were three from Dallas, all in the last twenty minutes.

"I'm sorry," he said. His voice lowered a notch. "Is there anything I can do to help?"

I scanned his messages asking me how I was doing and if we could get together tonight. It irked me that he had called to check up on me because I hadn't answered his texts. But maybe I had missed one from earlier. I double-checked and didn't see anything. "I see some messages from the last half hour. Did you try to send some earlier, 'cause I don't see anything."

"Usually you respond so quickly, and I knew you were home, so I thought I'd call."

"What do you mean, you knew I was home?" I tried to keep the edge out of my voice, unsuccessfully.

"I meant, I *figured* you would be home. It's nearly seven." He cleared his throat. "Sorry, I just hoped I could see you today." He paused, and I could hear the nervous tremor in his voice as he continued, "I miss you."

Man, this guy was a heartbreaker. I vacillated for a moment, thinking of his kisses. "I can't. I have a huge bridal shower in a couple of days, and Sylvia Rockfort cancelled her wedding today, but I have to wait until tomorrow to see if she reinstates. I'm really behind because of the trouble we had with the stolen dresses." I knew I was babbling, but I couldn't help it.

"I understand." Dallas sounded so vulnerable, I almost changed my mind and told him to come over. "Do you have any time tomorrow?"

My to-do list popped back into my head, and I remembered that I had been scanning it before I fell asleep. "Hmm." I stalled for a minute, trying to think how I could squeeze him into my schedule. I wanted to see him, but June was just the beginning of my busy season—I had three more weddings in July. I needed to drive up the mountain and make sure the area Natalie and Brock had selected for their outdoor wedding would work. I'd be taking Warm Springs Road, which led to Frenchman's Bend, a beautiful area with natural hot pools right in the middle of the creek. "Have you ever been up to the hot springs?"

"No. Those are the volcanic springs, aren't they, the ones that get boiling hot?" Dallas asked. "Do you hike there?"

"Actually, you can drive all the way up, but we could hike around as well. I have to go up there tomorrow to check out the site for a wedding, but it'll be around four." I needed to see how the light would fall at the same time as Natalie's wedding, which would be held at five o'clock.

"I have to be at the restaurant at six-thirty. Can we be back by then?"

"Sure. That should give us time to soak our feet in the hot pools, just so you can say you've tried it."

I could hear shuffling papers in the background and figured he must be calling from his realtor's office. "What time would you like me to pick you up?"

"How about if I drive this time? I'll be meeting with several vendors, and I don't want to make you have to hunt me down. Do you want me to stop at your office or your home?"

"My office would be great," Dallas answered.

"I'll try to be there by three-thirty."

"I'm looking forward to it already. Have a great night." He ended the call, and I stared at my phone for a moment, arguing with myself again over Jenna's suggestion that I didn't like Dallas. He definitely liked me and was persistent. A guy who wasn't really into me would've given up by now with my crazy schedule.

The kitchen beckoned, and I foraged for something to ease the gnawing hunger attacking my stomach. A hunk of cheese and some flour tortillas would make a great transformation into quesadillas. My mouth watered as I turned on the stove and flicked a tab of butter into a frying pan. My phone buzzed, and I noticed a text from Dallas. Feeling slightly irritated, I opened the message. It hadn't even been five minutes since we talked.

Check your doorstep.

I frowned. Had he come over, even though I explained how much work I had to do? I tiptoed to the front door and looked through the peephole. No one there. I opened the door and heard a rustling at my feet. I looked down to see a bouquet of beautiful coral roses wrapped in green tissue paper. I scanned the parking lot before bending over to pick up the delicate buds. There was a note tucked in among the dark green leaves.

Adri,

I wanted you to know that I think you're amazing, and your talents and dedication in the wedding business are exceptional. I'm sorry you're so busy, but thanks for letting me take up some of your time. I can't wait to see you again.

Love,

Dallas

I admit I let out a girly sigh, but who wouldn't? So that's how he knew I was home—he must have seen my vehicle outside when he brought the flowers. And I wouldn't let him come see me. I felt terrible that I had been upset at him for checking up on me. I grabbed my phone to send him a message—or maybe I should call and tell him to come back. But the pile of things I needed to do would not go away just because Dallas was sweet and thoughtful. He had honored my wishes, and that meant something to me. I sent him a text.

Thank you for the roses!!! They're beautiful!

Two seconds later, my phone pinged.

So are you.

I put my hand to my cheek, which lifted in a huge smile. The butter sizzled and popped, reminding me that I still hadn't eaten. While the quesadilla browned in the pan, I gathered up my supplies and spread them across the table. I ate and then worked for two hours until my neck ached and my brain felt like mush.

It was just after nine, so I decided it was time for a kitty litter run. Tux had hung around the patio, sticking his nose in the crack of the door and meowing. I bent down and opened the door so I could cuddle the sleek kitten in my arms. "I'll be back in a few minutes."

It creeped me out to go to Roxy's again, knowing that someone could be watching me. I shrugged off the worry and drove the speed limit, thinking that if Tony had been successful, maybe a few more cops would be patrolling my neighborhood. The entire trip took less than twenty minutes, since I speed-walked through the store and hit the express lane.

Once home again, I set up the tub of kitty litter, and then I used Tux's paw and sifted through the litter, showing him what to do. He sniffed at it and circled around it with his tail held high.

"Sorry, boy, but you'll have to stay out here for a couple more nights until I get things in the garage moved around for you."

Tux looked at me and then started crunching his cat food. He was easy to please, at least. I moved into the living room with my wedding organizer and made a checklist of things I needed to look for in the forest by the hot springs. A few years ago, a fire had devoured part of the woods. I would need to make sure that no burnt trees were in view of the site for the wedding ceremony. The background for the pictures was supposed to be majestic and calming, not blackened and charred.

My cell phone rang, and I answered on the second ring. "Hey, Mom. How are you?"

"You should see the little flowers I'm crocheting. They are darling and so easy!" I could hear the smile in my mom's voice. "I'm going to crochet a ring of them and see what you think about using them around one of your centerpieces."

"You mean kind of like a doily?"

"Sort of, but this is more fresh, modern. I can't wait to show you all the things we've been doing with them. Jenna sewed some onto a little shirt for Bryn—so cute."

"You need to get out more."

"Oh, hush. You'll be just as excited when you see them. I can make them look elegant, artsy, or cutesy."

I heard something in the background and then my mom shushing. "Did Dad just say artsy-fartsy?" I laughed.

"It's another blog I found with all kinds of great ideas. Of course, your father hasn't let up on that for a minute."

"Tell Dad hi. And make sure you're taking pictures so we can post a tutorial on the blog."

"Of course, what would your father make fun of if he didn't catch me photographing my crafts?"

I laughed and glanced at the notebook full of sketches and scribblings. "You know, I still haven't found that one special item for Natalie's wedding. I need you to brainstorm with me." For every wedding I'd organized—and that was more than fifty in the past three years—I had always given the bride and groom a special gift. Handmade and unique, my gifts took a lot of thought and also much of my mother's quirky inspiration. Sometimes ideas would just come to me during the planning stages. Other times, I had to rack my brain to come up with something that would be remembered.

A few of the gifts were worthy of repeating, and I thought of my favorites now, wondering if any would suit Natalie. Jenna and my mother had painstakingly découpaged rose petals of the same variety as the bride's bouquet to the outside of a journal. The first page said, "1,000 Reasons I Picked You." I filled in the first three reasons as given to me by the bride and the groom and wrote instructions for them to continue filling the journal over the next few years. I admit I repeated that one several times because it was so well received.

Another time, we used vinyl lettering and etching cream to engrave the couple's wedding date on a glass-enclosed shadow box to hold mementos from their life apart and then their life together.

Natalie would probably appreciate the decorative pillows my mom made, using scraps of fabric from the wedding dress, accent colors, tablecloths—anything to do with the wedding—and then embroidered with the couple's name and date. But still, it didn't seem like enough. Natalie was such a sweet person. I'd have to keep thinking.

"Natalie likes earthy things, right?"

"Yes, and she loves antiques."

"I think I have an idea based on something we featured recently on mashedpotatoesandcrafts.com."

"Really? Which project?"

"I think I'll surprise you," Mom said before ending the call.

I was nearly finished with my checklist when I heard a loud thud against the patio window. Goose bumps scattered across my arms. Holding perfectly still, I listened and heard a tapping, one, two more times. My heartbeat thrummed in my ears, and a war raged within—did I dare look?

The light was within reach. If I stretched my arm just right, I could extinguish it and then investigate the odd sound. I crept toward the light panel, fear tingling up my spine. With speed and stealth Hitchcock might have envied, I flipped off the light, dashed across the room, and turned on the patio light. A scream suspended in my throat as I watched Tux slam into the patio window—momentarily dazed by the light. He flipped around and batted at a grotesque June bug. The giant beetle lay stunned for a moment, the patio light reflecting off its glossy burgundy back.

Then it launched into the air directly into my line of vision and bounced off the window again. The scream released from my throat, and Tux jumped back as I curled my shoulders inward. "Ew! I hate those things. Kill it, Tux."

He hesitated, then pawed at the bug. I chided myself for my near-panic attack. Ticking antennas held the feline's attention, and I laughed when Tux jumped back at the bug's sudden movement. Turning off the light, I gathered up my lists and binders and walked toward my bedroom, hopeful for a good night's rest.

The next morning, I hurried to get ready for work. Tux rubbed against the patio door as I approached, and I could hear him meow through the glass. I reached for the door and stopped, my mouth dropping open. A piece of paper was taped to the outside of the glass door. I stubbed my toe on a stool and cursed as I leaned in for a better look. I closed my eyes when I saw the picture and tried to quiet the terror pumping my heart at double speed. I dialed Tony's number as I examined the picture of Natalie's wedding dress taped on my patio door above a note:

You have 24 hours to return the diamonds. Use the lunch bag and leave it at Rotary Park.

I noticed my lunch bag sitting at the far corner of the patio, and a cold river of fear ran through me. I closed my eyes and sent up a quick prayer that Tony could get me out of this mess.

Tony answered the phone. "This is Detective Ford."

"Houston, we have a problem."

Chapter 19

LAUREL'S SWEET FIVE-PETAL CROCHET FLOWER PATTERN

Use any size hook (depending on what size flower you want) and any weight yarn, but for delicate lace flowers use fingering 10-count crochet thread and a size 6, 7, or 8 hook.

Rnd 1: Ch 5, join into a ring w/sl st in 1st ch.

Rnd 2: Ch 3 (counts as first dc), work 9dc in ring, join to top of ch w/sl st—10 sts.

Rnd 3: **Ch 2, work 3dc in next st, ch 2, sl st in next st** five times. Fasten off.

For variety, you can create a different colored center by changing yarn colors after round 2. Experiment with different weight yarns and hook sizes. To layer a slightly smaller flower on top, use one hook size smaller than you used for the larger flower.

Courtesy of www.mashedpotatoesandcrafts.com.

"There's an undercover cop on your street. I want you to leave right now," Tony said after I told him what was taped to my patio door. "I'll meet you at your shop."

"What should I do about the lunch bag?"

"Leave it there for now. Act normal."

"Yeah, I'll do that." I fed Tux, grabbed my stuff, and hurried to my shop, not bothering with the speed limit this time.

I spotted Tony leaning against the back door when I arrived. He straightened as I approached. "What do you have planned for today?"

The bag on my shoulder probably weighed forty pounds, and I hefted it toward him. "Nothing that I'm willing to cancel for these crooks."

He grunted as he took the bag. "What do you have in here?"

"Wedding plans."

We stepped inside the store, and I punched the electronic keypad, disarming the security system. Tony set my bag on the floor and walked around the shop, checking things out. "I know you're trying to act tough, but we're not fooling around with these guys. Hamilton and I have a plan."

Acting tough didn't mean I felt tough. Dread came over me as I followed his train of thought. "You're going to use me as bait."

"You're already doing a great job of that yourself." Tony stood with his feet apart, and he didn't look happy. "Someone came right up to your patio door last night. Do you realize how easy it would have been for them to come inside and hurt you?"

I stepped back and sat in my office chair, dropping my head into my hands. "I know."

Tony crouched down and took hold of my hands. "I had an

officer patrolling your street all night, and he didn't notice anything out of the ordinary. Whoever is behind this isn't out to fail."

I furrowed my brow, angry again that the stupid crooks were making me sick to my stomach. "It just makes me so mad that they are messing with my plans."

Tony chuckled. "You're a spitfire. That's how I know you can see this thing through."

"What do I have to do?"

"Tonight you're going for another run, and I want you to get those diamonds."

"We can't hand them over."

"We won't. I'm pretty certain this person is tailing you, and they're planning to take the diamonds before you can put them in your cute little lunch bag."

"So I *will* be bait?" I didn't like the idea, even though Tony was right about the criminals already stalking me.

"It's a nice open area. I'll be running the trail as well as two other officers. Detective Hamilton will be in a car." Tony took out a notebook. "Now, fill me in on your plans for the day."

I sighed and flipped out my planner so I could show Tony every appointment I had set up.

"Can you postpone going to the hot springs?" Tony asked. "There are too many possibilities in that area—no way of keeping it secure."

"Sure." Dallas would be disappointed. I hoped he wouldn't think I was avoiding him. I would still stop by his office, even if I couldn't explain exactly why we weren't going to the springs.

"Can you be ready to run at about eight o'clock tonight?"

"I'll wear my pink running skirt, so I'll be easy to spot."

"Okay. You get the diamonds and then run back up the trail

a half mile. We hope he won't try to intercept you before then. You'll hand the diamonds off to me, but be obvious about it." He patted my knee. "So you'll only be partial bait. The idea is for him to go after me."

Fear dropped like a stone down my throat, and for a moment, I couldn't find my voice. "I'm scared."

"Good." His expression was stern. "Maybe it'll keep you from doing anything stupid."

"I'm sorry, Tony. I know I messed things up." I gave him my best apologetic look. "I should've brought the diamonds to you first thing."

"Maybe not. This way, we'll catch the smuggler. If you had turned them in already, we might not have had a chance." He held up a finger. "But don't do anything like this ever again."

I raised three fingers. "Scout's honor."

He stood. "I'll be keeping an eye on you, but please be careful." Tony left the shop through the back door, and I waited until I heard the latch click before I groaned and lowered my head to the desk.

Stiff with tension, I attempted to massage a few knots out of my neck while thinking how I could tell Dallas that I needed to cancel our date. He would probably want to try to do something else, and I didn't want to risk bringing him into my dangerous life—not that I had any extra time today anyway.

The shop was quiet because I had come in so early to meet Tony. It gave me a chance to work without interruption. I made several phone calls to check on the progress of Natalie's catering, flowers, cake, and limo service. Valerie from Decadent Catering said she would bring a sample of the dark chocolate truffles

Natalie requested, as well as a platter of cream cheese-stuffed strawberries that she wanted me to try.

Mom e-mailed her "Sweet Five-Petal Crochet Flower Pattern" complete with pictures, and I uploaded it to mashedpotatoesand crafts.com under our tutorial section. I rummaged around in the sewing supplies until I found some yarn and a crochet hook. Ten minutes later, I had made two that I thought might be a perfect embellishment for a thank-you card.

Lorea arrived with a happy glow that increased when she surveyed the remaining wedding gowns in her collection. "My sister called me this morning and said one of her friends wants to look at our dresses. She heard that Natalie bought her gown here. It's starting, Adri."

"Let's just hope Natalie gets more publicity than Sylvia." I didn't want to be a downer, but I felt like I should keep Lorea grounded in case the Rockforts retaliated.

"My bet is on Natalie. Sylvia will just be the jilted ex, no matter what she says."

"Good theory." And it was, especially considering Sylvia had moved to Ketchum to follow Brock Grafton. Rumor was, he hadn't even moved into the "log cabin on steroids" he'd built before Sylvia found out and the Rockforts came to town. They tried to make it look like it was Sylvia's parents who had come up with the idea to purchase a vacation home in Sun Valley, but the tabloids didn't take that spin.

Sylvia the stalker continued to surprise me with the lengths she would go in her quest to capture her man. For the millionth time, I wondered why Brock had dated her in the first place. He must have been attracted to her outward beauty but hightailed it when he discovered the snake within. I glanced at the clock—nearly ten. It was time to call Frankie and find out whether Sylvia's trumped-up wedding would be cancelled. I picked up the phone at the same time I heard the bells over the front door chime.

I turned around with a smile that immediately froze into place. Mrs. Bonnie Rockfort stood in the center of the shop with an imposing eyebrow arched over her fake lashes. She lifted a finely manicured finger and pointed it at me. The light glinted off the dark pink polish. "You have created great emotional turmoil in my home."

Just what I needed. Another torture session. I looked out the window behind Mrs. Rockfort. The caterer would be here in thirty minutes. That meant I needed to get this over with and excuse the leading lady in twenty. I sucked in a breath and put on my funeral face, as Lorea called it. "Mrs. Rockfort, I'm extremely sorry for all that Sylvia has had to go through. Lorea and I have stayed up nights trying to amend this. I even dug through the trash bins looking for clues."

Bonnie Rockfort blanched, and I continued before she could interrupt. "I just want your daughter to be happy, and it breaks my heart that someone would stoop so low as to steal her dress." Next I would hammer home the point I had rehearsed in my mind, appealing to her diva persona. "The only thing I can think of is that someone saw Sylvia here, perhaps a rabid fan. Somehow word got out, and they stole her dress because she's an actress who is also the daughter of one of the world's most renowned actresses." I stepped forward and took Bonnie's hand. "I've heard of people doing crazy things like this before. Once, someone stole a gown right after the bride left on her honeymoon."

Bonnie's fake eyelashes fluttered. "You think someone did this because of me—because we're famous?"

Scrunching up my eyes, I willed tears to come and felt a bit of moisture. The Rockforts weren't the only actors in town. I nodded. "It's terrible, isn't it? When people hear, I'm sure they'll be outraged."

Bonnie studied me for a moment and straightened. "I hadn't thought of it that way, but of course you're right. Sylvia must go on. Famous people must make sacrifices, and if she lets this setback throw her off course, then *they* have won."

Rustling from the back of the shop confirmed that Lorea had likely seen our visitor. I could almost feel her cheering. She had probably been hanging on every word since Bonnie spoke her first sentence.

"I couldn't agree with you more."

Bonnie pressed her lips together and smiled, revealing her too-white teeth. "Have you already cancelled everything?"

I grimaced and let her stew for five, four, three, two, one. "I couldn't reach everyone yet. But I did talk to Frankie."

"Yes, she called me. I told her that Sylvia was suffering, but she still wants to get married. We're thinking of postponing the wedding until August."

"We could arrange that. We'll just push everything back and have more time to make this the most spectacular wedding Sun Valley has ever seen." My smile was genuine this time.

"Sylvia hopes it might be enough time for the police to track down her dress or for a replacement to be shipped from China."

The authentic smile waned, and I struggled to replace it with another fake one. "Bonnie, it's important that she doesn't hang her hopes on that gown. If we find it in the same condition as the others, it would be devastating."

"We can still hope, though."

"You're right. And I'm working with the dressmakers to get a replacement, but Sylvia's was one of a kind, so it might take longer."

Bonnie tapped her foot. "I'm going to tell Sylvia what you said, about who might be responsible for the theft. Her manager would want to know, I think."

"Thank you for coming in, Mrs. Rockfort. Please have Sylvia call me when she finalizes the new wedding date."

"Ta-ta, darling." Bonnie waved as she exited. Her driver held open the door for her on the cream-colored Mercedes parked in front of my shop.

I turned around, and Lorea applauded. "I can't believe it! You just turned the whole thing around. She took the bait." She bounced up and down and then hugged me. "How did you come up with that?"

"I took a drama class in high school."

Lorea high-fived me, and we both giggled. "Your shop is probably going to be on the front page of the tabloids by next week. With the Sylvia-Brock angle *and* the wedding dress stolen by a rabid fan." Lorea grinned. "You're a genius."

At three o'clock, the alarm on my cell phone went off with a message telling me to get ready to pick up Dallas. I groaned and surveyed my office space. Three chocolate truffles and two cream cheese-stuffed strawberries were left on the silver platter Valerie had brought. I grabbed a decorative box that had once held place cards and arranged the treats inside. Then I sent a text to Dallas.

Coming early with a peace offering cuz I can't go up to the hot springs today like we planned. I'm sorry things are so crazy right now.

I wasn't sure how much of a sweet tooth Dallas had, but I figured the confections would do the trick to buy me some forgiveness. My phone pinged with a response.

I understand. No worries if the offering is you.

With a chuckle, I headed out the door. I glanced around the parking area before getting into the Mountaineer, wondering where Tony or his fellow officers might be. The temperature had warmed up significantly in the last few weeks, and I cranked up my air conditioning. It was less than a week into June, so the dry heat of summer hadn't officially descended on the Sun Valley area. On the docket for July would be mostly outdoor weddings held in the evening, but even then, the temperatures would still have a few of my brides glistening.

The realtor's office where Dallas worked was only half a mile from my condo. He had texted me this morning to tell me he had some showings, but he planned to be back early for our date. I pulled in front of a gingerbread-style house. Several of the businesses in our town had renovated old houses into cafés, insurance sales offices, and realty offices. As new businesses came in, they kept the charming village look with their décor.

The heavy wooden door had a glass pane at the top etched with Gold Realty Agency. I pushed the door open and was greeted by a blast of cool air and a hint of lemon scent. There were two desks in the main room, and I could see a couple of rooms-turned-into-offices down the hall. Dallas worked at a desk in the corner, and he looked up when I entered, his face brightening with a smile.

I held out the box of treats. "I'm sorry. Will you take a rain check?"

"Definitely, but this looks good too." He opened the flap to examine the truffles and strawberries and then closed it and set it on his desk. He stepped closer to me and clasped my hand. "Can I see you later tonight? I'm covering a half shift, so I get off at nine."

The bag of diamonds in the cemetery flashed through my mind. I had been trying not to think about my plans for the evening. "If it wouldn't be so boring for you, you could. I have twenty minutes if you want to walk around the block. That's the best I can come up with."

"Can I introduce you to my coworkers first?"

"Sure." I followed him down the hall into the first office. Two women who appeared to be in their forties were on either side of the large room working at computers.

"Kristie, Stephanie, this is my girlfriend, Adrielle Pyper." I struggled to hide my surprise. Our relationship was moving at lightning speed, and I wasn't sure I felt ready to refer to Dallas as my boyfriend.

The women greeted me. "Dallas is such a nice guy. You're a lucky girl."

I didn't think it was possible, but his smile widened. He turned to me. "I'm the lucky one."

"Oh, you're the wedding planner, right?" Stephanie asked.

I nodded.

"That's just perfect," the woman named Kristie said and gave Dallas an exaggerated wink. "She can plan your wedding."

I felt my face heat up, and I tugged on Dallas's hand. Thankfully, he took the cue.

"I'm going to walk around the block. Be back in twenty."

"It was nice to meet you," they said in unison.

"Thanks, uh—you—have a nice day," I stammered and felt my face go another shade of crimson as I followed Dallas out the front door.

"Sorry about that," he said. "I've been talking about you a lot."

"It's okay." It wasn't, though, because I hated how my face turned beet red when I was embarrassed.

We turned right and ambled along under several green ash trees—their branches fully dressed in dark green foliage that provided a cooling respite along the sidewalk. "I'm sorry about today."

"Don't worry about it." Dallas stopped and turned toward me. "I'm glad you came by."

"Now you know why I'm still single."

"I figured you just hadn't met the right person." He leaned closer and slipped his arm around my waist. His gaze was intense, and I stared at him a moment before he kissed me. My eyes fluttered as I gave into the kiss, but my mind wandered back to Dallas's office, thinking about how he'd called me his girlfriend. It took a lot more than three dates for me to classify someone as my boyfriend. Maybe that was because I'd always been too occupied with work for a serious relationship.

Dallas was a great kisser. I allowed myself to enjoy the closeness and warmth of his lips. He trailed his hands through my curls, resting them on my hips. I kissed him once more and then pulled away. "We'd better finish our walk so I can get back to the shop."

Dallas frowned. "You look like you need more mouth-to-mouth."

I laughed as he leaned toward me for another kiss. Then pulling his hand, I moved at a brisk pace around the block. His fingers interlaced with mine as he hurried to keep up with me.

"When can I use my rain check for that trip up to the springs?"

I'd figured he would ask, but I hadn't been able to think beyond the upcoming adventure in the cemetery. "I'm trying to see if I can move some things around this weekend. I might have time after Natalie's bridal shower."

"Are you going to bring your swimsuit?"

"It would be fun to soak, but I don't know if I have enough time."

We had completed the circle and stood in front of his office again. He turned toward me. "You have to take time for yourself."

"Now you sound like my mother."

"Sorry." He placed his hand on my cheek. "I care about you, that's all."

"Thanks. Anyway, summers are my most busy time."

He kissed me on the cheek and held onto my hand as he took a step toward the front door. "See you soon?"

I untangled my hand from his and blew him a kiss, leaving his question unanswered as I slid into the driver's seat.

I felt so confused. One part of me wished I had more time to hang out with Dallas, feel his lips caressing mine—the rest of me felt relieved to be heading back to work. Briette had always told me I hid in my work so I wouldn't have to deal with a real relationship. I wondered if the conflicted feelings I was experiencing lent truth to her evaluation.

Chapter 20

CREAM CHEESE-STUFFED STRAWBERRIES

Rinse one pound of large strawberries. With a paring knife, remove the tops and cores. In a mixing bowl, beat one package of cream cheese, ¼ to ½ cup powdered sugar, and one teaspoon vanilla extract until creamy. Fill a frosting bag with the cream cheese mixture and pipe it into the strawberries. Crush enough graham crackers to fill a ½-cup measure, and dip the strawberry tops in the crumbs, or sprinkle them over the tops. If not serving immediately, refrigerate the strawberries until serving.

Courtesy of www.mashedpotatoesandcrafts.com.

Barely two blocks from Dallas's office, I clicked the air conditioning up another notch and noticed a familiar person to my right. Luke Stetson stood in the front yard of a lovely two-story home painted a muted olive green. His Harley was parked in the driveway, so I figured he must live there.

Watching him water the flowerbeds with a high-powered sprayer attached to a yellow garden hose, I thought of how Luke had stopped during his run and apologized to me and then told me his secret. Before I had a chance to talk myself out of it, I stopped and hopped out of my Mountaineer.

"Hey, you're going to kill those flowers if you don't change the setting on that sprayer."

Luke startled and turned toward me—with the water still going full blast. I screamed as an icy stream hit my midsection.

"Oh, no!" He released the trigger and dropped the hose. "I'll grab a towel."

I didn't say anything, just sucked in my stomach away from the dripping fabric that was my new rayon blouse. At least it would dry quickly. The coral color had deepened from the water, and my khaki capris were a bit soggy around the waistline too.

Luke jumped down the last three steps of his porch and handed me a fluffy blue bath towel. "I'm so sorry. I wasn't thinking—you startled me." The worried look on his face added a few creases to his forehead, and he wiped his hand across it, as if subconsciously smoothing the tanned skin. "Did I ruin your shirt?"

"No, it'll dry quickly in this heat." I blotted at the water on my arms and held the towel awkwardly.

"Sheesh, I can't believe I did that." Luke's expression was contrite, and I couldn't stop myself from laughing.

"Don't worry about it." I handed him the towel. "I was just trying to save your flowers." I motioned to the petunias that had been taking a beating from his trigger finger.

Luke glanced at the flowers, and his shoulders drooped. "I'm not much of a gardener. One of my clients offered to do some landscaping in trade for a bill reduction. He said I needed to water them every day when it heated up."

I pressed my lips together to keep from smirking. The garden hose at my feet vibrated with the pressure from the water. I picked it up, and Luke immediately stepped back. "I'm not going to spray you. Let me show you how to water your flowers so you don't kill them."

"Hey, thanks." He moved closer so he could see the different nozzle settings. "I grew up on the east coast. You don't have to water much there."

"No problem. I grew up an hour and a half from here—in the desert. I know all about irrigating." I explained to him how and when to water the petunias and the few shrubs that banked the sides of his house. Then I handed him back the hose. "You could also install some drip lines, so you wouldn't have to do it by hand."

"Thanks, Adri." There was a question in his eyes, and I realized he probably wondered why I had stopped by his house.

"I didn't know you lived in this neighborhood." I stopped myself before I blurted out that the guy I was dating worked just around the corner.

"Yeah, I moved in two months ago. Bought the place through a realtor who works around the corner."

"No way." I hesitated, wondering if life could be this coincidental. "His name wouldn't be Dallas Reynolds, by chance?"

Luke rubbed the back of his neck with the damp towel. "Yes, do you know him?"

"I'm on my way back from his office right now." I was embarking on dangerous territory, and I could anticipate what the next question might be—boyfriend? The problem was, I didn't know how I would answer it. Luke was more tactful than I deserved.

"Thinking of buying some property?"

"No, I bought a condo three blocks from here." I pointed down the street. "You know the ones with the river rock and tan stucco and a one-car garage?"

"Yeah, that's a nice area. Are you close to the road or farther back?"

"Mine is the third one in the complex."

"Great location. So, how do you know Dallas?"

Here was where I needed to decide how much explanation I wanted to give. Smoothing the damp material of my blouse, I looked at the ground. "He wanted me to go to lunch." I raised my eyes to Luke's to gauge his reaction. "But this is the best I could do today."

"Huh. Small world." The skin around his eyes tightened, but then he straightened and gave me a look I was sure he'd used in court before. "Do you like him a lot?"

"We've been dating for about two weeks. He's very nice, and he likes weddings." I lifted my chin and waited to see how he would react to my little barb.

Luke laughed but remained focused. "You didn't answer my question."

He definitely was a lawyer. I nodded. "Yes. I like Dallas."

"But?"

"I didn't say *but.*"

"Yes, you did—I mean, you didn't *say* it, but you didn't have to. I could hear it in your voice. You're hesitant."

I narrowed my eyes. "What? Are you cross-examining me now?"

He laughed again. "I'm just trying to figure you out. What's so hard about admitting you're not into this guy?"

I swallowed and kept eye contact with Luke. "It's not that." I blew out a breath. Might as well get it off my chest. "It's just that he already refers to me as his girlfriend. I like him, but he's moving kind of fast."

Luke tilted his head and took a step closer to me. "So you'd be open to dating other guys?"

"Does that make me seem like a bad person?"

"No, it means you're careful and honest with yourself." He stared at me for a moment. The rich blue of his eyes held my focus. He lowered his voice. "It makes me want to ask you out."

I felt my face go slack, and I struggled to regain my composure.

"I don't want you to get the wrong idea about me." He twisted the towel between his hands. "I don't usually, uh, date, but you know my story. Anyway, I'd just like to hang out."

There it was again. I felt like he was talking himself out of liking me. He let go of the towel, and I watched it slowly unwind. It was about the least compelling invitation for a date I'd ever received, but something about the storm clouds in his eyes kept me riveted. I wanted to know more about him, in spite of Dallas. "This is an incredibly busy time for me. You know—June is the month for weddings."

Luke nodded and brushed his hand past mine. "Just dinner. I—well, you're the only one I've told . . ." His mouth opened as if to say more, but he clamped it shut. Then he touched my wrist and whispered, "Think about it."

I swallowed and looked at the ground, unsure of how to answer. Then I remembered why I had stopped in the first place.

"Mind your manners with those petunias, and they'll keep blooming into September." I had skirted his question, but it was the best I could do.

He saluted me. With a wave, I got into my car and hurried back to work. The detour had cost me another twenty minutes.

Luke's invitation for a date pressed against the back of my brain. He was both infuriating and attractive, but at the same time I wasn't sure if I should trust him. He said he just wanted to hang out and he had shared his past, but what if Luke's story was something he made up to gain my trust?

I mulled that over for a few blocks. No, the idea was silly. He was a divorce lawyer, not a criminal—depending on who you asked, of course. The encounter we'd had on the running trail had calmed my suspicions. I thought of the emotion I'd seen on Luke's face. He deserved an award if that was an act.

But still, there had to be more than one person involved with the diamonds. What if Luke was staking me out? It wouldn't be hard for him to take my picture. He knew what time I usually ran and was familiar with my route. My thoughts spiraled out of control as I tried to pin the blame on someone, anyone. The faceless enemy made me feel so much more vulnerable.

I was afraid to go home, so I worked until the last possible minute and then texted Tony that I'd be home in ten minutes to change into my running clothes and be on my way. Tux bumped up against the patio window when I got home, and I opened the door and cuddled him for a moment before refilling his cat dish. "Wish me luck," I murmured as I set him down.

Briette smiled up at me from the picture frame, and I touched it as I came into my bedroom. I could be brave tonight. Ten minutes later, I walked out to my vehicle, stretched, and climbed inside. Tony had told me to take a couple of switchbacks so it would seem like I was trying to throw the thief off my trail. I drove toward Warm Springs Road again, but this time I turned off onto a side street that didn't offer a hiding place. I turned around and drove to the park. I counted to one hundred before getting out, adjusted the laces on my shoes and headed for the path. Without a backward glance, I began running, hoping Tony and his gang were as close by as he said they'd be. I usually didn't run this late at night, so if the thief was as attentive as I thought, he would know the diamonds were on the move.

With each step, I felt my anxiety heighten. I kept reminding myself to breathe. My iPod was snug on my arm, but no sound came from the earbuds. I wanted to be alert to any strange noises along the way.

Fifteen minutes into my run, I could feel the tension from my shoulders radiating up my neck. *Relax, Adri.* I checked my watch—it was nearly eight twenty, and I was almost to the entrance of the cemetery. I had run way too fast. Tony planned to pass by me on the trail around eight forty. At this rate, I'd be on my way back, a mere half mile from my car. I worried I would pass the meeting point before Tony could get there. I needed to kill some time.

The cemetery had no visitors that I could see. I couldn't resist looking behind me as I entered. No one followed, but I couldn't shake the oppressive feeling of someone watching. I ran toward Hemingway's grave and darted between the large fir trees flanking the slab marked with the famed writer's name. I paused and looked around again.

A slight breeze lifted the pine boughs, and I could hear the tree creak in the stillness. My shoulders rippled in an involuntary shiver. Taking a deep breath, I ran across the cemetery toward the rusty bird feeder. As I approached the tree, my stomach clenched. The bird feeder was gone.

For a second I panicked, my eyes scanning the branches and the surrounding headstones. Then I caught sight of the feeder lying haphazardly in a mound of grass. I dropped to my knees and reached my hand inside. Rusty metal chafed against my skin as my hand closed around the Ziploc bag. I pulled it out and checked it carefully. I didn't dare unwind it, but I could tell it hadn't been touched.

Brushing off a few more flecks of rusty debris, I stuffed the bag into my sports bra and raised my body into a crouch. My heart pounded in my ears as I rotated slowly, peering out from under the tree. A brilliant sunset had tinged the clouds pink and purple. It was hard to ignore the particularly large cumulus cloud hovering right over the sun, tinged in gold from the last rays as the orb ducked beneath the horizon.

Dusky shadows erased the fine details of the day, making it harder for me to see clearly. Tony and I had talked about that. I didn't like running in semidarkness, but he insisted it would be to our advantage. A sudden movement to my right and a flapping sound nearly gave me a heart attack. I bolted and ran about twenty-five yards at a sprint before my senses caught up to each other. It was only a bird. I glanced behind me. I was still safe, but I didn't stop running.

With the cemetery behind me and the diamonds against my chest, I entered the unknown of the bike trail with its multitudinous bushes and weeds flanking the path. Every shrub seemed like the perfect place for a criminal to hide. I reminded myself that policemen were stationed at regular intervals. An officer had probably been at the cemetery, and I just hadn't seen him.

Checking my watch, I slowed my pace to a comfortable jog. I was still too early, so I stopped for a moment to adjust my shoes. Adrenaline buzzed along my nerves as I retied my laces. Every sound made my heart jump, and it took all my willpower to keep from sprinting down the trail again at full speed. My pace was much slower than usual, but I didn't want to slow to a walk. I hoped Tony would be early.

The paved bike trail was one of my favorite features of the Sun Valley area. It ran alongside the highway, and on more than one occasion I had followed the trail the full ten miles to Hailey, the town next to Ketchum. The road was quiet, and the lack of traffic added to the stillness of the encroaching night. Each footfall reverberated in my ears, and I strained my eyes for any sign of Tony or another police officer.

I had at least another half mile to go before the drop point with Tony, but I would still get there before eight-forty. With another glance behind me, I slowed my pace again. The trail appeared empty, but I could see only about twenty yards into the ever-darkening night. I faced forward again, concentrating on my breathing instead of the fear clawing at my insides.

The trail curved slightly to the right, and a formidable-looking bush in need of a trim reached for my bare legs. I sidestepped the branch and ran into something solid that hadn't been there a millisecond before.

Before I could react, strong arms pulled me off the trail and through the scraggly sagebrush. One hand reached up to cover my mouth, extinguishing my rising scream.

Rachelle J. Christensen

"I know you have the diamonds," a low voice spoke right next to my ear. "If you want to stay alive, you'll cooperate."

I felt something jab me in the back, and I recoiled. All of my self-assurances that this little operation would go off without a hitch left the instant I realized he had a gun.

He prodded me with the weapon, and I winced. "Now let's take a little walk."

I tripped through the undergrowth off the trail as we headed away from the road toward the mountain. Thoughts of struggling against him and biting his hand flitted through my mind, but the touch of cold steel against my back killed any courageous ideas. I held onto the hope that someone was coming. The police had been watching me, and this man didn't know it. As we moved farther from the path, I began to worry about how wide a surveillance they had set up.

The man pushed me up a rise and around a couple of large boulders. He shoved me to the ground and put his knee in my back. I grunted as my face hit the dirt. Tears stung my eyes as several rocks bit into my skin.

"Were you hoping to keep those diamonds for yourself?" I could feel his hot breath on my ear as he whispered, "Like you would even know what to do with them. Lucky me, you decided not to take them to the police first thing."

I did not need a reminder of how stupid I had been. I'm a fast learner. Tony would be the first to know if anything out of the ordinary happened from now on. At least he knew now—but where was he?

The man turned me over and grabbed my wrists so hard I cried out. "Don't try to fight, or things will get bad in a hurry."

Squinting, I tried to take in details of my abductor. His dark

234

hair brushed the tops of his shoulders. Close-shaved sideburns reached down and around his jaw and ended in a well-trimmed goatee. His fingers gripped the black gun that reminded me of Tony's weapon—I think he called it a Glock—and I didn't like the way the barrel was pointed at my head.

He straddled me and leaned forward. "Now, where are the diamonds?"

Chapter 21

COMFORT ME HOT COCOA

Heat one cup milk, two tablespoons sugar, one tablespoon cocoa, a pinch of salt, and ½ teaspoon vanilla in a saucepan at medium temperature. Do not allow to boil. When mixture is warm, add a little half-and-half or top with whipped cream and a sprinkle of cinnamon. Courtesy of www.mashedpotatoesandcrafts.com.

The darkness made everything fuzzy, but he was close enough that I could see his face. I studied him as I tried to catch my breath. With a hard swallow, I struggled to formulate an answer to his question.

I noticed a large diamond earring stud in each ear, and my heartbeat ratcheted up another notch. My mind fled to the incident with the silver Camry on my parents' canal bank. The man had turned to look at me, and the setting sun had glinted off something near his face. A chill cascaded down my spine.

"You've been following me the whole time." I wondered if

there was more than one guy, or if he was it. The police had figured a group of men were working together, and I had assumed the same thing, but only one man aimed a gun at me.

Some of my hair had come loose from the ponytail during the scuffle, and it hung down over one eye. I twisted my head, trying to get the hair to move, but froze when he reached his hand toward me. He pushed the hair away from my face and stared at me. "Observant little thing, aren't you? But not very smart to take something that doesn't belong to you."

"I was going to give them to you." My voice cracked, and I swallowed, trying to clear the fear that coated my vocal cords.

"Where are they?" He moved the barrel of the gun closer, and I couldn't stop the tears from leaking out the sides of my eyes.

"I was on my way to get them."

He let go of my hands and slapped my face. I cried out and struggled against him. He pressed his meaty palm against my mouth so hard I tasted blood. Then he removed his hand. "I'm not a killer, but there's a first time for everything."

"Please, I was just doing what you said."

"I said to give me the diamonds. I'm happy to strip-search you, or you can hand them over. What'll it be?"

The tears came now. I wanted to scream. He was going to win. After everything, he would get the diamonds, and then he'd kill me. He hadn't tried to hide his face. I could pick him out of a lineup. I could tell a sketch artist about the gold ring he wore in his eyebrow or the mole on his neck.

"Okay, I'll tell you where they are."

He narrowed his eyes, took my hands, and pushed them down by my sides. He knelt on my arms, and I cried out as the pressure of his legs pushed my hands against the hard ground until I felt my bones would break.

"Sorry about that, but you're taking too long." He shifted so he leaned back on his heels but still put enough weight on my arms to keep me immobile. The gun was an ever-present reminder of how helpless I was in the situation. He reached under my shirt and groped my chest.

"Stop! I said I'd tell you where they are," I cried.

But it was too late. He felt the bulge of the bag in my bra and reached inside. His hand strayed for a moment, and then he pulled the bag out with a grin. "That was fun. Maybe I should check for more hiding places."

"No, that's all of them. Please."

He laughed and carefully unrolled the bag. He flicked on a penlight, and the diamonds shimmered through the plastic. "See, that wasn't so bad. Now, what to do with you?" He leaned closer. "I have several ideas. Want to hear them?"

I didn't respond but dug through the recesses of my mind for any fighting techniques that might help me. Squeezing my eyes shut, I held my breath. That's when I heard something. My eyes flew open. The man kept talking about what he was going to do with me, but I heard another sound.

A crunching noise, like someone approaching through the weeds to the left. I kept perfectly still, praying for deliverance. The diamond thief stopped talking and turned his head toward the sound just as a body collided into him. They tumbled to the ground with grunts and cursing. Someone's foot connected with my left thigh as I rolled away, but I didn't stop.

I tried to stand up but fell forward as my legs tingled. My

attacker's weight had slowed my circulation. Sharp needles of pain pricked my feet as I rotated them, preparing to run.

The two men were still fighting, but it was too dark for me to see who was saving me. I could hear the impact of them hitting each other as I scrambled farther away. Then someone cried out, and the movement halted.

I paused and looked behind me. Who had won the fight? I wondered if I could hide somewhere until it was safe or if I should start running again. I heard a gurgling noise and felt the ground for something I could use to protect myself. My hand closed around a jagged rock, and I crept back toward the two men.

A light bounced along the trail ahead of me. Someone rushed past me as I approached. It was a police officer with a high-powered flashlight. The beam jogged back and forth and settled on the two men. One was on top of the other, his hands squeezing the man's throat.

"Stop! Don't kill him!" Tony shouted as he approached with his gun drawn. He stood next to an officer in running gear. Tony shone his flashlight on the man strangling the diamond thief. "Put your hands in the air."

"Dallas?" I cried out as the man doing the strangling turned his face toward me. The fury in his eyes vanished abruptly, and he became the kind and gentle Dallas I knew. He turned his gaze back to the man, at his hands squeezing the man's windpipe, and shuddered. He yanked his hands away.

Another officer shone his light toward me. "You know him?"

"That's Dallas Reynolds. He saved my life."

Dallas jumped off the man and ran to me. He opened his arms and pulled me tight to his chest. I could feel his heart racing against mine and a subtle trembling throughout his body.

The adrenaline rush flowed out of me in the form of tears, and I clutched Dallas and cried into the soft red cotton of his shirt. I could hear the police all around us, moving to examine the criminal.

"Adri, I'm so sorry I wasn't here sooner," Dallas murmured. "I got off work early and tried to call you, but I couldn't reach you."

I lifted my face toward his. "You came just in time." I started to ask him what he meant by not getting here sooner, but he covered my mouth with a tender kiss. A sob broke free from my throat. "Oh, Dallas. I was so scared."

"Me too." He patted my back. "I love you so much. Are you hurt? I couldn't bear it if something happened to you."

I leaned against him and felt the concern he had for me in the way he held me. "I'm okay now."

"But he hurt you." Dallas moved my hair from my cheek. "He hit you."

"I'm okay now, thanks to you."

"But did I get here in time?" Dallas stepped back and looked me up and down. "Did he . . . ?"

"He touched me, but you came just in time." I buried my face against his chest and murmured, "Did you kill him?"

"No, but I should have." The vengeance in his voice was powerful, and frightening.

"No. It's better to give him to the police."

Something passed through his eyes, and he shook his head. "Just so long as you're okay." He tipped his head down and caressed my lips with his. I kissed him back with more passion than I probably had ever felt before.

I still couldn't believe that Dallas had saved my life. He'd told me he loved me, and I knew he meant it. I had to admit, the way he held me at that moment made me feel something I hadn't before.

His hands moved in a slow circle on my back and then reached up to hold my head as he continued to kiss me. I pressed against him, feeling the warmth and security he exuded. Then he broke contact. "Why were you running so late at night?"

My shoulders drooped, and I took an uneven breath that caught on another sob. "It's a long story, but I'll tell you all about it."

Dallas pulled me close again, and I could hear his breath heaving in and out of his chest. I put my hand on his cheek and kissed him, moving my hand to his heart. "I need you to be calm for me."

"Sorry. I—he—I almost lost you." He glared in the direction of the man now standing, handcuffed, next to Tony.

He spoke the truth, but it wasn't something I wanted to dwell on. If Dallas had been a few minutes later, I might not be alive. "Thank you."

Tony stepped up and clapped Dallas on the shoulder. "I don't know how you happened to be in this area, but we're all grateful you were." Tony looked at me. "Are you all right?"

I nodded and put a hand to my swollen cheek.

Tony's brow creased with concern. "We have an EMT. Maybe you should get checked out."

"No, I'm just bruised and shaky." I let Dallas support some of my weight as I leaned against him. Tony studied Dallas, and I realized I hadn't introduced them. "Tony, this is—" I paused and glanced at Dallas. The word was on the tip of my tongue, but I still felt unsure. Obviously Tony had seen us lip-locked, so I might as well say it. "This is my boyfriend, Dallas Reynolds. Dallas, this is Detective Ford."

The look in Dallas's eyes made me thankful I had used the boyfriend label. I hadn't thought he'd noticed my lack of commitment, but he had. The two men shook hands, and Tony scrutinized Dallas. "How did you happen to be here? Did you see that man take Adri?"

With one arm Dallas held me tight to his side and then lifted his hand to the east. "I went for a drive and saw Adri running along the trail. I parked at the first pullout I came to and ran back to meet her. But then she wasn't there, and I heard a scream." He paused and looked down at me. "I didn't think. I ran as fast as I could and found that guy on top of her."

"I'm grateful you intervened, but that was a huge risk. He was armed."

"I knocked his gun loose when I jumped him," Dallas said.

Tony nodded and then looked at me as if considering something. "Adri, it's important that you not tell Dallas any of the particulars until we get things sorted out."

I felt Dallas's arm tense. I touched his hand and looked at Tony. "He deserves to know what's going on."

"I'm a witness, and I saved her. You can trust me," Dallas said.

"I know I can trust you, but I have to follow protocol," Tony said. He shook his head and looked at me. "Have you said anything to him?"

"There hasn't been time. Can't you tell him why we're out here? At least the basics?"

"I know it's hard to understand, but if you'll please hold off until we've taken everyone's statements, it would help."

Dallas nodded. "I can wait."

"Okay," I answered with a frown.

"Adri, I know this probably isn't the best timing, but we need to get a statement and ask you a few questions about your encounter with the suspect. And don't kill me, but I just called Wes to see if your parents could come up here to help."

"You didn't." I let my head drop to my chest. "My mom is going to freak."

"I don't want you to be alone after everything that's happened, and I figured you would refuse my help, so I went over your head."

"I can't believe you did that." A part of me felt angry, but the rest felt like crying because I really did need my mom. She would know how to comfort me.

"I can take care of her," Dallas offered. There seemed to be a challenge in his voice. "I could stay with you—sleep on your couch." There it was again. The love in his eyes was evident. I felt grateful that Tony had interfered because Dallas's offer sounded nice, but I was afraid of getting carried away in the moment and going too far down the relationship path. It was still a leap for me to refer to him as my boyfriend. I needed to keep my head clear.

"Thanks, Dallas, but as much as I hate to admit it, Tony did the right thing. I have a huge bridal shower tomorrow, and I'm going to need my mother's help."

"And we're going to need at least an hour of your time at the station," Tony added. "Dallas, there's an officer ready to take your statement now. Then you're free to go."

Dallas frowned. "I could drive Adri."

Tony shook his head. "Actually, I'd feel better if she came with me. We still don't know if this guy was working alone, or if there is someone else still waiting for an opportunity."

I sucked in a breath.

"I don't want to scare you," Tony said, "but I promised to be up front with you, and that's one aspect of this investigation. We'll know more once we question the suspect."

"Okay." I turned to Dallas. "I'm sorry."

Tony cleared his throat. "I'll give you two a minute before we go."

"I don't want to let you out of my sight," Dallas murmured. He pulled me close enough that I could feel his warm breath on my forehead. "Will you call me when you're finished at the station? I don't care how late it is."

"Of course. And I'll tell you everything as soon as I get the okay. I'm sorry I can't right now."

"That doesn't matter. You are the most important thing, and as long as you promise you'll be safe, I'll let you go with that officer."

I started to say that we didn't really have a choice, but the look in his eyes stopped me. "Thank you."

"I love you, Adri. I won't be able to think straight until I have you in my arms again."

I knew he was hoping for reciprocation, but I couldn't say the "L" word yet. Instead, I pressed my mouth against his, kissing the words away and hoping that would be enough until I figured things out. I wrapped my arms around his neck and deepened the kiss. His mouth moved against mine, and he tightened his hold on me.

He was strong—not with bulging muscles but a wiry build I hadn't really noticed until tonight. The fact that he had overpowered the man who'd attacked me attested to his strength. I could feel the smooth lines of his chest muscles as he held me, and I let one hand slide down his arm to feel the power in his bicep. I pulled away and smiled. "I'm glad you're stronger than you look."

Dallas chuckled. "I'm glad you're mine."

I pecked his cheek and stepped away. "I'll call you."

He grabbed my hand and held on to my fingertips for a moment. "I'll be waiting."

Tony helped me into a patrol car and gave me a scratchy

wool blanket. I draped it over my lap and took deep breaths as my body trembled. He put the cruiser in gear and glanced at me. "You could be experiencing some shock from everything that happened. I noticed you were shaking." He handed me a bottle of juice. "Drink this."

I unscrewed the cap and took a large swallow. "Where were you?" My voice raised in pitch, but I didn't care. "I thought you said there would be officers along the path watching out for me."

"There were, but that guy knocked one of our men out. He came out of nowhere. I'm sorry, Adri. I hate that you had to go through this." He patted the blanket over my leg. "If it helps, Wes already chewed me out."

"Thanks for calling my family. When do you think they'll be here?"

"Probably within the hour."

"I bet they're calling my cell phone every ten seconds. Can we stop by my car and get my stuff?"

"Sure, but if I were you, I'd plan on texting them that you're at the police station. That way, you won't be tempted to say anything yet."

I leaned my head against the seat. The tears were right under the surface, and I kept seeing that man's face leering at me. "I had the diamonds in my sports bra when he found them."

He swore. "That scum. We have the diamonds now, but I'm really sorry about what happened." He glanced at me. "He didn't do anything else, did he?"

"No." My voice sounded flat, and I could feel another lump of tears rising up my throat.

"Hang in there. This isn't something you're going to get over

RACHELLE J. CHRISTENSEN

in a day. We have a victims advocate I want you to see. You could talk to her after you're finished giving your statement."

"I don't have time for that. It's June, and I'm a wedding planner." I moaned. "And tomorrow night is Natalie's bridal shower."

"Take a deep breath, Adri. Drink some more of that juice."

I obeyed and stared ahead at the taillights of another vehicle. Tony pulled into Rotary Park next to my Mountaineer and hopped out with me. I grabbed my cell phone, purse, and a ratty sweatshirt I kept in the backseat, and Tony tucked me back in the police cruiser.

"Looks like you've found time to date somewhere," he said.

My stomach flipped when I thought about the way Dallas had kissed me good-bye. "Dallas is persistent and patient."

"He'd have to be. You're a hard one to nail down. So, how long have you been dating?"

"Only two weeks."

Tony whistled. "And he's already telling you he loves you." He glanced at me with raised eyebrows. "He obviously kisses up to your expectations."

I rolled my eyes. "He is a good kisser, but I'm not ready to be as serious as he wants me to be."

"Don't let him rush you. If he's the right one, he won't do that to you."

"When did you become an expert on relationships?"

"Ouch. Don't be mean—I'm trying here. My hours haven't been the best for socializing, and Ketchum isn't much of a party town, if you haven't noticed."

I laughed. "Unless you're picking up on tourists."

"Yeah, they don't like cops much. We give out too many speeding tickets."

When we arrived at the station, Tony led me into a cramped

246

office. I had pulled the sweatshirt on and kept the blanket over my legs. A perpetual chill had descended over me, and I couldn't seem to get warm. Tony explained that it was the aftereffects of too much stress on my system. Another police detective entered the room behind Tony.

"This is Detective Trevor Hamilton." He indicated the man who stood several inches below Tony's towering six-foot-three frame.

Detective Hamilton's dark hair was receding, and his brown eyes looked kind. "I'm sorry about what you've been through. Let's see if we can gather the info we need and get you home."

Hamilton asked me to recount everything that happened that evening. He turned on a handheld digital recorder and interrupted my narrative every few minutes to ask questions. An hour later, my story was told. I felt completely wiped out.

Tony led me out to the front of the station. I heard my mom before I saw her. "Adri, I've been worried sick!"

She came around the corner and hugged me. "Are you okay?"

I struggled to maintain my composure. "I'm glad you're here."

My dad put his arm around me. "You have some 'splainin' to do, young lady."

Tony approached and greeted my dad. They spoke in low voices, and then Tony turned to me. "It's okay to tell your parents what's going on, but it can't travel any further than that."

"Them but not Dallas?"

Tony frowned. "Look, I know you like the guy, but I still need to check him out. It's a bit of a coincidence that he happened along."

I bristled. "Good thing for me he did." Tony couldn't suspect Dallas, not after he'd just saved me.

"It's my job. I'm sure he's fine." He studied my face for a moment, and I reminded myself that Tony was a good cop.

I nodded. "Okay."

Tony turned to go, but Mom grasped his hand. "Thank you," she whispered.

Tony hugged my mom and met my eyes over her shoulder. "Call me if you think of anything else, Adri."

I nodded and let my parents guide me out to the parking lot. It was almost eleven by the time Mom and Dad drove me to my vehicle with a police officer following us. Dad insisted on driving the Mountaineer and commanded me to stay put. I obeyed, and he followed us to my condo. When we pulled up, I jumped out and motioned for Dad to park in front of the garage.

"You're still parking outside?" My dad jerked his thumb toward the garage. "Guess I know what I'll be doing tomorrow."

I opened my mouth to protest but thought better of it. Dad would need something to keep him busy, and I remembered the sturdy metal shelves I had purchased. "I bought some shelves that need to be put together and hung. That would help me clear some space to park."

"We'll worry about that later," Mom said. "Let's get you inside." They followed me up the front steps and into the house. "And you don't have to explain anything now. Go get cleaned up first."

"Thanks, guys. Make yourselves at home." I hurried to my bedroom and gasped when I paused in front of the large mirror hanging above my dresser. The right side of my face was swollen and scratched. Bits of mascara dotted my face, and my eyes were red and puffy.

I stripped down and jumped into the shower. Scrubbing at the places my attacker had touched, I wished that the remembered feel of his hands would go away. I wished that every trace of this night could wash down the drain like so many soap bubbles, but at least it was over.

The police had the diamonds, and they were contacting the FBI to continue the investigation into the shipping company that had brought in the wedding gowns. Walter Mayfield still couldn't be reached. When I thought of him, a nervous jolt ran through me. Had Walter been in the middle of this, or was he a victim?

Tony hoped the man who had attacked me would talk, but what if he didn't? I rinsed my hair and reminded myself that the diamonds were no longer in my possession and I didn't have to worry. I dried off and put on some cozy pajamas. Even though it was June, the temperatures in Ketchum dropped considerably because we were nestled against the mountains. The chill that had settled over me since Dallas rescued me was finally starting to subside.

That thought reminded me that I needed to update Dallas. I sent him a text apologizing that I couldn't share details yet. I ended by thanking him again for saving my life, and then I turned my phone off so if he responded, I wouldn't be tempted to say something Tony had asked me not to.

I found my parents in the kitchen. "I whipped up some home-made hot cocoa for you." Mom handed me a steaming mug. "It would be better with cream, but I found a few marshmallows."

I took a sip. "Thanks, Mom. You're the best."

My dad patted the chair next to him at my dinette table. "I'm ready for your story."

As I pulled the chair out, I heard a muffled meow.

"Oh, Tux. I bet you're hungry." I set down my mug of cocoa

and opened the patio door. Tux mewed again, and I picked up the kitten, holding his warm body close to me.

"I didn't know you had a cat," Dad said.

"Meet Tux." I patted the kitten's head. "He was hanging around my shop, so I brought him home." I refilled his food dish and set the kitten outside to eat.

"He's a cute little thing." My mom sat next to my dad and watched Tux through the window.

I settled into my chair and wrapped my hands around the warm mug. "I'll tell you my story if you promise not to tell me how foolish I've been."

My dad chuckled.

"It all started when I offered to help Lorea with some alterations. She was behind on the bridesmaids' dresses, so I told her I could pick out the hem of Natalie's wedding gown."

It was after two when we finally called it a night, and I could barely keep my eyes open. My parents had plenty more questions, but Mom told Dad he'd have to wait.

"She needs her strength for tomorrow."

"Yeah, Natalie's bridal shower starts at six. It's a good thing it's hers and not Sylvia's, or you'd have to commit me right about now." Natalie would be forgiving of the few last-minute items I hadn't completed.

"I'll help you. Don't worry yourself into a frenzy."

I hugged my mom and dad. "Thanks for being here."

My parents crashed in my guest room on an air mattress, and thanks to sheer exhaustion, I slept until eight the next morning.

Chapter 22

STRIKE A POSE

Set up a photo booth at the reception for a lasting memory of your guests. Select fun props that coordinate with the wedding theme and encourage guests to choose a prop and strike a pose. Courtesy of www.mashedpotatoesandcrafts.com.

The following afternoon Mom helped me load the Mountaineer with everything I needed to take to the shower. Natalie had selected a decorative box of chocolates and a hand-made bag for each of her five bridesmaids. Brock had offered to pay for everything, but she nonetheless had used her own hard-earned money for the gifts. Although she wanted a simple wedding, she had requested several elegant touches. For Brock's part, he tried to honor her wishes while pleasing his family and the public eye, so the wedding would be a bit larger than the original plan.

The florist, Melissa Catmull, stopped by at ten o'clock and

brought in a gorgeous arrangement of roses. I quirked my eyebrow as I looked at it. The roses were stunning, pink with white marbling through the petals, but they weren't the dinner-plate dahlias Natalie had ordered for today.

Melissa's strappy red heels clicked as she approached me with a smile. "These are for you. Special delivery." She indicated the white card tucked between the blossoms and then handed me the bouquet. "I'll be right back to have you check the arrangement for this evening."

My heart warmed as I reached for the card. Dallas was so thoughtful. He'd texted me several times that morning, checking to see if I was okay. I inhaled the strong scent that antique roses hold in rich abundance. The tissue paper crinkled as I pulled the card out of the tiny envelope. I scanned the note and sighed. It wasn't from Dallas, and I didn't like the way my heart flip-flopped with anticipation as I read the card.

Adri,
I'd better leave the watering to the professionals. Sorry about your shirt.
Please call me.
Luke

His phone number trailed after his signature, and a grin tugged at the corners of my mouth. Why was I even thinking of calling him?

Mom was in and out of the shop through the back entrance, loading the last of the supplies. I didn't want her to see the note from Luke. I could only imagine the discussion she and Jenna had about me after I left Sunday.

"Those are beautiful. Who sent them?" Lorea came up behind

me and snatched the card before I could hide it. She read it and then waved it in front of me. "What's this all about?"

"Turns out 'the hottie' lives just around the corner from me." I laughed when Lorea jumped up and down in place, waiting for more. "And Dallas was the agent who sold him his house."

"That's a crazy coincidence. So he knows your boyfriend, but he still asked you out?" Lorea narrowed her eyes. "You did tell him you were dating Dallas, didn't you?"

"Yes, give me some credit." I tipped a rose forward and sniffed. "He grilled me about Dallas—told me he could tell I wasn't serious about him and that I should date other people."

"Wow, he's presumptuous."

"Yeah, that too."

Lorea waved the card at me again. "Just go out with him. I can tell you want to."

I grabbed the card and tucked it under the vase of roses. "I even told Tony that Dallas is my boyfriend."

"So, is that what your heart wants?"

Leave it to Lorea to get straight to the point. I sighed. "I don't know. When he saved me—it was incredible. I felt so much love from him. I've never had someone be so attentive before. I like it."

"But you're not sure about him."

"We haven't known each other very long. At first he was painfully shy, but he got over that pretty fast, and now he's totally into me. He's a great kisser, but sometimes he seems too intense." I thought about it and swallowed. "He almost killed that guy with his bare hands."

"So I heard. I'd be kissing him too."

"I didn't think he was capable of something like that. He was so angry."

"You worry too much. Of course he'd be angry. The guy was going to kill you . . . or something."

I cringed, thinking of that man's hot hands on my chest.

"Either way, you have to call Luke." Lorea touched one of the velvety rose petals. "I don't think it would hurt anything to meet him for lunch. He already knows about Dallas. It's not like you're sneaking around. Maybe it will help you decide what to do."

"Please don't mention any of this to my mom."

"If you promise to call him."

With a huff, I moved the roses to my planning desk. "Okay, if I have time."

"Make time." Lorea returned to the back of the shop.

Dallas called me twenty minutes later. "I need to see you."

"I can't today. It's Natalie's bridal shower, remember? My parents are here to help me, and they might be staying the night again. We won't be home until later."

"I'd be happy to help."

"I appreciate that, Dallas. I really do, but I still feel kind of frazzled, and I can't have any distractions." Darn, that came out wrong. "What I mean is, if you're there, I'll want to be with you instead of running around like a madwoman."

Dallas chuckled. "I think I understand what you're trying to say."

"Forgive me. But at least I have an idea how to make it up to you."

"You don't owe me anything. You've told me again and again how busy this time of year is for you, and I keep pushing you."

Nothing like a guilt trip. Sheesh, he was good. "I'm glad. You've helped me a lot. And I do owe you—a trip to the hot springs. I wonder, are you available Thursday?"

"I'm available whenever you have an opening."

"Okay, let me get this shower over with, and then we can plan."

"Tomorrow sounds great, but I still need to see you, just to make sure you're okay. Can I stop by the shop for a minute?"

It was a good thing we were on the phone so he couldn't see the pained expression on my face. I glanced at the back where Mom was helping Lorea sort through tablecloths and candles for the evening. I wasn't ready to introduce Dallas yet—too many implications. "I'm leaving in half an hour to run some errands. I can make time for a quick lunch."

"That'd be wonderful. I'm in Hailey showing some property. Do you want me to grab a sandwich on my way into town and meet you somewhere?"

"Sounds perfect. Let's stop at the park just off First Street."

I ended the call and hurried back to check off the last of the table decorations. It took some ingenuity, but I told my mom I needed to run a few errands while she finished up with Lorea. An hour later, I met Dallas at the park and ate my sandwich like a ravenous beast.

"I never get to stop for a decent lunch break, so thank you. I need energy today."

Dallas put his arm around me and pulled me toward him. "Thank you. I guess persistence pays off." He kissed my cheek. I leaned my head against his shoulder.

Dallas was charming, and we had some great chemistry, so what was my problem with commitment? The bouquet of roses Luke sent came to mind, and I felt my cheeks grow warm with a twinge of guilt. He was not my type—a divorce attorney who was full of himself. But my initial impression of him had been revised, especially after he'd confessed the truth about his dislike of marriage. I truly didn't believe he'd told me that to reel me in, but it had had that effect on me, nonetheless. I smiled when I recalled the quick gardening lesson I'd given him.

"What are you thinking about?"

I jerked my head upright. "Oh, nothing."

"Must be something good, with a smile like that."

"Just a daydream." I knew my smile didn't hide the nerves playing around the edges of my mouth, but Dallas just smiled back and dipped his head. He kissed me, and his lips lingered on mine for a moment before he broke contact.

I crinkled my sandwich wrapper. "Not the best ingredient for the world's greatest kiss, but thanks."

Dallas chuckled. "I love you, Adri."

I choked. There were those words again. The ones I was so not ready to say. Dallas patted my back as I coughed. When I settled down, I took a big gulp of water. "Sorry, lettuce down the wrong pipe." I hugged him and then murmured, "I need to go. But I'll see you tomorrow afternoon."

Dallas kissed my forehead. "Can't wait."

Every one of the eight tables in Brock's backyard was decorated with a cream linen tablecloth. On top of that was sheer pink lace, and then the centerpieces added a touch of Natalie to the decorations. A round candle about six inches high sat in a hand-thrown pottery bowl. The bowl was half filled with water and lined with smooth river rocks. The candles flickered gently in the breeze that wasn't strong enough to cool my glistening forehead. I always got overheated at events, running back and

DIAMOND RINGS ARE DEADLY THINGS

forth triple-checking things, but as I stopped to admire the setup, I had to admit it was perfect.

The tables had been placed among Brock's wildflower and antique rose gardens. I admired the beautiful setting as I went on a hunt for a lighter. I'd used up the last of my matches relighting the candles.

My heels clicked against the stone pathway winding around the pool and up to the back entrance to the house. Natalie had said Brock kept a few torch lighters in a drawer beside the fridge. I pulled open one of the French doors, ready to make a beeline for the kitchen, and froze.

Brock and Luke turned toward me mid-laugh with glasses in their hands.

"What are you doing here?" Suddenly I remembered something that answered my own question. Luke must have been the lawyer friend Natalie mentioned who drew up the prenuptial agreement. I recalled how upset Natalie was when she first told Lorea, but then the lawyer had explained to her how it could protect both her and Brock from the high-profile life Brock led. She had signed the agreement a couple weeks ago.

"Don't worry. We'll be leaving soon." Brock tilted his head toward Luke. "This is Luke Stetson, my lawyer."

"One of them," Luke interrupted with a smirk. "And I know Adri."

"That's right." Brock snapped his fingers. "She's the wedding planner you were asking me about. Remind me how you two met—something about fried pickles?" Luke's eyes widened, and I caught the warning look he gave Brock. Unfortunately, the intended recipient didn't seem to notice.

Luke's tanned skin couldn't hide the pink on the tips of his ears. Brock laughed and slapped him on the back. "Dude, you've got it bad. What are you waiting for?" He continued, as if completely oblivious to the mortification he was inflicting on Luke. "You know, Natalie and I have been wanting to go on a double date with Luke, but we can't ever get him to commit. You should come, Adri."

My throat tensed. My voice box felt like a locked chest, and someone had just thrown away the key. Luke's expression was pained, and I gave a subtle shake of my head and moved toward the kitchen. "I'm in a hurry," I squeaked and dashed into the other room.

What were the chances I would see Luke here? I pawed through the drawers looking for a lighter and then stopped with a groan. Grabbing a paper towel, I soaked it in cold water and then wrung it out, lightly dabbing my hair line. I turned around and yelped when Luke sauntered into the kitchen.

"I'm sorry." He held up his hands. "I didn't mean to scare you."

I fumbled with the paper towel. "Just startled. I'm a little frazzled today."

"Sorry about Brock. He's pretty gung ho about love lately, if you haven't noticed."

The imported granite countertops had my complete attention.

Luke cleared his throat. "I heard about what happened. Are you okay?"

My head snapped up. "It already made the news?"

He nodded and took a step forward. "I could tell it was the watered-down version, but it mentioned an attempted kidnapping and assault."

"I wish I could give you more details, but everything's under investigation, so please don't ask."

Luke nodded. "I can't believe you're working today."

I lifted my hand to touch the bruised cheek that I had covered generously with concealer and foundation. "My parents came up to help me. My mom has been a lifesaver." I swallowed the nervous lump in my throat. "Thanks for the roses. They're beautiful."

"I'm glad you liked them." Luke gently traced two fingers along my cheek. "Are you sure you're okay?"

It was a struggle to keep from flinching, but when I saw the look in his eyes, any fear zipped out of my system, replaced with fireworks. "Yes, thank you."

"If you have a minute later, I'd love to talk." His voice was low, and his smile looked inviting.

"I'll be here late, cleaning everything up." Heading for the door, I struggled to ignore the curiosity welling up inside. He'd seemed embarrassed moments ago when Brock put him on the spot. What did he want to talk about now?

Luke followed me out past the pool and grabbed my hand. "Adri, this is new territory for me. I'm trying not to think about you, but you keep popping up despite my best efforts." He sighed and stepped closer. The breath of space between us was charged with electricity. "Think about it before you go too much further down that other road."

I scrunched my eyes in a question.

His brow creased, but I could see a twinkle in his eye. "The road that leads to Dallas Reynolds. There's something about him—I don't think he's the right guy for you."

"And how would you know anything about who is the right guy for me?" I tugged at my hand, but he held it, interlacing my fingers with his.

"Because I want to see you, Adri. I want to get to know you. Will you think about it?"

"I need to get back." I couldn't answer his question with my insides shaking like the creamed custard we were about to serve.

He released my hand. I shelved my feelings. There simply wasn't time to conquer the jungle of emotions Luke elicited.

Natalie glowed with happiness the entire evening. I managed to stay focused, and Luke and Brock were gone the next time I made a run to the house. A double success.

During the shower, my mom received a phone call from Wes. Jenna had been throwing up for more than twenty-four hours and couldn't stop, so her doctor wanted her to stay overnight in the hospital. They were putting her on some stronger medication to combat the morning sickness and help her recover from severe dehydration.

"You have to go," I told her.

"But I don't want to leave you," Mom said.

"I know, but Lorea will help me, and you can come back, right?"

Mom nodded and hugged me fiercely. "Please be careful."

She and Dad headed back to my house to grab their stuff so they could leave to take care of Bryn and help Wes with his work on the farm.

Lorea and I cleaned up everything after Natalie's bridal shower in record time. Dad returned to help us haul it all back to the shop before my parents headed back to Rupert.

"Sweetie, are you sure you don't want to come home with us?" Mom asked.

"I can't, Mom. I have so much going on this weekend, and I'm already behind. You go and take care of Jenna."

My dad hugged me. "I'll be back soon to complete your honey-do list."

"Give Brynnie a kiss for me, and thanks for cleaning up my garage." I kissed Dad's cheek.

Mom patted my arm. "I wish I could've met Dallas. Have fun tomorrow."

I didn't tell her I was grateful there hadn't been time to meet him, but I was. I knew Dallas probably wanted to meet my parents, but he wasn't about to push the issue. A part of me wondered if he knew I didn't want him to meet them.

So much had happened so fast. Only a week ago I had sat across from Luke for Thursday specials at Smokehouse BBQ. Since then, Dallas had moved me down the relationship path at lightning speed. It was a path littered with uncertainties that I wasn't sure I was ready to travel.

After my parents left, I drove home. It was almost nine-thirty, and I felt a sense of relief about the upcoming weekend. Natalie's bridal shower had been a success, and I was ready to indulge in a well-deserved bowl of chocolate peanut butter ice cream. My nerves tensed as I approached the front door. A piece of paper rustled in the breeze. It was a full sheet attached to the door with a strip of masking tape.

The oxygen turned heavy in my throat, and I struggled to breathe as I reached for the paper and ripped it off the door. It wasn't note paper. I stared at the glossy eight-by-ten photo and felt fear snaking down my spine. The photo was of Luke standing next to me beside Brock's pool, his hand covering mine. Someone had circled our hands with a black Sharpie marker and written an exclamation point next to the circle.

Tears stung my eyes as I read the message printed across the bottom, also with the black Sharpie:

Only a diamond ring will keep you safe.

I let the picture fall to the ground as I scrambled for my cell phone. By the time Tony answered, I was in hysterics. I struggled to put into words what I had just discovered.

"I'll be right there," Tony said. "Go wait out front."

The picture stared up at me menacingly with the fine hand penned beneath. My breath caught. "The handwriting is different."

"It's okay, Adri," Tony reassured me. "Are you outside?"

I pulled my eyes from the message on the picture. "I never made it inside. It was taped to my front door."

"Good. Hamilton and I are on our way. Can you wait in your car?"

"Yes." I hurried to my Mountaineer, and once inside, double-checked the locks and slid down in the seat. I covered my face with my hands and took ragged breaths. My mind raced through scenarios. Was this somehow connected to Sylvia's missing wedding gown? There must be more diamonds inside the dress, but I didn't know where the dress was.

I heard a tap at my window and screamed. Tony stepped back as I unlocked the door and pushed it open.

"I'm sorry, Adri. I stood there for a couple seconds because I didn't want to scare you, but you weren't moving."

"That's okay." I looked past him to see Detective Hamilton climbing the steps toward the photo.

Tony took my hand and helped me out of the vehicle. "You

look a little pale. Why don't you sit on the steps in the fresh air, and we'll talk?"

I held onto his arm as we walked the few feet toward my door. "I'd like to go in your house and check things out, if that's okay."

I thrust my keys into his hand. "Definitely."

Tony helped me sit and then hurried inside, while Hamilton waited with me. He studied me. "Are you okay? Do you need anything?"

"I'll be fine—just need to breathe." I gave him a weak smile.

Hamilton patted my shoulder. "We'll figure out who's behind this. It's good that you called us right away."

I nodded and leaned against the steps as I viewed the horizon. The last pinkish rays of light had retreated toward the mountains, replaced with pinpricks of glitter scattered across the sky. It was a beautiful night, and I was angry at the person who took the picture for ruining the evening.

"All clear," Tony said as he came back out.

"There must be more diamonds somewhere, and they think Adri has them," Hamilton said.

I flinched. "But I thought that criminal told you everything."

Tony's mouth was set in a grim line. "I thought he did. He said he named everyone involved. He didn't say anything about more diamonds."

"That scum was probably waiting for another package to get lifted out of here. Must be a boss man he hasn't named yet." Hamilton flipped open his notebook and scribbled for a moment before scrutinizing me. "No more secrets?"

I saw Tony's brow furrow in frustration as I opened my mouth to retort. Tony believed me, so I thought better and stepped down my defense. "I told you everything. I value my life, detective. I don't want to be involved in this anymore."

Tony studied the picture for a moment. "So tell me a little more about this."

I glanced at Luke's smile in the photo, and I could tell Tony was trying to piece together the situation, in light of the boyfriend he had met last night. "This is Brock Grafton's pool. I was there for Natalie's bridal shower. Luke was there hanging out with Brock."

"I thought you had a boyfriend. Why is Luke holding your hand?"

I started to explain but then clamped my mouth shut as a realization came over me. "Wait a minute. This picture was taken at Brock's house, on his private property."

That got Hamilton's attention. "That's right. It's a gated property—fenced, with surveillance."

"So the person who took this picture was at the party or found his way around Brock's security system," Tony said.

"But it was a bridal shower—all women—except for Luke and Brock. They were in the house, but they left shortly after things got started."

"How many in attendance?" Hamilton asked.

"Thirty-six." I knew the exact number of attendees because they had been asked to RSVP. "Forty-two were invited."

Tony stood. "We'll have to go over there and check things out in the morning."

"I'm sure Brock will be happy to help you," I said.

"I'm not sure what this means, but I don't think you should stay here tonight," Hamilton said before Tony could comment.

"Do you have somewhere else you could stay? Maybe your boyfriend's?"

My face reddened, and I shook my head. "I could stay with Lorea."

"Good. I'll follow you over." Tony seemed relieved with my answer. I almost asked him what was up before I thought better of it.

"Let me make a call while I grab my things." When I called Lorea and told her what had happened, she said to get myself over to her house. It took me only a few minutes to stuff a bag with overnight necessities and the clothes I planned on wearing up to the springs the next day. The freezer called to me as I passed through the kitchen—I still needed some ice cream. I gave it a longing look filled with chocolate peanut butter desire and then grabbed the carton out of the freezer. I ignored Tony's smile as I stuffed it in a sack and headed out the front door.

"Will you call me as soon as you find anything? And please don't tell Wes about this yet?" I asked Tony as he followed me to the car.

He gave my upper arm a squeeze. "I won't say anything. Please be careful and call me if you notice anything strange."

"We'll have someone posted here and at your friend's house tonight," Hamilton said.

I called Dallas on my way over. "I'm staying at Lorea's tonight, so I may have a bit of a late start in the morning." My voice wobbled, even though I tried to keep it steady.

"What's wrong?" Dallas sounded worried. That helped me relax a bit, for some strange reason.

"Someone left a picture of me on my front door with a cryptic message. The police are investigating." I left out the information of who else was in the picture with me, still not ready to mention his name.

"The police? Wow, you must be on good terms with that detective."

"Tony is a friend of my family's."

"I thought you said everyone relating to the assault was in custody," Dallas said.

"That's what we thought, but now the police aren't sure."

"Adri, I can come over to your house and stay with you."

"I know. But the police recommended I stay somewhere else."

"Would you rather come to my place? Space is at a premium, but I'd love to have your company."

A tingle of longing spread across my shoulders as I considered Dallas's offer. I trusted him to keep me safe, but I hadn't been able to get past my mixed-up feelings. "Thanks, but I think we both know what would happen if I did that, and I'm not quite ready—"

Dallas coughed. "I respect you, Adri. I understand. But if you change your mind, I promise to be on my best behavior."

I laughed. "You're tempting me."

"That's the idea." He chuckled. "Tell me what I can say to get you to change your mind. You already know I love you."

I sighed. Those words were enough to keep me on the path to Lorea's house. They were scary words—ones I wasn't ready to reciprocate. Every time he said them, I felt his disappointment at my inability to respond. "I know. Thanks for understanding."

"Okay." I heard melancholy filling Dallas's voice, but then he buckled down and continued in a chipper voice. "I'll be counting the hours until I see you tomorrow."

"Talk to you later." I tucked my cell phone into my purse, resisting the urge to bang my head against the steering wheel.

My life was an anomaly. I had a boyfriend spouting off his undying love for me every chance he got, and I had a love-hate relationship with Luke, who wanted to spend time with me as long as I understood there was no future. When I thought about it in those terms, it was a no-brainer, but then Luke flashed through my subconscious with the cute dimple in his chin. I remembered how charming he'd been on the day we first met, and I couldn't ignore the attraction I felt when he approached me at Brock's house.

I shuddered when I thought of the photo. What did it mean?

Chapter 23

ICE CUBE BLISS

Add an elegant touch to sparkling water or any bridal party beverage with these flavored ice cubes. Combine a small amount of lemon juice, several lemon slices, and water and then freeze in ice cube trays. You can also freeze fresh blueberries, mint leaves, or raspberries in ice cubes.

Courtesy of www.mashedpotatoesandcrafts.com.

My headlights illuminated the window of Lorea's front room. Lorea would know what to do. She always had the best answers, and tonight I was ready for her no-nonsense attitude. Tony made sure I was safely inside her house and flashed his lights as he drove away.

"Adri, you're like a magnet for danger lately!" Lorea hugged me and led me into her cozy living room. "Let me get you a drink of water."

I heard her rummaging around in the kitchen, and she

returned carrying a glass of water with something floating in it. Before I took a sip, I recognized the tiny green leaves frozen in the ice cubes. "Thanks. These are great."

"I know," Lorea said. "Natalie gave me a tray of those ice cubes from her bridal shower. I love the ones with the blueberries frozen inside, but they were all gone, so you get mint."

The ice clinked in my glass as I drank, and I felt a tiny bit of the tension easing out of my body as I savored the faint taste of peppermint.

"Okay, spill."

"First, I need some ice cream." I grabbed a spoon and plopped down on the couch with my carton.

Lorea grabbed an ice cream scoop and a bowl and handed it to me. "You'll just have to talk with your mouth full, 'cause I need details."

While I scooped ice cream into the bowl, I explained about the picture. I didn't leave out the part about Luke.

"Wait a minute. Luke? He was at the bridal shower, and he held your hand? I didn't see him there. You gotta spill *all* the details, chickee."

"It was nothing. I ran into Brock's house to get a lighter, and Luke was there hanging out with him. Apparently, Luke had mentioned me to Brock, and you know Brock—he doesn't beat around the bush. He wanted Luke and me to go on a double date with him and Natalie. I was embarrassed, and so was Luke, but not enough to reject Brock's invitation."

"He asked you out again?"

My shoulders slumped. "If he wasn't so hot, maybe I'd have the nerve to slap him, but half the time I want to kiss him."

"Ene, zodue zara?" Lorea put her head in her hands. "Yes, you are crazy."

"I'm not, really. I'm just confused. You know me. I've had a hard time dating since . . ."

Lorea touched my shoulder. "I'm not trying to be mean. This is tough, but I think you need to look in the mirror and quit trying to please everyone else. What does *Adri* want?"

I slouched farther down on her sofa. "I don't know."

"I know Dallas is a nice guy, but you have to admit that if Luke is looking that good, you must not be completely satisfied."

"If it had been up to me, I wouldn't have gone on a second date with Dallas. He was all nerves and awkwardness. Then it was like he drank some magic elixir and became this guy who persistently goes after the girl he wants. He's always been sweet, but now he seems to have come into a power of his own. It's kind of nice having someone want me like that, and I can tell he cares about me."

Lorea nodded. "He has done a great job of overcoming his shyness to woo you. But how long are you willing to stick around?"

Licking the back of my spoon, I gave Lorea a conspiratorial look. "He's not afraid to be affectionate anymore. He's a really great kisser."

"So you've mentioned." She raised one eyebrow.

"And it's been a long time since I've been close enough to any-one to make out."

"That's debatable. You were close enough to Luke."

"Lorea!" I reached over and pushed her off her perch on the arm of the sofa.

Lorea laughed and stood up. "Okay, here's the deal. Dallas

gets one more date. If you can't honestly say that you feel an in-kling of love or commitment for him, then you have to let him loose."

I wrinkled my nose. "That doesn't sound fun."

"That's probably because you don't even need to go on an-other date. You know the answer. What about Luke?"

"He's so irritating, such a know-it-all, a . . ." I struggled to find the word I wanted.

"A lawyer?" Lorea said and shrieked when I tossed a decorative pillow her way. "If he wasn't a lawyer, would that change things?"

"Of course." Then I thought of the conversation we'd had ear-lier and clenched my fist tight. "I guess not."

"Why?"

"Because he's still going on about how he's against marriage."

"I think that's just some weird mind game he's playing to keep you interested."

I wanted to tell Lorea about Luke's secret, but I decided to wait. For some reason, he trusted me, and I didn't want to break that trust. I thought of the way he and Brock had bantered with each other and wondered if Brock knew about Luke's wife. No. If he had, I didn't think he would have been so brazen about setting up a double date.

Lorea studied me, and I turned to her and smiled. "I don't think it's a mind game. I think he's committed to his plan. But it doesn't matter, because I'm not going to let that cloud my judg-ment concerning Dallas."

"Oh, really?" Lorea didn't look convinced.

"I'm going to take your advice. Tomorrow, Dallas and I are go-ing up to the hot springs. If I don't feel anything more for him, I'll break up with him."

Lorea held out her pinky. "Swear."

I frowned but hooked my pinky with hers. "I swear. I'll nip it in the bud if there's nothing there."

"It's a little late for nipping," Lorea said. "I wouldn't be surprised if he proposes before the night's over."

I gasped. There was no way we were even close to that.

Chapter 24

A TWIST ON THE RING PILLOW

Tie wedding rings to a vintage or family heirloom Bible using ribbons that match the wedding colors.
Courtesy of www.mashedpotatoesandcrafts.com.

The birds chirped outside the window of the breakfast nook while Lorea and I munched on extra-large apple-cinnamon muffins. I licked some streusel off my finger, figuring that one muffin would equal two meals if I was counting calories, but with the stress I'd had that week, I didn't care.

"Thanks, Lorea. It was fun to stay here." We had talked past midnight. Part of the conversation centered on my trying to convince her to give up her cynical views of love and romance. As usual, I didn't make much headway.

"I'm glad you decided to come. And I know you don't think I'm listening to you about love, but I am. Part of me would like to fall in love again, but until Mr. Right shows up, I'm not going to worry about it," Lorea said.

I definitely didn't want to argue with that progress. "I'll be here when you're ready to plan your wedding." I shied away when Lorea attempted to slug me in the arm.

I checked my phone again. I'd sent a text to Tony asking him for news, but he had yet to respond, which meant there probably wasn't any. My cell phone sang "Marry Me" as I pushed it back into my jeans pocket. I scrunched my eyebrows together when I didn't recognize the number.

"Pyper's Dream Weddings, where happily ever after is your destination."

Lorea snorted, and I pushed her off the stool.

"Hi, Adri. It's Necia."

"Hey. How are things at the store?" Necia owned a cute consignment store called Everybody's Closet, and I frequented it to look for unique pieces for wedding décor and fodder for my *Mashed Potatoes and Crafts* blog. Mom and Jenna had been on an upcycling kick for the past few months.

"I have something that might interest you."

"That's so nice of you to think of me."

"Could you come over this morning?" Necia sounded nervous.

"Uh—sure." It must be something big for Necia to want me to come right away. "How about I head over now?"

"That'd be perfect. Just come around back."

I ended the call and grabbed the rest of my muffin. "I'm going to Everybody's Closet. Necia found something she seemed anxious for me to see. Meet you at the store?"

"I'll be there in the next thirty minutes." Lorea waved as I hustled out the door.

The nice thing about living in a small, touristy town like Ketchum is that it hadn't taken me long to learn the lay of the land. I had made it my job to get to know the members of the Chamber of Commerce. Necia was on the board, so my reasons for making her acquaintance had been twofold.

The consignment store had been in business for more than ten years, and with the recent downturn in the economy, its popularity had risen. Necia always put new items out on Thursdays and Fridays, and the committed thrifters were usually waiting for her store to open at ten. The dashboard on the Mountaineer read fifteen to nine, so she had called me in time to check out whatever she had found before anyone else had a chance to see it.

I had scored major points with Natalie when I bought an old family Bible from the store to use in her wedding ceremony. She planned to tie the rings to the Bible instead of to a ring pillow.

I signaled to turn left into the tiny parking lot and eased over the dip in the pavement. A horn blared behind me, and my heart jumped as I slammed on the brakes. A familiar brown truck showed up in my rearview mirror. I frowned. Why was Colton honking at me? He had stopped his truck alongside the road, so I put the Mountaineer in park and turned to see what he was up to. He jumped from his truck and grabbed a box, heading toward me with a grin.

With a shrug, I opened my door and leaned out as he approached. "Morning, Colton."

"Adri, I'm so glad I saw you. I have a package for you. I think it could be that cupcake stand you ordered the other day. I'm really sorry about how I acted." He held out the box. "I thought it might help if you had it before you opened your shop."

"That's really kind of you, Colton, but you didn't need to

worry. Let me pop the back." I pressed the button to release the liftgate and followed him around to the back of my Mountaineer.

He set the box inside and wiped his hands on his pants. "I hope that helps. I even stopped by your house this morning, but you'd already left. I feel better knowing this is delivered and it won't be knocking around my truck all day."

"Wow, thanks," I said. "Wait—how do you know where I live?" All my packages were delivered to the shop, so I didn't have boxes sitting on my doorstep at home.

Colton grinned. "I'm the delivery man. I know where everyone lives." He winked. "Your neighbor—Lily Rowan—she gets a lot of packages, and I've seen you coming and going a few times."

"Well, thank you again. I appreciate you looking out for me."

"No problem. Tell Lorea hello for me."

I waved and got back in my vehicle. Colton's truck roared by a second later. I hadn't had the heart to tell Colton that Sylvia had postponed her wedding. He'd caught me off guard when he mentioned stopping by my house. It bothered me that he knew where I lived and had made a special trip to deliver this package. I couldn't decide if he was trying to make a good impression on me in the hopes I'd convince Lorea to go out with him someday or if he really was that friendly. *Chill out, Adri!* I thought as I drove across the parking lot and around to the back of Necia's store.

Too much anxiety had me questioning everything lately, even a delivery man's good will. After locking my vehicle, I hurried down the alley. I knocked three times on the large gray metal door, and it echoed across the clear morning. Necia must have been waiting for me because the door swung open just as I pulled my hand away.

"I'm so glad you could come down." She motioned for me to

follow her through the back of the store and then swept a lock of her straight brown hair over her shoulder. "I read the paper this morning. You poor thing. First the stolen wedding gowns, and then to have that awful man attack you. Are you okay?"

"I am now. It's been a stressful couple of weeks." The scent of lavender floated in the air as we passed aisle after aisle of knick-knacks, old books, baskets, ceramics, and antique dolls.

"I'll say. That's why when I found this, I called you right away."

We turned the corner, and my breath caught in my throat. The morning light streaming through the side window caught the rhinestones sewn onto the dress and created a dazzling sparkle. The gown intended for Sylvia Rockfort had somehow ended up in the consignment store.

I hadn't thought of Sylvia for two full days. It had been a wonderful reprieve, since Miss Nostril had haunted my days for the past eight weeks. When I saw her dress, intact, its train billowing down from a second hanger, my knees wobbled. I grabbed a wicker chair for support and sucked in a breath. "Where did you get that?"

"It was in a box out back. Someone left it there last night." Necia watched me. "It's one of yours, isn't it? One of the stolen gowns?"

"We need to call the police." I had learned my lesson. I didn't even want to look at Sylvia's dress without Tony. I dialed his number. "I have a minor emergency, and I need you at Everybody's Closet. Now."

"Are you hurt?" Tony asked.

"No, I'm fine—no danger. I'll explain when you get here."

"Is everything okay?" Necia asked after I hung up.

"I'm glad you called me. The man who attacked me did it because of the wedding gowns."

Necia's eyebrows shot up.

"It's a long story, but I have to wait for Tony's permission before I fill you in."

Tony arrived at the store five minutes later. "Adri, do you have my number on speed dial yet?"

With a smirk, I tipped my head toward the wedding gown.

"Is that . . ."

"Yes. It's Sylvia Rockfort's stolen wedding dress."

"But how did it get here?" He crouched and lifted the bottom of the dress with a closed pen. "And it's in perfect condition, isn't it?"

"I didn't check it over fully. I called you first."

He stood and patted my back. "Good girl. Why don't you take a look now?"

I nodded toward Necia. "She doesn't know what's going on. I didn't tell her. But she called to tell me about this."

Tony pressed his lips together and turned to Necia. "How did you get this dress?"

"Someone left it out back last night. I saw the box first thing this morning. I have no idea where it came from."

Tony scrutinized Necia until I interrupted. "She didn't steal it. Why would she call me?"

"I know, it's just . . ." He hesitated. "This goes no further." He indicated the three of us, and Necia nodded. "We have a big investigation going on with these dresses. Adri found diamonds sewn into the hem of one of them."

Necia's eyes widened, and she covered her mouth. Her gaze flicked toward me and then back to the dress. "Diamonds?"

With a nod, I sat in the wicker chair and reached for the hem of the dress, carefully pulling the satin material through my hands. Tony gave Necia a few more details about the rough diamonds as I studied the fabric. There weren't any odd bulges, and I couldn't find any damage, not even a broken stitch.

Tony watched me examine the fabric and crouched to look at the hem. "Will you be able to tell if anything has been altered?"

"You mean, like if someone already took the diamonds and sewed it back up?"

He nodded.

"Possibly. Lorea's the expert on those things. She would definitely be able to tell if there was any inferior stitching going on."

"This doesn't make any sense." Tony's forehead wrinkled as he studied the dress.

I started to agree but then stopped and considered the gown again. A thought tickled the back of my brain. A few random bits of conversation from Lorea, Sylvia, and her mother congealed into something suspicious.

Lorea and I always believed that Sylvia's wedding was set up to make Brock jealous in some insane hope that he'd break off his engagement to Natalie. We'd made bets on how soon after the nuptials an annulment would come about. Lorea had joked that they'd stop at a drive-through annulment office on the way to their honeymoon and then go their separate ways.

"From the viewpoint of the diamond smuggling, it doesn't make sense, but if we think about it in terms of Sylvia Rockfort, it might."

He stood. "What do you mean?"

I smoothed the dress back down and put one hand on my

hip. "Are you aware of the gossip surrounding Sylvia, Brock, and Natalie?"

Tony rolled his eyes. "Yes, that she's crazy about Brock and hates Natalie, or some such nonsense."

"That would be correct. But have you also read anything about how Sylvia's engagement was invented to make Brock jealous?"

"I don't think she's that crazy," Tony said.

Necia made a choking sound, and I could see that she was trying not to laugh.

"I'm starting to wonder if she ever intended to take it this far." I fingered an embroidered rose on the sleeve of the dress.

"I did ask our perp about this gown, and he acted like he didn't know anything about it. At first I thought he was lying, but then he gave me quite a bit of intel about the other gowns. I didn't understand why he would withhold information about this dress unless it had more diamonds."

He fiddled with the radio clipped to his belt. "I planned on calling you later this morning. I interrogated Jerry—that's his name—last night and again this morning. He doesn't know anything about the picture left on your door. Hamilton and I were getting ready to head out to the Grafton residence to check their security footage, but it looks like that'll have to wait."

That didn't help my mood, but I didn't want to think about the picture and veiled threat. I wanted to figure out why Sylvia's dress had gone missing in the first place. "What if we're looking at two separate thefts?"

"Like, someone stole this dress so she couldn't get married?" Necia asked.

"Not someone. *Sylvia* stole this dress so she couldn't get

married." I paced back and forth in front of the dress, watching how the light reflected off the rhinestones. It was exquisite.

Tony shook his head. "That's a little too far-fetched for me." He reached for the gown.

"I'm going to take this back to the station—,"

"What? But you—"

Tony held up his hand to stop my outburst. "I want you and Lorea to come help me search every square inch of this fabric for hidden diamonds. Once we know it's clear, it will be returned to you."

"Fair enough." I sighed. "I'll call Lorea and see if she can meet us there." Lorea was going to flip her lid if I dragged her to the police station.

For more than an hour, Lorea, Tony, and I examined and reexamined every stitch of that blasted wedding gown. Lorea picked out sections of the hem. There were no diamonds. Tony filled out a report, took some pictures, and lifted a brow. "The dress is yours—or Sylvia's?"

"We refunded her money," Lorea said.

"Probably what she planned on all along," I added.

Tony shook his head. "There's no proof Sylvia took it."

"She was there the next morning," I said. "She's never that early. Then the first chance she got, she called off the wedding."

"Not even circumstantial," Tony continued.

Clenching my hands into fists, I spouted off the thought that had been running through my mind for the past hour. "I've invested a lot of time and resources into planning Sylvia's wedding, and I don't intend to be cheated out of my work. The Rockforts put down a $25,000 deposit, and I'm not giving one cent of it back."

"I think that's fine. They signed a contract with you, didn't they?" Tony asked.

"Yes, but they have a way of dragging people through the mud when they don't get what they want." I glanced at Lorea, and she nodded her agreement. "My business is new, and I can't afford bad reviews—the same goes for Lorea's dress business. Sylvia has already put her through hell over the stolen gown."

"If you want to dance with celebrities, you have to protect your toes. I wouldn't recommend pursuing this," Tony said.

"If she *is* behind this, I want to make sure she's caught and pays restitution."

"But if she already paid for the wedding dress, is it really a crime for her to steal it?" Lorea asked.

"Good point," Tony said. "I think you'd have a difficult time pressing charges against her."

"Then what about letting her know that I know she was behind this?" I could feel the frustration seeping into my tone.

Tony sucked in a breath through his teeth. "Sounds dangerous unless you can find something really solid."

I took a step forward and lowered my voice. "Do I have your permission to use my detective skills?"

Tony groaned, and Lorea laughed.

"I'll take that as a yes. Now let's get this dress back in business, Lorea." I had a few ideas to start my investigation and even a pretty good guess as to how the dress had left my shop.

"I have one more piece of information for you," Tony said. "Jerry, the diamond smuggler, gave us a couple names of people he worked with, but we think they were aliases, so we still don't know who was involved."

"Did he say if they were in Sun Valley?"

"Jerry said he didn't think they were." Tony's phone rang, but before he answered it, he gestured toward us. "Please be careful. We're heading out to Brock's later today to investigate how this person was able to take the picture in the first place."

I followed Lorea out of the station, mulling over the information Tony had shared with us. The revelation that there could be more criminals in the vicinity looking for diamonds or a wedding planner who imported dresses shoved aside my indignant attitude toward Sylvia. Maybe I needed to hope for the best when it came to Sylvia and just give myself a different outlook. The important thing was that we had the dress, and it hadn't been vandalized. But if Jerry, the man in custody, wasn't telling the truth about the whereabouts of his accomplice, what was the diamond smuggler's next move?

Chapter 25

CHOCOLATE CHIP RASPBERRIES

Place one chocolate chip in the center of each raspberry and fill
serving cups with berries. Garnish with mint leaves.
Courtesy of www.mashedpotatoesandcrafts.com.

Dallas entered the shop a few minutes before four o'clock,
looking delicious in dark blue jeans and a gray V-necked shirt. He
had taken extra care in styling his hair. The shiny black strands
were spiked in the front and combed neatly around his ears. His
hands were behind his back, and he grinned when he caught me
staring. I lifted one eyebrow as he stepped forward and surprised
me with a bouquet of white daisies.

"Thank you." I moved to kiss him on the cheek, but he turned
his head and intercepted my mouth. I noticed the intensity in
his eyes again. It made my stomach clench with apprehension,

remembering what Lorea and I had discussed. "Let me put these in a vase."

The daisies were lovely, but as I went to put them in water, it took all my willpower not to glance at the roses blooming on my desk. I shook off thoughts of Luke and concentrated on what Dallas had to offer and how he made me feel. It was nice to be loved. I hoped that spending time with him would help me make a decision. I smiled as I returned to the front of the shop and extended my hand. "Ready?"

"Definitely."

I laughed and tugged on his arm as we headed to the Mountaineer. "Let's go."

"Are you sure you don't want me to drive?" he asked.

"I actually prefer to drive so I don't have to worry about getting carsick on the winding roads." I breathed in deeply. "It's a beautiful day today. I'm so glad we're going up the mountain."

He opened the door for me. "You're in a good mood today."

The compliment made me realize just how much stress I'd been under recently. I hadn't been hiding it as well as I thought. Maybe that was the reason my brain was so muddled when it came to dating. I waited for Dallas to buckle up before pulling out of the parking lot. "I'm trying hard to forget that someone is stalking me. Concentrate on the good things, you know."

"Good things?"

"Like, the last of our stolen dresses was recovered at a consignment store today."

"That is good news. It must not have been ripped to shreds like the others, if you're happy about it."

"In perfect condition." That part still amazed me and was the most significant clue that Sylvia's dress was not part of the diamond smuggling operation. I explained to Dallas how Necia had called me and my resulting suspicions regarding Sylvia's involvement.

"But steal her own dress? I don't think she'd take that risk," he said.

"I agree. I think someone nabbed it for her. I know the why. I just have to figure out the who."

"Does your mind ever stop?"

"Not even when I sleep. If you could see my dreams . . ." I winked at him. "Thanks for coming with me today."

"Thanks for making time for me."

I felt a little guilty. Dallas had done so much to show he cared, and I hadn't been able to reciprocate much. His patience was probably the biggest reason why I had given him so many chances. I glanced at him and then cleared my mind of relationship worries for the moment.

Natalie and Brock had met at the hot springs off Warm Springs Road, and they wanted to exchange vows in a meadow not far from there. In March, I had gone with Natalie and Brock in his Hummer through mud and snowy vegetation to scope out the area. Now I needed to see how everything looked in bloom. It would be much more fun with Dallas tagging along—I was determined to put the disturbing photo of Luke and me out of my mind and enjoy the day with Dallas.

I filled Dallas in on a few of the details of my wedding planner life as we drove, and he shared a funny story about a house he had shown that turned out to be inhabited by bats. We followed Warm Springs Road and entered the Sawtooth National Forest on a bumpy, graveled road. Dallas leaned forward when he saw the wooden sign that read "Frenchmen's Bend Hot Springs 6.5 miles."

"Almost there," he said with a smile.

"On this road, it'll take us at least another fifteen minutes," I said. "But check out this next sign."

Dallas read aloud, "'Entering burned area. Beware of falling trees, rockslides'—when did this happen?"

"A couple of years ago. The burn pattern is really interesting. You'll see." And he did, a few minutes later, as we drove farther into the forest. Black scorch marks reached up the sides of several trees. The fire had devoured parts of the east side of the mountain, but in some areas, the scorch marks took a curious hit-and-miss attitude. We passed entire sections of burned-out forest with fallen logs and then other spots where the fire had merely danced through the trees, licking the dry bark. The charred remnants stood out among the new growth of wildflowers and grasses. I pointed out the creek winding close to the road and veering off only to meet back up with us after a few more switchbacks.

"Pretty amazing that the whole forest didn't burn up," Dallas said.

I nodded. "I know. I'm grateful it didn't." We rounded another bend and left the remnants of the forest fire behind. "Okay, I need to be in wedding planner mode for a bit."

"What does that mean?"

"I want you to take everything in as a potential guest. See what you notice on the way to the wedding ceremony." I tossed him one of my notebooks. "Feel free to jot stuff down."

He picked up the pen from my console and twirled it in his fingers. I could feel him staring at me, and I glanced in his direction. "What?"

"I notice you. You will be a beautiful bride."

I nearly snorted but choked instead, because I realized

he wasn't joking. "Thanks." Okay, time to change the subject. "Natalie and Brock have limited the guest list, but there will still be plenty of the elite in attendance. I want you to help me notice potential problems—things people might complain about because this setting is so different."

"It is a ways out here," Dallas said. "I guess it will make it harder for people to crash the wedding."

"Exactly."

I pulled the Mountaineer off to the side of the road and grabbed my camera. "This is nature's chapel, according to Natalie." I motioned to the meandering creek making its way through a grassy meadow.

"Are you going to haul dance floors and tables out here?" Dallas stepped from the vehicle into the meadow.

"No, the reception will be held at Brock's house—triple the attendance of the ceremony." I clicked a few pictures and surveyed the site. The open expanse of flat land against the backdrop of the mountain was a beautiful setting. Blue wildflowers peeked above the grasses, as if a child had interwoven the blossoms in a stunning design.

The ground felt firm, save a few marshy spots near the creek that I figured would dry up in the next two weeks of higher temperatures. Dallas and I walked the perimeter of the meadow, and I noted the natural backdrop of two blue spruce trees growing above the scrubby bushes by the creek. "We'll set up chairs and place stepping-stones as a walkway to the altar. That way Natalie's heels won't sink into the ground."

"I'm surprised she isn't going barefoot," Dallas said with a smirk.

"Natalie is definitely not someone you can fit into a mold.

She constantly surprises me. I think that's why Brock loves her so much." I followed the course that Natalie would take and stood under the shade of the tree. It would be warm, but the shade would keep the bride and groom from sweating. Hopefully, the wedding party wouldn't melt. A large gauzy canopy would dull the sun's rays, but I planned on breezy summer weather to come through with some light air-conditioning.

Dallas crouched and examined a few wildflowers while I continued to snap pictures and take notes. It cheered me to think of Natalie's special day. She would get the small, private wedding ceremony she wanted, and the reception would placate Brock's megastar friends. "I think I've taken enough pictures. Should we go on up to the springs?"

"I'm ready." Dallas twirled a yellow wildflower in his fingers. He reached forward, and I moved to take the flower, but he held it out of my grasp and proceeded to weave it into my hair. He stood back and studied me for a moment. "Beautiful. Let me take your picture."

I handed him my camera. "You have to hold that button down—" I stopped when Dallas snapped a picture. "Hey, I wasn't ready."

Dallas laughed. "You're cute, though. Ready—one, two, three." I grinned, and he snapped another picture. Then he set the camera on a rock, pushed a couple of buttons, and put his arm around me. The timer blinked, and we waited for another shot.

He flipped the camera around so we could view the picture. "What a great couple."

I tickled his side. "You look great, as usual. And you're good with a camera." Lorea still hadn't figured out how to focus my Canon DSLR.

He pulled me close and planted a kiss on my cheek. "It's easy when the subject is breathtaking."

I gave him a light kiss on the lips. Then I took his hand and tugged it. "Let's go."

Ten minutes later, we pulled into the makeshift parking area in the woods. "Here we are." I indicated the sign for the springs that banned parking beyond that point. A person could drive farther up the trail, but the road was too narrow to park next to the springs. "It's less than a five-minute walk."

Dallas took my hand as we hiked up the gravel road. The rushing of the creek brought back so many good memories. "My family used to come up here nearly every summer with our old camper. We'd fish upstream and then sit in the hot pots. It's pretty much the same now as it was twenty years ago."

We stopped in front of the rocks surrounding the first hot springs we came to. Dallas helped me down near the bank of the creek. "That's incredible it's still here. So how many springs are along this stretch?"

"They're mostly in this area—not more than a hundred yards. Look there." I pointed to a wisp of rising steam. "You can see where the hot water is flowing right out of the mountain into the stream."

Dallas looked in the direction of the boiling volcanic water coming from underground. I sat on a large boulder and kicked off my sandals. Three main pools had been created long ago when someone moved large rocks to block the flow of the frigid creek water from diluting the hot water of the springs. As I dipped my toe in the water, I breathed in the sulfur-scented air and wrinkled my nose. Dallas watched me and laughed.

"That part hasn't changed." I rubbed my nose. "I remember complaining of that stink to my parents."

Dallas sank his feet into the water beside me. "I guess that's the price you pay for a hot tub in the mountains."

"A lot of people come here for health benefits and the healing properties of the springs. I think it doesn't hurt to relax." The water lapped gently at my calves, and I could feel some of the tension of the last few weeks trickling out. "Did you know this is where Natalie and Brock met?"

"Really? How?"

"Natalie and Lorea were up here soaking in that pool right there." I indicated a group of rocks across the creek. "A lot of people don't like to cross because it's so cold, but that pot is hotter. So last year, they were soaking, and along comes Brock. Turns out he'd been coming once a week for some solitude. Natalie was sitting in his preferred spot. She says it was meant to be."

"Kind of like how we met." Dallas put his arm around me and pulled me close. "I wasn't supposed to work that night, but someone called in sick."

The look in his eyes hinted as to what his next words would be, and then we'd be back to that awkward place with me struggling to say the 'L' word. I let my feet slip on the smooth river rock, and I lurched forward out of his grasp with a little shriek.

Dallas grabbed me and helped me to a standing position. "Easy there."

"Thanks—I didn't bring my swimsuit. Guess I should have."

"I agree."

I shook my head. "Tempting, but I didn't feel like I had the time."

"You really need to slow down and let someone help you." His hands rested on my arms, and he drew me in to his chest. "You have amazing talent. You don't want to burn yourself out."

"You sound like my mother."

"Sorry." He brought his face closer to mine, tilting his head slightly as our lips met. He kissed me and then pulled back. "I'm not your mother."

I laughed and looked into his green eyes. "I know." My mouth was a breath apart from his, and my heart beat double time. I parted my lips and kissed him, feeling his hold on me tighten. He sucked gently on my bottom lip, and I relaxed into him, allowing the kiss to deepen. The hot springs swirled around our feet, and the steam enveloped us in its mist.

"I love you, Adri."

My eyes dropped down to the rippling water. Dallas put a finger under my chin and lifted it so I had to meet his gaze. "I know you're not comfortable yet with those words, and it's okay. I can see you're having trouble deciding what your heart wants. I've tried not to push you with all the stress you've been under, but I can't help telling you how I feel."

I hesitated. My heart warmed at his honest evaluation of me. He was so kind. I thought about forcing myself to say what he wanted to hear, but he stopped me.

"You don't have to say anything." He kissed me again and let his words sink into my heart as his lips lingered over mine. "Can I come over to your house tonight?" he murmured.

I thought about it for a moment. Holding on to his arms, I stepped back and swallowed. Through the strong sulphur-coated air, I suddenly smelled the light scent of roses. Pink-and-white antique roses—from Luke. His face flashed through my mind, and my heart somersaulted with a new emotion.

I looked at Dallas. He was right. I couldn't say that I loved him, but what he didn't know was I'd never be able to say it. No matter how kind and gentle he was, the connection wasn't there. His devotion to me was sweet, but it wasn't Dallas's face that kept flitting through my mind at random moments during the day. Why did I keep thinking about Luke?

Dallas rubbed his thumb in a slow circle on the back of my hand. The look in his eyes made me feel guilty about my realization. Remembering the deal I'd made with Lorea, I nodded. "Sure. Thanks for understanding my feelings."

He embraced me again. "Thanks for letting me share mine."

I stepped out of his embrace and smiled brightly. "Are you hungry? I brought sandwiches from the deli."

"Starving." Dallas rubbed his stomach, and I mentally compared his lean physique to Luke's chiseled abs before scolding myself to stay in the moment.

We ate our sandwiches, sitting on the bank of the creek as the sun sped across the sky, nearing its descent. I pulled out a container of raspberries dotted with chocolate chips and handed it to Dallas. "Try these. It's one of the appetizer ideas we came up with for our July wedding."

He popped a few in his mouth and nodded. "Those are delicious. They look nice, too."

I smiled and ate a handful. "Glad you like them."

Dallas finished off his raspberries and then put his arm around me. "Do you have tons of work to do tonight? I don't want to bother you."

"It'll be fine. I need to go over my notes and the pictures I took to put everything in line with the plans for the wedding, but I'm allowing myself some time off for you." Hopefully, I could work up the nerve to tell Dallas that I didn't see a future with him.

Part of me wanted to tell him how I felt right then, before I had a chance to chicken out, but it would be awkward to have to ride together another thirty minutes after that, especially if Dallas wasn't too keen on breaking up. My nerves buzzed with my hidden worries as we got into the Mountaineer. If only he weren't so sweet, it would be easy to let him go.

"Are the police still watching your house?"

"I need to call and check. I wonder if they've found out anything about that picture." I brought up Tony's number and waited for the call to go through. When he answered, I got right to the point. "Do I have the okay to go back to my house? Dallas is with me." He wouldn't be staying the night, but I didn't want to go into details with Dallas listening to my end of the conversation.

"Do you trust him?"

"Obviously."

"I'd feel better if you stayed somewhere else," Tony grumbled. "I'll still have someone drive by your place, but we're short staffed tonight because of the ice show and a couple officers out sick."

"Thanks. I appreciate it."

"And, Adri . . ." Tony hesitated.

"Yes?"

"We found the area where the camera was set up. It was just outside Brock's fence. Looks like the perp climbed a tree and probably used a high-powered zoom."

"Oh." The information sent a shiver down my spine. I was already creeped out. Why was Tony telling me this?

"We're still operating under the suspicion that the photographer is a male, but that means he doesn't weigh more than two hundred pounds. The tree branches couldn't support more than that. Hamilton climbed partway up and broke a couple of branches."

"So it could be a woman?"

"Anything is possible. I'm telling you this because I want to scare you in hopes that you'll be extra cautious."

"That's nice of you," I replied, letting an edge of sarcasm into my voice.

Tony laughed. "What would be nice is if we can figure out who's stalking you and why, especially since the diamonds have been recovered."

The unsettling feeling of the danger that lurked somewhere unknown sent a chill down my spine. "Okay, you win. I'm scared to death."

Dallas raised his eyebrows, and I gave him a weak smile.

"I'll call you as soon as we know more," Tony said.

I ended the call and slowed to ease the bumps of the washboard road. "Tony said they're not sure if the person taking pictures is a man or a woman."

"I'm glad you trust me. I want to keep you safe, since the police can't seem to do their job."

"They're doing their job." I bristled at his comment. Tony had gone above and beyond to protect me and solve the crimes, and I didn't want him discredited.

"Well, they're not doing it fast enough to satisfy me." Dallas put his hand on my knee and squeezed gently. "But you're right. They're doing what they can. The perpetrators must be smarter than they are."

I bit my tongue because I couldn't think of a good reply to his statement. "Can we change the subject?"

"Sure. Tell me more about Natalie's wedding plans."

I smiled and began talking. And Dallas listened. He really was interested in how hard I was working to make Natalie's dream wedding a reality. That's why I felt so wishy-washy about breaking up with him. He cared about me and had made a continuous investment in our relationship—working overtime to get to know me and the intricate details of the wedding business that made me who I am. That thought derailed my smile as I remembered that I still didn't know much about him.

Dallas was a clever conversationalist. Every time I tried to delve into his background, he found a way to turn the question back at me. I kept thinking that maybe he'd open up more after we spent more time together. I decided to make another attempt to get to know him better before I let him go.

"Thanks for listening. I don't mean to bore you, so why don't you tell me *your* deep, dark secrets?"

Dallas licked his lips and rolled his shoulders back. "Now, that *would* be boring. You already know my secrets."

"I do?"

"You know—the one about how I fell in love with a wedding planner?"

"And?"

His face reddened, and he focused on his hands. "I have another secret, but I planned to tell you later. That's why I wanted to go to your house."

"Gee, I'm not curious at all now." My anxiety level ratcheted up a few more notches.

He touched my knee. "No, it's something good—really good. I just wanted to surprise you."

"Okay, I'll be a good girl and be surprised, if you give me one hint." I parked in front of his realty office so he could get his car.

"How about, I love you?"

"That's a hint?"

Dallas jumped out of the car and hurried around to my side. I rolled down the window, and he leaned in and kissed me. "I won't make you wait long."

Chapter 26

WEDDING QUESTION CARDS

Create six to eight questions that members of the wedding party can answer about the bride and groom (questions that encourage brief answers are best). Print one question each on a sheet of cardstock. In place of just signing a guest book, encourage guests to pick a question to answer and then sign.

Some examples of questions:

"What is the best marriage advice you have ever received?"

"What is the most romantic place we should visit?"

"What should we name our kids?"

"Where do you see us in twenty-five years?"

Courtesy of www.mashedpotatoesandcrafts.com.

The five-minute drive to my house wasn't long enough to calm my nerves or steel my defenses against what I knew I needed to do. Lorea told me it was cruel to get Dallas's hopes up by continuing to date him when I wasn't committed, but I wasn't the one who spouted the "L" word on the third date. I had hoped for a slow, easy relationship where we both took time to get to know each other before jumping into the messy stages. When I had told Lorea that, she laughed at me and said, "Now who's the cynic?"

I wondered about Dallas's surprise. There wasn't any reason for him to buy me a gift, but that was probably what he had done. I parked in front of my house and stepped out, looking for police cars in the vicinity. They would drive by once each hour, according to Tony. I texted him a description of Dallas's gray Hyundai so the police would know he was an expected visitor. My phone pinged, and I read the text from Tony and laughed.

Stay out of trouble!

I hurried to unlock my door and turn on some lights before Dallas arrived. Brushing at a spot on my capris, I wondered if I should change but decided against it. Dallas would be here any minute, and his shorts had some grass stains from the meadow anyway.

Tux pawed at the patio window, and I refilled his dish with cat food. He purred as I stroked his back and scratched behind his ears. For a moment, I wished I could escape out my back door with some wedding emergency so I wouldn't have to face the breakup with Dallas. With a sigh, I stood and slid the door shut before heading back toward my front door.

The hall mirror was a great checkpoint for me as I left my house each morning. I stood in front of the oval-shaped glass now and smoothed out my hair. As my fingers worked through a tangled curl, I thought about how many times I had told my brides that love would set them on a path that would change their lives forever.

For a short moment, I wished I did love Dallas so I could be on that road with someone by my side. I straightened my shoulders and gave myself a solemn look in the mirror. My brown eyes remained serious, and they didn't light up when I thought of a future with Dallas. It was time to let him go. The doorbell rang, and I dredged up the last of my courage, opening the door with a smile.

Dallas carried a gift sack, and my heart sank down to my toes. "Thanks again for giving me a tour of the springs today." He stepped inside, his eyes bright.

He had bought a gift. Blast. As much as I wanted to tell him right then, I wimped out.

"The night is young. What would you like to do?" It was just after seven, and I had hoped to send him home by eight and get to work on the wedding plans for Natalie, but I would have to stall until I could figure out what to do about his gift. I didn't have the heart to tell him as he walked casually into my living room and set the gift bag on the floor. I didn't want to date him anymore, but I didn't want to crush him, either.

"I want to kiss you senseless, and then I want to sate your curiosity by letting you open this gift." Dallas patted the cushion next to him.

"Okay, but let's do those things in reverse, since I am dying to know your secret." I sat down, and he scooted closer until our legs touched. He picked up the gift sack and let the handles swing gently on his fingertips. The bag was made of some kind of silver iridescent paper, and I noticed flecks of multicolored glitter embedded in the tissue. The sack was medium sized, so the possibilities were endless.

"This is my secret," he murmured.

I reached for the sack, but he held it just out of my reach. "Just one kiss?" He leaned toward me.

Kissing him now didn't seem right. I'd made my decision. I hated it when I had to upset nice people. "Dallas, I wanted to tell you—"

He covered my mouth with his, cutting off my explanation. I changed my mind again. One last liplock wasn't going to hurt anything. But Dallas had more than a kiss in mind. He deepened the kiss, and I tasted peppermint on his tongue. I heard the gift sack slide onto the floor as he put his other arm around me and held me tight. Perfect timing. I reached for the sack and grabbed one handle with my index finger. Pulling my head back, I whispered, "Gotcha."

Dallas nuzzled my neck. "Cheater."

I giggled. "Please, can I open it?"

Dallas released me and sat up. He put his hand over mine, and my eyes were again drawn to the stump of his ring finger. "Yes. Open it."

The tissue paper crinkled as I pulled it out of the sack. I reached inside, and my fingers grazed a velvet-covered box. With a gasp, I lifted it out, hating myself for not saying something to him the minute he walked in the door. I hoped it was just jewelry, but the size was exactly like every ring box I'd ever seen. I could feel tears pricking at the corners of my eyes.

"Close your eyes."

"But . . ."

"Please, Adri. This is special. Just close your eyes."

I took a ragged breath and closed my eyes. He took my left hand and gently uncurled my fingers. I heard the box snap open, and I held my breath as I felt Dallas slip something onto my ring finger. This couldn't be happening. It would crush him, but I had to tell him. I couldn't force myself to love him.

"You can open your eyes now."

I realized I was squeezing my eyes tight and still holding my breath. I relaxed my eyelids and lifted them slowly. With a glance at Dallas, I examined my ring finger just as I was about to suck in some much-needed oxygen. My lungs convulsed as I focused on the ring.

"Adrielle Pyper, will you marry me?"

The ring glittering on my finger sent a shudder through my body. I took short gasps and blinked several times, trying to cover the absolute terror that had overtaken my senses.

"What's wrong?" Dallas looked at me, followed my gaze toward the ring, and then back to my face. "Don't you like it?"

I wiped my eyes. There was nothing I could say now. Everything had changed. I couldn't breathe right. Briette's engagement ring—the ring on my finger belonged to my best friend. The setting was one of a kind with the swirl of diamonds surrounding the emerald. Briette had loved the ring so much that she chose emerald green as an accent color for her wedding. I could never forget how I spent hours searching for just the right florist who could tint white roses with an emerald hue.

I hesitated. There was so much love in Dallas's eyes that I doubted myself for a moment. Maybe he'd bought the ring—maybe the murderer had sold it. My breath stilled as I focused on the emerald.

When Briette was murdered, the police searched for any clues to why she had been killed. When they discovered her twenty-five-thousand-dollar engagement ring was missing, they decided that was motive enough. But I had never been satisfied with that explanation—it had to be more than theft. And now I'd discovered I was right all along. The police said if the murder wasn't related to the ring specifically, the killer most likely held onto it as a keepsake, a memento of the crime.

The blood pumping in my ears increased as I thought of Briette's picture. It sat in plain sight on my dresser. If he'd seen it, he would know I recognized the ring. Maybe I could pretend I didn't know the truth. Unless—my heart pulsed with new fear as I lifted my eyes to meet his gaze—Dallas already knew that Briette was my best friend.

My chin trembled, and I worked to make my voice sound normal. "It's Briette's ring."

"Isn't it beautiful? I'm sure you're happy to see it again."

He was absolutely crazy, but I knew that if I wanted to breathe a few more minutes, I needed to play along. "It's just so sudden. I didn't expect this."

"But I love you."

"I know, but we've only been dating for two weeks." My voice trembled, and I tried to swallow, but fear coated my throat, making it difficult to breathe.

"Almost three weeks since I met you." He smiled. "When you find the right one, you can't let them get away."

My skin prickled with goose bumps. I hesitated, mentally screaming at myself to calm down and be rational. I had to play along if I was going to get out of this. "You're right. I always overanalyze things." I glanced at the ring again and lifted my hand to examine the emerald solitaire surrounded by five diamonds. With a hard swallow, I struggled to keep my composure. I had to hide the cord of fear winding itself around my body. "I love it." I leaned forward and kissed Dallas and then hugged him.

"I thought you were going to say no there for a minute." He kissed me gently. "I would've been very unhappy."

I started to speak but didn't trust my voice. My lips caressed his while my mind spun out of control.

Dallas traced my jaw with his thumb and leaned closer. He kissed me, almost reverently, and pulled me close. "You will make me so happy." He stroked my hair. "You'll be such a beautiful bride."

He kissed me again, and my pulse quickened. I leaned into him, deepening the kiss and threading my arms around his neck. He lifted me up and swept my legs over his arm. Uh-oh. I had to do something, but fear paralyzed me. I stopped and pulled back with a question in my eyes.

He kissed my cheek. "Is it all right if we go to your bedroom?"

I wanted to say no, but I reminded myself again that I needed to act normal. To act as if I was excited that Dallas had just proposed to me. "I—it's kind of a mess, and I need to use the bathroom first. Do you mind waiting a few minutes?" I wriggled from his arms to a standing position.

He chuckled. "You're never messy, but if you want to change into something . . ." He winked. "I'll still act surprised."

I couldn't answer him, so I forced a smile.

Dallas gave me one more passionate kiss, his hands trailing down my back and resting on my rear end. "I'll try to be patient."

I dipped my head and brushed my lips across his ear. "It'll be worth the wait," I whispered and broke free from his grasp.

My throat tightened with fear, and I struggled to keep the panic from showing in my eyes. I glanced at my cell phone lying on the coffee table in front of us. I forced a smile to my face as I picked up the phone. "I want to call my parents and tell them the good news."

Dallas grabbed my hand. "Not yet. Let me keep you to myself for a few hours."

"But—"

Dallas took my phone and set it back on the table. He smiled at me and licked his lips. "It can wait an hour, can't it?"

Acid boiled in my stomach. The way Dallas acted only confirmed my fears that anything might set him off. I sucked in a breath and made one final attempt. "Lorea texted me about Natalie's wedding site just before you came. I'll need her help later to sort out some of my notes." I grabbed the phone and began texting before he could reply. My mind spun as I tried to think of a cryptic message I could send to Lorea in case Dallas took my phone again.

> Hey, I need your help. For Natalie's wedding, could you call Wes's best friend for a quote? I'm home.

I moved to put the phone in my pocket, but Dallas grabbed it. "You know she'll text you right back. This way you won't be distracted."

Forcing myself not to react to the adrenaline telling me to run, I nodded.

Dallas slid my phone into his pocket. "I'm so happy you said yes."

I attempted a smile. "I'll be right back."

It took all my willpower to walk demurely from the room and resist sprinting down the hall. Grabbing Briette's picture off my dresser, I hurried to my bathroom and locked the door. *I didn't say yes*, I thought. I looked at the sparkling diamonds and bit back tears. Clutching the picture frame, I slid open the bottom drawer and placed Briette out of sight. Removing memory triggers might help me to deal with Dallas.

I could feel my body trembling. Lorea was my one hope. I prayed that she would understand the text. With a shaky breath I stared at myself in the mirror. My eyes were dark with fear. If I could just wipe the panic from my face, I would be able to continue this charade until the police arrived. But what if Dallas reacted violently when he heard the sirens coming? If someone *was* coming. My stomach churned, and for a moment I thought I might be sick. I took deep, steadying breaths and tried to think of my options. They were few.

Dallas might wonder what was taking so long. I should've taken my phone back, but I was too afraid of how he might react. Maybe I could tell him I needed five more minutes—make up some excuse to get my phone and call 911. Rolling my shoulders back, I lifted the corners of my mouth and opened the bathroom door.

Dallas stood in front of me, his hand resting on the doorframe. I jumped and tried to repress the scream climbing up my throat.

"You scared me!" I forced a shaky laugh.

Dallas narrowed his eyes. He grabbed my arm, jerked me forward, and dangled my cell phone in front of me.

"Were you trying to tell Lorea something?"

"No, I just—"

He gripped my arm tighter.

"Stop it, Dallas." I tried to grab my phone, but he held it out of my reach.

He glared at me and threw my phone against the wall. I screamed as the glitter case popped off and the phone fell behind my headboard. I couldn't hide my fear as he shook his head, making a tsking sound with his tongue. "Oh, Adrielle. I thought you would be happy to see that ring again." He reached for my hand, but I pulled it away. The ring was the only proof I had of his identity as Briette's murderer. I wouldn't let him take it from me now.

"Dallas, what's wrong?"

He held up a wedding planning book, and I took a step back, covering my mouth to suppress a whimper. He had found Briette's binder. It had been sitting in plain sight on my bookshelf. Of course I'd kept it. Inside were pictures of her exotic engagement ring, her dress, Caleb and Briette together. Seeing her again might have triggered some new level of insanity for Dallas.

He squeezed the spine of the book until his fingertips turned white. "I'm not in this book, but I was there every step of the way." He spoke in a low voice that left me petrified. "Briette went out on a date with me right before she met him. I'm certain things would have worked for us, if Caleb hadn't gotten in the way." The fury in his eyes dissipated as he looked at me. "But maybe it was all for the best, so I could find you." He flipped open the wedding binder and held it so I could see.

The air in my lungs felt as if it had turned to ice. He dragged his finger down the page until it rested on a picture of me and Briette. We were sitting in the grass, wiggling our freshly painted purple toenails, and laughing at the camera.

"That's why I picked you. Briette talked about you all the time—it was natural to love you. She said you wanted to get married but hadn't met the right person yet." He looked down at the picture again and back at me. "It was hard to find you at first—you disappeared. And I had to wait for the right time. But look at us now. Briette would be happy to see us together."

"She was my best friend." Tears ran down my face, but I didn't move to wipe them away.

"I loved her. I tried to help her, but she couldn't see how she was throwing her life away for that scumbag." He took a step forward, and I cowered. I had seen his strength when he rescued me from the diamond thief. I didn't stand a chance against him. "Come here, Adri. It will be different with you. You have a better understanding of what marriage means."

Dallas flipped his wrist, and I saw a gleam of silver in his hand.

"Dallas, please. I'm sorry it took me so long to say it, but I do love you. I've been scared. It's hard for me, working with so many couples and then seeing those marriages fail. I'm cautious."

He inched closer, the blade of his knife reflecting the light toward my face. "But you're just like her. You want to be with someone else."

"What are you talking about? I haven't dated anyone else."

"What about Luke Stetson? You always seem to find a reason to run into him."

"No." How did he even know about Luke? Then I realized how Dallas had kept tabs on me. "The photos? That was you?" No wonder he was so good with a camera.

"That's how I found you that night and saved you from that man. I followed you to take more pictures. And you repaid my love by spending time with that dirtbag lawyer."

"No. It's not what you think." I shook my head. I needed to stay calm, but I could hear the hysteria underlying the soft tones of my voice. I needed to come up with something quick. "I was consulting Luke about a potential lawsuit. Sylvia threatened to sue my business over her stolen wedding dress."

"I saw you. The way you looked at him. Smiled at him. Laughed with him. Wanted him." Each word came out heavy, punctuated with pained emotion, and he moved closer. The knife in his hand jerked back and forth as if he were warring within himself whether to stab me or slice me.

I did not want to die in my bathroom. Or any place, for that matter. I needed to keep moving. Deciding on a new approach, I stepped toward him. "If you really love me, you should trust me. I was scared when I saw this ring, but I understand now. Every moment I've spent with you has made me feel more alive." I made one small movement toward him. His throat constricted, and he swallowed. We stood in the doorway of the bathroom.

"Could we sit on my bed for a minute?"

"Why?" He glanced at the bed and then back at me.

"Because every time you kiss me, it makes me go weak in the knees. I thought you'd noticed."

His lips twitched. I forced myself not to look at the knife in his hand.

"I want you to hold me again, Dallas. Make me feel safe."

He hesitated, and I took another step toward my bed. When he didn't stop me, I continued forward. I patted the quilt and held up my left hand. "I don't deserve this. I don't deserve you. I was scared because I didn't think it could be true."

Dallas studied me, and I kept my eyes focused on his, refusing to look at the knife. His eyes narrowed. Something rubbed up against my legs. I heard a meow and jumped back. "Oh, it's just you, Tux."

"You have a cat?" Dallas looked at Tux and then glared at me. "Where has he been?"

"He hangs out in my laundry room. He sleeps a lot, but he usually finds me around now to fill up his food dish." I tried to keep from rambling as I struggled for an explanation.

I knew exactly where Tux had come from—the patio.

Someone must have opened the sliding glass door, and I needed to alert that person that we were in the bedroom and Dallas had a knife. I prayed that it was Tony.

"You said you were going to kiss me, but I'm worried about that knife. Could you please put it down?" I emphasized the word *knife* as loudly as I dared. Dallas studied me for a moment, and I saw his biceps quiver as he clenched the knife tighter.

"I tried to convince her. I didn't want to—but it was the only way to save her." The side of his face twitched.

My body was shaking, and my breaths were shallow. I glanced at the knife and directly into his eyes. "You killed Briette, but you don't have to kill me."

Dallas pressed his lips together and closed the distance between us. He held the blade near my throat. "I loved her."

"Dallas, please don't do this." My ears perked up at the sound of the creaky floorboard in my hallway. Someone was there to save me, but how could they when Dallas held me at knifepoint?

I could feel the cool metal against my skin, and I struggled to hold perfectly still. He narrowed his eyes, pressing the flat edge of the blade down my throat toward my collarbone.

"I love you," he said and flicked the tip of the knife downward. A stinging sensation ran across my chest. Pain sparked up my throat. I screamed and fell back on the bed at the same moment Luke sprang forward. He clubbed Dallas across the head with my Mag flashlight. Dallas stumbled forward and fell to his knees.

I pressed a hand to my wound. Blood trickled over my fingers and onto my shirt as I moved to the far side of my bed. My chest throbbed, and the knife wound seeped dark red. I grabbed my running shorts off the bed and put pressure on the cut.

"You're hurt." Luke's eyes widened in fear as he approached

me. Dallas brandished the knife as he struggled to stand. Luke hit him again with the flashlight, and the skin above Dallas's brow split. Blood trickled down his face as he staggered forward. Luke kicked Dallas on the side of his knee and his leg buckled. The knife fell to the floor as Dallas collapsed with a grunt. His head hit the side of my dresser as he fell. Luke kicked him again, but Dallas didn't move. "I think he's out."

A cry escaped my throat. I lifted one of my hands from the cut on my chest and pointed toward the blood dripping from Dallas's hairline. My other hand felt tingly, and I dropped my blood-soaked running shorts. Luke grabbed a washcloth and held it against the wound on my chest. I winced and felt the room spin. "I think I'm gonna pass out."

"Hold on. We need to get you to the hospital." Luke cradled me in his arms, lifting me off the bed and heading for the door. "I'm sorry. I came as fast as I could. I didn't know what to do when I heard you say he had a knife."

"Thank you." I leaned my head against his shoulder. Then everything went black.

I came to in the ambulance, completely disoriented. Fear overcame rational thought, and I thrashed and cried until Luke's face appeared above me. He gripped my hand. "It's all right. Hold still. They said you just need a few stitches." He brushed my hair back from my face with his other hand and leaned in close. "Shh—try to relax."

Focusing on the feel of his fingertips against my clammy skin reminded me that I was alive. "He killed Briette." I sobbed, and the pressure from my heaving chest caused pain to arc through my body.

"We're going to have to sedate her."

"No." Luke's voice was firm as he spoke to the EMT. Then he turned to me and put both his hands on the sides of my face. "Adri, look at me. You have to stop moving. Breathe. You're safe now. I know Dallas hurt you, but you'll be okay." He kept one hand on my face, and the other clasped my fingers. "Can you lie still?"

I nodded as tears rolled down my cheeks. I closed them and took a few shallow breaths. When I opened them, Luke was still right there, worry lines crinkling his brow. "The police have Dallas in custody. They showed up right after you blacked out."

I took a minute to absorb that and then asked, "How did you know?"

"That you needed help?" He smiled. "Lorea called me. She said you sent her some weird text to call Tony, but she couldn't reach him on his cell. She was freaked out and said she was calling 911. She knew I lived nearby, so she told me to run to your house and go in through your patio door. She told me where you kept the spare key."

"Dallas was watching me. I couldn't call for help." My voice sounded raspy, and I coughed to clear my throat.

"I told her to call the police, and I would come to your house. When I got there, I saw Dallas's car and had a bad feeling. I know it's crazy, but I never liked him. He was strange."

"Why didn't you say so?"

He raised his eyebrows. "I did. Remember at Brock's house? You were pretty ticked at me. Anyway, I'm thankful I found the key." Emotion flickered across his face, and he stopped talking.

I was about to say thank you again when the doors to the

ambulance flew open and the EMTs carried me inside the hospital. Eleven stitches and some pain meds later, I rested on a hospital bed in recovery. Tony had taken my statement and questioned me on specific details.

"Adri, I'm really sorry about this." He patted my arm. "It shouldn't have happened."

"It's over now. Luke saved me." I closed my eyes. The medicine took the rough edges off my pain, and I began to relax.

"I'll follow up with you later." Tony stepped away from the bed. "Luke wondered if he could talk to you for a minute when I'm through taking his statement."

"Of course," I answered. "He saved my life."

Tony grinned. "You said that already, but I'm sure glad he did."

My eyelids felt heavy, and I dozed off until I heard the scraping of a chair against the floor. My breathing relaxed, and it took some effort to open my eyes. Luke sat beside my bed. He leaned forward in his chair and grasped my hand.

"How do you feel?"

"Like I've been stabbed by a psychotic boyfriend."

Luke shook his head. "I'm really sorry. In my defense, I did ask you out."

Laughing would surely hurt, so I smiled instead. "It's not your fault." Then I changed my teasing tone to the more serious thought that had been buzzing through my mind. "I only dated him because I felt Briette wanted me to."

Luke leaned forward in his chair. "Who's Briette?"

"She was my best friend. Dallas killed her." I could feel my lip trembling. "I kissed him. I kissed the man who murdered Briette."

"Don't do that to yourself. How do you know he killed your friend?"

I covered my mouth with my hand and saw the glint of diamonds. The ring was still on my finger. I held my hand out in front of me. "This was her engagement ring. That's how I knew. Dallas asked me to marry him and gave it to me." I slid the ring off my finger and cupped it in my palm. "When Briette was murdered, her ring was missing. The police thought the crime was connected to the theft."

Luke stared at the ring. "That's horrible."

"I didn't know. I wouldn't have known if I hadn't seen this ring." I shuddered. "Every time I would think about whether or not to go on another date with him, I would remember how Briette tried to convince me to give guys a chance to show their best selves."

Luke was quiet for a moment, and Briette's words hit me again with new meaning when I looked in his eyes.

He rubbed the back of his neck and spoke softly. "You solved her murder. Don't you think that's what she would want?"

I thought about Luke's words and closed my eyes. Could it be true? Did Briette have a hand in bringing Dallas and me together so she could finally be at rest? My fingers tingled, and I opened my eyes.

The diamonds surrounding the emerald flashed as I moved my hand. I looked toward the window to see a bright ray of sunlight coming through the half-open shades. The light reflected off the gems, and warmth filled my body. An image of Briette came to mind, and this time when I thought about her, it felt different. I studied Luke, sitting quietly at the edge of the bed.

"I think you're right," I whispered. "I kept giving Dallas another chance—going out with him even though I wasn't sure. I made myself like him. I think Briette brought Dallas to me. She wanted me to date him so that her fiancé could finally have peace. She loved Caleb so much."

Luke put his arm around me, and I leaned into his side and sobbed. "She was my best friend. He killed my best friend."

He didn't say anything. He just held me and lowered his head to mine, rubbing my back as I cried. My throat hurt, my chest was sore from the stitches, and I felt completely exhausted, but the tears wouldn't stop. After my cries subsided, he handed me a tissue and offered me a drink of juice from a Styrofoam cup. I set Briette's ring on the table beside my bed. The police would want to see it, and hopefully it could be returned to Caleb.

Luke watched me release the ring, and he grasped my hand. The raw pain in his eyes mirrored my own. He knew what I was feeling. That's why he didn't say anything, because he knew there were no words that would help me feel better. Nothing would bring Briette back.

When I had drained my reservoir of tears, and my body was left trembling, he embraced me gently and whispered, "I'm sorry."

I lifted my head so I could see his face. "Thank you. Me too."

He nodded and handed me another tissue.

Lorea burst into the room. "Adri. *Nide lagune*—my friend, I was so worried." Dark lines of mascara were smeared across her cheeks. She moved as if to hug me, then stopped when she saw the bandage.

"It's okay. I'm—Luke saved me."

Chapter 27

KEY TO MY HEART

Add this special touch to the ceremony. Attach a key to the groom's boutonniere and the matching lock to the bride's bouquet. Courtesy of www.mashedpotatoesandcrafts.com.

Lorea hugged Luke and cried. "If you hadn't gone to her house . . ." She covered her mouth and sank to the edge of the hospital bed.

"Lorea, you saved Adri," Luke said.

I reached my hand out to her, and she clasped it. "I'm so sorry that he hurt you."

"He would've killed me if it weren't for you and Luke."

"But still, look at what he did to you." She indicated the bandage poking out of the top of the hospital gown.

"You did the right thing," Luke said. "I think Adri likes me now."

I grimaced. "But how did you even know where to reach Luke?"

"I took the card out from under the vase and put his number in my phone. Just in case you tossed it." She ducked her head. "Then he came by the shop, wanting to talk to you, so I told him where you lived and that he needed to try harder."

"Thank goodness you're so bullheaded."

We all laughed.

"I'm going to take you back to my house. And I passed Tony on the way in. He said your parents are coming."

"My poor family. My mom will never let me out of her sight again."

"I guess she can help us with preparations for Natalie's wedding." Lorea lifted a sack onto the bed. "The doctor said that I could take you home with me—you need supervision. Your parents are going to stay with me too. I brought some of my things for you to change into, unless you want to wear that lovely outfit home."

I wrinkled my nose and reached for the sack. "Thanks."

Luke cleared his throat. "I guess that's my cue." He stood, pushing his hands into the pockets of his jeans and looking at me.

"Actually, stay right here. I need to get Adri some water." Lorea gave him a pointed look as she left. I followed her gaze to Luke, and his face broke into a wide grin.

"What's that about?" I asked.

"Well, as she mentioned, I stopped by your shop earlier today when you were out. You really have done a great job with your wedding business."

"Thank you. That means a lot, coming from someone who doesn't believe in marriage."

Luke's shoulders dropped. "I thought you'd forgiven me for all my past sins."

I couldn't help but smile. "You're right. But that doesn't mean I won't try my best to convert you from your unholy beliefs."

He held out his hand. "You're on."

"For what?"

"I'd like you to try to convert me." He stepped closer and grabbed my hand. "Would you go out with me?"

He still wanted to date me after every crazy thing we'd been through? My mouth started to drop open, but I clamped it shut. I didn't understand Luke or his persistence in asking me out. He watched me with a smile on his face—that cute dimple in his chin made him even more endearing. I pulled my hand from his and touched the edge of the bandage—it felt itchy against my neck. My heartbeat sped up, and I closed my eyes, not wanting to go where my thoughts were taking me. Luke was quiet until I opened my eyes.

"You didn't call, so I thought I'd give it one more shot." He shifted from one foot to the other. "Lorea made me promise that the next time I saw you I would ask you out and that I couldn't take no for an answer."

I lifted my eyes to the ceiling. "That girl." My heart raced as Luke took my hand again.

"I thought this was bad timing, but apparently she's holding me to my promise." He blew out a breath. "I always keep my word. Adri, I'd really like a chance to get to know you. When you get feeling better, would you consider going out with me?"

I blinked back tears. There were too many emotions swirling around me. I had worked so hard to convince myself to like Dallas that now I didn't trust my feelings. The movement it took to lift my head off the pillow caused more pain in my sore chest than I'd bargained for. I winced and sucked a breath through clenched teeth.

Luke put his hand on the small of my back and helped me to an upright position. "What do you need? You sound like you're in pain."

"It's just really sore." I indicated my chest.

"I heard the doc say it would be pretty tender for the next few days. You'll need to take it easy."

"Yeah, about that." My lips twitched with the feelings I struggled to express. "I think I should take it easy in the dating arena as well."

The disappointment in his eyes was obvious, but he recovered quickly. "I understand."

"But that doesn't mean I wouldn't like to treat my hero to something special, like his own order of fried pickles."

"You're on." Luke held out his hand. "As soon as you're feeling better, we'll go."

I shook his hand but didn't release it. "Seriously, though, I think you're a great guy. You are a hero. I'm just really mixed up right now. Thanks for understanding."

He nodded. "Before I leave, I want to give you one piece of advice, if that's okay?"

"Shoot."

"Don't blame yourself. For anything. You're a fantastic person, and you deserve to be loved." He gave my hand a squeeze and backed away. "Just think about it. I'm worried for you."

His forehead was creased with lines of concern. Those deep blue eyes were fixed on mine.

"Thank you. And thank you for saving my life."

I felt tears threatening again as he walked toward the door. He lifted his hand as he exited and flashed me one more smile.

When Lorea returned, I wiped the wet sheen from my cheeks and swallowed a sob.

"Where's Luke, and why are you crying?"

"He asked me out. I told him I couldn't right now."

Lorea opened her mouth to protest but then closed it. She set a cup of water on the table and gave me a gentle hug. "Whatever you need."

There was a tap on the door, and Tony poked his head inside. "Would you like some help out to the car?"

Lorea smiled in his direction. "Yes, I'm taking her to my house so she can rest."

"I hope you can keep her out of trouble," he replied.

I closed my eyes and took a shallow breath, trying not to feel the pressure of my stitches. It was definitely time for a rest.

Chapter 28

I HEART YOU REFRESHMENTS

Freeze ice cream in a 9 x 13 pan, then use heart-shaped cookie cutters to create individual servings. Drizzle ice cream hearts with hot fudge and top with a selection of berries. Garnish with a chocolate cookie and a mint leaf.

Courtesy of www.mashedpotatoesandcrafts.com.

I found out later that Dallas had confessed his love for me in his irrational state as the police hauled him away. He also inadvertently confessed to Briette's murder. Tony reported that he had kept saying how much he loved Briette and tried to save her and that he was trying to save me, too. After the police presented the evidence of his babbling confession, plus Briette's engagement ring, the district attorney charged Dallas with theft, murder, and attempted homicide.

My parents arranged for new carpet to be installed in my bedroom. The blood from my knife wound and Dallas's head injury had ruined mine. They scrubbed and cleaned and removed every trace of Dallas from my life, but my heart still felt damaged by the betrayal.

I found myself focusing daily on the memory of tingling warmth I felt in the hospital when Luke suggested that Briette was at peace. It comforted me, but it didn't help me sort through my feelings about Luke.

Four days after Dallas tried to kill me, Lorea helped me move back to my home. A stunning bouquet of zinnias caught my attention.

"I want to meet your hero," Mom said.

The flowers must have been from Luke. I admired the fuchsia-colored petals and plucked the card from the vase.

Adri,
Be happy. I like your smile.
Your hero,
Luke

"Mom, you've read it."

"Just wanted to make sure it was for you."

I frowned and stuck the card in my pocket. The flowers were beautiful, and I was touched by Luke's thoughtfulness. We hadn't gotten off to a great start, but I felt like we were at least getting to be friends now.

"So tell me about him."

"His name is Luke Stetson."

"I know, I know. It's that divorce lawyer you've had a crush on but didn't want to admit it, right?"

"Mom, I'm injured here. Can you give me a break?"

"You'll get to meet him, Laurel. I'll make sure it happens." Lorea waggled her eyebrows in my direction.

I decided not to comment. I didn't have the energy to reckon with my mom and Lorea's combined persistence. I reclined on my sofa for about ten minutes before I was accosted again.

"Try these, Adri." Mom handed me a plate with some kind of heart-shaped ice cream.

"Ice cream therapy?" I asked as I picked up the spoon.

"Yes, and a test run for your next bridal shower. I let the ice cream start to melt and then scooped it into a 9x13 pan and refroze it." She motioned to the heart shape. "Then I used a cookie cutter. Aren't they sweet?"

I scooped a bite of the strawberry-flavored ice cream into my mouth. Mom had drizzled the heart with chocolate sauce and accented it with chocolate cookies. "Yummy."

"There's more in the freezer." Mom gave my shoulder a squeeze. She was trying her best to keep my mind off my worries.

"Thanks, Mom. I love you."

"I love you too." Her voice cracked a little, and she hurried into the kitchen to tidy up.

The ice cream soothed my parched throat, but my mind returned immediately to the memory of Briette.

The story of the wedding planner who solved her bride's murder hit the Associated Press within the week. My cell phone rang constantly with reporters, brides-to-be, and every busybody in town. My parents helped field the calls and sift through requests. After only six days, Lorea reported that we had eleven potential clients for fall weddings.

Caleb called as soon as he heard the news about Dallas. His voice cracked as he struggled to speak. "Adri, are you okay? This is the craziest thing! I didn't believe it when I first heard. I talked to your mom. She told me what happened."

"I'm healing. Eleven stitches from a knife wound have set me back a little."

"I'm so sorry that you were hurt. I just keep thinking, what are the chances that Briette's best friend would solve her murder?"

"I guess you *could* call it solving—or something."

"It's a miracle. I know you might not think so right now, but you have helped me and Briette so much. This past year has been hell for me. I couldn't sleep knowing that the man who had killed her was out there, living life. But it's over now. It's really over." He hesitated. "Do you know what I mean? Does any of this make sense?"

"I do. I think she's at peace. I'll always miss her, but when I think of her now, it feels . . . better."

"Thank you, Adri. It will never be enough, but thank you for all you've done."

We talked for a few minutes longer, and Caleb told me about the work he was doing for his father's business in an effort to get through another day, another week. We wished each other luck, and I clutched my phone until it started ringing again, and my mom came running to answer it.

Fortunately, another news story overshadowed mine a couple of days later. It involved Sylvia Rockfort. Lorea and I were able to piece together most of the details through tabloids, Twitter, and Tony.

Sylvia had hired someone to steal her dress so she could call off her wedding. When she heard the news story about how I was attacked while running, she felt incredibly guilty—like stealing the dress in the first place didn't make her feel guilty? Anyway, she was afraid I was going to be killed over her conniving plan, so she had the wedding dress dropped off at Necia's consignment store.

After Dallas tried to kill me, she came clean over the whole thing. She mistakenly thought my attempted murder had something to do with the diamonds and stolen gowns. I didn't press charges, but I did tell Tony "I told you so" plenty of times. Then I made him promise to let my detective skills have their freedom.

Lorea stopped by with a few wedding binders from my shop. The empty binders filled me with hope and excitement as I thought of the new growth in my business. "So, what's the latest on Sylvia?"

"They left town right after she spilled the beans. I think she didn't want to give you a chance to change your mind about pressing charges," Lorea said.

"Good plan."

"Sylvia has a contract for a new reality TV show—and a book deal."

I sat up. "A book? About what?"

"I think they're calling it *How I Sabotaged My Own Wedding.*"

"Get out." I snorted. Lorea raised one eyebrow and cocked her head to the side. "Wait. You're serious?"

"The Rockfort mansion is up for sale."

"Thank goodness." We indulged in a good belly laugh, and I got back to work.

Tony stopped by the next day with bittersweet news. Jerry had identified a man named Roland Mayfield as an accomplice in the diamond smuggling ring. It had taken the feds longer to figure it out because he'd been using an alias. "Apparently, they were supposed to intercept the diamonds before they arrived at your boutique, but some of the boxes got mixed up." Tony frowned.

"Roland is in custody now, and we found out that Walter is okay. Roland stole Walter's cell phone and encouraged Walter to go out of the country. It was the only way to shield him from the diamond smuggling operation."

I saw tears well up in Lorea's eyes. "Poor Walter. He'll be so upset."

Tony nodded. "At least he wasn't involved directly. It's still a shame, though."

Thinking of Walter and the way his cousin had used him made my chest feel heavy with sadness. Tony said Walter would be arriving home in Ketchum in a few days. I hoped that he would still be able to continue with his business, but I was afraid that his genuine smile and light step might be forever affected.

By the time my stitches were removed, Natalie's wedding was only nine days away. I struggled with overcoming the paralyzing fear that haunted me each night. My mom planned on traveling back and forth from Rupert every few days to help me until I felt like the "old Adri" again. Each day brought me closer to recovery, and I soon immersed myself in the business of weddings. Luke honored my wish to give me time to straighten things out in my head, but I found myself thinking of him more often than I would ever admit.

Chapter 29

GUEST-BOOK STONES

Collect or purchase small river rocks (nothing larger than about three inches in diameter) and arrange on a table beside permanent markers (both black and lighter colors, such as silver). Invite guests to sign the "Stepping-Stones to a Happy Marriage" with brief words of advice. Present the bride and groom with a large (sturdy) glass container filled with the guest-book stones.

Courtesy of www.mashedpotatoesandcrafts.com.

I checked the seating of the wedding party one last time and gave a thumbs-up to Lorea. My eyes flicked to the center of the meadow, where Brock stood dressed in a gorgeous charcoal-gray tuxedo. I had instructed the photographer and videographer to capture his face when Natalie entered. She was beyond beautiful, glowing with happiness, and I was so happy to see this day come.

I could feel someone staring at me, and I turned slowly to meet Luke Stetson's gaze. Of course I knew he would be present. The guest list was on my computer, and he and Brock were friends, but my stomach still flipped when he smiled at me. I smiled back, and it was sincere. Saving someone's life gave a whole new motivation for full forgiveness—Lorea had ceased calling him "tontua"—and I could see the possibility of friendship between us. Smoothing out an invisible wrinkle in the cream ruffled skirt that brushed my knees gave me a moment to catch my breath. I lifted my hand to cover the scar that the doctor had assured me would fade, and I turned away.

Every layer of Natalie's gorgeous dress was in place as she seemed to float down the aisle of stepping-stones. A light breeze brushed the tendrils of soft brown curls around her face as she gazed at Brock and took his hand.

Lorea smoothed out the train as bride and groom took their places at the altar, the remnants of a burned-out log from the forest fire. The hem of the gown moved easily, but it was hard for me to grasp all that had happened since I discovered the diamonds.

I caught Walter's eye and he smiled, but I could tell he still carried the weight of his cousin's crimes. Walter had returned from Belgium just a few days before with a batch of legal diamonds he planned to sell in his jewelry store. He was crushed when he learned of the attempt on my life and the crimes surrounding the wedding gowns he'd helped bring to our peaceful valley.

Lorea and I were looking into other options for specialty wedding gowns we could carry in the shop, and she had ordered some beautiful fabric with the idea of trying her hand at creating her own designs.

My wedding planning business looked solid for the next year. None of the bookings would be as lucrative as Natalie's, but they would pay the bills. The happy thought was that none of the prospective brides came close to Sylvia's attitude or penchant for trouble.

Things were definitely looking better, except in the matter of my confused emotions. I'd been too busy to spend much time feeling sorry for myself. That thought brought my attention back to the present. The pastor was nearing the end of the vows, and I perked up, watching the photographer to make sure he would get a clear shot of their first kiss as a married couple.

Brock whooped and then punched the air as he covered Natalie's mouth with a kiss. Everyone laughed and cheered for the new Mr. and Mrs. Grafton. I felt truly happy for Natalie. She deserved to have her dreams come true. I caught Lorea wiping her eyes—maybe her hardened shell had a few cracks in it.

The rest of the evening was a blur as I ran from one person to the next, supervising the takedown of the wedding and moving guests to the reception at Brock's home. When I pulled around to Brock's six-car garage, I took a moment to admire the fantastic sunset tinting the sky with dark orange and pink highlights. I hurried to Brock's garden and pool house and appreciated the joint effort of so many highly skilled workers.

Twinkle lights wound through the rose garden and across the canopy over the seating area. Once the sun disappeared and darkness set in, the place would be stunning. The table near the entrance to the backyard was covered with smooth river rocks of varying sizes and permanent markers. Each guest would be invited to sign the "Stepping-Stones to a Happy Marriage" and include some advice. Natalie loved the idea of incorporating the setting of their ceremony into the "guest book" and planned on using the stones to line one of Brock's rose gardens.

"How are you holding up?" Lorea asked as she came up behind me with a box of supplies for last-minute touchups.

"I feel good. This turned out better than I could've imagined."

"I've been worried about you." Lorea paused. "I'm sure it's hard seeing Luke."

I started to shake my head, but she held up her hand. "I just wanted to tell you that you can trust your heart. Dallas can't hurt you anymore." She studied my face with a half smile. "Enough about that. I also wanted to say that you outdid yourself. The wedding was perfect."

I followed Lorea into the house, saving the response I wanted to give to the sigh hanging on the end of her words. When she set the box down, I hugged her instead. "Thank you for looking after me. I know it's been hard, but I appreciate it."

"What are friends for?" Lorea said. "Now, let's go party."

She pulled me outside to do the final check before the guests arrived. I grabbed the bulky wedding gift I had prepared for the happy couple. Usually, I presented my gift to the couple just before their big day, but my creative juices had run dry after Dallas's attack. I turned to my mom and her Craft Monster for inspiration, and she had finished the gift just in time.

We found Natalie and Brock moving into place under an archway of pink climbing roses. They would have an old-fashioned receiving line for the first hour, and then the dancing would begin.

Brock had his arm around his bride. He nuzzled her cheek, and she giggled. Natalie's smile widened as I approached. "I don't know how this day could get any better."

"I do." Brock tightened his grip on Natalie, and she blushed.

"I brought you a gift." I held the box wrapped in silver paper. "I apologize that I couldn't find a better time to give it to you."

"Adri, that's so kind of you—and this is great timing," Natalie responded as she and Brock opened the gift. "Oh, how did you find something so perfect?"

Brock lifted out the antique window frame by the silk ribbons attached to the back. The light caught the black vinyl lettering of their wedding date and "Brock & Natalie Forever." Natalie traced her finger over the pressed wildflowers and leaves between the panes of glass that we had carefully arranged and sealed as a memento. "I love it."

"My mom helped me make it. She's really craftsy."

"So that's where you learned it." Natalie hugged me. "Thanks."

"Thank you, ladies, for making this day exceptional," Brock said.

"I wish every couple was as fun to work with as you two have been."

"Me too," Lorea said. "But enough wishing. Let's get out of the way so the photographer can take more pictures. Guests should be here in fifteen."

Two hours later, exhaustion rode along every one of my nerves, and it was only nine thirty. I had pretty much run myself ragged keeping up with the caterer, the florist, the live band, and the few press people allowed in, not to mention mentally checking off my list a hundred times. The send-off for the new couple was scheduled for ten. Brock was surprising Natalie with honeymoon plans. I didn't even know what continent they were headed to, and I was glad. Hopefully they would have time to themselves.

I stopped at the refreshment table and downed two bottles of exotic spring water before sampling one of Valerie's concoctions. Platters of cream cheese-stuffed strawberries alternated with dainty butter cookies in the shape of flowers. I wanted to eat more than one of the melt-in-your-mouth sweets, but I needed to prepare for the send-off.

Someone tapped my shoulder. "You must be the wedding planner."

I looked into the smiling face of a beautiful dark-haired young woman. Brushing the crumbs off my fingers, I extended my hand. "Yes, I'm Adrielle Pyper."

She gave me a firm handshake. "I'm so happy to meet you. My name is Malia Wright, and I just got engaged last week." A rather large ring balanced on her slender finger.

"Congratulations," I said, and I meant it. The glow in her face was evident, and I couldn't help smiling back at her perma-grin. Her eyes were a deep blue, lined by heavy lashes that I figured were false, in defense of my own puny eyelashes.

"After I saw Natalie's wedding, I told my fiancé that this—" She motioned to the elaborate decorations and gauzy tent covering with sparkling starlight—"is exactly what I want."

"Thank you. I'm glad you like it." I studied her closer now: a prospective client. My mom said I had a gift because I could get a vibe from someone in just a five-minute conversation that was usually pretty accurate. Malia seemed nice. I'd probably compare everyone to Sylvia for the rest of my career. As long as they weren't up to her level of snobbishness, I would consider them.

Malia smiled at me and continued. "But I want this—my wedding—in Hawaii, and I want you there to make my dreams come true."

I struggled to keep my mouth from falling open. "Hawaii?"

"Of course. February is just too cold here in Sun Valley. So what do you think?" She took a step closer, and I could see the flawless creamy texture of her skin and subtle auburn highlights in her hair.

Think? I couldn't think. I'd always wanted to go to Hawaii—who doesn't? But a destination wedding with barely six months lead time? I wasn't sure if it would be too big a commitment on the heels of my hectic summer. I grinned at Malia, resisting the urge to chew on my bottom lip as my brain whirred around the proposal she'd just given me.

"Oh, I'm sorry. You need a reference, I'm sure. You'll probably be swamped with requests. I have a few, but the most important . . ." She stopped and dug through her sequined purse for a moment before pulling out a business card with a flourish. "Here you are."

I read the card and my eyes widened.

Luke Stetson, Attorney at Law
Serving your needs in Sun Valley, Idaho

Scrawled underneath in a blue ball-point pen, Luke had added: *Specializing in Divorce!*

"Did Luke put you up to this?"

Malia laughed. "No, Luke is my cousin. He's not keen on weddings, but he said he might come if I got you to be my wedding planner." She glanced at the card and back at me. "So what do you think?"

I looked past her to a tall, dark-haired man leaning casually against a tree. He lifted his head slightly. When our eyes met, his face broke into a wide grin. I studied him for a moment and then returned my attention to Malia. Hawaii was the dream destination for weddings. Lorea would flip. "I think we should make an appointment and see if I might be the right person to help make your dreams come true."

Malia grinned and hugged me. She handed me a green index card with her name and number written on it. "Is it all right if I call you Monday?"

I nodded and glanced at Luke, still leaning against the tree. He straightened and gave me a thumbs-up sign. I laughed as Malia turned and caught his eye. She waved at Luke, and as he made his way toward us, I said, "You really think it's a good idea to invite a divorce lawyer to your wedding?"

"Oh, Luke is doing our prenup, and he's such a great guy. He probably has you fooled, just like everyone else, but once you get past his prickly cover, he's a blast."

"He's making progress." I said, "He came to Brock's wedding."

"Two weddings in six months." Malia whistled. "Maybe you'll be next, Luke?"

"In your dreams." Luke tugged on one of Malia's curls. "Or one of those books that end with 'happily ever after.' "

"But that's what I specialize in, right, Malia?" I handed Luke one of my business cards and said, "Pyper's Dream Weddings, where happily ever after is your destination."

He laughed as he read the card and then lifted his blue eyes to mine. "Guess you have your work cut out for you." He elbowed Malia and held the card toward her. She took it, and her eyes lit up as she broke into another mega-watt grin.

"Adri, we need to get ready for the send-off." Lorea tugged on my arm, and I took a step back. "Is it all right if I steal her away?" she asked.

Malia nodded. "Sure, as long as you convince her to plan my wedding."

"It was nice meeting you, Malia. Talk to you soon." I waved as Lorea pulled me along.

At first I thought Luke was referring to Malia when he said I had my work cut out for me, but as I followed Lorea, I turned back to catch him staring at me with a half smile.

The send-off for Natalie and Brock brought a happy warmth to my heart. Lorea had handed out baskets of rose petals for people to throw as the couple made their way across the lawn to a stretch limo parked in front of the house. The result was a fragrant snowstorm of velvet petals cascading in every direction.

Brock stepped back to make room for his bride to toss a bouquet—a mini version of Natalie's wedding arrangement with cream and wine-colored roses wrapped in a dark green ribbon and adorned with an antique pearl brooch.

My neighbor Lily Rowan elbowed several ladies out of the way to catch the bouquet. She cheered and held the roses high in triumph. I didn't even mind when I caught Luke rolling his eyes. Natalie brushed by with Brock holding her close. I saw her reach out and squeeze Lorea's hand before climbing into the limo. Brock pushed aside some of the frills on Natalie's gown and with a whoop slid onto the seat next to her.

Everyone cheered, including me. The smile that encompassed my face was a well-deserved one, and I basked in the glory of my wedding planner dreams for a moment. The crowd jostled me a bit as people hurried back to the party to nab one last drink and finish off the refreshment table. But I stood there in the quiet, watching the rose petals twirl across the lawn, lifted by the cool mountain breeze.

"So that's how it's done," Luke's voice tickled my ear. I turned and bumped right into him. He had crept up behind me, and as I moved to step back, I stumbled. My heels sank into the grass, but as I fell backward, Luke grabbed my arms. At the same moment I clutched his white dress shirt.

"Oh, sorry," I said. Releasing his shirt, I smoothed out the fabric and then realized that I was touching those rock hard abs I'd admired for so long. My cheeks flushed, and I pulled my hands back.

"No harm done," Luke answered, but he didn't let go of me. "I didn't mean to startle you. I just wanted to tell you that you did a great job."

His compliment and his closeness lit off the grand finale of emotions in my chest. I lifted my head, feeling the breath of space between us charged with fireworks. He glanced at my mouth and then back to my eyes.

"Do I detect a hint of admiration in the divorce lawyer's tone?" I struggled to make my voice light and teasing.

Luke grinned. "You do, but your friend Tony told me you're not supposed to do any more detecting."

I shook my head. Tony was one of the many guests at the reception. I wondered how long a conversation he'd had with Luke. "Did he tell you that I pegged Sylvia as the thief of her own wedding gown?"

Luke chuckled. "He mentioned something about you making him eat his words with the wedding cake."

I laughed. "I'm so happy to be rid of her."

"I'm happy for you." Luke hesitated, studying my face before he continued. "How are you doing, Adri, really?"

My chin wobbled as I opened my mouth to answer that I was fine—the answer I gave to everyone who asked—but I could see I couldn't fool Luke. The way he scrutinized me, I realized that he really saw me. Somehow he'd gotten past my façade of *everything is all better now.* Tears stung the corners of my eyes. "It's hard," I whispered.

Luke nodded, and before I could think about my wounded heart and crazy emotions, he had pulled me into an embrace. My cheek rested against his chest, and tears dripped onto his crisp white shirt, leaving trails of black mascara.

"It hurts, but it's okay to feel that pain once in a while." Luke's voice rumbled in his chest, and the vibrations caressed my cheek. "It doesn't go away just because other people are happy."

With a sniff, I pulled back. "I don't know what's wrong with me. I'm sorry."

"Don't be." Luke didn't move to release me. "You are an incredibly strong woman. Just don't be so strong that you can't feel."

I heard what he was saying, and at the same time I realized that he was telling me something about himself. I nodded, and we stood staring at each other for a moment. The breeze shifted, bringing with it music from the band playing in Brock's backyard. Luke tilted his head toward the sound. "Would you like to dance?"

"That sounds like a great idea." My hands rested on his forearms as I leaned forward to kiss his cheek. "Thank you." I thought about saying more, but I knew he understood what I meant in those two little words.

Luke smiled and took my hand as we walked toward the dance floor. I could feel Malia's index card in the inner pocket of the linen dress jacket I wore over a blush-colored silk top. The prospect of a new challenge had me excited to meet with Malia next week. A wedding in Hawaii. I wondered if she would want to be married on the beach.

Luke squeezed my hand, and I turned my head to meet his

gaze. We began dancing, moving through the crowd of people. Luke wouldn't travel all the way to Hawaii for his cousin's wedding, would he? For a moment, I let my mind wander to the sand and surf. What would it be like to spend time with Luke? There was depth to him, emotion that he kept hidden from the rest of the world, but for some reason he had let me see.

I felt his hand on the small of my back, guiding me along the dance floor. Even though he was a divorce lawyer, Luke had saved me. He made me feel safe. He twirled me and drew me in close to his chest. I allowed myself to relax and lean my head on his shoulder. A breeze cooled the back of my neck as it sent more rose petals scattering across the dance floor. For a moment, I could hear Luke humming along to the song. With my face so near his chest, I wondered if wounded hearts could ever really heal. But then I remembered something Briette had always said: "Love makes everything new."

I believed her. There would be time to figure out the destination of my heart. For now, I was content to dance with "the hottie" and envision wedding vows in Hawaii.

Book Club
Discussion Questions

1. When Adri finds the diamonds, she's faced with a dilemma that could ruin the business she and Lorea are building. Do you think she made the right decision? What would you have done?

2. In the dating arena, Adri has a difficult time discerning what her heart really wants. She feels some understandable pressure for a healthy, romantic relationship because she's a wedding planner. Do you think that at times we force ourselves deeper into situations or relationships because of what we feel is expected of us?

3. How did you feel about Dallas Reynolds and his interactions with Adri? Did your feelings about him change? If so, how did they change and at what point in the novel did that change happen?

4. This novel is set in Sun Valley, Idaho, in the shadow of the Sawtooth Mountains. Discuss how the setting affected the story and the choices the characters made.

5. What was your first impression of Luke Stetson? How did

that impression change when you learned more about him? How often do you think this happens in life?

6. Adri experiences a lot of joy and family bonding through her crafts and wedding planning business, and she's also quite successful. What activities in your life provide joy, happiness, and feelings of success and self-mastery?

7. Adri undergoes a traumatic life-threatening incident that is linked to a painful part of her past. Discuss your feelings about the situation and how she handled it. How do you think this event will affect her in the future?

8. What would your fairy-tale wedding look like?

Learn more about Adri and her crafts at www.mashedpotatoes andcrafts.com

Photo by Erin Summerill

About the Author

Rachelle was born and raised in a small farming town in Idaho not far from the setting of her mystery *Diamond Rings Are Deadly Things*. She graduated cum laude from Utah State University with a degree in psychology. She enjoys singing and songwriting, playing the piano, running, motivational speaking, and of course reading. Rachelle has an amazing husband and five cute kids. To learn more about her, visit www.rachellechristensen.com.